CALDWELL COLLEGE

BETWEEN TWO AGES

By the same author

Political Controls in the Soviet Army (editor and contributor)

The Permanent Purge—Politics in Soviet Totalitarianism

Totalitarian Dictatorship and Autocracy (with Carl J. Friedrich)

The Soviet Bloc—Unity and Conflict

Ideology and Power in Soviet Politics

Africa and the Communist World (editor and contributor)

Political Power: USA/USSR (with Samuel P. Huntington)

Alternative to Partition: For a Broader Conception of America's Role in Europe

Dilemmas of Change in Soviet Politics (editor and contributor)

BETWEEN TWO AGES

America's Role in the Technetronic Era

Zbigniew Brzezinski

THE VIKING PRESS / NEW YORK

First published in 1970 by The Viking Press, Inc.
625 Madison Avenue, New York, N.Y. 10022

Published simultaneously in Canada by
The Macmillan Company of Canada Limited

SBN 670-16041-5

Library of Congress catalog card number: 76-104162

Printed in U.S.A. by H. Wolff Book Mfg. Co.

Prepared under the auspices of the Research Institute
on Communist Affairs, Columbia University

Second printing October 1970

Portions of this book appeared in *Encounter*
in different form

For Ian, Mark, and Mika

Acknowledgments

Though this book deals with communism only in part—and then primarily in relation to the broader issues with which I am concerned—the Research Institute on Communist Affairs of Columbia University provided me with invaluable research assistance and with a congenial and stimulating setting. My colleagues at the Institute little realize how very helpful they have been in the gradual process of shaping my ideas, testing my views, and enlarging my perspectives.

The manuscript was read and criticized by a number of friends and colleagues. I am especially grateful to Professor Samuel P. Huntington for his trenchant criticisms and very helpful recommendations; to Professor Albert A. Mavrinac, who maintained our friendly tradition of his questioning my arguments and of forcing me to rethink some of my propositions; to Mrs. Christine Dodson, the former Administrative Assistant of the Research Institute, who prepared a very constructive and highly perceptive chapter-length critique of the entire draft; and to Professor Alexander Erlich for steering me away from some economic pitfalls. I am also most obliged and grateful to Miss Sophia Sluzar, currently the Administrative Assistant, who very ably supervised the over-all preparation of the manuscript and who earlier was instrumental in preparing the tables and assembling the needed data. Miss Toby Trister, my research assistant, was indefatigable in exposing my inaccuracies, in filling bibliographic gaps, and in completing the research. Miss Dorothy Rodnite, Miss Michelle Elwyn, and Mr. Myron Gutmann amiably and efficiently—even when under great pressures of time—devoted their energies to the completion of the manuscript. To all of them I owe a debt which I am pleased to acknowledge.

I also wish to note my obligation to Mr. Marshall Best of The Viking Press, on whose experience and wise counsel I often relied, and to Mr. Stanley Hochman for his sensitive editorial assistance.

A special mention is due to my wife. In all my writing I have never come across a more conscientious reader, a more ferocious critic, and a more determined—dare I say obstinate?—perfectionist. I have no hesitation in saying, though only now I say it with relief, that any merit this essay may have is in large measure due to her efforts.

Z.B.
October 1969

Contents

Introduction

Perhaps the time is past for the comprehensive "grand" vision. In some ways, it was a necessary substitute for ignorance, a compensation in breadth for the lack of depth in man's understanding of his world. But even if this is so, the result of more knowledge may be greater ignorance—or, at least, the feeling of ignorance—about where we are and where we are heading, and particularly where we should head, than was true when in fact we knew less but thought we knew more.

I am not sure that this need be so. In any case, I am not satisfied with the fragmented, microscopic understanding of the parts, and I feel the need for some—even if crude—approximation of a larger perspective. This book is an effort to provide such a perspective. It is an attempt to define the meaning—within a dynamic framework—of a major aspect of our contemporary reality: the emerging global political process which increasingly blurs the traditional distinctions between domestic and international politics. In working toward that definition, I shall focus particularly on the meaning for the United States of the emergence of this process, seeking to draw implications from an examination of the forces that are molding it.

Time and space shape our perception of reality. The specific moment and the particular setting dictate the way international estimates and priorities are defined. Sometimes, when the moment is historically "ripe," the setting and the time may coalesce to provide a special insight. A perceptive formula is easier to articulate in a moment of special stress. Conditions of war, crisis, tension are in that sense particularly fertile. The situation of crisis permits sharper value judgments, in keeping with man's ancient proclivity for dividing his reality into good and evil. (Marxist dialectic is clearly in this tradition, and it infuses moral dichotomy into every assessment.) But short of that critical condition—which in its most extreme form involves the alternatives of war or peace—global politics do not lend themselves to pat formulations and clear-cut predictions, even in a setting of extensive change. As a result—in most times—it is extraordinarily difficult to liberate oneself from the confining influence of the immediate and to perceive—from a detached perspective—the broader sweep of events.

Any abstract attempt to arrive at a capsule formula is bound to contain a measure of distortion. The influences that condition relations among states and the broad evolution of international affairs are too various. Nonetheless, as long as we are aware that any such formulation inescapably contains a germ of falsehood—and hence must be tentative—the attempt represents an advance toward at least a partial understanding. The alternative is capitulation to complexity: the admission that no sense can be extracted from what is happening. The consequent triumph of ignorance exacts its own tribute in the form of unstable and reactive policies, the substitution of slogans for thought, the rigid adherence to generalized formulas made in another age and in response to circumstances that are different in essence from our own, even if superficially similar.

Today, the most industrially advanced countries (in the first instance, the United States) are beginning to emerge from the industrial stage of their development. They are entering an age in which technology and especially electronics—hence my neologism "technetronic"*—are increasingly becoming the principal determinants of social change, altering the mores, the social structure, the values, and the global outlook of society. And precisely because today change is so rapid and so complex, it is perhaps more important than ever before that our conduct of foreign affairs be guided by a sense of history—and to speak of history in this

* To be more fully discussed in Part I.

context is to speak simultaneously of the past and of the future.

Since it focuses on international affairs, this book is at most only a very partial response to the need for a more comprehensive assessment. It is not an attempt to sum up the human condition, to combine philosophy and science, to provide answers to more perplexing questions concerning our reality. It is much more modest than that, and yet I am uneasily aware that it is already much too ambitious, because it unavoidably touches on all these issues.

The book is divided into five major parts. The first deals with the impact of the scientific-technological revolution on world affairs in general, discussing more specifically the ambiguous position of the principal disseminator of that revolution—the United States—and analyzing the effects of the revolution on the so-called Third World. The second part examines how the foregoing considerations have affected the content, style, and format of man's political outlook on his global reality, with particular reference to the changing role of ideology. The third part assesses the contemporary relevance of communism to problems of modernity, looking first at the experience of the Soviet Union and then examining the over-all condition of international communism as a movement that once sought to combine internationalism and humanism. The fourth part focuses on the United States, a society that is both a social pioneer and a guinea pig for mankind; it seeks to define the thrust of change and the historical meaning of the current American transition. The fifth part outlines in very broad terms the general directions that America might take in order to make an effective response to the previously discussed foreign and domestic dilemmas.

Having said what the book does attempt, it might be helpful to the reader also to indicate what it does not attempt. First of all, it is not an exercise in "futurology"; it is an effort to make sense of present trends, to develop a dynamic perspective on what is happening. Secondly, it is not a policy book, in the sense that its object is not to develop systematically a coherent series of prescriptions and programs. In Part V, however, it does try to indicate the general directions toward which America should and, in some respects, may head.

In the course of developing these theses, I have expanded on some of the ideas initially advanced in my article "America in the Technetronic Age," published in *Encounter*, January 1968, which gave rise to considerable controversy. I should add that not only have I tried to amplify and clarify some of the rather condensed points made in that article, but I have significantly revised some of my views in the light of constructive criticisms made by my colleagues. Moreover, that article addressed itself to only one aspect (discussed primarily in Part I) of the much larger canvas that I have tried to paint in this volume.

It is my hope that this essay will help to provide the reader with a better grasp of the nature of the political world we live in, of the forces shaping it, of the directions it is pursuing. In that sense, it might perhaps contribute to a sharper perception of the new political processes enveloping our world and move beyond the more traditional forms of examining international politics. I hope, too, that the tentative propositions, the generalizations, and the theses advanced here—though necessarily speculative, arbitrary, and in very many respects inescapably inadequate—may contribute to the increasing discussion of America's role in the world.

In the course of the work, I have expressed my own opinions and exposed my prejudices. This effort is, therefore, more in the nature of a "think piece," backed by evidence, than of a systematic exercise in social-science methodology.*

---

* In this respect, I share the view of Barrington Moore, Jr., that "when we set the dominant body of current thinking against important figures in the nineteenth century, the following differences emerge. First of all, the critical spirit has all but disappeared. Second, modern sociology, and perhaps to a lesser extent also modern political science, economics, and psychology, are ahistorical. Third, modern social science tends to be abstract and formal. In research, social science today displays considerable technical virtuosity. But this virtuosity has been gained at the expense of content. Modern sociology has less to say about society than it did fifty years ago" (*Political Power and Social Theory*, Cambridge, Mass., 1958, p. 123).

Finally, let me end this introduction with a confession that somewhat anticipates my argument: an apocalyptic-minded reader may find my thesis uncongenial because my view of America's role in the world is still an optimistic one. I say "still" because I am greatly troubled by the dilemmas we face at home and abroad, and even more so by the social and philosophical implications of the direction of change in our time.

Nonetheless, my optimism is real. Although I do not mean to minimize the gravity of America's problems—their catalogue is long, the dilemmas are acute, and the signs of a meaningful response are at most ambivalent—I truly believe that this society has the capacity, the talent, the wealth, and, increasingly, the will to surmount the difficulties inherent in this current historic transition.

BETWEEN TWO AGES

"Human life is reduced to real suffering, to hell, only when two ages, two cultures and religions overlap. . . . There are times when a whole generation is caught in this way between two ages, two modes of life, with the consequence that it loses all power to understand itself and has no standard, no security, no simple acquiescence."

—Hermann Hesse, *Steppenwolf*

PART I
The Global Impact of the Technetronic Revolution

The paradox of our time is that humanity is becoming simultaneously more unified and more fragmented. That is the principal thrust of contemporary change. Time and space have become so compressed that global politics manifest a tendency toward larger, more interwoven forms of cooperation as well as toward the dissolution of established institutional and ideological loyalties. Humanity is becoming more integral and intimate even as the differences in the condition of the separate societies are widening. Under these circumstances proximity, instead of promoting unity, gives rise to tensions prompted by a new sense of global congestion.

A new pattern of international politics is emerging. The world is ceasing to be an arena in which relatively self-contained, "sovereign," and homogeneous nations interact, collaborate, clash, or make war. International politics, in the original sense of the term, were born when groups of people began to identify themselves—and others—in mutually exclusive terms (territory, language, symbols, beliefs), and when that identification became in turn the dominant factor in relations between these groups. The concept of national interest—based on geographical factors, traditional animosities or friendships, economics, and security considerations—implied a degree of autonomy and specificity that was possible only so long as nations were sufficiently separated in time and space to have both the room to maneuver and the distance needed to maintain separate identity.

During the classical era of international politics, weapons, communications, economics, and ideology were all essentially national in scope. With the invention of modern artillery, weaponry required national arsenals and standing armies; in more recent times it could be effectively and rapidly deployed by one nation against the frontiers of another. Communications, especially since the invention of the steam engine and the resulting age of railroads, reinforced national integration by making it possible to move people and goods across most nations in a period of time rarely exceeding two days. National economies, frequently resting on autarkic principles, stimulated both the awareness and the development of collective vested interest, protected by tariff walls. Nationalism so personalized community feelings that the nation became an extension of the ego.*

All four factors mentioned above are now becoming global. Weapons of total destructive power can be applied at any point on the globe in a matter of minutes—in less time, in fact, than it takes for the police in a major city to respond to an emergency call. The entire globe is in closer reach and touch than a middle-sized European power was to its own capital fifty years ago. Transnational ties are gaining in importance, while the claims of nationalism, though still intense, are nonetheless becoming diluted. This change, naturally, has gone furthest in the most ad-

* This was a major change from the earlier feudal age. At that time weapons were largely personal, communications were very limited and primarily oral, the economy was primitive and rural, and ideology stressed direct, religion-based obeisance to a personally known chief. These conditions thus reinforced and reflected a more fragmented "intranational" political process.

vanced countries, but no country is now immune to it. The consequence is a new era—an era of the global political process.

Yet though the process is global, real unity of mankind remains remote. The contemporary world is undergoing a change in many respects similar to that prompted by the earlier appearance of large population centers. The growth of such centers weakened intimate and direct lines of authority and contributed to the appearance of many conflicting and crosscutting allegiances. A typical city dweller identifies himself simultaneously with a variety of groups—occupational, religious, leisure, political—and only rarely operates in an environment that is exclusively dominated by a single system of values and a unilinear personal commitment. American metropolitan politics are typically messy: special-interest and pressure groups, ethnic communities, political organizations, religious institutions, major industrial or financial forces, and even the criminal underworld interact in a pattern that simultaneously includes continuous limited warfare and accommodation.

Global polities are acquiring some analogous characteristics. Nations of different sizes and developmentally in different historical epochs interact, creating friction, variable patterns of accommodation, and changing alignments. While the formal rules of the game maintain the illusion that it is played only by those players called "states"—and, when war breaks out, the states become the only significant players—short of war the game is truly played on a much more informal basis, with much more mixed participation. Some states possess overwhelming power; others, the "mini-states," are overshadowed by multimillion-dollar international corporations, major banks and financial interests, transnational organizations of religious or ideological character, and the emerging international institutions that in some cases "represent" the interests of the minor players (for example, the UN) or in other cases mask the power of the major ones (for example, the Warsaw Pact or SEATO).

The methods for coping with international conflicts are hence becoming similar to those for dealing with urban discord. A characteristic feature of concentrated humanity is the routinization of conflict. Direct violence becomes increasingly regulated and restricted, and ultimately comes to be considered as a deviation from the norm. Organized mechanisms, in the form of uniformed, salaried personnel, are established to confine violence to socially tolerable limits. A certain measure of crime is accepted as unavoidable; for the sake of order, therefore, organized crime is generally preferred to anarchic violence, thus indirectly and informally becoming an extension of order.

The routinization of conflict on a global scale has been the goal of statesmen for many decades. Agreements, conventions, and pacts have sought to govern it. None of these could prove effective in a system of relatively distinctive and sovereign units; but the appearance of rapid communications, which created not only physical proximity but also instant awareness of distant events, and the onset of the nuclear age, which for the first time made truly destructive global power available to at least two states, fundamentally altered the pattern of international conflict. On the one hand these factors depressed its level, and on the other they heightened its potential and increased its scope.

Urban underworld wars do not give rise to much moral revulsion nor are they seen as major threats to social peace. Only outbreaks of violence directed at that peace, as represented by human life and major vested interests—banks, shops, or private property, for example—are resolutely combated. Similarly, in the more advanced portions of the world there is a tendency among the establishment and the middle class of the "global city" to be indifferent to Third World conflicts and to view them as necessary attributes of a low level of development—provided, of course, that such conflicts do not feed back into the relations among the more powerful states. Wars in the Third World thus seem tolerable as long as their international scale is contained at a level that does not seem to threaten major interests.*

* ". . . during the post-1945 years, the development of nuclear weapons, the formation of power blocs and multilateral alliance systems, and the in-

In our time the routinization of conflict has also meant a shift from sustained warfare to sporadic outbreaks of violence. Sustained, prolonged warfare was made possible by the industrial age. In earlier times armies confronted each other, fought pitched, head-on battles, and, like gladiators of old, scored decisive victories or went down in defeat. The industrial age permitted societies to mobilize their manpower and resources for prolonged but indecisive struggles resembling classical wrestling and requiring both skill and endurance. Nuclear weapons—never used in conflict between nuclear powers—pose the possibility of such mutual annihilation that they tend to freeze their possessors into passive restraint, with sporadic outbreaks of violence occurring on the peripheries of the confrontation. Though, in the past, violence tended to result in the use of maximum available power, today those states possessing maximum power strive to employ a minimum in the assertion of their interests.

Since the appearance of nuclear weapons, relations between the superpowers have been governed by a rudimentary code of restraint forged by trial and error in the course of confrontations ranging from Korea through Berlin to Cuba. It is likely that in the absence of these weapons war would long since have broken out between the United States and the Soviet Union. Their destructive power has thus had a basic effect on the degree to which force is applied in the relations among states, compelling an unprecedented degree of prudence in the behavior of the most

---

creasing financial cost of modern warfare, have all been factors inhibiting the outbreak of formal warfare between the advanced, industrial nations. The majority of 'conflicts' during these years have taken place in Africa, the Middle East and Asia, the so-called Third World. And a large number of them have followed on or been associated with the break-up of colonial empires, whether Ottoman, British, French or Japanese, and the subsequent emergence of new states which are often small, poor and insecure" (David Wood, "Conflict in the Twentieth Century," *Adelphi Papers,* June 1968, p. 19). The above study contains a list of eighty conflicts that have occurred in the years 1945–1967. All but eight of these conflicts involved Third World participants on both sides.

The analogy with metropolitan politics is also made by Theodore H. Von Laue in his thoughtful book *The Global City* (New York, 1969). Von Laue is particularly stimulating in his analysis of the impact of the Western "metropolitan" system on world politics during the last century.

powerful states. Within the fragile framework in which the contemporary transformation of our reality occurs, nuclear weapons have thus created an entirely novel system of deterrence from the reliance on overwhelming power.

In the case of urban politics, the weakness of accepted and respected immediate authority is compensated for by the sense of higher allegiance to the nation, as represented by the institutional expression of state power. The global city lacks that higher dimension—and much of the contemporary search for order is an attempt to create it, or to find some equilibrium short of it. Otherwise, however, global politics are similarly characterized by the confusing pattern of involvement, congestion, and interaction, which cumulatively, though gradually, undermines the exclusiveness and the primacy of those hitherto relatively watertight compartments, the nation-states. In the process, international politics gradually become a much more intimate and overlapping process.

Eras are historical abstractions. They are also an intellectual convenience: they are meant to be milestones on a road that over a period of time changes imperceptibly and yet quite profoundly. It is a matter of arbitrary judgment when one era ends and a new one begins; neither the end nor the beginning can be clearly and sharply defined. On the formal plane, politics as a global process operate much as they did in the past, but the inner reality of that process is increasingly shaped by forces whose influence or scope transcend national lines.

1. The Onset of the Technetronic Age

The impact of science and technology on man and his society, especially in the more advanced countries of the world, is becoming the major source of contemporary change. Recent years have seen a proliferation of exciting and challenging literature on the future. In the United States, in Western Europe, and, to a lesser degree, in Japan and in the Soviet Union, a number of systematic, scholarly efforts have been made to project, predict, and grasp what the future holds for us.

The transformation that is now taking place, especially in America, is already creating a society increasingly unlike its industrial predecessor.[1] The post-industrial society is becoming a "technetronic" society:* a society that is shaped culturally, psychologically, socially, and economically by the impact of technology and electronics—particularly in the area of computers and communications. The industrial process is no longer the principal determinant of social change, altering the mores, the social structure, and the values of society. In the industrial society technical knowledge was applied primarily to one specific end: the acceleration and improvement of production techniques. Social consequences were a later by-product of this paramount concern. In the technetronic society scientific and technical knowledge, in addi-

* The term "post-industrial" is used by Daniel Bell, who has done much of the pioneering thinking on the subject. However, I prefer to use the neologism "technetronic," because it conveys more directly the character of the principal impulses for change in our time. Similarly, the term "industrial" described what otherwise could have been called the "post-agricultural" age.

tion to enhancing production capabilities, quickly spills over to affect almost all aspects of life directly. Accordingly, both the growing capacity for the instant calculation of the most complex interactions and the increasing availability of biochemical means of human control augment the potential scope of consciously chosen direction, and thereby also the pressures to direct, to choose, and to change.

Reliance on these new techniques of calculation and communication enhances the social importance of human intelligence and the immediate relevance of learning. The need to integrate social change is heightened by the increased ability to decipher the patterns of change; this in turn increases the significance of basic assumptions concerning the nature of man and the desirability of one or another form of social organization. Science thereby intensifies rather than diminishes the relevance of values, but it demands that they be cast in terms that go beyond the more crude ideologies of the industrial age. (This theme is developed further in Part II.)

New Social Patterns

For Norbert Wiener, "the locus of an earlier industrial revolution before the main industrial revolution" is to be found in the fifteenth-century research pertaining to navigation (the nautical compass), as well as in the development of gunpowder and printing.[2] Today the functional equivalent of navigation is the thrust into space, which requires a rapid computing capacity beyond the means of the human brain; the equivalent of gunpowder is modern nuclear physics, and that of printing is television and long-range instant communications. The consequence of this new technetronic revolution is the progressive emergence of a society that increasingly differs from the industrial one in a variety of economic, political, and social aspects. The following examples may be briefly cited to summarize some of the contrasts:

(1) In an industrial society the mode of production shifts from

agriculture to industry, with the use of human and animal muscle supplanted by machine operation. In the technetronic society industrial employment yields to services, with automation and cybernetics replacing the operation of machines by individuals.

(2) Problems of employment and unemployment—to say nothing of the prior urbanization of the post-rural labor force—dominate the relationship between employers, labor, and the market in the industrial society, and the assurance of minimum welfare to the new industrial masses is a source of major concern. In the emerging new society questions relating to the obsolescence of skills, security, vacations, leisure, and profit sharing dominate the relationship, and the psychic well-being of millions of relatively secure but potentially aimless lower-middle-class blue-collar workers becomes a growing problem.

(3) Breaking down traditional barriers to education, and thus creating the basic point of departure for social advancement, is a major goal of social reformers in the industrial society. Education, available for limited and specific periods of time, is initially concerned with overcoming illiteracy and subsequently with technical training, based largely on written, sequential reasoning. In the technetronic society not only is education universal but advanced training is available to almost all who have the basic talents, and there is far greater emphasis on quality selection. The essential problem is to discover the most effective techniques for the rational exploitation of social talent. The latest communication and calculating techniques are employed in this task. The educational process becomes a lengthier one and is increasingly reliant on audio-visual aids. In addition, the flow of new knowledge necessitates more and more frequent refresher studies.

(4) In the industrial society social leadership shifts from the traditional rural-aristocratic to an urban-plutocratic elite. Newly acquired wealth is its foundation, and intense competition the outlet—as well as the stimulus—for its energy. In the technetronic society plutocratic pre-eminence is challenged by the political leadership, which is itself increasingly permeated by individuals

possessing special skills and intellectual talents. Knowledge becomes a tool of power and the effective mobilization of talent an important way to acquire power.

(5) The university in an industrial society—in contrast to the situation in medieval times—is an aloof ivory tower, the repository of irrelevant, even if respected, wisdom, and for a brief time the fountainhead for budding members of the established social elite. In the technetronic society the university becomes an intensely involved "think tank," the source of much sustained political planning and social innovation.

(6) The turmoil inherent in the shift from a rigidly traditional rural society to an urban one engenders an inclination to seek total answers to social dilemmas, thus causing ideologies to thrive in the industrializing society. (The American exception to this rule was due to the absence of a feudal tradition, a point well developed by Louis Hartz.) In the industrial age literacy makes for static interrelated conceptual thinking, congenial to ideological systems. In the technetronic society audio-visual communications prompt more changeable, disparate views of reality, not compressible into formal systems, even as the requirements of science and the new computative techniques place a premium on mathematical logic and systematic reasoning. The resulting tension is felt most acutely by scientists, with the consequence that some seek to confine reason to science while expressing their emotions through politics. Moreover, the increasing ability to reduce social conflicts to quantifiable and measurable dimensions reinforces the trend toward a more pragmatic approach to social problems, while it simultaneously stimulates new concerns with preserving "humane" values.

(7) In the industrial society, as the hitherto passive masses become active there are intense political conflicts over such matters as disenfranchisement and the right to vote. The issue of political participation is a crucial one. In the technetronic age the question is increasingly one of ensuring real participation in decisions that seem too complex and too far removed from the aver-

age citizen. Political alienation becomes a problem. Similarly, the issue of political equality of the sexes gives way to a struggle for the sexual equality of women. In the industrial society woman —the operator of machines—ceases to be physically inferior to the male, a consideration of some importance in rural life, and begins to demand her political rights. In the emerging technetronic society automation threatens both males and females, intellectual talent is computable, the "pill" encourages sexual equality, and women begin to claim complete equality.

(8) The newly enfranchised masses are organized in the industrial society by trade unions and political parties and unified by relatively simple and somewhat ideological programs. Moreover, political attitudes are influenced by appeals to nationalist sentiments, communicated through the massive increase of newspapers employing, naturally, the readers' national language. In the technetronic society the trend seems to be toward aggregating the individual support of millions of unorganized citizens, who are easily within the reach of magnetic and attractive personalities, and effectively exploiting the latest communication techniques to manipulate emotions and control reason. Reliance on television—and hence the tendency to replace language with imagery, which is international rather than national, and to include war coverage or scenes of hunger in places as distant as, for example, India—creates a somewhat more cosmopolitan, though highly impressionistic, involvement in global affairs.

(9) Economic power in the early phase of industrialization tends to be personalized, by either great entrepreneurs like Henry Ford or bureaucratic industrial officials like Kaganovich, or Minc (in Stalinist Poland). The tendency toward depersonalization of economic power is stimulated in the next stage by the appearance of a highly complex interdependence between governmental institutions (including the military), scientific establishments, and industrial organizations. As economic power becomes inseparably linked with political power, it becomes more invisible and the sense of individual futility increases.

(10) In an industrial society the acquisition of goods and the accumulation of personal wealth become forms of social attainment for an unprecedentedly large number of people. In the technetronic society the adaptation of science to humane ends and a growing concern with the quality of life become both possible and increasingly a moral imperative for a large number of citizens, especially the young.

Eventually, these changes and many others, including some that more directly affect the personality and quality of the human being himself, will make the technetronic society as different from the industrial as the industrial was from the agrarian.* And just as the shift from an agrarian economy and feudal politics toward an industrial society and political systems based on the individual's emotional identification with the nation-state gave rise to contemporary international politics, so the appearance of the technetronic society reflects the onset of a new relationship between man and his expanded global reality.

Social Explosion/Implosion

This new relationship is a tense one: man has still to define it conceptually and thereby render it comprehensible to himself. Our expanded global reality is simultaneously fragmenting and thrusting itself in upon us. The result of the coincident explosion and implosion is not only insecurity and tension but also an entirely novel perception of what many still call international affairs.

Life seems to lack cohesion as environment rapidly alters and human beings become increasingly manipulable and malleable. Everything seems more transitory and temporary: external reality

---

* Bell defines the "five dimensions of the post-industrial society" as involving the following: (1) The creation of a service economy. (2) The pre-eminence of the professional and technical class. (3) The centrality of *theoretical knowledge* as the source of innovation and policy formulation in the society. (4) The possibility of self-sustaining technological growth. (5) The creation of a new "intellectual technology." (Daniel Bell, "The Measurement of Knowledge and Technology," in *Indicators of Social Change,* Eleanor Sheldon and Wilbert Moore, eds., New York, 1968, pp. 152–53.)

more fluid than solid, the human being more synthetic than authentic. Even our senses perceive an entirely novel "reality"—one of our own making but nevertheless, in terms of our sensations, quite "real." * More important, there is already widespread concern about the possibility of biological and chemical tampering with what has until now been considered the immutable essence of man. Human conduct, some argue, can be predetermined and subjected to deliberate control. Man is increasingly acquiring the capacity to determine the sex of his children, to affect through drugs the extent of their intelligence, and to modify and control their personalities. Speaking of a future at most only decades away, an experimenter in intelligence control asserted, "I foresee the time when we shall have the means and therefore, inevitably, the temptation to manipulate the behavior and intellectual functioning of all the people through environmental and biochemical manipulation of the brain." [3]

Thus it is an open question whether technology and science will in fact increase the options open to the individual. Under the headline "Study Terms Technology a Boon to Individualism," [4] *The New York Times* reported the preliminary conclusions of a Harvard project on the social significance of science. Its participants were quoted as concluding that "most Americans have a greater range of personal choice, wider experience and a more highly developed sense of self-worth than ever before." This may be so, but a judgment of this sort rests essentially on an intuitive —and comparative—insight into the present and past states of mind of Americans. In this connection a word of warning from an acute observer is highly relevant: "It behooves us to examine carefully the degree of validity, as measured by actual behavior, of the statement that a benefit of technology will be to increase the number of options and alternatives the individual can choose

---

* Charles R. DeCarlo, in "Computer Technology" (*Toward the Year 2018*, New York, 1968, p. 102), describes the use of "holography" to create the sensation of living presence—as well as the actuality of conversations—by long-range laser beams from a satellite.

from. In principle, it could; in fact, the individual may use any number of psychological devices to avoid the discomfort of information overload, and thereby keep the range of alternatives to which he responds much narrower than that which technology in principle makes available to him." [5] In other words, the real questions are how the individual will exploit the options, to what extent he will be intellectually and psychologically prepared to exploit them, and in what way society as a whole will create a favorable setting for taking advantage of these options. Their availability is not of itself proof of a greater sense of freedom or self-worth.

Instead of accepting himself as a spontaneous given, man in the most advanced societies may become more concerned with conscious self-analysis according to external, explicit criteria: What is my IQ? What are my aptitudes, personality traits, capabilities, attractions, and negative features? The "internal man"—spontaneously accepting his own spontaneity—will more and more be challenged by the "external man"—consciously seeking his self-conscious image; and the transition from one to the other may not be easy. It will also give rise to difficult problems in determining the legitimate scope of social control. The possibility of extensive chemical mind control, the danger of loss of individuality inherent in extensive transplantation, the feasibility of manipulating the genetic structure will call for the social definition of common criteria of use and restraint. As the previously cited writer put it, ". . . while the chemical affects the individual, the person is significant to himself and to society in his *social* context—at work, at home, at play. The consequences are social consequences. In deciding how to deal with such alterers of the ego and of experience (and consequently alterers of the personality after the experience), and in deciding how to deal with the 'changed' human beings, we will have to face new questions such as 'Who am I?' 'When am I who?' 'Who are *they* in relation to me?' " [6]

Moreover, man will increasingly be living in man-made and rapidly man-altered environments. By the end of this century approximately two-thirds of the people in the advanced countries will live in cities.* Urban growth has so far been primarily the by-product of accidental economic convenience, of the magnetic attraction of population centers, and of the flight of many from rural poverty and exploitation. It has not been deliberately designed to improve the quality of life. The impact of "accidental" cities is already contributing to the depersonalization of individual life as the kinship structure contracts and enduring relations of friendship become more difficult to maintain. Julian Huxley was perhaps guilty of only slight exaggeration when he warned that "overcrowding in animals leads to distorted neurotic and downright pathological behavior. We can be sure that the same is true in principle of people. City life today is definitely leading to mass mental disease, to growing vandalism and possible eruptions of mass violence." † [7]

The problem of identity is likely to be complicated by a generation gap, intensified by the dissolution of traditional ties and values derived from extended family and enduring community relationships. The dialogue between the generations is becoming a dialogue of the deaf. It no longer operates within the conservative-liberal or nationalist-internationalist framework. The breakdown in communication between the generations—so vividly evident during the student revolts of 1968—was rooted in the irrelevance of the old symbols to many younger people. Debate implies the acceptance of a common frame of reference and language; since these were lacking, debate became increasingly impossible.

Though currently the clash is over values—with many of the

---

* In 1900 there were 10 cities with populations of one million or more; in 1955 the number had grown to 61; in 1965 there were over 100 cities with populations of one million or more. Today in Australia and Oceania three-quarters of the people live in cities; in America and Europe (the USSR included) one-half do; in Africa and Asia one-fifth live in cities.

† G. N. Carstairs, in "Why Is Man Aggressive?" (*Impact of Science on Society*, April-June 1968, p. 90), argues that population growth, crowding, and social oppression all contribute to irrational and intensified aggression. Experiments on rats seem to bear this out; observation of human behavior in large cities seems to warrant a similar conclusion. For a *cri du cœur* against this congested condition from a French sociologist, see Jacques Ellul, *The Technological Society*, New York, 1965, p. 321.

young rejecting those of their elders, who in turn contend that the young have evaded the responsibility of articulating theirs—in the future the clash between generations will be also over expertise. Within a few years the rebels in the more advanced countries who today have the most visibility will be joined by a new generation making its claim to power in government and business: a generation trained to reason logically; as accustomed to exploiting electronic aids to human reasoning as we have been to using machines to increase our own mobility; expressing itself in a language that functionally relates to these aids; accepting as routine managerial processes current innovations such as planning-programming-budgeting systems (PPBS) and the appearance in high business echelons of "top computer executives." [8] As the older elite defends what it considers not only its own vested interests but more basically its own way of life, the resulting clash could generate even more intense conceptual issues.

Global Absorption

But while our immediate reality is being fragmented, global reality increasingly absorbs the individual, involves him, and even occasionally overwhelms him. Communications are the obvious, already much discussed, immediate cause. The changes wrought by communications and computers make for an extraordinarily interwoven society whose members are in continuous and close audio-visual contact—constantly interacting, instantly sharing the most intense social experiences, and prompted to increased personal involvement in even the most distant problems. The new generation no longer defines the world exclusively on the basis of reading, either of ideologically structured analyses or of extensive descriptions; it also experiences and senses it vicariously through audio-visual communications. This form of communicating reality is growing more rapidly—especially in the advanced countries*

* For example, Hermann Meyn, in his *Massen-medien in der Bundesrepublik Deutschland* (Berlin, 1966), provides data showing cumulatively that an

—than the traditional written medium, and it provides the principal source of news for the masses (see Tables 1–3). "By 1985 distance will be no excuse for delayed information from any part of the world to the powerful urban nerve centers that will mark the major concentrations of the people on earth." [9] Global telephone dialing that in the more advanced states will include instant visual contact and a global television-satellite system that will enable some states to "invade" private homes in other countries* will create unprecedented global intimacy.

The new reality, however, will not be that of a "global village." McLuhan's striking analogy overlooks the personal stability, interpersonal intimacy, implicitly shared values, and traditions that were important ingredients of the primitive village. A more appropriate analogy is that of the "global city"—a nervous, agitated, tense, and fragmented web of interdependent relations. That interdependence, however, is better characterized by interaction than by intimacy. Instant communications are already creating something akin to a global nervous system. Occasional malfunctions of this nervous system—because of blackouts or breakdowns—will be all the more unsettling, precisely because the mutual confidence and reciprocally reinforcing stability that are characteristic of village intimacy will be absent from the process of that "nervous" interaction.

Man's intensified involvement in global affairs is reflected in, and doubtless shaped by, the changing character of what has until now been considered local news. Television has joined newspapers in expanding the immediate horizons of the viewer or reader to the point where "local" increasingly means "national," and global affairs compete for attention on an unprecedented scale. Physical and moral immunity to "foreign" events cannot be

---

average West German over the age of fifteen read each day for fifteen minutes, listened to the radio for one and one-half hours, and watched television for one hour and ten minutes.

* It is estimated that within a decade television satellites will carry sufficient power to transmit programs directly to receivers, without the intermediary of receiving-transmitting stations.

TABLE 1. RADIO AND TELEVISION RECEIVERS PER 1000 POPULATION; ESTIMATED CIRCULATION OF DAILY NEWSPAPERS PER 1000 POPULATION

	1960			1966		
	Radios	TV	Newspapers	Radios	TV	Newspapers
United States	941	310	326	1,334	376	312
Canada	452	219	222	602	286	212*
Sweden	367	156	(1962) 490	377	277	501
United Kingdom	289	211	514	300	254	488
West Germany	287	83	307	459	213	332
Czechoslovakia	259	58	236	269	167	288
France	241	41	(1962) 252	321	151	248*
USSR	205	22	172	329	81	274
Argentina	167	21	155	308	82	128*
Japan	133	73	396	251	192	465
Brazil	70	18	54	(1964) 95	30	33
Algeria	54	5	28	(1964) 129	(1965) 13	(1965) 15
India	5	—	11	13	—	13

Source of Tables 1 and 2: *UNESCO Statistical Yearbook,* 1967, Tables 5.1; 8.2; 9.2.
* Statistics from *UN Statistical Yearbook,* 1968.

TABLE 2. ABSOLUTE INCREASE PER 1000 POPULATION IN RADIO, TELEVISION, AND NEWSPAPER CIRCULATION, 1960–1966

	Radios	TV	Newspapers
United States	+393	+66	−14
Canada	+150	+67	−10
Sweden	+10	+121	+11
United Kingdom	+11	+43	−26
West Germany	+172	+130	+25
Czechoslovakia	+10	+109	+52
France	+80	+110	−4
USSR	+124	+59	+102
Argentina	+141	+61	−27
Japan	+118	+119	+69
Brazil	+25	+12	−21
Algeria	+75	+8	−13
India	+8	—	+2

TABLE 3. APPROXIMATE USE OF MEDIA FOR EACH OF THE FOUR AUDIENCE GROUPS

Per cent of U.S. population that:	Mass Majority (50–60%)	Peripheral Mass (20–40%)	College Graduates (10–25%)	Elites (less than 1%)
Read any nonfiction books in the last year	5	15	30	50
Read one issue a month of *Harper's, National Review,* etc.	½	2	10	25
Read one issue a month of *Time, Newsweek,* or *U.S. News*	5	10	45	70
Read one issue a month of *Look, Life,* or *Post*	25	50	65	30
Read a daily newspaper	70	80	90	95
Read the *New York Times*	⅕	½	5	50
Read national or international news first in paper	10	20	30	50
Want more foreign news in paper	10	20	30	50
Listen to radio daily	60	70	85	?
Hear radio news daily	50	60	65	?
Use television daily	80	75	65	?
Watch TV news	45	45	45	?
Favor TV as news medium	60	35	20	?
Favor news as TV show	5	15	30	50

Source: *Television Quarterly,* Spring 1968, p. 47. These figures are for the most part derived from data in John Robinson, *Public Information about World Affairs,* Ann Arbor, Mich., 1967.

very effectively maintained under circumstances in which there are both a growing intellectual awareness of global interdependence and the electronic intrusion of global events into the home.

This condition also makes for a novel perception of foreign affairs. Even in the recent past one learned about international politics through the study of history and geography, as well as by reading newspapers. This contributed to a highly structured, even rigid, approach, in which it was convenient to categorize events or nations in somewhat ideological terms. Today, however, foreign affairs intrude upon a child or adolescent in the advanced countries in the form of disparate, sporadic, isolated—but involving—events: catastrophes and acts of violence both abroad and at home become intermeshed, and though they may elicit either positive or negative reactions, these are no longer in the neatly compartmentalized categories of "we" and "they." Television in particular contributes to a "blurred," much more impressionistic—and also involved—attitude toward world affairs.[10] Anyone who teaches international politics senses a great change in the attitude of the young along these lines.

Such direct global intrusion and interaction, however, does not make for better "understanding" of our contemporary affairs. On the contrary, it can be argued that in some respects "understanding"—in the sense of possessing the subjective confidence that one can evaluate events on the basis of some organized principle—is today much more difficult for most people to attain. Instant but vicarious participation in events evokes uncertainty, especially as it becomes more and more apparent that established analytical categories no longer adequately encompass the new circumstances.*

The science explosion—the most rapidly expanding aspect of

* To provide one simple example, for about twenty years anticommunism provided the grand organizational principle for many Americans. How then fit into that setting events such as the confrontation between Moscow and Peking, and, once one had become accustomed to think of Moscow as more "liberal," between Moscow and Prague?

our entire reality, growing more rapidly than population, industry, and cities—intensifies, rather than reduces, these feelings of insecurity. It is simply impossible for the average citizen and even for men of intellect to assimilate and meaningfully organize the flow of knowledge for themselves. In every scientific field complaints are mounting that the torrential outpouring of published reports, scientific papers, and scholarly articles and the proliferation of professional journals make it impossible for individuals to avoid becoming either narrow-gauged specialists or superficial generalists.* The sharing of new common perspectives thus becomes more difficult as knowledge expands; in addition, traditional perspectives such as those provided by primitive myths or, more recently, by certain historically conditioned ideologies can no longer be sustained.

The threat of intellectual fragmentation, posed by the gap between the pace in the expansion of knowledge and the rate of its assimilation, raises a perplexing question concerning the prospects for mankind's intellectual unity. It has generally been assumed that the modern world, shaped increasingly by the industrial and urban revolutions, will become more homogeneous in its outlook. This may be so, but it could be the homogeneity of insecurity, of uncertainty, and of intellectual anarchy. The result, therefore, would not necessarily be a more stable environment.

---

* It is estimated, for example, that NASA employs some fifteen thousand special technical terms—all of which are compiled in its own thesaurus (*CTN Bulletin* [Centres d'études des conséquences générales des grandes techniques nouvelles, Paris], June 1968, p. 6). It is also estimated that "the number of books published has about doubled every twenty years since 1450, and some 30 million have by now been published; the projected figure is 60 million by 1980" (Cyril Black, *The Dynamics of Modernization,* New York, 1966, p. 12) and that "science alone sees the publishing of 100,000 journals a year, in more than 60 languages, a figure doubling every 15 years" (Glenn T. Seaborg, "Uneasy World Gains Power over Destiny," *The New York Times,* January 6, 1969).

2. The Ambivalent Disseminator

The United States is the principal global disseminator of the technetronic revolution. It is American society that is currently having the greatest impact on all other societies, prompting a far-reaching cumulative transformation in their outlook and mores. At various stages in history different societies have served as a catalyst for change by stimulating imitation and adaptation in others. What in the remote past Athens and Rome were to the Mediterranean world, or China to much of Asia, France has more recently been to Europe. French letters, arts, and political ideas exercised a magnetic attraction, and the French Revolution was perhaps the single most powerful stimulant to the rise of populist nationalism during the nineteenth century.

In spite of its domestic tensions—indeed, in some respects because of them (see Part IV)—the United States is the innovative and creative society of today. It is also a major disruptive influence on the world scene. In fact communism, which many Americans see as the principal cause of unrest, primarily capitalizes on frustrations and aspirations, whose major source is the American impact on the rest of the world. The United States is the focus of global attention, emulation, envy, admiration, and animosity. No other society evokes feelings of such intensity; no other society's internal affairs—including America's racial and urban violence—are scrutinized with such attention; no other society's politics are followed with such avid interest—so much so that to many foreign nationals United States domestic politics have become an essential extension of their own; no other society so massively disseminates its own way of life and its values by means of movies, television, multimillion-copy foreign editions of its national magazines, or simply by its products; no other society is the object of such contradictory assessments.

The American Impact

Initially, the impact of America on the world was largely idealistic: America was associated with freedom. Later the influence became more materialistic: America was seen as the land of opportunity, crassly defined in terms of dollars. Today similar material advantages can be sought elsewhere at lower personal risk, and the assassinations of the Kennedys and of Martin Luther King, as well as racial and social tensions, not to speak of Vietnam, have somewhat tarnished America's identification with freedom. Instead, America's influence is in the first instance scientific and technological, and it is a function of the scientific, technological, and educational lead of the United States.*

Scientific and technological development is a dynamic process. It depends in the first instance on the resources committed to it, the personnel available for it, the educational base that supports it, and—last but not least—the freedom of scientific innovation. In all four respects the American position is advantageous; contemporary America spends more on science and devotes greater resources to research than any other society.†

---

* As a sweeping generalization, it can be said that Rome exported law; England, parliamentary party democracy; France, culture and republican nationalism; the contemporary United States, technological-scientific innovation and mass culture derived from high consumption.

† According to a 1968 congressional report, "Current spending on research and development in the United States amounts to some $24 billion annually —about two-thirds financed by the Federal Government—in contrast to a mere $6 billion in all of Western Europe." The Soviet figure has been estimated to be in the vicinity of 8 billion rubles, but, American costs being higher, one ruble buys approximately $3 of research. In 1962, according to the Organization for Economic Cooperation and Development (OECD), the United States was spending $93.70 per capita on research and development;

In addition, the American people enjoy access to education on a scale greater than that of most other advanced societies. (See Tables 4 and 5.) At the beginning of the 1960s the United States had more than 66 per cent of its 15–19 age group enrolled in educational institutions; comparable figures for France and West Germany were about 31 per cent and 20 per cent, respectively. The combined populations of France, Germany, Italy, and the United Kingdom are equal to that of the United States—roughly two hundred million. But in the United States 43 per cent of college-age people are actually enrolled, whereas only 7 to 15 per cent are enrolled in the four countries (Italy having the low figure and France the high). The Soviet percentage was approximately half that of the American. In actual numbers there are close to seven million college students in the United States and only about one and a half million in the four European countries. At the more advanced level of the 20–24 age bracket, the American figure was 12 per cent while that for West Germany, the top Western European country, was about 5 per cent. For the 5–19 age bracket, the American and the Western European levels were roughly even (about 80 per cent), and the Soviet Union trailed with 57 per cent.[11]

Britain $33.50; France $23.60; and Germany $20.10. As a percentage of gross national product, the United States' expenditure on research and development amounted to 3.1; Britain's to 2.2; France's to 1.5; Poland's to 1.6; Germany's to 1.3; and the Soviet Union's to 2.2. The number of scientists, engineers, and technicians engaged in research and development totaled 1,159,500 in the United States; 211,100 in Britain; 111,200 in France; 142,200 in Germany; 53,800 in Belgium and Holland; and somewhere over 1,000,000 in the Soviet Union (C. Freeman and A. Young, *The Research and Development Effort in Western Europe, North America and the Soviet Union,* OECD, 1965, pp. 71–72, 124. Source for Poland: a speech by A. Werblan, published by Polish Press Agency, October 15, 1968. The Poles expect to reach 2.5 per cent only by 1975. For a higher estimate of Soviet scientific manpower, see *Scientific Policy in the USSR,* a special report by the OECD, 1969, especially pp. 642–47). On a global scale, the United States accounts for roughly one-third of the world's total supply of scientific manpower ("The Scientific Brain Drain from the Developing Countries to the United States," *Twenty-third Report by the Committee on Government Operations,* House of Representatives, Washington, D.C., March 1968, p. 3; hereafter cited as *Report* . . .).

TABLE 4. ACCESS TO HIGHER-LEVEL EDUCATION PER 100,000 OF TOTAL POPULATION (1950, 1965)

	1950		1965	Absolute Increase 1950–1965
United States	1,508		2,840	+1,332
West Germany	256		632	+376
France	334		1,042	+708
Japan	471		1,140	+669
USSR	693		1,674	+981
Poland	473		800	+327
India	113	(1963)	284	+171
Indonesia	8	(1963)	95	+87
Brazil	98		189	+91
Algeria	52		68	+16

Source: *UNESCO Statistical Yearbook,* 1967, Table 2.10, pp. 185–99.

TABLE 5. NUMBER OF GRADUATES FROM HIGHER-LEVEL INSTITUTIONS PER 100,000 OF TOTAL POPULATION (1964)

United States	(1965)	349
West Germany		109
France		96
Japan		233
USSR		177
Poland		81
India	(1962)	45
Indonesia		—
Brazil		25
Algeria		—

Source: *UNESCO Statistical Yearbook,* 1967, Table 2.14, pp. 259–68.

As a result, the United States possesses a pyramid of educated social talent whose wide base is capable of providing effective support to the leading and creative apex. This is true even though in many respects American education is often intellectually deficient, especially in comparison with the more rigorous standards of Western European and Japanese secondary institutions. Nonetheless, the broad base of relatively trained people enables rapid adaptation, development, and social application of scientific innovation or discovery.* While no precise estimates are possible,

* America's scientific lead is particularly strong in the so-called frontier industries that involve the most advanced fields of science. It has been estimated that approximately 80 per cent of all scientific and technical discoveries made during the past few decades originated in the United States. About 79 per cent of the world's computers operate in the United States. America's lead in lasers is even more marked. The International Atomic Energy Agency has estimated (in its report *Power and Research Reactors in Member States,* Vienna, 1969) that by 1975 the United States will utilize more nuclear power for peaceful uses than the next eleven states combined (including Japan, all of Western Europe, Canada, and the Soviet Union).

some experts have suggested that a present-day society would experience difficulties in rapid modernization if less than 10 per cent of its population in the appropriate age bracket had higher education and less than 30 per cent had lower education.

Moreover, both the organizational structure and the intellectual atmosphere in the American scientific world favor experimentation and rapid social adaptation. In a special report on American scientific policies, submitted in early 1968, a group of experts connected with OECD concluded that America's scientific and technical enterprise is deeply rooted in American tradition and

---

To measure innovating performance, OECD analysts checked to see where one hundred and thirty-nine selected inventions were first used. Nine industrial sectors that depend heavily on innovation were surveyed (i.e., computers, semi-conductors, pharmaceuticals, plastics, iron and steel, machine tools, non-ferrous metals, scientific instruments, and synthetic fibers). The results showed that in the last twenty years the United States has had the highest rate of innovation, since approximately 60 per cent of the one hundred and thirty-nine inventions were first put to use in the United States (15 per cent in Great Britain, 9 per cent in Germany, 4 per cent in Switzerland, 3 per cent in Sweden). The United States collects 50–60 per cent of all OECD-area receipts for patents, licenses, etc.; the United States predominates in trade performance, accounting for about 30 per cent of the world's export in research-intensive product groups (J. Richardson and Ford Parks, "Why Europe Lags Behind," *Science Journal,* Vol. 4, August 1968, pp. 81–86).

It is striking to note, for example, that while Western Europe still slightly exceeds the United States in the number of patents registered annually, industrial application of patents is roughly eight times higher in the United States.

American leadership is also marked in pure science. In an unusually assertive—but not inaccurate—report, the National Academy of Sciences stated in late 1968 that the United States enjoys world leadership in mathematics, citing as evidence that 50 per cent of the prestigious Fields Medals awarded since 1945 went to Americans, that American mathematicians play the leading role in international mathematics congresses (delivering more than 33 per cent of all scientific papers), and that American mathematical research is cited most frequently in foreign mathematics journals (*The New York Times,* November 24, 1968).

American preponderance in Nobel Prizes in Physics, Chemistry, and Medicine has also become more marked. Thus, between the years 1901 and 1939 the United States and Canada won 13 prizes, while France, Germany, Italy, Benelux, and the United Kingdom won a total of 82, Scandinavia won 8, the USSR won 4, and Japan won none. Between 1940 and 1967 the respective figures were 42, 50, 6, 8, and 2.

history.* Competitiveness and the emphasis on quick exploitation have resulted in a quick spin-off of the enormous defense and space research efforts into the economy as a whole, in contrast to the situation in the Soviet Union, where the economic by-products of almost as large-scale a research effort have so far been negligible. It is noteworthy that "the Russians themselves estimate that the productivity of their researchers is only about half the Americans' and that innovations take two or three times as long to be put into effect." [12]

This climate and the concomitant rewards for creative attainments result in a magnetic pull (the "brain drain") from which America clearly benefits. America offers to many trained scientists, even from advanced countries, not only greater material rewards but a unique opportunity for the maximum fulfillment of their talents. In the past Western writers and artists gravitated primarily toward Paris. More recently the Soviet Union and China have exercised some ideological attraction, but in neither case did it involve the movement of significant percentages of scientific elites. Though immigrating scientists initially think of America as a platform for creative work, and not as a national society to

---

* "Since the first hours of the Republic, the right of citizens to the 'pursuit of happiness,' formulated in the Declaration of Independence, has been one of the mainsprings of American society; it is also the foundation of a social policy inspired by the prospect of new benefits issued from the scientific and technical enterprise. How can one fail to hope that these benefits, which have in fact contributed so much to national defense or the race for world prestige, will make an essential contribution to the achievement of other great national goals? It is this propulsion which has given science, the mother of knowledge, the appearance of a veritable national resource. The enterprise is indissolubly linked to the goals of American society, which is trying to build its future on the progress of science and technology. In this capacity, this society as a whole is a consumer of scientific knowledge, which is used for diverse ends: in the last century, to increase agricultural productivity and to facilitate territorial development, and then to back the national defense effort, to safeguard public health and to explore space. These are activities which have an impact on the destiny of the whole nation, and it seems natural that all skills should be mobilized to cooperate. In this way industry and the universities and private organizations are associated with the Government project" (conclusion of a report prepared by the Secretariat of the OECD, January 1968, as quoted by *The New York Times,* January 13, 1968, p. 10).

which they are transferring political allegiance, in most cases that allegiance is later obtained through assimilation. America's professional attraction for the global scientific elite is without historic precedent in either scale or scope.*

Though this attraction is likely to decline for Europeans (particularly because of America's domestic problems and partially because of Europe's own scientific advance), the success of J. J. Servan-Schreiber's book, *The American Challenge,* reflects the basic inclination of concerned Europeans to accept the argument that the United States comes closest to being the only truly modern society in terms of the organization and scale of its economic market, business administration, research and development, and education. (In contrast, the structure of American government is viewed as strikingly antiquated.) European sensitivity in this area is conditioned not only by fear of a widening American technological lead but very much by the increasing presence on the European markets of large American firms that exploit their economic advantages of scale and superior organization to gradually acquire controlling interests in key frontier industries. The presence of these firms, the emergence under their aegis of something akin to a new international corporate elite, the stimulation given by their presence to the adoption of American business practices and training, the deepening awareness that the so-called technol-

---

* In the words of E. Piore, vice president and chief scientist of I.B.M., "The United States has become the intellectual center of the world—the center of the arts, the sciences, and economics" ("Towards the Year 2000," *Daedalus,* Summer 1967, p. 958). It is symptomatic that in the early 1960s, 44 per cent of the Pakistani students studying at institutions of higher education in fifteen foreign countries were studying in the United States; 59 per cent of the Indians; 32 per cent of the Indonesians; 56 per cent of the Burmese; 90 per cent of the Filipinos; 64 per cent of the Thais; and 26 per cent of the Ceylonese (Gunnar Myrdal, *Asian Drama,* New York, 1968, p. 1773). In 1967 the United States granted 10,690 M.D.s at its own universities, and admitted in the same year as permanent immigrants 3457 physicians (*Report. . . ,* p. 3). In that same year 10,506 scientific, engineering, and medical personnel from the developed countries emigrated to the United States ("The Brain-Drain of Scientists, Engineers and Physicians from the Developing Countries to the United States," Hearing before a Subcommittee on Government Operations, House of Representatives, Washington, D.C., January 23, 1968, pp. 2, 96; hereafter cited as *Hearing . . .*).

ogy gap is in reality also a management and education gap[13]—all have contributed both to a positive appraisal of American "technostructure" by the European business and scientific elite and to the desire to adapt some of America's experience.

Less tangible but no less pervasive is the American impact on mass culture, youth mores, and life styles. The higher the level of per-capita income in a country, the more applicable seems the term "Americanization." This indicates that the external forms of characteristic contemporary American behavior are not so much culturally determined as they are an expression of a certain level of urban, technical, and economic development. Nonetheless, to the extent that these forms were first applied in America and then "exported" abroad, they became symbolic of the American impact and of the innovation-emulation relationship prevailing between America and the rest of the world.

What makes America unique in our time is that confrontation with the new is part of the daily American experience. For better or for worse, the rest of the world learns what is in store for it by observing what happens in the United States: whether it be the latest scientific discoveries in space and medicine or the electric toothbrush in the bathroom; pop art or LSD; air conditioning or air pollution; old-age problems or juvenile delinquency. The evidence is more elusive in such matters as style, music, values, and social mores, but there too the term "Americanization" obviously implies a specific source.

Similarly, foreign students returning from American universities have prompted an organizational and intellectual revolution in the academic life of their countries. Changes in the academic life of Germany, the United Kingdom, Japan, and more recently France, and to an even greater extent in the less developed countries, can be traced to the influence of American educational institutions. Given developments in modern communications, it is only a matter of time before students at Columbia University and, say, the University of Teheran will be watching the same lecturer simultaneously.

This is all the more likely because American society, more than any other, "communicates" with the entire globe.[14] Roughly sixty-five per cent of all world communications originate in this country. Moreover, the United States has been most active in the promotion of a global communications system by means of satellites, and it is pioneering the development of a world-wide information grid.* It is expected that such a grid will come into being by about 1975.[15] For the first time in history the cumulative knowledge of mankind will be made accessible on a global scale—and it will be almost instantaneously available in response to demand.

New Imperialism?

All of these factors make for a novel relationship between the United States and the world. There are imperial overtones to it, and yet in its essence the relationship is quite different from the traditional imperial structure. To be sure, the fact that in the aftermath of World War II a number of nations were directly dependent on the United States in matters of security, politics, and economics created a system that in many respects, including that of scale, superficially resembled the British, Roman, and Chinese empires of the past.[16] The more than a million American troops stationed on some four hundred major and almost three thousand minor United States military bases scattered all over the globe, the forty-two nations tied to the United States by security pacts, the American military missions training the officers and troops of many other national armies, and the approximately two hundred thousand United States civilian government employees in foreign posts all make for striking analogies to the great classical imperial systems.[17]

Nevertheless, the concept of "imperial" shields rather than reveals a relationship between America and the world that is both

---

* It is estimated (by the Institute for Politics and Planning, Arlington, Virginia) that the volume of digital communication will shortly exceed human conversation across the Atlantic; it has already done so in the United States. Moreover, within the next decade the value of information export from the United States to Europe will exceed the value of material exports.

more complex and more intimate. The "imperial" aspect of the relationship was, in the first instance, a transitory and rather spontaneous response to the vacuum created by World War II and to the subsequent felt threat from communism. Moreover, it was neither formally structured nor explicitly legitimized. The "empire" was at most an informal system marked by the pretense of equality and noninterference. This made it easier for the "imperial" attributes to recede once conditions changed. By the late 1960s, with a few exceptions the earlier direct political-military dependence on the United States had declined (often in spite of political efforts by the United States to maintain it). Its place had been filled by the more pervasive but less tangible influence of American economic presence and innovation as they originated directly from the United States or were stimulated abroad by American foreign investment (the latter annually yielding a product considerably in excess of the gross national product of most major countries).[18] In effect, ". . . American influence has a porous and almost invisible quality. It works through the interpenetration of economic institutions, the sympathetic harmony of political leaders and parties, the shared concepts of sophisticated intellectuals, the mating of bureaucratic interests. It is, in other words, something new in the world, and not yet well understood."[19]

It is the novelty of America's relationship with the world—complex, intimate, and porous—that the more orthodox, especially Marxist, analyses of imperialism fail to encompass. To see that relationship merely as the expression of an imperial drive is to ignore the part played in it by the crucial dimension of the technological-scientific revolution. That revolution not only captivates the imagination of mankind (who can fail to be moved by the spectacle of man reaching the moon?) but inescapably compels imitation of the more advanced by the less advanced and stimulates the export of new techniques, methods, and organizational skills from the former to the latter. There is no doubt that this results in an asymmetrical relationship, but the content of that asymmetry must be examined before it is called imperialism. Like every society, America no doubt prefers to be more rather than less advanced; yet it is also striking that no other country has made so great an effort, governmentally and privately, through business and especially through foundations, to export its know-how, to make public its space findings, to promote new agricultural techniques, to improve educational facilities, to control population growth, to improve health care, and so on. All of this has imperial overtones, and yet it is misleading to label it as such.[20]

Indeed, unable to understand fully what is happening in their own society, Americans find it difficult to comprehend the global impact that that society has had in its unique role as disseminator of the technetronic revolution. This impact is contradictory: it both promotes and undermines American interests as defined by American policymakers; it helps to advance the cause of cooperation on a larger scale even as it disrupts existing social or economic fabrics; it both lays the groundwork for well-being and stability and enhances the forces working for instability and revolution. Unlike traditional imperialistic powers, which relied heavily on the principle of *divide et impera* (practiced with striking similarity by the British in India and more recently by the Russians in Eastern Europe), America has striven to promote regionalism both in Europe and in Latin America. Yet in so doing, it is helping to create larger entities that are more capable of resisting its influence and of competing with it economically. Implicitly and often explicitly modeled on the American pattern, modernization makes for potentially greater economic well-being, but in the process it disrupts existing institutions, undermines prevailing mores, and stimulates resentment that focuses directly on the source of change—America. The result is an acute tension between the kind of global stability and order that America subjectively seeks and the instability, impatience, and frustration that America unconsciously promotes.

The United States has emerged as the first global society in history. It is a society increasingly difficult to delineate in terms of its outer cultural and economic boundaries. Moreover, it is unlikely that in the foreseeable future America will cease to exercise the innovative stimulus that is characteristic of its current relationship with the world. By the end of this century (extrapolating from current trends) only some thirteen countries are likely to reach the 1965 level of the per-capita gross national product of the United States.[21] Unless there is major scientific and economic stagnation or a political crisis (see Part IV), at the end of the century America will still be a significant force for global change, whether or not the dominant subjective mood is pro- or anti-American.

3. Global Ghettos

The Third World is a victim of the technetronic revolution. Whether the less developed countries grow rapidly or slowly, or not at all, almost inevitably many of them will continue to be dominated by intensifying feelings of psychological deprivation. In a world electronically intermeshed, absolute or relative underdevelopment will be intolerable, especially as the more advanced countries begin to move beyond that industrial era into which the less developed countries have as yet to enter. It is thus no longer a matter of the "revolution of rising expectations." The Third World today confronts the specter of insatiable aspirations.

At one time in history seemingly insoluble problems prompted fatalism because they were thought to be part of a universal condition. Today similar problems stimulate frustration because they are seen as a particular phenomenon by which others, more fortunate, are not afflicted. The plight of the urban ghettos in the United States provides an appropriate analogy to the global position of the less developed countries, particularly in Africa and Asia. Their problem is not that of the absence of change.* In some cases it is not even that of insufficiently rapid change, because in recent years several underdeveloped countries have attained impressive and sustained rates of growth (South Korea, Taiwan, and Ghana, for example). Rather, their problem arises from an intensifying feeling of relative deprivation of which they are made more acutely aware by the spread of education and communications. As a result, passive resignation may give way to active explosions of undirected anger.

Prospects for Change

It is extremely difficult to predict the economic and political development of the underdeveloped countries. Some of them, especially in Latin America, may make respectable progress and may, within the next two decades, reach the economic levels of the currently more advanced states. Islands of development may increasingly dot the maps of Asia and Africa, assuming that there is relative peace and political stability in the region as a whole. But the over-all prognosis is not hopeful. Medium projections for several of the more important underdeveloped countries point to a per-capita annual gross national product in 1985 of $107 for Nigeria, $134 for Pakistan, $112 for Indonesia, $169 for India, $185 for China, $295 for the United Arab Republic, and $372 for Brazil.

---

* "The growth rate of these countries during the Development Decade has not reached the annual figure of 5 per cent which was set as the minimum target. Actually the average rate for fifty-four countries, representing 87 per cent of the population of the developing world as a whole, was only 4.5 per cent *per annum* from 1960 to 1965. . . . Among the fifty-four countries mentioned, there is a group of eighteen with an average growth rate of 7.3 per cent *per annum,* while the rate for fifteen countries was scarcely 2.7 per cent *per annum.* . . . Between these two extremes there were twenty-one countries whose average growth rate was 4.9 per cent" ("Towards a Global Strategy of Development," a report by the Secretary-General of the United Nations Conference on Trade and Development, New York, 1968, p. 5).

(By way of contrast, the prospective per-capita figure for 1985 for the United States is $6510, for Japan $3080, for the USSR $2660, and for Israel $2978.)[22] What is even more striking is that while the per-capita GNP in the above advanced countries is likely to double during the years 1965–1985, for a single Nigerian the per-capita GNP will have increased by only $14, for a Pakistani by $43, for an Indonesian by $12, for an Indian by $70, for a Chinese by $88, for an Egyptian by $129, and for a Brazilian by $92 during the same two decades of development.

The threat of overpopulation to economic growth—indeed to existence itself—has been widely discussed in recent years. That threat, it should be added, involves a crucial social-political dimension. Overpopulation contributes to the breakup of landholdings and thereby further stratifies and complicates the rural class structure, widening disparities and intensifying class conflicts. Staggering problems of unemployment are also highly probable. According to the International Labor Organization, by 1980 the labor force of Asia's developing nations will have increased from 663 million to 938 million. During this same period the number of new jobs in these countries will increase by only 142 million, according to projections of current growth rates.[23]

Even if it is assumed that the problem of overpopulation will be met by greater acceptance of birth control, the economic picture in terms of the per-capita GNP for underdeveloped countries becomes only marginally brighter when it is compared with the figures projected for the more advanced societies. For example, in the unlikely event that by 1985 Indonesia's population will not have increased since 1965, its per-capita GNP will be approximately $200 instead of the projected $112; under similar circumstances, for Pakistan it will be $250 instead of the projected $134, and for the United Arab Republic almost $500 instead of $295. Since some population growth is unavoidable, the above figures actually represent unattainable levels, even though they are in themselves singularly unimpressive when compared with the figures for the more advanced portions of the world.

To point to these figures is not to exclude the probability that progress will be made in some fields. It is probably true that "the picture of the world in 1985, despite the large pockets of poverty that will still exist, is far from grim. Indeed, by 1985 mass starvation, mass homelessness, and the rampant spread of diseases that have historically decimated entire populations will be generally eliminated. Although the underdeveloped countries will still be comparatively poor, they will have greater and more immediate access to worldwide transportation and communications systems and to the provision of drugs, medical care, food, shelter and clothing through international assistance in the event of disaster. The surplus commodity production of the United States will be an important element in the feeding of underprivileged nations." [24] One may assume that the appearance of greater international planning in terms of international commodity agreements, transport arrangements, health regulations, finance, and education will make for more orderly and deliberate approaches to the problems posed by backwardness, slow growth, and the widening disparity in standards of living. The increasing communications intimacy will permit instant responses to sudden emergencies and allow for continuous long-distance visual consultations by specialists. In the event of need, aid could be mobilized and ferried across the globe in no more time than is now needed to respond to an internal national calamity—or even an urban one.

The agricultural revolution in Asia is already challenging the recently fashionable predictions of mass hunger and starvation. Mass educational campaigns and the introduction of new cereals and fertilizers have prompted an impressive upsurge in productivity. Within the next few years Pakistan, the Philippines, and Turkey may become grain-exporting states; Thailand and Burma already have. The cumulative effect of such successes may well be to "bolster the confidence of national leaders in their ability to handle other seemingly insoluble problems. It may also strengthen the faith in modern technology and its potential for improving the well-being of their people." [25]

Yet even allowing for these more hopeful developments, the fact remains that though the material conditions of life in the Third World are in some respects improving, these improvements cannot keep pace with the factors that make for psychic change. The basic revolutionary change is being brought about by education and communications. That change, necessary and desirable to stimulate an attitude receptive to innovation (for example, the acceptance by peasants of fertilizers), also prompts an intense awareness of inadequacy and backwardness.

In this regard, a comparison of the contemporary socio-economic transformation of the Third World with that of Russia at about the turn of the century is revealing. In Russia the industrial revolution outpaced mass education; literacy followed—rather than preceded—material change.* The revolutionary movements, particularly the Marxist one, strove to close the gap by politically educating—hence radicalizing—the masses. Today in the Third World a subjective revolution is preceding change in the objective environment and creating a state of unrest, uneasiness, anger, anguish, and outrage. Indeed, it has been observed that "the faster

---

* Between 1887 and 1904, Russian coal-mining output rose by 400 per cent (from 5 million to 21.5 million tons) and iron smelting by 500 per cent; between 1861 and 1870, 5833 miles of railway were constructed, and between 1891 and 1900, 13,920 miles. "Coal production in Russia rose 40 percent in the period 1909–1913, as against a growth rate of 24 percent in the United States, 28 percent in Germany, 7 percent in Britain, and 9 percent in France in the same period. In the case of pig iron, Russian output rose by 61 percent in the period 1909–1913, while the rate of increase in the United States was 20 percent, in Germany 33 percent, in Britain 8 percent, and in France 46 percent. Although the economic backwardness of Russia had not disappeared on the eve of the war, it was clearly disappearing. The standard of living was not high, but it was rising. In the twenty years preceding the war the population of Russia increased by about 40 percent, while the domestic consumption of goods more than doubled" (S. Pushkarev, *The Emergence of Modern Russia 1801–1917*, New York, 1963, p. 280). Yet on the eve of World War I there were only 117,000 students in higher education in a country of some 160 million people, and 56 per cent of the people were illiterate (Pushkarev, pp. 286, 292). Of the children in the 8–11 age bracket, 49 per cent were not receiving any education, while the percentage of literates among military inductees rose between 1874 and 1913 at a rate of only slightly more than one per cent per annum (A. G. Rashin, *Formirovanie Rabochego Klassa Rossii*, Moscow, 1958, p. 582).

the enlightenment of the population, the more frequent the overthrow of the government." *

This gap between awakening mass consciousness and material reality appears to be widening. In the years 1958–1965 the income per capita of an Indian rose from $64 to $86† and that of an Indonesian from $81 to $85; the income of an Algerian declined from $236 to $195.[26] The percentage of the economically active population in fields other than agriculture grew substantially only in Algeria (from 10 per cent to 18 per cent). Housing, physicians per thousand inhabitants, and personal consumption did not show significant advances for the major backward areas. In some they even showed a decrease.[27] (See Table 6.)

The Subjective Transformation

Although objective conditions changed slowly, the subjective environment altered rapidly. Spectacular advances came primarily in two fields: communications and education. The number of radios in India quadrupled between 1958 and 1966 (from 1.5 million to 6.4 million); elsewhere in the Third World the figures have doubled or tripled. The television age is only beginning in these regions, but both transistor radios and television will no doubt become generally available there in the next two decades.‡

* "For 66 nations, for example, the correlation between the proportion of children in primary schools and the frequency of revolution was –.84. In contrast, for 70 nations the correlation between the rate of change in primary enrollment and political instability was .61" (Samuel P. Huntington, *Political Order in Changing Societies*, New Haven and London, 1968, p. 47).

† It should be noted that these are average figures. "A survey for 1965–66 indicated that half of India's population was living on R14.6 or less per month (about 10¢ in U.S. currency per day). . . . In short the very low average income does not begin to plumb the depths of misery in India" (Myrdal, p. 565).

‡ The Chairman of the Indian Atomic Energy Commission estimated that community television for all the five hundred and sixty thousand villages in India could be transmitted by satellite in five years at a cost of only $200 million (*The New York Times*, August 15, 1968). In September 1969 the United States concluded an agreement with India for the creation by 1972 of a satellite that will provide television programs on agriculture and birth control for approximately five thousand villages in four Hindi-speaking states (see also our earlier discussion of the American impact).

Access to higher education has also grown rapidly: in India between 1958 and 1963 the increase was roughly 50 per cent (from 900,000 to 1.3 million students), and by 1968 there were about 1.9 million students in 2749 colleges and 80 universities; in Indonesia the increase was 30 per cent (from 50,000 to 65,000) between 1958 and 1964; and in the United Arab Republic it was more than 50 per cent (83,000 to 145,000) during the same half decade. Enrollment in India's primary schools jumped from 18.5 million in 1951 to 51.5 million in 1966, according to UNESCO statistics. (See Table 7.)

Increased access to education gives rise to its own specific problems. On the one hand, access to advanced training, particularly of a technical nature, is too limited to sustain extensive and intensive modernization.* The Third World is still woefully backward in intermediate technical education. On the other hand, the capacity of many of the less developed countries to absorb trained personnel is inadequate; the result is a class of dissatisfied college graduates, composed especially of those from the legal and liberal-arts faculties, who are unable to obtain gainful employment compatible with their expanded expectations. Although this problem is already acute in several countries,[28] it could be made worse by the introduction of automation into the overmanned factories and bureaucracies of the less developed countries.†

The problem is aggravated by the frequently low level of what is officially described as higher education. According to one ad-

---

* See the tables on page 27, as well as the more extensive comparisons between the Third World and the United States and Western Europe (both current figures and projections for the year 2000) contained in *Higher Education*, Committee on Higher Education, London, 1963, especially Appendixes I and V.

† "As the scientific processing of information will be under way in the urban centers of Asia, Africa and Latin America by 1985, large numbers of clerks, runners, sorters, and filers that today account for the weight of public and private bureaucracy in India, Nigeria or Brazil will begin to be threatened with displacement and the insecurities of unemployment" (*The United States and the World in the 1985 Era*, p. 91). It is estimated that by 1970 roughly one-half of Ceylon's expected one million unemployed will have certificates of higher education ("The International Report," *The Economist*, June 15, 1968, p. 47).

TABLE 6

	Per-capita GNP in U.S. Dollars			Per Cent of Population Employed Outside Agriculture		
	1958	1966	Increase (in percentages)	1950	1960	Increase (in percentages)
United States	2,602	3,842	48	90.4	93.5	3.1
West Germany	1,077	2,004	86	74.2	86.6 (1961)	12.4
France	1,301	2,052	58	72.5 (1954)	80.2 (1962)	7.7
Italy	598	1,182	98	60.5 (1951)	71.8 (1962)	11.3
Soviet Union	1,100	1,500 (1965)	36	52.0	60.8 (1959)	8.8
Poland	800	1,100 (1965)	38	42.8	46.6	3.8
Czechoslovakia	—	—	—	61.4	80.5 (1965)	19.1
Japan	344	986	187	—	74.0	—
India	72	105	46	27.0 (1951)	27.1 (1961)	0.1
Indonesia	84	95 (1963)	13	—	32.0 (1961)	—
United Arab Republic	120	179 (1965)	49	37.3 (1947)	43.3	0.6
Brazil	310	333	7	51.9	48.4	−3.5

	Per Cent of Population in Localities over 20,000 Inhabitants			Average Number of Persons per Room		
	1950	1960	Increase (in percentages)	1950	1960	Increase (in percentages)
United States	41.4	46.9	5.5	0.7	0.7	0.0
West Germany	41.5	47.6	6.1	—	0.9	—
France	33.3 (1954)	—	—	1.0 (1954)	1.0 (1962)	0.0
Italy	41.2 (1951)	—	—	1.3 (1951)	1.1 (1961)	−0.2
Soviet Union	—	35.5 (1959)	—	—	1.5 (1956)	—
Poland	25.5	31.9	6.4	—	1.7 (1961)	—
Czechoslovakia	21.0 (1947)	25.3 (1961)	4.3	1.5	1.3 (1961)	−0.2
Japan	—	72.0	—	—	1.2 (1963)	—
India	12.0 (1951)	—	—	—	2.6	—
Indonesia	9.1 (1955)	—	—	—	—	—
United Arab Republic	29.1 (1947)	29.1 (1955)	0.0	—	1.6	—
Brazil	20.1	28.1	8.0	1.3	1.3	0.0

TABLE 7

	Number of Students in Institutions of Higher Learning			Number of Radios		
	1958	1965	Increase (in percentages)	1958	1966	Increase (in percentages)
United States	3,042,200	5,526,325	81.6	161,000,000	262,700,000	63
West Germany	173,320	372,929	115	15,263,000	27,400,000	79
France	186,101	509,764	174	10,646,000	15,861,000	49
Italy	216,248	300,940	39	6,112,000	11,163,000	83
Soviet Union	2,178,900	3,860,500	77	36,667,000	76,800,000	109
Poland	111,820	251,864	125	4,465,000	5,593,000	25
Czechoslovakia	48,805	141,687	190	3,317,000	3,829,000	15
Japan	566,551	1,116,430	97	14,610,000	24,787,000	70
India	913,380	1,310,000 (1963)	43	1,560,000	6,485,000	316
Indonesia	49,557	65,635 (1964)	32	631,000	1,250,000	98
United Arab Republic	83,251	177,123	113	792,000	1,613,000 (1965)	104
Brazil	86,868	155,781	79	4,000,000	7,500,000 (1964)	88

	Number of Television Receivers			Number of Telephones		
	1958	1966	Increase (in percentages)	1958	1966	Increase (in percentages)
United States	50,250,000	74,100,000	47	66,630,000	98,789,000	48
West Germany	2,125,000	12,720,000	499	5,090,102	9,532,417	87
France	989,000	7,471,000	655	3,703,578	6,554,441	77
Italy	1,098,000	6,855,000	524	2,988,465	6,467,597	116
Soviet Union	1,767,000	19,000,000	975	2,370,000	4,459,000 (1965)	88
Poland	85,000	2,540,000	2888	446,236	1,411,481	216
Czechoslovakia	328,000	2,375,000	624	789,679	1,582,852	100
Japan	1,600,000	19,002,000	1088	4,334,602	16,011,745	269
India	400 (1962)	4,000	900	367,000	926,617	153
Indonesia	—	4,600	—	90,968	116,332	28
United Arab Republic	128,000 (1962)	375,000	193	185,452	335,000	81
Brazil	700,000	2,500,000	257	928,117	1,431,653	54

Sources for Tables 6 and 7: *UN Statistical Yearbooks,* 1960–1967; *UNESCO Yearbook,* 1967.

mittedly impressionistic but perceptive account, "At a generous estimate, perhaps 5 per cent of the mass of Indian students in institutions of higher education are receiving decent training by recognizable world standards. . . . In most places academic standards have fallen so low that they can hardly be said to have survived." [29] This condition is by no means limited to India. "Teaching in South Asian schools at all levels tends to discourage independent thinking and the growth of that inquisitive and experimental bent of mind that is so essential for development. . . . The South Asian peoples are not merely being insufficiently educated; they are being miseducated on a huge scale." [30] Similarly in Latin America: "By now it is fully recognized that education in Latin America has fundamental shortcomings, that there is a high illiteracy rate, and that the educational system bears no relation to the requirements of economic development, quite apart from the serious deficiencies that exist in other basic cultural respects." [31] "Education" of this sort contributes to the emergence of an inadequately trained class of younger people whose frustrations, increasing radicalism, and susceptibility to utopian appeals have many parallels in those of the nineteenth-century intelligentsia of the more backward regions of Europe, particularly Russia and the Balkans.

To obtain quality education, a small percentage of the students —either because they are unusually gifted and can obtain scholarships, or because they come from wealthy families—go abroad. As a result, they are tempted to adapt to foreign styles and modes of life, and even to remain abroad; in effect, they opt out of their own society either by emigrating internally on their return, or simply by never returning. In 1967, for example, 26 per cent of the Chinese students studying sciences and engineering in the United States chose not to return to Taiwan; for India the percentage was 21, and for Korea and Pakistan it was 15 and 13, respectively.[32] It is a staggering fact that the underdeveloped countries supplied almost exactly one-half of the total number of engineers, scientists, and medical personnel who emigrated to the

United States in the year ending June 1967: 10,254 out of 20,760.[33] It is expected that this proportion will actually rise in the years to come.[34] At the same time, many of those who do return to their native lands do so after having become "immersed in values and an educational system which prepares individuals to fit in an advanced country and may unfit them for developing an appropriate personality for an active life in their own community." [35]

The cumulative effect of these factors makes for a highly turbulent and extremely amorphous political pattern. Without allowing for specific differences among Third World countries, it can be said in general terms that the political pyramid in the less developed countries has at its base the peasant masses, still primarily engaged in manual labor and largely illiterate* but no longer parochially restricted to their immediate environment, since transistor radios establish intimate contact with the national society and help develop awareness of their material or national deprivation;† next in order is a rapidly increasing urban population,‡

---

* As of 1960, approximately 70 per cent of the males over 15 and 90 per cent of the females over 15 in Pakistan were illiterate; in India the percentages were 60 per cent and 85 per cent, respectively; in Indonesia 40 per cent and 70 per cent; and in Burma 20 per cent and 60 per cent. In Latin America in 1960, 35.6 per cent of the males and 42.6 per cent of the females in Brazil were illiterate; in Argentina 7.5 per cent and 9.7 per cent; in Chile 15.1 per cent and 17.6 per cent; in Peru 25.6 per cent and 52.4 per cent; and in Venezuela 30.2 per cent and 38.3 per cent (Myrdal, pp. 540, 1672; *UN Statistical Yearbook*, 1965).

† It is therefore too late to suggest that since participation is running ahead of the effective institutionalization of political processes, it might be desirable—in order to prevent chaos—to either limit or delay programs that stimulate higher levels of participation—for instance, by slowing down drives against illiteracy so that literacy does not outpace economic and political development. Even if the latter were practicable, the dissemination of transistor radios (and soon television) is beginning to have the same politically activizing effect that literacy had on the urban proletariat of the late nineteenth century. Thus, Frantz Fanon quite correctly observed in his *Studies in a Dying Colonialism* (New York, 1965) that "since 1956 the purchase of a radio in Algeria has meant, not the adoption of a modern technique for getting news, but the obtaining of access to the only means of entering into communication with the Revolution, of living with it" (p. 83).

‡ Cities with populations of over a hundred thousand have been increasing in Asia at a rate three times that of the general population growth of the countries concerned (Myrdal, p. 469).

composed to a large extent of first-generation post-peasant city dwellers searching for new sources of authority;[36] then comes a pseudo-intelligentsia, which accounts for roughly two to three per cent of the population and is composed of relatively young people who during the last decade have acquired some formal advanced education—often of very poor professional quality—and who, because they live badly and feel that society does not offer them the opportunity to which they are entitled, are highly susceptible to militant xenophobic causes; at the top of the pyramid is a relatively well-educated but narrow-gauged elite class, struggling to achieve both stability and progress (Iran), or sometimes to delay or prevent reforms (some Latin American countries), because, as a Brazilian scholar put it, they "want it that way. In order to maintain their privileges, they are dependent on the perpetuation of the status quo." [37] These privileges are either those of property or, more frequently in the case of the new nations, of bureaucratic position.

The ghettos of the global city have, accordingly, some parallels to the racial slums of the United States. In American cities the problem is not the absence of development or change; it stems from the perception by the poor that even rapid change will not change much for many in the near future, and from their growing realization that those who are richer are themselves becoming morally uneasy over the material gap. This combination of factors creates a sense of acute deprivation that results in intensified political hostility toward the outside world.[38] The mobilization of that hostility in the United States was made possible by the increase in the number of black Americans receiving higher education and therefore capable of providing on a socially significant scale the energizing leadership for the expression of hitherto suppressed grievances. Another factor was the rapid growth in the number of black Americans living in cities* and therefore re-

* The proportion of all Negroes living in the North and West almost quadrupled from 1910 to 1960, when 73 per cent of all Negroes resided in urban areas and thus represented a more urbanized population than the whites,

leased from the lethargy of traditional, white-dominated rural existence and brought into direct contact with the white community, which, although essentially conservative, has become increasingly ambivalent in its values. Within this context, attempts at reform contributed to further tension and friction, prompting some, in the dominant community, to adopt a reactionary posture against change, and others, especially among the deprived, to argue that no change was meaningful within the framework of the existing system.

American racial slums have grown in a pattern not unlike the expansion of the huge impoverished urban centers of Asia. Blacks from the South have tended to move to northern cities more in reaction to their poverty and felt injustice than because of the actual employment available there. The rate of unemployment in large American cities is several times more than the national average. In Asia, cities inhabited by impoverished and unproductive masses have grown rapidly in recent years not because of employment opportunities but because of rural poverty and insecurity. "Instead of standing as a symptom of growth, as it was in the West, urbanization in South Asia is an aspect of continued poverty." [39]

The parallel between the ghettos of the global city and the racial slums of the United States can be extended to the problems faced by the intellectual political elite of the Third World. In the United States "integration" has so far tended to mean the selective assimilation of a few individuals who can conform to the prevailing norms of the dominant community; however, their assimilation also means the loss of talent and expertise to the black community, in which the less educated, more militant "pseudo-intelligentsia" increasingly provides charismatic leadership to the masses by exploiting reverse racism. In like manner, the established social elites of the Third World have tended to emulate

---

only 70 per cent of whom resided in urban areas (Philip M. Hauser, "Demographic Factors in the Integration of the Negro," in *The Negro American*, Talcott Parsons and Kenneth B. Clark, eds., Boston, 1965, pp. 74–75).

the life styles of the more advanced world, and to emigrate into it either directly or vicariously.

The Political Vacuum

The resulting vacuum is filled by an indigenous pseudo-intelligentsia, whose views are influenced by doctrines advocated by Frantz Fanon, Regis Debray, Che Guevara, and others. Nineteenth-century European Marxism, originally addressed to an urban proletariat only recently divorced from rural life, is romantically adapted to the conditions of industrially backward twentieth-century global ghettos. "The revolutionary intellectual is a virtually universal phenomenon in modernizing societies. 'No one is as inclined to foster violence as a disgruntled intellectual, at least within the Indian context,' Hoselitz and Weiner have observed. 'It is these persons who compose the cadres of the less responsible political parties, who make up the narrower entourage of demagogues and who become leaders of millenarian and messianic movements, all of which may, when the opportunity is ripe, threaten political stability.' In Iran extremists of both the left and the right were more likely than moderates to be products of the city, to come from the middle economic strata, and to be better educated." [40]

Given this emotional context, external aid, designed to overcome the specific condition of backwardness and poverty, becomes an additional point of friction, and—even when it helps to improve the objective situation—stimulates further subjective tension. In the urban ghettos of the United States, governmental and private aid programs administered by whites have been resented by the blacks; when administered by the blacks, however, they have often become targets of white charges that funds designed for specific development programs have been used to advance black militancy. On the global scale, "neo-colonialism" has been the formula used to stimulate suspicion by the masses of the political motives of economic aid from the advanced countries;* graft, corruption, and inefficiency have been the charges made by donor countries against the recipients of economic assistance.

The shift toward economic assistance on an international basis is a response to this danger—at least in part. It poses another danger, however. Aid can at best be only a partial response to a condition that has profoundly psychological as well as material roots. Economic assistance can be effective only if, in addition, the recipient country's emotional resources are mobilized and a sense of popular enthusiasm and purpose is created. This requires native leadership that knows both how to stir the masses and how to utilize foreign aid intelligently. Such leadership is rare; where it does exist it frequently tends to be unresponsive to foreign interests and advice, and thus stimulates foreign resentment. The difficulties faced by the United States in dealing with Nasser or Ayub Khan, who were not only promoting but also responding to the emotionalism of their own masses, are cases in point.

Moreover, even if those in authority are determined to promote social change, they are faced with the intractable fact that their reality can be changed only very gradually, while popular mobilization on behalf of change can be attained only by stimulating mass enthusiasm and emotion. The rulers thus confront a dilemma.

---

* On a more sophisticated level, the economic system of the advanced countries is condemned as inherently incapable of providing true assistance. "Thus, Furtado [the Latin American economist] points out, the corporation is designed to fit the needs of profit-making in an advanced economy, and when one tries to transplant its technology to impoverished, developing lands, furious contradictions result. The newest machines save manpower—a blessing in the US and a curse in a country with rampant underemployment. Mass production requires a huge market nonexistent in an archaic agricultural society. So, Furtado concludes, the very structure of economic life in the new nations—forced upon them in the last century—makes it difficult for them to absorb the benefits of scientific and technical progress on those rare occasions where they might have the opportunity to do so. Thus, the rich nations specialize in activities which make work easier, goods more abundant, leisure more widespread, and living standards higher. The poor nations are left with the grubby tasks of primary production and with a stagnant or declining market; they must sell cheap and buy dear from the booming factories" (Michael Harrington, *American Power in the Twentieth Century,* New York, 1967, p. 9).

To admit the reality of the slowness of change is to deprive themselves of the support of the masses and to yield the political initiative to radical demagogues; to mobilize the masses on behalf of unattainable goals is to court an eventual explosion—unless that mobilization becomes a vehicle for subordinating the masses to centralized, bureaucratic control of the sort that communist leaders provide most effectively. Furthermore, to obtain the support of the propertied and more educated groups, the reform planners often have to "tread most warily in order not to disrupt the traditional social order . . . they permit the laws to contain loopholes of all sorts and even let them remain unenforced."[41] The distance between promise and attainment thus tends to widen.

The prospect is that feelings of intensive resentment will most likely grow as the gap between the Third World and the developed world widens.* Indeed, they will probably intensify as by the year 2000 the spectrum expands and ranges from the few most advanced post-industrial technetronic states (the United States, Japan, Sweden, Canada), to the dozen or so mature industrial states (only then approaching the present levels of the United States), to the ten to fifteen currently underdeveloped states that by 2000 will have reached the levels of the currently less advanced early-industrial states, to the large group (about sixty) still in the pre-industrial stage, and finally to those remaining still in extremely primitive conditions. The third and fourth groups, those containing the majority of the world's population and experiencing at best only partially effective progress, will in all likelihood be the centers of volatile political activity, resentment, tension, and extremism.[42]

In that context, it is difficult to conceive how democratic institu-

* In 1965 the per-capita production of the developed world exceeded that of the less developed by twelve times; it is estimated that by the year 2000 the proportion will be eighteen times greater (Herman Kahn and Anthony J. Wiener, *The Year 2000*, New York, 1967, p. 142). In 1965 Illinois alone had a larger gross product than all of Africa; California, more than all of China.

tions (derived largely from Western experience but typical only of the more stable and wealthy Western nations) will endure in a country like India—or how they will develop elsewhere.* "Much will depend on the pace of economic development itself, and in this respect the omens are far from favorable."[43] The likely consequence is sporadic turbulence in individual countries and a turn toward personal dictatorships. The latter will be based on more internally oriented, though socially radical, unifying doctrines in the hope that the combination of xenophobia and charisma may provide the minimum stability necessary for imposing social-economic modernization from above.

As in the case of urban ghettos in the United States, this may make for a tenser relationship with the more prosperous and advanced world. The latter has in recent years come to accept—at least as a general proposition, and still grudgingly—a moral obligation to assist materially the development of the Third World. This "new morality" was doubtless stimulated by Cold War rivalry, which made the two developed camps compete in providing assistance to the backward nations. It is far from certain that these feelings of conscience will persist if the Cold War wanes;† they certainly will not if East-West rivalry is replaced by intensifying North-South animosity. The peoples of the developed world may well take refuge in the self-serving argument that the irrational fanaticism of the leaders of the global ghettos precludes cooperation. Such a negative posture will ensure both the further widening of the gulf and a more bitter split among mankind, which is for the first time beginning to live in subjective intimacy.

---

* "Like the states of seventeenth-century Europe the non-Western countries of today can have political modernization or they can have democratic pluralism, but they cannot normally have both" (Huntington, pp. 136–37).

† This has been duly noted by some Third World spokesmen. The Algerian delegate to the UN Economic and Social Council meeting in Geneva said in July 1966, "Even as the détente in the Cold War has permitted an attenuation of the conflict between blocs with different social systems, one must fear that the East-West opposition will revolve on its axis and become an antagonism of North against South" (cited by Harrington, p. 20).

4. Global Fragmentation and Unification

The cumulative effect of the technetronic revolution is contradictory. On the one hand, this revolution marks the beginnings of a global community; on the other hand, it fragments humanity and detaches it from its traditional moorings. The technetronic revolution is widening the spectrum of the human condition. It intensifies the gulf in the material condition of mankind even as it contracts mankind's subjective tolerance of that disparity.

Though differences among societies gradually developed in the course of human history, it was not until the industrial revolution that these differences became sharp. Today some nations still live under conditions not unlike those of pre-Christian times, and many live in circumstances no better than those of the Middle Ages. Yet soon a few will live in ways so new that it is now difficult to imagine the social and personal ramifications. The result could be a profound three-way split in the attitudes and views of mankind. The coexistence of agrarian, industrial, and new technetronic societies, each providing different perspectives on life, would make understanding more difficult at the very time it becomes more possible, and it would render the global acceptance of certain norms less likely even as it becomes more imperative.

Fragmented Congestion

This three-way global split could further strain the already weak fabric of social and political order and result in domestic and, therefore, possibly international chaos. Growing anarchy in the Third World would very likely involve racist and nationalist passions. At the very least, this would create major pockets of disruption and chaos in the world; at worst, Third World instability could draw the more developed nations into potentially antagonistic forms of involvement that could have the same effect on American-Soviet relations as Balkan conflicts had on the European order prior to World War I.

In the most advanced world the tension between "internal" and "external" man—between man preoccupied with his inner meaning and his relationship to the infinite, and man deeply involved in his environment and committed to shaping what he recognizes to be finite—prompts an acute crisis of philosophic, religious, and psychic identity; this crisis is aggravated by the fear that man's malleability may permit what was previously considered immutable in man to be undermined. The explosion in scientific knowledge poses the danger of intellectual fragmentation, with uncertainty increasing in direct proportion to the expansion in what is known. The result, especially in the United States (see Part IV for a more extended discussion), is an accelerating search for new social and political forms.

The impact of the United States as the first global society reflects these conflicting tendencies. Though the United States searches for global stability and devotes its enormous resources to preventing revolutionary upheavals, its social impact on the world is unsettling, innovative, and creative. Even as it provokes violent antagonism to itself, it sets off expectations that are measured by American standards and that in most countries cannot be met until well into the next century. It accelerates the unification of other societies—not only because regionalism has since the 1960s become Washington's professed foreign-policy formula but also because other nations see in unification the best weapon for combating American influence. In its role as the first global society, it thus unifies, changes, stimulates, and challenges others—often against its own immediate interests. "Americanization" thus creates common aspirations and highly differentiated reactions.

In the Third World the effect of United States influence is to intensify social contradictions and conflict between the generations. Mass communications and education create expectations—for which the material wealth of America provides a vague standard—that simply cannot be met by most societies. Since neither communications nor education can be contained, it is to be expected that political tensions will mount as purely parochial, traditional attitudes yield to broader global perspectives. In the advanced world the contemporary challenge increasingly focuses on the identity of man, but in the Third World social fragmentation looms as the principal problem—one which is in a historic race with the advanced societies' only slowly maturing sense of their global responsibility for helping develop the Third World.

Even nationalism is subject to contradictory influences. Nationalism has never been stronger and has never before enjoyed such extensive, aroused, and conscious support from the popular masses as well as from the intelligentsia. The interaction of nation-states still determines matters affecting war and peace, and man's primary self-identification is still on the basis of nationalism. The non-Russian states in the Soviet Union are perhaps the only exception to nationalism's successful dissolution of colonial empires. Yet precisely because this is so, nationalism is ceasing to be the compelling force that determines the broad character of change in our time. Though still the source of many tensions, it is tempered by the growing recognition, shared even by the most nationalist elites, that today regional and continental cooperation is necessary to the fulfillment of many purely national goals. The success of nationalism makes the nation a principal object, but no longer the vital subject, of dynamic processes.

Because he finds himself living in a congested, overlapping, confusing, and impersonal environment, man seeks solace in restricted and familiar intimacy. The national community is the obvious one to turn to, and a definition of what a national community is may well become more restrictive as broader transnational cooperation develops. For many peoples the nation-state was a compromise dictated by economics, by security, and by other factors. An optimum balance was eventually struck, often after centuries of conflict. Today the balance is becoming unsettled, because newer and larger frameworks of cooperation are emerging, and the effective integration of much smaller, more cohesive units into much larger wholes is becoming increasingly possible because of computers, cybernetics, communications, and so on.

As a consequence, the Flemings and the Walloons in Belgium, the French and English Canadians in Canada, the Scots and the Welsh in the United Kingdom, the Basques in Spain, the Croats and the Slovenes in Yugoslavia, and the Czechs and Slovaks in Czechoslovakia are claiming—and some of the non-Russian nationalities in the Soviet Union and the various linguistic-ethnic groups in India may soon claim—that their particular nation-state no longer corresponds to historical need. On a higher plane it has been rendered superfluous by Europe, or some other regional (Common Market) arrangement, while on a lower plane a more intimate linguistic and religious community is required to overcome the impact of the implosion-explosion characteristic of the global metropolis.

This development is thus not a return to the emotions or to the ecstatic style of nineteenth-century nationalism, even though there are many superficial analogies to it. It takes place, by and large, in a context that recognizes the current necessity for broader cooperation on a level above the national. It accepts as an ideal the functional integration of regions and even of whole continents. It is a reflection of the desire for a more defined sense of personality in an increasingly impersonal world, and of the changed utility of some of the existing state structures. This can even be said of Gaullism, which has often been described as a throwback to nineteenth-century nationalism. Nevertheless, Gaullism's major ambition was to construct a Europe that would be "European" and not dominated by an external hegemony, though, to be sure, France would exercise political leadership in it.

The "new" nationalism has many elements of the old nationalism, especially in some of the new nations. There nationalism is still a radical, changing force creatively mobilizing community feelings but also prompting ethnic exclusiveness and conflicts.* Yet it is generally true, as the author of a suggestive paper notes, that "the vision and objectives of society [have] changed. Today a new concept of man and his world is challenging the concepts of the Renaissance which have guided man's behavior for the past five hundred years." The nation-state as a fundamental unit of man's organized life has ceased to be the principal creative force: "International banks and multinational corporations are acting and planning in terms that are far in advance of the political concepts of the nation-state."[44] But as the nation-state is gradually yielding its sovereignty, the psychological importance of the national community is rising, and the attempt to establish an equilibrium between the imperatives of the new internationalism and the need for a more intimate national community is the source of frictions and conflicts.

The achievement of that equilibrium is being made more difficult by the scientific and technological innovations in weaponry. It is ironic to recall that in 1878 Friedrich Engels, commenting on the Franco-Prussian War, proclaimed that "weapons used have reached such a stage of perfection that further progress which would have any revolutionizing influence is no longer possible."[45] Not only have new weapons been developed but some of the basic concepts of geography and strategy have been fundamentally altered; space and weather control have replaced Suez or Gibraltar as key elements of strategy.

---

* ". . . . In spite of all the parallels to European nationalism, the new nationalism in South Asia is something very different. It differs in many more respects and for more fundamental reasons than appears from the qualifications just listed. The fundamental reason is that an historical process that in Europe spans centuries is telescoped within a few decades and that the order of the happenings is deranged. . . . Nationalism there is needed to provide the impulse for change—indeed, for all the necessary changes, and concurrently. The difficulties in this syncopation of policies, the historical necessity of which is seen by all the enlightened intellectual and political leaders in the region, are immense" (Myrdal, pp. 2118–19).

In addition to improved rocketry, multi-missiles, and more powerful and more accurate bombs, future developments may well include automated or manned space warships, deep-sea installations, chemical and biological weapons, death rays, and still other forms of warfare—even the weather may be tampered with.* These new weapons could either encourage expectations of one-sided, relatively "inexpensive" victory; permit proxy contests that will be decisive in their strategic political outcome but will be fought by only a few human beings (as in the Battle of Britain) or even by robots in outer space;[46] or simply create such mutual instability that the breakdown of peace will become inevitable, in spite of man's rational recognition of the futility of war.

In addition, it may be possible—and tempting—to exploit for strategic-political purposes the fruits of research on the brain and on human behavior. Gordon J. F. MacDonald, a geophysicist specializing in problems of warfare, has written that accurately timed, artificially excited electronic strokes "could lead to a pattern of oscillations that produce relatively high power levels over certain regions of the earth. . . . In this way, one could develop a system that would seriously impair the brain performance of very large populations in selected regions over an extended period. . . . No matter how deeply disturbing the thought of using the environment to manipulate behavior for national advantages to some, the technology permitting such use will very probably develop within the next few decades."[47]

Such technology will be available primarily, and to begin with

---

* As one specialist noted, "By the year 2018, technology will make available to the leaders of the major nations a variety of techniques for conducting secret warfare, of which only a bare minimum of the security forces need be appraised. One nation may attack a competitor covertly by bacteriological means, thoroughly weakening the population (though with a minimum of fatalities) before taking over with its own overt armed forces. Alternatively, techniques of weather modification could be employed to produce prolonged periods of drought or storm, thereby weakening a nation's capacity and forcing it to accept the demands of the competitor" (Gordon J. F. MacDonald, "Space," in *Toward the Year 2018*, p. 34).

exclusively, to the most advanced countries.* But it is likely that in the coming decades some states in the Third World will have taken major steps toward acquiring—or will have acquired—highly destructive weaponry. Even if they are not capable of using it against the major powers without bringing about their own extinction, they may be able and tempted to use it in "underworld" wars among themselves. The question then arises whether such wars would be interpreted by the major powers as posing a direct threat to the fabric of peace, and whether a joint response by them would be effectively mounted and imposed. The absence of accepted global institutions could temporarily be overcome by *ad hoc* arrangements and agreements designed to meet specific threats, but it is conceivable that in some cases there will not be sufficient unanimity to permit joint reactions. The mutual annihilation of some lesser states thus remains at least a possibility.

Toward a Planetary Consciousness

Yet it would be wrong to conclude that fragmentation and chaos are the dominant realities of our time. A global human conscience is for the first time beginning to manifest itself. This conscience is a natural extension of the long process of widening man's personal horizons. In the course of time, man's self-identification expanded from his family to his village, to his tribe, to his region, to his nation; more recently it spread to his continent (before World War II it was not as customary as it is now for university students or intellectuals to describe themselves merely as Europeans or Asians).

---

* This has led one concerned scholar to comment, "Whether it is used to kill, hurt, nauseate, paralyze, cause hallucination, or to terrify military personnel and civilians, the systematic use of biological and chemical warfare will require the resolution of major moral and ethical problems" (Donald N. Michael, "Some Speculations on the Social Impact of Technology," mimeographed text of address to the Columbia University Seminar on Technology and Social Change, p. 6).

During the last three centuries the fading of the essentially transnational European aristocracy and the successive nationalization of the Christian church, of socialism, and of communism have meant that in recent times most significant political activity has tended to be confined within national compartments. Today we are again witnessing the emergence of transnational elites, but now they are composed of international businessmen, scholars, professional men, and public officials. The ties of these new elites cut across national boundaries, their perspectives are not confined by national traditions, and their interests are more functional than national. These global communities are gaining in strength and, as was true in the Middle Ages, it is likely that before long the social elites of most of the more advanced countries will be highly internationalist or globalist in spirit and outlook. The creation of the global information grid, facilitating almost continuous intellectual interaction and the pooling of knowledge, will further enhance the present trend toward international professional elites and toward the emergence of a common scientific language (in effect, the functional equivalent of Latin). This, however, could create a dangerous gap between them and the politically activated masses, whose "nativism"—exploited by more nationalist political leaders—could work against the "cosmopolitan" elites.

Increasingly, the intellectual elites tend to think in terms of global problems. One significant aspect of this process is the way in which contemporary dilemmas are identified: the need to overcome technical backwardness, to eliminate poverty, to extend international cooperation in education and health, to prevent overpopulation, to develop effective peace-keeping machinery.* These

* "We are discovering the need for coordination at the world level, for looking ahead so that the pieces can be fitted together more precisely. This has brought us to the beginning of global planning. FAO is a pioneer: its Indicative World Plan is the first such attempt, the prototype version of which will be ready in 1969. The ILO is working hard on a World Employment Plan.

"The U.N.'s Center for Development Planning, Projections and Policies (CDPPP) is preparing what could well be called the framework for a master

are all global issues. Only thirty years ago they were simply not in the forefront of public attention, which was riveted at the time on much more specific regional, national, or territorial conflicts.

The technetronic revolution creates conditions that increasingly make possible global responses to these needs and to human suffering in general. Indeed, a rudimentary framework of global social and economic institutions has already taken shape.* The availability of the means to cooperate globally intensifies the sense of obligation to act. Conscience is easily pacified by a feeling of futility. An uneasy conscience is usually one that knows that it can act differently. The sense of proximity, the immediacy of suffering, the globally destructive character of modern weapons all help to stimulate an outlook that views mankind as a community.

It is a hopeful sign in this connection that the yardsticks by which the public measures international competition are undergoing a constructive change. In the recent past, and even in the present, territorial expansion, population, and vague national claims of cultural and ideological superiority, as well as military power in general and victory in direct contests in particular, have provided the criteria for measuring status and influence. Gradually these are giving way to rivalry in GNP figures, per-capita income and consumption data, educational opportunities, creative and scientific attainments, research and development, standards of health and nutrition, and even competitive national Olympic scores, to say nothing of the space race between the two superpowers. To anyone living in 1914 the current international rivalry

---

plan covering all such activities. This is part of the task imposed on it by assembly resolutions which request the secretary-general, in plain words, to prepare future development efforts which are an improvement on the present development decade" (Jan Tinbergen, "The Way Out of the Labyrinth," *Ceres* (FAO Review), Vol. 1, No. 3, May-June 1968, p. 20).

* To list but a few: a world health organization, a world food and agricultural organization, a world labor organization, a world educational and cultural organization, a world bank, a global meteorological organization, an international atomic-energy agency, an international civil-aviation organization, an international agency for the peaceful uses of outer space, an agency for tapping the ocean beds, etc.

in producing more impressive charts and in defining new indices for measuring national status would be well-nigh incomprehensible; at that time nationalist geopolitics provided a more direct appeal.

Today a different orientation is becoming dominant. Social problems are seen less as the consequence of deliberate evil and more as the unintended by-products of both complexity and ignorance; solutions are not sought in emotional simplifications but in the use of man's accumulated social and scientific knowledge. Increasingly, it is felt that the variations in both scientific development and the human psyche do not lend themselves to doctrinal solutions formulated in advance; in addition, the unanticipated consequences of the discoveries of science have produced, especially in the more advanced countries, an awareness that the basic issues facing man have a common significance for human survival, irrespective of international internal diversity.

The concern with ideology is yielding to a preoccupation with ecology. Its beginnings can be seen in the unprecedented public preoccupation with matters such as air and water pollution, famine, overpopulation, radiation, and the control of disease, drugs, and weather, as well as in the increasingly non-nationalistic approaches to the exploration of space or of the ocean bed. There is already widespread consensus that functional planning is desirable and that it is the only way to cope with the various ecological threats.[48] Furthermore, given the continuing advances in computers and communications, there is reason to expect that modern technology will make such planning more feasible; in addition, multi-spectral analysis from earth satellites (a by-product of the space race) holds out the promise of more effective planning in regard to earth resources.

The new global consciousness, however, is only beginning to become an influential force. It still lacks identity, cohesion, and focus. Much of humanity—indeed, the majority of humanity—still neither shares nor is prepared to support it. Science and technology are still used to buttress ideological claims, to fortify national aspirations, and to reward narrowly national interests. Most states are spending more on arms than on social services, and the foreign-aid allotment of the two most powerful states is highly disproportionate to their asserted global missions.* Indeed, it can be argued that in some respects the divided, isolated, and compartmentalized world of old had more inner cohesion and enjoyed greater harmony than the volatile global reality of today. Established cultures, deeply entrenched traditional religions, and distinctive national identities provided a stable framework and firm moorings; distance and time were the insulators against excessive friction between the compartments. Today the framework is disintegrating and the insulants are dissolving. The new global unity has yet to find its own structure, consensus, and harmony.

---

* It was estimated that in 1966 global arms spending was 40 per cent greater than the world's outlays for education and was more than three times greater than the world's public-health budget. In that same year the total foreign aid extended by the United States was approximately $4 billion, by the Soviet Union approximately $330 million (both sets of figures from "World Military Expenditures, 1966–1967," U.S. Arms Control and Disarmament Agency, Washington, D.C., 1968, especially pp. 9–12).

PART II
The Age of Volatile Belief

The age of volatile belief is intimately linked with the impact of the technetronic revolution on existing ideologies and outlooks on life. What man thinks is closely related to what man experiences. The relationship between the two is not causal but interacting: experience affects thought, and thought conditions the interpretation of experience. Today the dominant pattern seems increasingly to be that of highly individualistic, unstructured, changing perspectives. Institutionalized beliefs, the result of the merger of ideas and institutions, no longer appear to many as vital and relevant, while the skepticism that has contributed so heavily to the undermining of institutionalized beliefs now clashes with the new emphasis on passion and involvement. The result for many is an era of fads, of rapidly shifting beliefs, with emotions providing for some the unifying cement previously supplied by institutions and with the faded revolutionary slogans of the past providing the needed inspiration for facing an altogether different future.

Several broad phases can be discerned in the formation of the collective human consciousness that conditions our response to reality and provides the framework for intellectually structuring that reality. The great religions of recorded history were crucial in establishing a perspective that linked man's individual preoccupation with his inner life to a universal God, who was the source of a standard of behavior binding upon all. Reality was God-given, and the line between the finite and the infinite was blurred.

The ideological phase associated with industrialization and the spread of literacy involved a much higher propensity toward social activism and emphasized more immediate goals, as defined either in terms of the nation or some other collective good, the external condition of man being the primary focus. Activism called for a more explicit definition of our reality, and systematic, even dogmatic, intellectual frameworks were meant to meet that need.

In our time the established ideologies are coming under attack because their institutionalized character, which was once useful in mobilizing the relatively uneducated masses, has become an impediment to intellectual adaptation, while their concern with the external qualities of life is increasingly felt to ignore the inner, more spiritual dimension. Commitment to individual action, based on moral indignation and stimulated by a much higher level of general education, has become a substitute for highly organized activity, though it avoids the passivity and indifference to external reality that was characteristic of the pre-ideological age.

Compelling ideologies thus are giving way to compulsive ideas, but without the eschatology that characterized other historical eras. Yet there is still a felt need for a synthesis that can define the meaning and the historical thrust of our times. In that search the dominating passion is equality—among men within institutions, within societies, among races, and among nations. Equality motivates both the rebels in the universities—in the West and in the East—and the new nations in their struggle against the better established and richer ones. This emphasis, as well as the fear of personal obsolescence, causes concern in many that the new post-industrial age will require even greater differentiation in skills, competences, and intellectual preparation, thereby widening the disparities within the human condition at a time of ever intensifying global interaction.

1. The Quest for a Universal Vision

"Man came silently into the world." [1] But though his coming is shrouded in mystery—in the sense that we still know little about the actual beginnings of human existence—from earliest known history man has given evidence of an intense yearning to understand himself and his environment. However crudely and primitively, man has always sought to crystallize some organizing principle that would, by creating order out of chaos, relate him to the universe and help define his place in it.[2]

Despite the disappearance in earlier times of entire cultures,[3] human evolution—or social development—has involved both an expansion in man's awareness of himself and his fellows as a human entity endowed with certain common qualities and an increasingly systematic intellectual effort to define and organize his external reality meaningfully. There has thus been at work what Teilhard de Chardin has called "an augmentation of consciousness . . . a stream whereby a continuing and transmissible tradition of reflection is established and allowed to increase." [4]

In terms of the entirety of human existence, that "stream" may indeed be a short one, as the critics of the notion of historical progress readily point out. Nevertheless, recorded history does provide strong evidence of growth—often halting and uneven, but growth nonetheless—in man's consciousness of a common human fate, of certain universal cravings, and of common moral standard.* Even when they compete, religions and ideologies have increasingly done so in terms of and for the sake of principles that seem, when viewed from a historical perspective, more and more to involve semantic and not substantive differences. This is not to deny that practice has often widely differed; it is, however, remarkable that conflicts have been waged over competitive claims to a superior interpretation and application of such universal values as democracy, welfare, individual dignity, and personal freedom.

The Universal Religions

The crucial breakthrough in the development of human self-awareness on a mass scale came with the great religions—the first universal syntheses that simultaneously expanded man's vision both vertically and horizontally: vertically, to define in extended and complex terms man's relationship to a God that was not a small group's alone *but everyone's*; horizontally, to articulate a series of imperatives that governed man's obligations to man on the grounds that all shared the divine spark. Universalism thus emerged as a state of mind even at a time when man was still

* We are talking here about *our* history—of our historical civilization. Claude Lévi-Strauss is otherwise quite right in pointing out that ". . . it is forgotten that each of the tens or hundreds of thousands of societies which have existed side by side in the world or succeeded one another since man's first appearance, has claimed that it contains the essence of all the meaning and dignity of which human society is capable and, reduced though it may have been to a small nomad band or a hamlet lost in the depths of the forest, its claim has in its own eyes rested on a moral certainty comparable to that which we can invoke in our own case. But whether in their case or our own, a good deal of egocentricity and naïvety is necessary to believe that man has taken refuge in a single one of the historical or geographical modes of his existence, when the truth about man resides in the system of their differences and common properties" (*The Savage Mind,* Chicago, 1966, p. 249).

provincial and isolated in mutually exclusive social-cultural compartments.

Accordingly, the birth of the universal religions represents the appearance of humanity *qua* humanity. The assertion of man's equality before God in terms of his spirit, his conscience, or his soul, laid the basis for the transcendental importance of the human being and for the much later assertion of the equality of men in their political and social dimensions. In that sense, proselytizing Christianity, which universalized the more limited Greek and Judaic tradition, was a particularly revolutionary force and was viewed as such by established authority, in spite of the distinction it made between equality before God and obeisance to Caesar on Caesar's terms. If human history can be said to involve both a struggle and an evolution toward the progressive liberation of man, then the attainment of equality before the supernatural was the first major step on that road.

But early man could neither control nor comprehend either himself or his environment. Both were essentially a mystery, a given to be accepted, whatever the pains of life might be. As a consequence, the distant future became a much more intense object of preoccupation than the immediate present. The inability to cope effectively with disease, plagues, infant mortality, a short life span, or natural disasters such as floods and crop blights prompted man to seek refuge in all-encompassing definitions of his reality. These in turn provided at least partial justification for the view that human endeavor was futile and for the necessity of accepting events with fatalism. By taking refuge in an autonomous, distant, divine future, man relieved himself of the obligation to struggle intensely with the present under circumstances he was neither intellectually nor practically prepared for.

Even the notion of "free will"—a central component of the most activist of the great religions, Christianity—basically involved an inner act of conscience necessary for the state of grace, rather than a point of departure for morally motivated external action. No stress was placed on the struggle to improve external conditions, because the unstated assumption was that they could not be fundamentally improved. The emphasis was on the inner man; by riveting his attention on the universal and the divine future, man could master the present by simply ignoring it. Minimum social action was matched by maximum commitment to the supernatural.

To meet the central need of their time—mainly, to provide man with a firm mooring in a world which could not be comprehended—and to assert firm control over man's spirit, religious beliefs crystallized into dogmas and were organized into institutions.* The more individually demanding the religion, the higher was the degree of institutionalization.† (This has prompted the analogies made by a number of scholars between Islam and Christianity on the one hand and communism on the other.)[5] With the institutionalization came more activism (the Crusades and the holy wars of Islam) and the exercise of muscle by religious organizations on their environment. Power was asserted, however, to extend the conquest of the spirit, not to effect social change. The institutionalization of belief thus combined two functions: it was the zealots' self-defense mechanism against a non-believing environment, and it was a tool for sustained proselytization, one designed not only to win over adherents but to overcome the inertial

* I do not propose—nor do I feel qualified—to become involved in the debate among Marxists, Freudians, and Jungians concerning the autonomy and the functionality of religious development. My concern here is with the emergence of a conceptual and institutional framework for defining man's relationship to his reality.

† An extreme example is provided by the Catholic Church's insistence on celibacy. As one scholar has noted, "Celibacy ensured for it an exclusive loyalty of its personnel that was unavailable to other modern religious institutions. It often contributed to its amazing capacity to resist secular authority. It is worth noting in passing that churches with married priesthoods, be they Lutheran, Anglican, or Greek Orthodox (the latter allowing marriage only for the lower orders of priests), have not been able to stand up against secular authority in a way comparable to that of the Catholic Church. The Protestant and Orthodox churches have typically been servants and appendages of secular authority. They rarely could afford to resist it. One reason for this was precisely that their clerical personnel was deeply involved in the mesh of civil social life" (Lewis A. Coser, "Greedy Organizations," *European Journal of Sociology*, Vol. 7, 1967, p. 206).

resistance of the masses, who were largely indifferent to spiritual requirements.[6]

Although Christianity has been the most activist of the great religions and has thereby laid the basis for the subsequent secular revolutionary movements that have dominated Western history, the process of institutionalization—and hence the emergence on the part of organized religion of a stake in the *status quo*—has tended to mute the radical message in the Christian concept of history: the movement toward salvation "on earth as in Heaven." Thus in practice the Christian churches have gradually come to accept social stratification and even to benefit from it (as in Latin America), and some Lutheran varieties have even come to sanction in dogma concepts of racial inequality that are at extreme variance with the initial egalitarian revolution represented by the new Christian relationship between God and man.

The other great religions have been more passive—both in practice and in theory. Buddhism does not contain imperatives for social change but offers salvation from reality. Unlike Christianity, nirvana did not serve as a springboard for temporal activism. Similarly, Islam's dominant strain of fatalism has worked against the presence of at least that element of tension between "eternal peace" and "heaven on earth" that is so strong in Christianity and that has prompted its repressed activism.[7]

The National Identity

With the growth in the West of man's ability to master his environment, secular rationalism, accompanied by a greater awareness of social complexity as well as by a breakdown in the existing structure of religious allegiance, emerged to challenge institutionalized religion. That religious allegiance simultaneously rested on the narrowness and on the universalism of man's horizons: the narrowness derived from massive ignorance, illiteracy, and a vision confined to the immediate environment by limited communications; the universalism was provided by the acceptance of the idea that man's destiny is essentially in God's hands and that the limited present is but a steppingstone to an unlimited future. Emerging secularism challenged both dimensions, and in so doing required for the external projection of man's identity an intermediary focus of loyalty—something in between the immediate and the infinite. The nation-state and nationalism were the responses.

The doctrine of sovereignty created the institutional basis for challenging the secular authority of established religion, and this challenge in turn paved the way for the emergence of the abstract conception of the nation-state. Sovereignty vested in the people, instead of sovereignty vested in the king, was the consummation of the process which in the two centuries preceding the French and American revolutions radically altered the structure of authority in the West* and prepared the ground for a new dominant concept of reality. The nation-state became simultaneously the embodiment of personal commitments and the point of departure for analyzing reality. This development marked a new phase in man's political consciousness.

Nationalism did not seek to direct the individual toward the infinite, but to activate the impersonal masses for the sake of immediately proximate goals. Paradoxically, these concrete goals were derived from the still intangible and transcendental, though

* "In both its religious and its secular versions, in Filmer as well as in Hobbes, the import of the new doctrine of sovereignty was the subject's absolute duty of obedience to his king. Both doctrines helped political modernization by legitimizing the concentration of authority and the breakdown of the medieval pluralistic political order. They were the seventeenth-century counterparts of the theories of party supremacy and national sovereignty which are today employed to break down the authority of traditional local, tribal, and religious bodies. In the seventeenth century, mass participation in politics still lay in the future; hence rationalization of authority meant concentration of power in the absolute monarch. In the twentieth century, the broadening of participation and the rationalization of authority occur simultaneously, and hence authority must be concentrated in either a political party or in a popular charismatic leader, both of which are capable of arousing the masses as well as challenging traditional sources of authority. But in the seventeenth century the absolute monarch was the functional equivalent of the twentieth century's monolithic party" (Huntington, p. 102).

new, object of worship: the nation. The nation became the source of ecstatic, lyrical affection, and it was this highly emotional relationship, symbolized by the new anthems ("La Marseillaise"), flags, and heroes, that served to energize the populace. The concrete goals took the form of massive preoccupation with frontiers, irredenta, "brethren" to be regained from foreign captivity, and, more generally, the power and the glory of the state as the formal expression of the nation. The state thus became the institutional form for the new dominant belief, with a monopolistic claim on the active dedication to it of man, now designated, first and above all, as the citizen.

The designation "man the citizen" symbolically marks another milestone in the evolution of man as a social being. Equality before God was now matched by equality before the law; spiritual egalitarianism was now reinforced by legal egalitarianism. It is of note that legal equality was asserted both by the American Revolution, which supplemented its stress on equality before the law with a strong attachment to religious values—indeed, it derived the former from the latter—and by the French Revolution, which constructed its pantheon of human equality by explicitly rejecting the religious tradition. In both cases the legal equality of the citizen was postulated as a universal principle—and thus it marked another giant step in the progressive redefinition of man's nature and place in our world.

With nationalism, the distinction between the inner contemplative man, concerned with his relationship to God, and the external man, concerned with shaping his environment, became blurred. Nationalism as an ideology was more activist; man's relations to man were objectivized externally by legal norms and were not dependent, as was man's relation to God, on personal conscience; yet at the same time the definition of man as a "national" was based largely on abstract, historically determined, and highly emotional criteria. This outlook involved considerable vagueness and even irrationality when used as a conceptual framework within which relations between nations and developments within nations might be understood. Nationalism only partially increased men's self-awareness; it mobilized them actively but failed to challenge their critical faculties; it was more a mass vehicle for human passion and fantasizing than a conceptual framework that made it possible to dissect and then deliberately reassemble our reality.

Ideological Universalism

That is why Marxism represents a further vital and creative stage in the maturing of man's universal vision. Marxism is simultaneously a victory of the external, active man over the inner, passive man and a victory of reason over belief: it stresses man's capacity to shape his material destiny—finite and defined as man's only reality—and it postulates the absolute capacity of man to truly understand his reality as a point of departure for his active endeavors to shape it. To a greater extent than any previous mode of political thinking, Marxism puts a premium on the systematic and rigorous examination of material reality and on guides to action derived from that examination.

Though it may be argued that this intellectually rigorous method was eventually subverted by its strong component of dogmatic belief, Marxism did expand popular self-awareness by awakening the masses to an intense preoccupation with social equality and by providing them with both a historical and a moral justification for insisting upon it. More than that, Marxism represented in its time the most advanced and systematic method for analyzing the dynamic of social development, for categorizing it, and for extrapolating from it certain principles concerning social behavior. It did so in a manner that lent itself to translation into highly simplified principles that provided even the relatively uneducated with the feeling that their understanding of phenomena had been basically sharpened and that their resentments, frustrations, and vague aspirations could be channeled into historically meaningful actions.

Because of this, Marxism appealed simultaneously to man's ethical, rational, and Promethean instincts. The ethical component, sustained by man's emotions, drew on the Judaeo-Christian heritage; the rational responded to man's increased desire to comprehend the dynamic of his material environment more systematically; and the Promethean stood for "man's faith in his powers, for the notion that history is made by the people and that nothing can hem in their advance to perfection." [8]

In this sense, Marxism has served as a mechanism of human "progress," even if its practice has often fallen short of its ideals. Teilhard de Chardin notes at one point that "monstrous as it is, is not modern totalitarianism really the distortion of something magnificent, and thus quite near to the truth?" [9] Elsewhere he observes that "all the peoples, to remain human or to become more so, are inexorably led to formulate the hopes and problems of the modern earth in the very same terms in which the West has formulated them." [10] What he does not say is that for many outside the immediate influence of the West and its Christian tradition it has been Marxism that has served to stir the mind and to mobilize human energies purposefully.

Moreover, Marxism has decisively contributed to the political institutionalization and systematization of the deliberate effort to define the nature of our era and of man's relationship to history at any given stage in that history. Emphasis on this question has compelled reflection on the relative importance of different forces of change, the weighing of alternative historical interpretations, and at least the attempt at tentative judgment. Moreover, it has provoked a series of subordinate questions, all helpful in forcing recognition of change and in compelling adjustments to it: Within the given era, what particular phases can be deciphered? Is any given phase one of international tension, of greater stability, of shifting locale of conflict, of a new set of alliances? Who are our present principal foes—subjectively and objectively? Who are now our allies? What are the sources of principal, secondary, and tertiary dangers?

Periodic, formal, purposeful examination of such questions compels systematic probing of the international scene. This is not to say that contemporary communists have always been successful in accurately perceiving the meaning of new international phenomena. Indeed, their conviction that their analytical tools provide a faultless guide to the inner meaning of things has often led them astray. Unwilling to accept the notion of the relativity and elusiveness of truth, they have elevated their inescapably partial insights into absolute dogmas and reduced complex issues to gross oversimplifications.

Nonetheless, to define communism—the institutionalized expression of Marxism—primarily as "a disease of the transition from traditional to modern status," [11] or to assert that "Marxism is, in fact, nothing but an epiphenomenon of technical development, a phase of the painful marriage of man and technique," [12] is to neglect what will probably remain the major contribution of Marxism: its revolutionary and broadening influence, which opened man's mind to previously ignored perspectives and dramatized previously neglected concerns. To say as much is not to ignore the subsequently enslaving effect of institutionalized Marxism—especially when in power—or its analytical inability to cope with the problems of the advanced twentieth-century world; it is to assert that in the gradual evolution of man's universal vision Marxism represents as important and progressive a stage as the appearance of nationalism and of the great religions.

In all three cases—religion, nationalism, and Marxism—the breakthrough had many antecedents and did not suddenly come about as the result of an entirely autonomous act of creative genius. Marx capitalized on the intellectual achievements of his immediate predecessors, for some of whom socialism had a strong religious basis.* Similarly, nationalism and the great religions were the articulate syntheses of moods, of attitudes, and of a cer-

---

* Pierre Leroux (1797–1871) was among the first to analyze the term "socialism" conceptually and to use it in his writings. He saw in socialism the fulfillment of religious imperatives.

tain social receptivity that had matured over a very long period of time. Also, in all three cases the breakthrough in perception was followed by perversion in practice: religious wars and the Inquisition; national hatreds expressed in unprecedented mass slaughter; brutal terror, purges, and totalitarian subjugation of the mind as well as the body in the name of a "humanist" ideology.

Nevertheless, in all three cases the intellectual horizons of man, once widened, could not again be narrowed. Equality before a universal God and the emphasis on individual conscience, equality before the law and a commitment to a social entity larger than the immediate one, social equality and a concern for analytically dissecting the dynamic thrust of history—all have cumulatively helped to refine and enlarge man's political and social consciousness. Given the dominant role of the activist West in shaping the outlook of our times, now, in the second half of the twentieth century, almost everyone—often without knowing it—is to some extent a Christian, a nationalist, and a Marxist.

2. Turbulence within Institutionalized Beliefs

It is increasingly difficult for institutions to assert dogmatically the pristine purity of the doctrines that they claim to embody. This is as true of the Christian churches as of communist parties; in some of the more advanced countries this difficulty also involves—especially on the part of the young—a crisis in allegiance to the procedures of liberal democracy.

Today the relationship of ideas to institutions is turbulent: institutions resist ideas lest they lead to changes that undermine the institutions, and the exponents of ideas rebel against institutions because of the intellectual constraints said to be inherent in their existence.

This development is part of the progressive secularization of our life. An important role in this process is played by the changed character of contemporary communications, which permits rapid dissemination of ideas and images, and requires less reliance on an organized effort to proselytize. Today, more people are exposed to impressions that are both more fluid and more volatile than ever before. There is no longer the same need to challenge rigid and traditional taboos with alternative and more appealing visions, or to overcome social inertia with organized mobilization of effort. All this puts institutionalized beliefs on the defensive: more and more their efforts are designed to retain the positive loyalty of their adherents and to combat influences that are inimical to structured, formalized, and highly institutionalized beliefs.

Writing almost a century ago, Marx observed that "up till now it has been thought that the growth of the Christian myths during the Roman Empire was possible only because printing was not yet invented. Precisely the contrary. The daily press and the telegraph, which in a moment spread inventions over the whole earth, fabricate more myths (and the bourgeois cattle believe and enlarge upon them) in one day than could have formerly been done in a century." [13] When to the press and telegraph is added the contemporary global role of radio and television, and to religion are added contemporary ideologies, Marx's observations become even more pertinent.

In addition to developments connected with the means of dissemination and the pace of technologically induced social change, another factor is at work. In the view of many concerned people, especially among the younger generation, the fusion of religions or ideologies with institutions has resulted in bureaucratic rigidity as well as distortion in values. The long tradition of institutionalized religion's concentration on the inner man has prompted social passivity and *de facto* indifference to concrete human dilemmas, in spite of stated commitments to humanitarianism; the more contemporary ideological preoccupation with mobilizing the external man has resulted in political systems whose practice refutes the moral significance of their often proclaimed humanitarian objectives. If in the first case the spiritual elevation of man has permitted his social deprivation, in the second the assertion of man's social primacy has precipitated his spiritual degradation.

Institutional Marxism

Moreover, many people feel that both on the external, environmental level of human existence and on the inner, contemplative one, current institutionalized beliefs no longer provide adequate responses to contemporary problems. Despite the intellectual advance that Marxism represents in our thinking, it does not suffice as the sole basis for meaningful comprehension of our reality. Discoveries in modern science, advances in the study of the human psyche, and even contemporary socio-economic developments can no longer be satisfactorily interpreted by exclusive reliance on the Marxist framework. At the same time, the neglect of the spiritual element and the renewed search for the true nature of inner man—a search made more urgent because of scientific developments concerning the nature of the human brain and personality—have further exposed the limitations of Marxism as the sole basis for defining the meaning of human existence.

That limitation is accentuated by the link between Marxist ideas and institutions in the form of bureaucratic and dogmatic communist parties. Precisely because Marxism as a body of ideas and as a socio-economic method has become so much a part of the Western intellectual heritage, its intellectual vitality and political significance—the latter conceived of in broad terms as a source of influence for social programs—no longer depend on an organization of zealots. Such organization was needed to proselytize, to seize power, and to hold it. Specific Russian conditions led to the Leninist formulation of the historical utility of such a party and of the absolute necessity of subordinating the individual to it.

Subsequently, the bureaucratic elements that unavoidably gained control over the organization once it had come to power naturally tended to put a higher priority on the organization than on the ideas that the organization was supposed to uphold and, presumably, to nourish. As a result, the existence of communist parties has come to be an effective impediment to the further acceptance and development of Marxist thought. The parties' bureaucratic organization, their inherent concern for their institutional vested interests—even at the expense of the Marxist doctrine that they are said to embody—their fear of intellectual exploration, all have cumulatively stimulated both opposition on the outside and ideological sterility on the inside.

Characteristic of this sterility is the striking fact that the Soviet communist party has not produced a *single* creative and influential Marxist thinker in the fifty years since it seized power in 1917. (Moreover, its leading intellectual lights, the beginnings of whose creativity antedated 1917, were physically liquidated under Soviet rule.) This is remarkable, considering the significance officially attached to "creative" Marxism-Leninism by the first communist party ever to have come to power. Elsewhere probing and influential Marxist philosophers—George Lukacs, Ernst Bloch, Adam Schaff, or Leszek Kolakowski—have invariably either come into sharp conflict with party discipline or have eventually been driven out of the party.

As long as Marxism was an isolated school of thought, the party could serve as an effective mechanism for carrying it to the masses and, more generally, as the self-appointed agent of history, the direction of which Marxism claimed to have correctly identified. But once Marxism had become part of the world's historic mainstream, to insist on its separate, institutional identity and exclusivity was to diminish its influence and to stifle its creativity. Yet that is precisely what the communist parties have continued to do, and the Communist Party of the Soviet Union has even extended that claim by asserting its right to pass on the correctness of other parties' interpretations.

The result has been increasing indifference to doctrine among the general membership and increasing disaffection among the more creative Marxist thinkers. This is not to say that socialist ideas have become discredited. On the contrary, even in Eastern Europe, where communism has had to compete with anti-Soviet nationalism, the admittedly limited and very fragmentary data available on public attitudes indicate that socialism—broadly conceived of as an attempt to create a more just society through public welfare, mass access to education, social services, public ownership of the principal means of production, and social egalitarianism—has wide popular support, whereas communism as an institutionalized belief has not.* Similarly, in the West most non-socialist parties now accept the welfare society as desirable and

---

* Data to that effect come from polls taken both within a given country and among Eastern European travelers to the West. Thus, in a 1961 poll conducted in Warsaw among university students, 2 per cent identified themselves as "definitely Marxist" in outlook and 16 per cent as "on the whole, yes." One may assume that these two categories would represent the upper limit of student willingness to accept the official ideology, although many among the 16 per cent presumably would rebel against excessive party orthodoxy; 27.5 per cent said "definitely no" and 31 per cent "on the whole, no" to the question "Do you consider yourself a Marxist?" At the same time, however, 28.1 per cent expressed the definite desire to see the world "evolve toward some form of socialism" and 44.5 per cent responded "on the whole, yes," for a total of 72.6 per cent expressing a generalized preference for socialism (*East Europe,* April 1966, p. 19).

The gap between the generalized acceptance of socialism and the self-identification as Marxists is probably a good measure of the distinction made above.

Similarly, in a sample of 490 Polish visitors to the West in 1960 (people who were subsequently *returning* to Poland), 61 per cent defined communism as "a bad idea, badly carried out," while 14 per cent felt that it was "a good idea, badly carried out." The overwhelming majority however, endorsed postwar programs providing for a welfare state, education for all, agrarian reform, and nationalization of heavy industry (*Some Aspects of the Social-Psychological and Political Climate in Poland,* Audience Research Survey, Radio Free Europe, Munich, 1961, pp. 21, 24). A similar poll conducted among 119 Hungarians yielded 73 per cent and 8 per cent, respectively, and again there was considerable endorsement of the measures adopted after World War II (*Political Attitudes and Expectations of 119 Hungarians,* Audience, pp. 38, 43).

normal, though not necessarily requiring extensive nationalization. The Catholic Church expressed much the same point of view in the remarkable papal encyclical "Mater et Magistra" (1961).

Accordingly, "institutional Marxism," or communism, no longer confronts an intellectual reality that is hostile either to its social aspirations or even to some of the underlying assumptions. It no longer faces a world that intellectually rejects Marxism—that is, a virgin territory to be attacked by zealous missionaries collectively organized. By the same token, the only historical function of the closed Leninist-type party now appears to be to help communists who are in power to stay in power. As a result, a Marxist thinker can no longer be a communist if he wishes to remain a thinker.

That Leninist link between ideas and power—with all the inherent restraints and predispositions toward dogmatism that it involves—drives away from communism both the "truth-seeking" and the "efficiency-seeking" intellectuals.[14] The former group—typically the philosophers, humanists, and writers—reacts against the excessive concern with the external, active man; it seeks to restore and renew concern with the inner meaning of life and to confront such socio-psychic phenomena as alienation; it also sees a basic incompatibility between the quest for personal freedom that Marxism is said to embody and Marxism's institutionalization as a system of power. The most articulate and moving condemnations of the system have usually come from this group. In noncommunist countries, this group also contains much of what has come to be called the "New Left," which is intellectually preoccupied with the "larger" questions concerning the individual. Cohn-Bendit—the radical leader of the French students in 1968—characteristically reserved his sharpest barbs for the French Communist Party.[15]

Another threat to the established link between ideology and institution is the challenge from the "efficiency-seeking" intellectuals—typically the economists, the scientists, and the new managers. They are primarily concerned with socio-economic efficiency, and they see in the elevation of dogmas and in the subordination of ideas to institutions—with the resulting conservative dogmatism—a major impediment to positive social change. Less concerned with the inner man, more preoccupied with satisfying the demands of the external man, they do not pose a head-on challenge to the system. But because their attack is oblique—and because the attackers themselves are becoming both more numerous and socially more indispensable to an industrial society—their challenge is more difficult to suppress. The truth-seekers confront head on; in the case of weaker, more disorganized systems they have occasionally been successful, only to be later crushed by the application of superior power. The efficiency-seekers do not confront; they seek to erode. Both their successes and their defeats—seen in the cycle of communist economic reforms and subsequent retreats—are less visible, less extensive, but perhaps more tangible.

At some point, however, even the efficiency-oriented group will have to address itself to the more basic questions concerning the nature of man and the purpose of social existence. Until it does so, there is always the likelihood that the ruling elite can at least temporarily succeed in compartmentalizing the scientific community, in extracting its talents, and in corrupting it with a system of rewards—all the while reserving to itself the definition of the larger objectives.

Conscious of this danger and reacting against the dogmatic bureaucratic tradition, contemporary Marxist philosophers have been inclined to assert the primacy of human reason and conscience over vested organizational interests and to point out the inescapable limitations of any ideological framework one may apply to reality. Leszek Kolakowski, writing in 1956, reflected a widespread mood when he attacked the degraded notion of "Marxist" as no longer meaning "a person who recognizes a definite, meaningful view of the world, but a person of a definite intellectual make-up who is distinguished by his readiness to recognize the views established institutionally."[16] Rejecting "institutional Marxism," Kolakowski asserted that party interference in scientific pursuits is, by definition, un-Marxist, since it contradicts the essence of Marxism: a deliberate, scientific, and rational inquiry aiming at the closest approximation of the truth. In a similar vein, Yugoslav philosophers associated with the Zagreb philosophical journal *Praxis*—a magazine noted for its insistence that "Marxism" and "institutional truth" are contradictory terms—ridiculed the views of a Soviet philosopher who had "asserted that the Party's Central Committee formed the best solutions to the most important theoretical questions, including philosophical ones; in his opinion, the most important philosophical task today is 'the amalgamation of all forces within the socialist camp.'" In response to the Soviet view a Yugoslav philosopher noted that "the resolutions passed by the Central Committee are no philosophy whatsoever."[17]

More fundamental still has been the challenge to the notion that Marxism as a science of history provides both practical and ethical guides to the future. The more critical revisionists and the more outspoken opponents of the fusion of Marxist thought and a Leninist-type party have challenged that premise as well. Kolakowski put it particularly eloquently:

> A philosophy of history worthy of consideration describes only what has existed, the past, and not the creative future of the historical process. For this reason, those who wish to subordinate their own engagement in future processes to the pronouncements of the philosophy of history are only tourists who write their names on the walls of dead cities. Everybody can, if he wishes, interpret himself historically and discover the determinants to which he was subject in the past. But he cannot do so with respect to the self he has not yet become. He cannot deduce his own future development from the pronouncements of the philosophy of history in which he trusts. To work such a miracle would mean to become the irrevocable past oneself; that is, to cross the river of death which, the poet says, no one ever sees twice.[18]

Even relatively orthodox Marxist thinkers—such as Adam Schaff—who have actively defended the fusion of ideas and institutions have eventually had to confront the choice between intellectual subordination to institutional loyalty and intellectual integrity at the expense of good standing in the party. In belatedly opting for the latter, Schaff freely conceded that his own thinking could no longer be confined to the conservative, dogmatic—and hence institutional—definition of Marxism and that he now had to acknowledge that his more developed understanding of the sociology of Marxism required reliance on non-Marxist perspectives and insights.[19] A mere decade earlier, Schaff had still been one of the most effective orthodox critics of views expounded by his fellow Pole, Kolakowski, by the East German Wolfgang Harich, and by the Yugoslav revisionists.*

It has been said earlier that Marxism, disseminated on the popular level in the form of communism, represented a major advance in man's ability to conceptualize his relationship to his world. It ended an epoch in man's history that might be called that of historical unconsciousness. It gave man a sense of the social dynamic and stimulated a conscious concern with it. In spite of its materialistic determinism, it carried—and that was the source of much of its appeal—an essentially ethical message. It did so on the basis of a doctrine that asserted that it was derived from a totally rational method of inquiry. Its success, therefore, helped to stimulate a reaction against truths derived from seemingly irrational beliefs and against institutions asserting a monopoly on the truth. But that which was necessary to help terminate the age of historical unconsciousness—especially on a popular level—became counterproductive in the age of science, rapid dissemination, and accelerating change.

Initially the ideology of a narrowly based, weak, and relatively isolated intellectual class that aspired to harness both history and the popular masses, institutionalized Marxism has become the official doctrine of nonintellectual bureaucrats who are supported

---

* For another example among many, see the December 1968 issue of *Partelet* (the Hungarian party journal), containing a communiqué on the expulsion from the Budapest Philosophical Institute of several Hungarian philosophers, some of whom had advocated a "pluralist" concept of Marxism.

by millions (roughly ten per cent of the adult population in most communist countries) for whom formal membership is more often an expression of conservative social orthodoxy or professional opportunism than an ideological or an intellectual commitment. To buttress an institution from which the creative intellectual content is increasingly drained, the presiding officials have more and more taken refuge in state nationalism as the principal emotional bond with the masses. The effect—paradoxical and cruel in its historical irony—is to make communism in power increasingly reliant on the unconscious and the emotional factors which Marxism had sought to supersede.[20]

Organized Christianity

Equally dramatic, though different in substance, is the problem confronted today by established religions, especially Christianity. Unlike communism, contemporary Christianity is no longer a system of power; its temporal authority is not only limited but shrinking. On the other hand, it is both a system of doctrines and an institution, particularly in its Catholic expression. The tension between the beliefs and the institution is ancient, often painful, history for the Church, but the problem has been given a new dimension by the efforts initiated by Popes John XXIII and Paul VI, and expressed by the Second Ecumenical Council (Vatican II), to reinvigorate the Church.[21] These efforts are taking place in a setting that simultaneously involves both unprecedented interest on the part of concerned Christians (not only Catholics) and widespread evidence of increasing indifference to the prescribed religious forms. In other words, there is both massive involvement in change, which means that the official guardians of the institution cannot fully control it, and uncertainty concerning the best ways to make the Church again truly relevant, without diluting its spiritual identity.

The fundamental dilemma confronted by the Church, in the words of Unamuno, is that "Catholicism oscillates between mysticism, which is the inward experience of the living God in Christ, an intransmittable experience, the danger of which, however, is that it absorbs our own personality in God, and so does not save our vital longing—between mysticism and the rationalism which it fights against; it oscillates between religionized science and scientificized religion." [22] To opt for one is to be deprived of the other. Yet neither will do by itself: mysticism would mean withdrawal from the contemporary world; scientism would mean absorption by it.

This is an old dilemma for the Church, and it has been posed and answered in different ways at different historical stages. "Mater et Magistra" and Vatican II—occurring in an age shaped by ideological conflict, scientific innovation, mass popular awakening, political passion, and religious quiescence—can be viewed as an effort to satisfy three broad objectives: first, to update the Church's institutional structure, so that it is not an impediment to the vitality of the ideological component (to use a term applied throughout the chapter) and so that the institutionalized beliefs again become meaningful to both the inner and external dimensions of human life; second, better to focus the energies of the Church as a whole on social problems that range from personal poverty and social injustice to international inequality; and, finally, to heal doctrinal splits within Christianity and end the era of bigotry and conflict between Christianity and non-Christian religions.

The effort—precisely because it did move the Church somewhat in the desired directions—produced new strains in the relationship between ideas and institutions. Institutional reform, conducted at a time when pressures for theological adjustments have increasingly come from the Church hierarchy itself (as in the case of communism, these pressures have more often come from the periphery than from the center: what Yugoslavia has been to the Kremlin the Netherlands has become to the Vatican!), has prompted a profound crisis of papal authority. Pope Paul's reiteration of the ban on artificial contraception (in "Humanae Vitae,"

1968), which came shortly after the adoption by Vatican II of the concept of collegiality in Church affairs, provoked strong negative reactions from various national Councils of Bishops; these reactions in turn prompted the Pontiff to warn against "attitudes which departed more than a little from the traditional doctrine of the Church and menaced order in the bosom of the Church herself." * [23]

Yet the Vatican could not stifle the theological unrest. Almost echoing the demands of Marxist philosophers for an unfettered Marxist dialogue, Catholic theologians (notably in a public statement released in December 1968 by forty of the leading theologians) denounced efforts by the Vatican Curia to resolve theological issues by administrative fiat. They asserted their right to complete freedom of inquiry, subject to no institutional limitations whatever.

The increased emphasis on social questions—articulated with compassion in "Mater et Magistra"—presented a different challenge. Intense involvement in the affairs of the world, and particularly in the struggle against social injustice, could not help but focus the attention of the Church on external man, often placing the Church in direct competition with socialist or communist movements. Younger, more socially involved Catholics saw in that competition—especially in Latin America—the only possible salvation for the Church's mission; conservatives feared the transformation of the Church into merely another temporal radical movement. Particularly bitter was the conflict in those areas where the issue had immediate relevance, such as northeast Brazil.[24] There, as elsewhere, conservatives felt that what the Church would gain in the short run would cost it too much in the long run: social relevance would be gained at the cost of loss of identity. More generally, they argued that social success—no less

* The Pope was not alone in facing this quandary. *The New York Times* of January 16, 1969, reported that Dr. Eugene Carson Blake, general secretary of the World Council of Churches, discussed "the crisis of authority" with Pope Paul VI. It cited Dr. Blake as having said, "We find ourselves facing the same issues in both the World Council and in the member churches."

than economic success—could be detrimental to spiritual values. It may be assumed that from their point of view the experience of Protestantism in the United States was not reassuring.*

Ecumenism also prompted both institutional and doctrinal tension. Purists feared that it would accelerate the dilution of doctrinal content and transform the Catholic Church in the more advanced countries into a vague ethical organization engaged, together with other similar bodies, in social good works. Even more perplexing to the purists was the appearance of an "ecumenical" dialogue between Christians and communists, in which Catholics took an active part. That such a dialogue could develop, even though it received relatively little notice, was itself proof of the extent to which exclusivistic claims to absolute truth—though not formally abandoned by either side—no longer dominated either the Western mind or even those institutions that were themselves the products of the Manichaean tradition.†

---

* "Protestantism has become so identified with economic success, respectability, and middle-class virtues that large numbers of the clergy and laity alike appear to have lost sight of basic spiritual goals" (Gerhard Lenski, *The Religious Factor*, Garden City, N.Y., 1963, p. 352).

† "Without us, Communists, I fear that your Christian love, marvellous though it is, will continue to be ineffective; without you, Christians, our struggle risks again confinement to a horizon without stars" (Roger Garaudy, as quoted by *Le Monde* (*Hebdomadaire*), May 5–11, 1966). These words of a leading French Communist ideologue, once a strong Stalinist and a member of the Politburo, addressing a mixed Christian-Marxist colloquium organized by the Catholics, convey the extent to which previously frozen views are today in flux. Of the many meetings between Christians and Marxists, perhaps the most significant have been those organized by the Paulus Gesellschaft, starting in Salzburg in 1965, followed by meetings in Herrenchiemsee in 1966 (where the above remark was made) and in Marianske Lazne, Czechoslovakia, in 1967. The third meeting brought together two hundred and one Christian and Marxist philosophers, theologians, and scientists from sixteen European countries and the United States (but not from the Soviet Union, which chose to abstain).

The theme of the third meeting was "Creativity and Freedom in a Human Society" (the first two having dealt with "Christianity and Marxism Today" and "Christian Humaneness and Marxist Humanism"). At this meeting both sides expressed the view that the human personality can develop only in a setting of freedom; that both Christianity and Marxism must revitalize and open up their institutions and their doctrines; that the human personality cannot be fully understood on the existential and particularly the material

It would, however, be misleading to construe this dialogue as a fundamental breakthrough in the doctrinal relationship between Christianity and Marxism. The participants involved were individuals who, given their intellectual concerns, themselves reflected the tension between institutions and ideas; they inherently resented institutional efforts to limit the scope of philosophical inquiry. Both sides thus represented the intellectual fringes and not the very centers of bureaucratic power. The centers themselves displayed some ambivalence, not so much about the meetings—which they tolerated, in part, for reasons of political tactics—but about the degree to which differences between the two systems of thought were said to have been obscured by the respective spokesmen.*

These limitations notwithstanding, the discussions, which doubtless will continue and expand, had broad significance. They

---

level; that the state ought to be neutral on ethical and philosophical problems and that humanist Marxism must guarantee pluralism as the precondition for human freedom; and, finally, that both Christianity and Marxism involve a continuous, never-ending search for the most complete fulfillment of human freedom. (The above is a paraphrase of the conclusions reached by Charles Andras in his research paper on "Christians and Marxists in Marianske Lazne," RFE, July 10, 1967, which contains the best analysis of this meeting that I have seen. See also the valuable study by Kevin Devlin, "The Catholic-Communist 'Dialogue,'" *Problems of Communism,* May-June 1966, and especially the additional material on Latin America contained in the Spanish edition; and Charles Andras, "The Christian-Marxist Dialogue," *East Europe,* March 1968.)

One outgrowth of this dialogue was a remarkable little volume dealing with the philosophical and social problems of modernity, authored jointly by a leader of the French Communist Party and by a member of the Society of Jesus (Roger Garaudy and Quentin Lauer, S.J., *A Christian-Communist Dialogue,* New York, 1968).

* Subsequent to the meetings, there were reaffirmations from both sides, e.g., by the leadership of the French Communist Party, by the French Council of Bishops, and by Vatican spokesmen, that the dialogue could not be construed as involving any change in basic doctrinal attitudes. In a sense, these statements confirmed the point made by one of the more prominent Catholic participants that a true dialogue will not be possible until each side surmounts the tradition of "monolithism," which elevates both the "ecclesiastical society" and the party into the centers of history (Father Giulio Girardi of the Salesian University of Rome, as cited by *Le Monde* [*Hebdomadaire*], May 5–11, 1966; he repeated the same themes at Marianske Lazne [Andras, "The Christian Marxist Dialogue," p. 13]).

indicated that it is becoming increasingly difficult to confine the search for a more meaningful universal vision within institutionally defined frameworks, since the very existence of the institutions depends on the maintenance of their distinctive and exclusive identity. That is why what appears on the surface to be modest and limited has in fact been a major step away from the traditional Western view of such dialogue as anathema.[25]

The reforms and the debates within Catholicism have already had the effect, in many areas of personal life, of supplanting the authority of the institution by the rule of one's conscience. (Such, for example, has been the reaction of many bishops and Catholic laymen to the issue of birth control.) To a spiritually motivated person, conscience can be a stricter teacher than Church authority, but for most people reliance on conscience inescapably has the effect of making the Church increasingly irrelevant. It was this dilemma which more and more led Pope Paul VI to adopt a position—in spite of his earlier commitment to innovation—molded by the need for institutional defense: "Today, as anyone can see, orthodoxy, that is the purity of doctrine, does not seem to occupy first place in the psychology of Christians. How many things, how many truths are questioned and put up to doubt? How much liberty is claimed as regards the authentic heritage of Catholic doctrine, not only in order to . . . better explain it to the man of our time, but at times to subject it to that relativism in which profane thought . . . seeks its new expression, or to adapt it . . . to contemporary taste and the receiving capacity of modern mentality?" [26]

The Pope was right in noting that "orthodoxy . . . does not seem to occupy first place in the psychology of Christians." This is so not only on the level of formal, overt compliance with certain established rituals but even in regard to the more basic substance of belief, as is shown by Table 8, constructed from 1968 Gallup polls. The relatively low level of regular church attendance—while significant in revealing increasing disregard for the most basic but also the minimal ritualistic requirement—

was not as revealing as the striking gap between those who believe in God and those who believe in life after death. The essence of the Christian faith is that the former guarantees the latter. God without belief in life after death is something entirely different from the Christian God.

The poll data, though fragmentary and superficial, nevertheless highlight a problem. On the one hand, the poll indicates a crisis of institutionalized belief. On the other hand, however, it suggests that it would be misleading to conclude that low church attendance and disbelief in life after death mean pervasive irreligiosity. On the contrary, it suggests that authentic irreligiosity—that is

TABLE 8

	Do you believe in God?	Do you believe in life after death?	Do you attend church once per week?
	Yes	Yes	Yes
United States	98%	73%	43%
Greece	96	57	28 (Athens)
Uruguay (cities)	89	42	24
Austria	85	38	38
Switzerland	84	50	30
Finland	83	55	5
West Germany	81	41	27
Netherlands	79	50	42
Great Britain	77	38	—
France	73	35	25
Norway	73	54	14
Sweden	60	38	9

to say, a deeply felt rejection of a reality beyond the finite—does not exist, or at least not yet. A belief in God to which one cannot give substance may merely be a holdover from a more traditional society in a context that emphasizes immediate life, but it could also reflect the search for a highly personal, inner, and direct relationship between the individual and God.

Privatization of Belief

In fact, the waning of the Church as an institution may be a symptom of intensifying religiosity. The Church was a necessary intermediary between God and man in the phase of man's spiritual poverty and historical unawareness. It provided a rigid code of behavior, institutionalized sanctions (which gradually declined in severity as mankind was socialized on the level of personal, though not international, coexistence), and a link to the eternal. As the Church fades, for some the disintegration of its controls will doubtless mean license; for many it will simply be a matter of indifference; but for others it will be the beginning of a much more direct, more personal, less ritualized relationship to God.

This could mean the emergence of highly pluralistic religious responses—of cults, sects, believers' groups, each with a somewhat different form of expressing its faith, to say nothing of a much more personalized form of worship—even within the Catholic Church.[27] For most people the organized Church will continue to provide the basic mooring, but for many the relationship to God will be expressed much more individually and in keeping with their specific intellectual and psychological needs. The popularity of Teilhard de Chardin is, for example, symptomatic of our age's felt need to combine ecstasy with science, mystic belief with knowledge of the material world.*

The present ferment in Christianity is hence part of the general aversion toward the institutionalized belief that characterizes our time. This aversion reflects the nature of our intellectual style and

---

* A French thinker poses the issue more strongly, emphasizing the interdependence of science and ecstasy: "We must conclude that it is far from accidental that ecstatic phenomena have developed to the greatest degree in the most technicized societies. And it is to be expected that these phenomena will continue to increase. This indicates nothing less than the subjection of mankind's new religious life to technique. It was formerly believed that technique and religion were in opposition and represented two totally different dispensations. It was held that, with the development of a purely materialistic society, a struggle was inevitable between the machine and the economy, on the one side, and the ideal realm of religion, art, and culture, on the other. But we can no longer hold such a boundlessly simplistic view. Ecstasy is subject to the world of technique and is its servant. Technique, on the most significant level, integrates the anarchic and antisocial impulses of the human being into society. These impulses take their influence and receive their diffusion strictly by virtue of the technical means brought into play. The ecstatic phenomena of the human psyche, which without technical means would have remained completely without effect, are deployed throughout the world" (Ellul, p. 423).

the fragmented and impressionistic way we ourselves become exposed to reality, as well as the instinctive feeling that ideas are only relevant as long as they can successfully relate to a reality that is dynamic. To institutionalize an idea is to impede its capacity to adjust to change. The further evolution of the idea then becomes dependent not on the capacity of the mind to sense the speed and the significance of change but on the rate of change within the bureaucratic organization which has come to embody the idea. Vested power interests thus become more important than either ethical or intellectual imperatives.

The crisis of institutionalized beliefs is the last stage in the progressive secularization of life; that is, in the detachment of one's social existence from a framework of belief. Work, play, and now, increasingly, introspection have gradually separated themselves from formal Christian belief,[28] and they are beginning to detach themselves from Marxism under communism as well.

It was easier to establish institutional belief in an age of geographical, cultural and hence also psychological isolation. Religious fanaticism could thrive in such a context, and religious wars had profound moral meaning. Physical exhaustion (after the Thirty Years War and after the Battle of Vienna of 1683) as well as growing skepticism have made religious wars unfashionable. In our age communism has been the last great absolutist dogma, for it could use power to assure exclusiveness. It is not accidental that isolated China has lately been its most fanatic proponent—or that ideological conservatism in the communist states is usually accompanied by efforts to cut society off from contact with the external world by radio-jamming and other devices.* Global congestion—though not necessarily conducive to mutual comprehen-

* Nonetheless, these external controls are increasingly incapable of masking the evident lack of commitment within. It is revealing to note that in 1968, when the anti-intellectual and anti-Semitic purge in communist Poland compelled some communist intellectuals, until that moment quite orthodox in their loyalty, to leave the country, a number of them immediately moved to the "capitalist" United States, seeking employment in various institutions specializing in the study of communism and viewed in the East as intrinsically anti-communist.

sion—is simply inimical to institutions and ideologies relying on exclusivistic conviction.

Ideally, in this setting man should seek complete fulfillment by combining spiritual introspection with the moral imperative of social justice. Harvey Cox argues in his thoughtful book that "if men rather than metaphysical phantoms bear the meaning of historic life, then purposes other than those of one's own clan can be appreciated rather than repudiated. Separate world-views present the occasion not for mutual destruction but for fashioning a societal framework within which such variance can be encouraged and nourished. Ideally the secular city is such a society. It provides a setting in which a hodgepodge of human purposes and projects can thrive because each recognizes itself as provisional and relative. Authentic secularity demands that no world-view, no tradition, no ideology be allowed to become *the* officially enforced world-view beside which no others are tolerated. This in turn requires pluralistic social and political institutions." [29]

The shaping of the ideal secular city demands enormous social maturity and responsibility. It also calls for philosophical depth and a sense of restraint, since the transition from the tradition of dogma to the condition of diversity is not easy. Diversity of belief is certainly the prerequisite for freedom, and it may even be the concomitant of creativity (though the Middle Ages as well as the Orient argue against it). But carried to its extreme—to the point at which diversity itself becomes the substance of belief—it creates its own dangers. The healthy reaction against institutionalized doctrines is not complete unless it also involves the formulation of alternative principles of social contract and alternative views of the role of the individual. Fluid, fragile, and fragmentary ideas cannot provide either lasting insight or an enduring basis for action. Popular notions, shifting with the wind, may accurately reflect the underlying psychological and social tensions of our rapidly changing reality, but do they provide an enduring basis either for understanding it or for mastering it? Intellectual relativism may not suffice to meet the challenge of subjective activism, which is intensely intolerant because it is derived from purely personal criteria for evaluating reality.

This problem not only arises in systems in which formalized beliefs play a decisive role. It also confronts the Western liberal democratic states. These, too, depend on a symbiosis of ideas and institutions, though in much less formal, more implicit ways. The turbulence afflicting communism and Christianity is visible and direct, with restless ideas confronting unyielding institutions; the crisis of allegiance to liberal democracy is much more elusive but not less real. The effective working of a liberal democratic state requires a combination of social devotion to the abstract idea of democracy and of legalism in practice that can easily be strained by conditions of stress and crisis. A democratic process, moreover, is difficult to dramatize, in contrast to such notions as revolution, injustice, and freedom. Instead, it calls more prosaically for a high degree of procedural commitment: that is, a concern with the means as well as with the end of the process. Unless infused with new moral content, procedural commitment may not suffice in a confrontation with issues that are posed as absolutes and that are said to require passion—rather than procedure—for their resolution.

3. Histrionics as History in Transition

"We reject the world, we are no longer even 'traitors,' since this would imply an affinity with what we are betraying. We are the Viet Cong of thought. . . . The philosophy of tomorrow will be terrorist: not a philosophy of terrorism but a terrorist philosophy allied with an active policy of terrorism." [30] These words of a young Sorbonne philosopher convey the degree to which emotion has come to substitute for reason as a result of the reaction to what many feel has been the failure of rationalism in action. The "rejection" of the world is in essence the rejection of prevailing modes of thought and the substitution of ecstasy and action in the service of an abstract concept of revolution. Yesterday's "escape from freedom" has its equivalent in today's escape from reason.

Escape from Reason

In its extreme form, this mood—dramatized by the student riots in California, at Columbia University, throughout France, in West Berlin, in London, Rome, Belgrade, Warsaw, Tokyo, and much more lethally at the University of Mexico (where scores of students were killed in the fall of 1968), to say nothing of the many less publicized imitations elsewhere—has elevated action for action's sake into a moral principle. "Action is the only reality; not only reality but morality as well," proclaimed Abbie Hoffman, the leader of the American Yippies.[31] He was echoed both more belligerently and more ecstatically by his German counterpart, Daniel Cohn-Bendit, the leader of the 1968 French student strike who declared that "violence is happiness."[32] As two observers sympathetic to the new radical movements explained it, the contemporary rebels "think that the ivory-towered men of ideas have cheated them, lied to them, and that action and spontaneous experience will show them the truth."[33]

From this attitude is derived the view that reason by itself is suspect, that it must be buttressed by emotion, and that if a choice has to be made, emotion is a better guide than reason. Seeing in the world around them both hypocrisy and the failure of reason —with reason in the service of evil, which either makes it a slave of ideology or employs it as a scientific tool to improve war-making efficiency—even moderate dissenters condemned contemporary liberals for their lack of passion.* In cold reason they saw,

* In December 1968, at a major international conference held at Princeton on the subject of America's future, one of the accusations made by a student

more than a mere absence of moral indignation, a commitment to the *status quo*, a willingness to effect only marginal change, and a determination to avoid confronting the more basic moral issues.*

Reliance on passion and action had the added advantage of not requiring a programmatic blueprint. In contrast, the old ideologies offered both a critique of the present and a blueprint for the future, thus opening themselves to criticism on the level of both practicality (Is their utopia attainable?) and performance (Why hasn't the utopia been achieved?). The politics of ecstasy do not require a program to generate action, and their adherents were therefore not greatly troubled by the patronizing criticism of their programmatic vacuity advanced from the socialist old left and from the established communist parties.† On the contrary, they argue that it is not through institutional reforms spelled out in programs but through the creation of a community of emotion

---

leader was that the established liberal participants tend to rely on reason at the expense of passion. This charge prompted Arthur Schlesinger to remark, "Reason without passion is sterile, but passion without reason is hysterical. I have always supposed that reason and passion must be united in any effective form of public action. I can imagine nothing worse for our society than a rejection of reasoned analysis by the young. If we succeed in destroying the discipline of reason, if we make politics a competition in passion, a competition in emotion, a competition in unreason and violence, the certain outcome would be the defeat of the left."

* This charge has even been leveled against scholars engaged in studies of the future, and their "futurism" has been interpreted by critics as an immoral escape from the social dilemmas of the present. It has led to some unconsciously humorous situations, such as the one at the above-mentioned Princeton conference, where a millionaire radical attacked "futurists" for neglecting the role of wealth in American society. Shedding his sartorial elegance in favor of the more revolutionary open-necked-shirt uniform, he urged the assembled to "choose equality and flee greed."

† Max Eastman spoke for many old socialists when he expressed himself as "kind of sorry for these young rebels today. . . . They have an emotion not unlike ours. . . . They want to make a revolution but they have no ultimate purpose. I have a certain emotional sympathy for them, but they are rather pathetic because they have no plan. They just seek a revolution for its own sake" (as cited by *The New York Times*, January 9, 1969). Communist spokesmen expressed themselves more pungently, condemning the aspirations of the new rebels as "half-baked pie peppered with sexualism and narcomania" (*Trybuna Ludu*, May 9, 1968).

that true freedom can be attained. By creating that emotional state, the rebels of the late 1960s hoped to overcome the sexual oppression and "one-dimensional" quality of modern industrial society. Herbert Marcuse's *One Dimensional Man* has provided them with an intellectual frame of reference (much as Frantz Fanon's books exalting racial violence have done for the rebels in some areas of the Third World), though his advice and program are limited: "For the moment the concrete alternative is still only the negation." [34]

The call for "true freedom," however, permits the subversion of conventional freedom, and herein lies one of the basic contradictions of the movement. Leopold Labedz perceptively noted the striking resemblance between the romantic anarchism of the contemporary student revolution and the views of Max Stirner, who asserted in 1845 that "a people cannot be free otherwise than at the individual's expense." [35] Thus, the rebellion against the "oppressive freedom" of the West can entail both limitation on the freedom of those who do not share the ideals of "true" freedom and relative indifference to the suppression of freedom in the East. Moreover, the right to speak or write freely can be denied and its exercise disrupted by violence, since that violence is motivated by an emotional commitment to freedom and is designed to assert it. The definition of freedom is thus derived from a subjective inner conviction that one is right and not from the external pattern of relations guaranteeing choice and protection to the individual, whatever his views.

The intellectual—though not the social—seriousness of this phenomenon was further diluted by a certain artificiality on the level of political expression. Though every genuine revolution inescapably partakes of the past, it acquires its own distinctive character, style, and rhetoric precisely because it is a revolution: a sharp break with the past. The Paris Commune differed in these respects from the French Revolution, and the Commune in turn was not reproduced by the Bolshevik Revolution. Yet in recent years a great deal of the student rhetoric, symbolism, and personal behavior has taken the self-conscious form of a histrionic "happening" designed as a historical re-enactment.

At times it was the French Revolution that seemed to provide the scenario—especially in France—but more often it was Petrograd and Havana that were being re-enacted. The student leaders imagined themselves as historical figures, but in their imitativeness they often verged on the absurd. During the 1968 crisis at Columbia University, the leader of the student militants issued a pamphlet bearing Lenin's title, "What Is to Be Done?," and students occupying one of the buildings proclaimed themselves "a commune." The headquarters of the West Berlin militants were called "Smolny." Revolutionary beards (in styles ranging from Lenin to Castro to Marx) and combat fatigues à la Guevara were almost mandatory costumes against a decor of either red or black flags.

Even the violence was often more theatrical than real. In Tokyo it took the form of stylized battles, in which armored combatants employed shields and spears; in Paris a tacit agreement between the police and their opponents limited weapons to those used in the Stone Age: rocks, cobblestones, and clubs.* Only in Mexico was violence genuine in the sense that all available means were employed, as is true in real revolutions.†

---

* In all of France—despite the apparent temporary collapse of authority in May 1968—only one person died, and somewhat accidentally at that.

† But though the style and the format of the student rebellion was contrived and its aspirations almost deliberately unattainable (one of the most popular slogans of the May 1968 outbreak in Paris was "Be realists, demand the impossible!"), at least its youthfulness was authentic. The same cannot be said of the middle-aged admirers of the militants, who—though most often physically passive—outdid themselves in their efforts to drink again at the fountain of youth by vicarious identification with youth's exuberance. Verbal excess was most often the means used to attain this identification. Thus, one American scholar accused those critical of the abuses perpetrated by some militants of literally waging "a war against the young," which he compared to the war in Vietnam; he called for a "cultural revolution" in America! (Richard Poirier, "The War against the Young," *The Atlantic*, October 1968).

Cases of middle-aged exuberance were not isolated phenomena. As Labedz put it, "There can be little doubt that in many cases *les parents terribles* are worse than *les enfants terribles.* Some of them have moved from revolt against 'poverty amidst plenty' in the thirties to a revolt against affluent

To define the historical significance of these events, it is necessary to look beyond the violence and the slogans, beyond the superficial similarity among the outbursts that swept so many cities in so many parts of the world in so short a time. A closer analysis immediately reveals an important distinction: some aspects of the manifestations were clearly political in character and purpose; others—though linked with the political, though sharing with it a certain universality of aspirations, and though providing it with a mass emotional base—were much more socio-psychological in origin and vaguely moral and ethical in content. Linked together, each tended to obscure the specific character of the other.

The Political Dimension

The distinction between the two is important to an understanding of what was involved and of what it portends. The political manifestations are in some respects easier to dissect and analyze. Broadly speaking, they fell into two categories. In the West, and particularly in the United States, the politically motivated militants drew on both the ideological legacy of the old left's attack against capitalist society and on the more recent sense of outrage about the war in Vietnam. As the "imperialist" and "capitalist"

---

society in the sixties, at the time as they themselves moved from poverty to affluence, to practice alienation at 50,000 dollars a year. The revolutionary Establishment of New York and London, thrilled with revolutionary prospects, and displaying the characteristic *Salon-Maoismus,* contributes to the orgy of snobbery attendant upon the current Utopian wave. Long before the 'Black Power' spokesmen asked the students assembled at the London School of Economics to establish the Revolutionary Socialist Student Federation, whether they know how to make a petrol bomb, the *New York Review of Books* published a diagram of and a recipe for a Molotov cocktail on its cover page. This has not prevented, of course, its political writers from deploring 'American violence.' In France the self-abasement of the elderly 'progressives' reached its peak during the May 'revolution.' At the meeting of Jean-Paul Sartre with the students at the Sorbonne, Max Pol-Fouchet exclaimed with pathos appropriate to the occasion: 'Representing a generation which has failed, I ask you not to fail!' " (Leopold Labedz, "Students and Revolution," *Survey* [London], July 1968, pp. 25–26).

society par excellence, the United States provided the major target. The war served as a catalyst for emotions, as the basis for international unity among the young militants, as a bond between the old leftists and the new, and as a link between the politically-minded and the ethically concerned.*

Those motivated by strictly political concerns appear to have been a relatively small minority of the restless youth, but they provided influential leadership. It was the politically-minded who resuscitated the anarchist critique of organized society, who revived the Trotskyite slogan of the permanent revolution; and it was they who defined the more specifically political objectives (such as the call for immediate United States withdrawal from Vietnam). As the movement gained momentum and broadened its appeal, the political objectives—perhaps responding to the less clearly defined ethical and psychological needs of the following—were widened and became both vaguer and more demanding. It was no longer a matter of ending a particular governmental policy or of effecting a specific reform; the underlying "system"—capitalist in character and hence fundamentally irremediable—had to be undone before true reforms could be achieved. The specifics remained obscure, while the programmatic language ranged from Cohn-Bendit's exaltation of action—and rejection of communism†—to a rather simplistic repetition of Marxist cant.‡

---

* The war thus served the same function as the earlier campaigns against nuclear bombs in allowing for the expression of essentially moral concerns by the adoption of an anti–United States political posture. Frank Parkin, in his *Middle-Class Radicalism: The Social Bases of the British Campaign for Nuclear Disarmament* (Manchester, 1968), shows how the British CND mobilized middle-class support, drawn from among those with a tradition of moral concern, into a campaign against "evil." The campaign relied heavily on small symbolic gestures, such as eccentric dress, beards, and other forms of distinctive behavior.

† Because of this: the *Pravda* propagandist Yuri Zhukov, with his customary crudeness, characterized Cohn-Bendit as a "werewolf" (*Pravda,* May 30, 1968).

‡ The following may serve as an example: "Marxism is coming more and more to be the common denominator of all student movements in North America and Western Europe, even so in the new left SDS in the United States. I think this is inevitable and is a tribute to the growing sophistication

In the initial phases of the campaign against the Vietnam war, communist support—judging from approving communist pronouncements—was perhaps involved, but communist approval waned rapidly when the anti-institutional character of the movement became increasingly evident. In the eyes of many political militants, the communist system also represented bureaucratic conservatism, since its original revolutionary ideals had fossilized into institutional beliefs. Communist endorsement gradually shifted to criticism and then to condemnation; the views of the militant New Left were characterized by a Soviet writer as "Mamaism, which incorporates ideas of Marx, Marcuse and Mao, a completely artificial combination." [36]

Though the political manifestations in Mexico City, Madrid, Prague, and Warsaw partook of the same reaction against institutionalized belief and similarly capitalized on some of the ethical and psychological strains in modern society, they were much more specific in focus, less predisposed toward emotion, and more inclined toward a programmatic political approach. In all four cases, the demonstrators' demands were concerned with the loosening of direct political restraints, and the leaders did not have to construct an elaborate "one-dimensional man" thesis to prove that liberal democracy can also be oppressive and that its tolerance is in fact a masked form of constraint.[37] As a result, at least on the political level, their demands took the familiar form of the rejection of overt political dictatorship: abolition of censorship, the right of free assembly, freedom to travel, political democracy, and the abandonment of both ideological monopoly and oppression by

---

and maturity of the international student new left, inasmuch as Marxism is the most developed, refined and coherent revolutionary philosophy or world-view today and one that as a systematic social theory corresponds to the objective realities of the capitalist era, and inasmuch as it testifies to the realization by the student movements that they must align themselves with the working class in order to achieve the type of social transformation requisite to break the power of monopoly capital and create a new, non-repressive and truly free social order" (Stanley Gray, "Student Radicalism: An American Import?" a speech delivered to the 1968 Couchiching Conference, *McGill News,* November 1968, p. 22).

secret police. The similarity of the politically libertarian demands of the students in these four cities is striking.[38]

It should also be noted that the students who demanded direct political freedom acted in the context of a much more hostile political environment. The student militants in the United States, in Western Europe, and in Japan literally basked in publicity: front-page pictures, television interviews, ecstatic endorsements by middle-aged supporters, epic songs immortalizing their deeds, and books in which the various confrontations were recorded in prose and in photographs.* Given the pluralistic nature of the Western societies and the competitive character of their communications media, youthful militancy was rewarding to the ego—and thus also infectious.

This factor must be taken into account both in analyzing the dynamics of events in the West and in comparing them with events in less pluralistic societies.[39] There the mass media either ignored the demonstrations or condemned them. The student leaders were abused and arrested. Communications between institutions—not to speak of cities—required great personal effort, sacrifice, and risk. Youthful militancy was not rewarded with social acclaim; Madrid and Warsaw responded with prison sentences for the leaders and university expulsion for the participants.

The political environment clearly helped to shape the emphasis and the scope of the students' demands. In a strict authoritarian context, the demands had a politically libertarian content. In a looser, more pluralistic environment, the demands were either focused on more immediate university affairs or took on the form of a broader—and thus inevitably somewhat vaguer—social cri-

---

* The publicity bestowed on three female college militants (Peter Babcox, "Meet the Women of the Revolution," *The New York Times Magazine*, February 9, 1969) was characteristic. Similar deference was not paid to girls serving in the Peace Corps or in the war on poverty. In this connection, it was revealing to observe the satisfaction with which the militants would watch themselves on television replays or specially prepared documentaries. The publicity surrounding the militants brought considerable social pressure to bear on those who were less involved.

tique. Accordingly, the more specific and libertarian character of the demands made by the student leaders in the authoritarian states provided little basis for a common front with the militants of the West. In fact, there does not appear to have been much actual contact and coordination, although it was charged in Poland's political youth trials in late 1968 that the Brussels headquarters of the IV International (Trotskyite) provided ideological assistance to some Polish activists. If the charge is true, the Trotskyite link was perhaps the sole connection between political activists in the West and in the East.

The two movements appear to have been independently led and to have been motivated by profoundly different political aspirations. The slight direct contact that there was between the respective leaders turned out to be abortive. In 1968, in a BBC discussion of the student rebellion, the leader of the English militants attacked the spokesman of the Yugoslav students, while the head of the West Berlin SDS (Sozialistischer Deutscher Studentenbund) received a rather cool reception from Prague students, who found his political views primitive.* [40]

Nevertheless, important similarities between the respective political youth movements should also be noted. In both cases they were led by the abler students, who on the whole came from more socially established families. According to a study conducted at the University of California, the arrested undergraduate and graduate students tended to have much better than average grades; many of them held scholarships or had won awards.[41] In Poland official comment made much of the fact that the activists came from the relatively well-to-do homes of officials, and some

---

* It is also noteworthy that strictly politically oriented student movements in Mexico, Spain, or Poland avoided such manifestations as the "foul language" splinter that developed in California in the aftermath of the crisis, the fascination with drugs, and the deliberate adoption of deviant social behavior as in the case of the Yippies. To be sure, these manifestations were also the product of peculiarly American conditions, but their appearance as a side effect of the student rebellion was made possible by the less focused and also less oppressed character of the rebellion.

university professors stressed the fact (in conversation with this writer) that their best students were involved. After the demonstrations were suppressed, measures were taken to favor the admission into the university of workers' and peasants' children. Even in Rumania, where student unrest was suppressed relatively quickly, official reaction emphasized the fact that the young "hooligans" were in the main children of "building-site managers, university professors, instrumentalists in the Philharmonic Orchestra, physicians, engineers, white-collar workers, militia staff members." [42]

As in the West, the political leadership for the restless young was in many cases provided by the offspring of former left activists; hence not by rebels against the older generation but, rather, by young people who shared the ideals of their parents but felt that these had been corrupted in practice by the ruling communist elite. In Poland the most outstanding student rebels included the children of high party officials, while in the United States children of the old left formed a high percentage of the activist leaders at Columbia and Berkeley. In both the East and the West the rebel leaders came from environments that were not indifferent but ideologically concerned.

Another similarity between the student militants in the West and in the East was the vagueness of their long-range objectives. Though the specific and immediate goals of the students in the more politically oppressive regimes were somewhat more precise, their "demands" rarely went beyond a statement of immediate complaints. To be sure, the transformation of a police dictatorship into a multi-party democracy, or at least into something resembling the Yugoslav model, was a more defined objective—with experiential examples available—than the Western students' plea for a participatory democracy; however, the more specific ramifications of the desired social and political systems tended to be vague in the East as well as in the West.*

* One of the more extensive critiques of the existing Polish system was prepared by two young Warsaw sociologists, J. Kuron and K. Modzelewski, sev-

Though this may have been a weakness from the strictly political point of view—as was charged by the critics of the militants—it also helped to provide a wider bridge between the political leadership and the more generally restless younger generation. It is doubtful—and this is especially true of the more pluralistic societies—whether a highly specific political program would have attracted the wide support generated by the more undifferentiated attack against the Establishment, vested interests, the *status quo*, and institutionalized beliefs. The reliance on emotion rather than on reason, on felt aspirations rather than on concrete programs, struck a more responsive chord in a generation that was the most directly affected by the pace of contemporary change and that was the very product of that change.

Historical Discontinuity

In our time the student generation represents one of the most dynamic variables of change. The growth in their number as well as the simultaneous growth in the number of radios, televisions, telephones (all items that affect personal relationships, both making possible and encouraging the rapid dissemination of ideas) make for a subjectively dynamic mood that stands in sharp contrast to the relatively slower rate of change in such items as income (national or per-capita), the switch from rural to urban

---

eral years prior to the student outbreaks of March 1968. (The authors were promptly sent to prison.) Entitled "Open Letter to the Party," it became the source of much of the theoretical inspiration for the political-minded leadership of youth. Written from a Marxist point of view, it provided a scathing critique of the degeneration of Polish communism into an institutionalized bureaucratic despotism, with vested interests suppressing the egalitarian idealism of socialism. When it came to offering a program, however, the authors confined themselves to urging a new revolution led by workers and intellectuals determined to create a new social order characterized by few institutions, workers' self-government, and true social egalitarianism. In late 1968 Kuron and Modzelewski were again sentenced to prison for having allegedly inspired the March events in collusion with the IV International (Trotskyite).

employment, the population shift to larger urban centers, or the average number of people living in a room. The over-all result is the contradiction, already noted in the preceding chapter, between the pace of change in the state of mind and in material reality. (See Tables 6 and 7, pp. 42–43.)

In the words of a student of modernization, contemporary man —and this is especially true of the younger generation—"is less under the domination of his environment . . . and to this extent he is freer, but at the same time he is less certain of his purpose and in times of great unrest he is prepared to surrender his freedom in the interest of purposeful leadership." [43] In that fluid setting the present becomes difficult to comprehend, since it is no longer defined by either religion or nationalism or historical-ideological perspectives.[44]

Writing about the waning of the Middle Ages, the historian Johan Huizinga described a world of discontinuity, a world marked by the collapse of traditional beliefs, uncertainty about eternal salvation, widespread pessimism, and intense violence. Psychological refuge was sought by many in mystical cults, while individual behavior was dichotomized, ranging from emphasis on the saintly to indulgence in depravity and cruelty. Shifts from one extreme to the other were common, as men desperately sought social anchorage in absorbing commitment.[45]

A similar crisis, marked by much more secular forms of expression, occurred again in the West when nationalism and industrialization combined to change the character of society. Massive national and class conflicts, as well as acute social and psychological tension, spawned all-encompassing ideologies that seemed to provide both authority and a sense of direction. Writing about the cataclysm of World War II, Czeslaw Milosz, in *The Captive Mind,* drew perceptive portraits of Eastern European intellectuals as they moved from one faith to another in a search for the personal stability that their environment failed to provide.

Today's mood has many parallels, but it also differs significantly in scope and content. The industrial revolution, to say nothing of the culture of the Christian Middle Ages, was territorially confined, and only gradually—in the course of more than a century and a half—did it spill over to affect more and more societies.[46] Its appearance was accompanied by the rise of nationalism and other secular ideologies, in which broad concepts were reinforced by the institutions embodying them. In contrast, the current crisis of institutionalized belief takes place in the context of the technetronic revolution, a revolution which is not territorial but spatiotemporal.

This new revolution almost simultaneously affects the entire globe, with the result that fads and new forms of behavior move rapidly from society to society. The student generation lives in this new technetronic age, even if in some cases their immediate societies do not. Unlike the industrial age, which required that a society undergo extensive industrialization before the new proletarian class could become socially significant, the spatiotemporal technetronic revolution directly reaches those receptive to it because they have access to communications and because their state of mind is formed by factors outside their immediate social context. The contemporary student mass is precisely such a group, and that is why forms of behavior peculiar to Berkeley were within a year repeated elsewhere (West Berlin students even wore sandals in the cold November Central European weather!). American student activists studying abroad—and highly critical of American society—have tended to play an important energizing role in this process, and are evidence of the extent to which America, the first to experience the technetronic age fully, has replaced Europe as the principal source of social change.

The problem facing the rebels of a century and a half ago was how to integrate meaningfully the unprecedented, incomprehensible changes wrought by the industrial revolution. The same problem is posed by the onset of the technetronic age, with its apparent threat to human values, its impersonality, its overrationalization, its simultaneous intensification of personal experience, and its spatial immediacy to every human suffering anywhere on the globe. For many in the nineteenth century—especially those who were most affected, either vicariously or directly, by the industrial revolution (that is, the intellectuals and the workers)—Marxism provided the integrative response. Today the search is on for some new source of intellectual mooring, and the searchers have begun by rejecting established answers.

The younger generation is the one most directly affected by the transition into the new age, and it contains the most active opponents and includes the majority of those who feel themselves to be victims of the technetronic revolution. In their reliance on emotion and violence, many of the opponents are reminiscent of the Luddites of early-nineteenth-century England, who reacted to the machine age with primitive passion, destroying that which they did not understand well enough to harness. Often supported by local public opinion, the Luddites—well organized and highly motivated—shattered machines and decried the frequently very real injustices that the machines' appearance had precipitated. The fear, hatred, and incomprehension of the computer current among some people echoes the denunciations of the textile machine a century and a half ago.*

Like the Luddites, the contemporary opponents of the technological and electronic revolution represent, especially in the more advanced Western states, a response to the new modes of life. The Luddites were threatened by economic obsolescence and reacted against it. Today the militant leaders of the reaction, as well as their ideologues, frequently come from those branches of learning which are most sensitive to the threat of social irrelevance.[47] Their political activism is thus only a reaction to the more basic fear that the times are against them, that a new world is emerging without either their assistance or their leadership.†

---

* In early February 1969, rioting students in Montreal vented their anger at the "system" by destroying with fireaxes a one-million-dollar university computer.

† The insistence on total solutions prompts, at the same time, their characteristic unwillingness to become involved in the more mundane process of

The attraction that a segment of the younger generation in the more developed world now feels toward poetry, lyricism, and emotion—and their contempt for reason and intellectual concepts—may be indicative not so much of one tradition replacing another but rather of a clash between emotion and necessity. On the one hand are the feelings and attitudes prompted by the breakdown of institutionalized beliefs and intensified by the new modes of communication—all stimulating or creating an overwhelming desire for emotional escape, or at least emotional release through "concrete" feelings and associations. On the other hand is the tedious necessity to master by intensive conceptualization the techniques of computers, mathematics, systems control, and the like, on which the resolution of many contemporary social problems depends.*

Though this clash may be a profound one, it is doubtful whether the student generation represents a new revolutionary class of the twentieth century. A truly revolutionary class must

---

making partial improvements, of gradually adapting new techniques, of really becoming involved in the world. John Ardagh, in *The New French Revolution* (New York, 1969), notes this paradox in regard to the French intellectual left: "Sartre and his friends have preached that literature must be *engagée*—but in practice they have always shied away from realistic political action. . . . Sartre and his friends have always demanded utopia or nothing . . . So the technocrats have stolen the Sartrians' clothes" (p. 358).

* Compare, in this connection, Noam Chomsky's attacks on the new breed of American intellectual-experts (*American Power and the New Mandarins*, New York, 1968) with the attacks on Plato, who was accused of the sin of "intellectualizing" reality. There are other tantalizing parallels to ancient Athens. The author of a recent study of the impact of Plato's philosophy on the society of his time argues that the term "philosopher" was relatively new and was used by Plato to identify "the man who is prepared to challenge the hold of the concrete over our consciousness, and to substitute the abstract" (Eric A. Havelock, *Preface to Plato*, Cambridge, Mass., 1963, p. 281). The concentration on the abstract was associated with the appearance of a new technique of communication—the written, which first supplemented and then displaced the antecedent oral tradition (pp. 292–95). Epic poetry relied on narrative, which both stimulated and depended on emotionally shared experience; the more abstract categorization of reality became possible with the introduction of the alphabet and writing, and it opened the doors of history to conceptualization. Both Christianity and Marxism stepped through these doors.

master the contemporary techniques of social organization, rather than reject them. This may be difficult for the student "revolutionary class" to do, since it is necessarily transitional in character and subject to constant change. This does not preclude the possibility that student militants might well opt out of society permanently and become—especially after hardening prison experience—professional revolutionaries and that the inflow of new students may keep alive the feelings of restlessness and rebellion. It is not, however, certain that the older ex-student revolutionaries will be able to maintain their ties with the new generation of younger students, from whom they will be increasingly separated by age. They will run the risk of becoming rebels outside of a "class." Each student generation will then have to create its own leadership, its own aspirations and techniques, before it too fades from the scene. It is perhaps no accident that history is, after all, a cemetery of revolutionary youth movements.

Moreover, the coming waves of students may enter an environment gradually becoming more willing to tolerate the existence of altogether deviant subcultures and offering social support even to those who choose to divorce themselves from society. Many of the contemporary younger rebels—especially those who are pathological rather than political in their motivation—may well choose that path. Finally, as social change contributes to the spread of education and knowledge, the distinctive characteristics of the student may be blurred; as society becomes more knowledge-oriented and the student more socially involved, the gap between student life and society will narrow.

Nevertheless, the challenge of the student generation as a whole to rigid hierarchies and institutionalized beliefs and to the social order of the industrial age has had the effect of reopening the more basic questions concerning the purposes of social organization. What should be the balance between the internal and the external qualities of life? What is the relationship of personal liberty to social equality? These questions acquire new meaning and call for new definitions whenever a major historical crisis dominates our consciousness of reality.

4. Ideas and Ideals beyond Ideology

The nineteenth century can be said to represent the intellectual supremacy of the idea of liberty, but the twentieth century is witnessing the triumph of equality. For most people liberty found its political embodiment in the nation, and only for relatively few was it in procedural guarantees for the individual. The last century was, therefore, primarily the time of nationalism, and only secondarily of liberal democracy. The search for forms in which the idea of equality can be expressed is currently the strongest motivating impulse behind the activities of university students in the West and of youthful critics of the privileged communist elites; it also guides relations between blacks and whites both in the United States and in Africa, and between the richer and the poorer countries.

We have thus reached the stage in mankind's history where the passion for equality is a universal, self-conscious force. What is more, since equality is not likely to be attained on the objective plane, it may be sought more and more on the subjective plane. With real equality impossible, equality through emotion becomes a substitute, with passionate conflict and hostility creating the illusion of equality.

The Quest for Equality

The passion for equality is strong today because for the first time in human history inequality is no longer insulated by time and distance. Nationalism spread during a century and a half as populations gradually became politicized as a side effect of literacy and industrialization, but the rejection of inequality within and between nations has become the dominant mood in a mere matter of decades. In this regard, as in the rebellion of the younger generation, the appearance of global communication and of newly educated masses is the decisive stimulus.

Accordingly, the relationship between the technetronic age and the passion for equality—if not the idea of equality itself—is quite causal. From the standpoint of generating social and political motivation, it is a matter of enormous import that "the poor live as much in the new software multibillion dollar service environment of world information as the wealthy do." [48] National oppression and class oppression had to be direct and personal before they could generate counterreaction. Today the sense of inequality can be vicarious and nevertheless extraordinarily intense, because it can be magnified beyond the level of personal experience.

But though the commitment to the idea of equality currently commands the greatest allegiance, the definition of equality remains elusive. In the communist states the struggle for political equality involves the desire to do away with the right to rule as a privilege of only a few; with the right to read and to travel freely as a professional prerogative of only those at the top of the power elite; with the right to buy what one desires as an advantage enjoyed only by those on governmental assignments abroad or with access to special stores for high officials. Nevertheless, communist party leaders, who have long assumed that the elimination of propertied classes would automatically ensure social equality as the basis for personal liberty, find this desire for libertarian equality difficult to comprehend.

In the new and developing states, the difficulty in defining equality is compounded by the fact that in most cases complaints result not only from immediate social inequities but from an acute sense of deprivation vis-à-vis the developed world. The small size of many of the new states further intensifies their feeling of impotence and complicates the task of redress.* Their economic

---

* "The median population of all states independent before 1776 is today 22.6 million, of those emerging from the first anticolonial revolution and the

dependence on unstable commodity markets and foreign capital means that their liberty is highly relative and tenuous. The result is a condition in which liberty seems threatened by the absence of international equality.

It is the desire for equality that has made most of the leaders of the new states embrace socialism. They see in socialism a vehicle for ensuring the objectives which most of them share: the flowering of their nations' own distinctive cultures, national economic development, and the gradual erosion of internal and external inequality. Their socialism shares the Marxist analysis of capitalism and the Leninist description of imperialism, though the leaders tend to stress that their economic approach avoids the errors not only of capitalism but of communism as well.[49] Indeed, some leaders have claimed that their socialism—less dogmatic and enriched by indigenous traditions—would provide the world with a more humane alternative than either the doctrinaire materialism of communism or the social indifference of the corporate West.[50] Writing just before the attainment of independence in Kenya, Tom Mboya, in discussing the African concept of socialism, declared that eventually Africa "will show the rest of the world what freedom really means." [51]

These views, however, remain essentially unstructured and unsystematized. Though they have been described by some scholars as an ideology, they tend to lack the systematic, coherent, integrated, and intellectually sustained character of either socialism or communism, and there is an absence of formal dogmas and institutional embodiment. Though they back their views by undemocratic political power and phrase them in a terminology largely derived from Marxism, and though they are necessarily preoccupied with improving man's economic life, the leaders of the new

---

dissolution of dynastic empires (1776–1945), 5.2 million, and of those that won their independence in the last two decades, only 3.4 million. There may be some disagreement on the optimum size of a nation-state, but there is little doubt that it is above three or four million. The very size of the newly proclaimed states, particularly in Africa, makes it difficult for them to realize those aspirations of modernity and power, of dignity and prosperity, which their leaders profess" (Dankwart Rustow, *A World of Nations*, Washington, D.C., 1967, p. 247).

nations tend to lay stress on the pre-eminence of nationhood and of the spiritual importance of the human being. This is also true of the new indigenous intellectuals—those in the social layer immediately below the present Third World leaders—who tend to be even more radical in their outlook, more susceptible to racist appeals, and highly emotional in behavior.[52] Their ecstatic Marxism is a far cry from either the scholasticism of Marx or the organizational single-mindedness of Lenin.

Moreover, the experience of several years of independence has had a chilling effect on those who originally saw in the new nations an expression of a more humane vision and an example for others. In many of the new states the ruling elites have restricted liberty on the ground that such restriction is necessary to fight inequality by eliminating privilege on the home front and by mobilizing national efforts to bridge the widening gap between the nation and the outside world.[53] The passion for equality has in some places been debased into a racial nationalism that finds its expression in the expulsion of nonnative tribesmen (Chinese from Indonesia, Asians from East Africa) and more generally in a xenophobic and even racial resentment of the developed white world as the principal exploiter. The new political elites have shown a strong propensity toward conspicuous consumption, at some expense to their social consciousness.

The problem of equality poses itself rather differently in the more developed and prosperous countries. There, particularly in the United States, it has taken the form of opposition to "bigness" in institutions and vested interests. Opponents of "bigness" argue that the political process is deceptive because the "one man, one vote" formula merely obscures the underlying inequality of power between the individual and, for example, the corporations. More specifically, the notion of equality—rather than that of liberty—has been at the heart of the civil-rights struggle in the United States. Formal "liberty" has been gradually and painfully obtained by the blacks with the passage of civil-rights legislation, particularly legislation guaranteeing the right to vote. That "liberty," however, hardly assures the blacks equality in America, and the black man's struggle today is to obtain the "equality" that the white man already possesses. Defining that "equality" is precisely what perplexes the college president or the city manager, to whom liberty has traditionally been synonymous with equality.

The social tensions in the developed world—and this is true of some communist countries as well as of more pluralistic societies —highlight the difficulty of seeking equality purely on the external and material plane. After several centuries of social activism —which emphasized the external man—contemporary man in the advanced industrial countries confronts a crisis of self-definition for which he finds no satisfactory answers in either established religion or ideology. With the gradual fading of nationalist and ideological passions, inner certitude and external commitment have yielded to inner ambiguity and external uncertainty.

Syncretic Belief

When Michel Foucault proclaimed "the death of man," he was expressing in almost Nietzschean terms the pessimism inherent in the reaction against Promethean ideologies.* That reaction, in

* This pessimism has been summarized in Robert Bailey's *Sociology Faces Pessimism* (The Hague, 1958, pp. 116–17) in ten propositions, contrasting the European *Zeitgeist* of a hundred years ago with that of today:

EUROPEAN ZEITGEIST	
One hundred years ago	*Today*
1. There is progress.	1. There is no progress.
2. Social evolution is linear.	2. Social evolution is cyclical.
3. Western civilization is moving continually toward greater heights in cultural and social development.	3. Western civilization is in a period of disintegration and decline.
4. Man is rational.	4. Man is nonrational or irrational.
5. Society is composed of individuals who, being rational or capable of becoming rational, shall boost mankind to new levels of accomplishment.	5. Society is composed of masses who, being nonrational and easily influenced, shall reduce mankind to mediocrity.

turn, reflects the scientific complexity of modern society, which stimulates a feeling of futility and impotence on the part of the individual. Foucault's views, associated with a school of thought called "structuralism," have been characterized by a critic as the ideology of contemporary technocracy, for Foucault sees man as the object of a process which deprives him of any autonomy and rules him impersonally, according to a structural dynamic.[54] The rejection of conscious history—thus striking at the heart of the ideological-religious approach that has dominated Western thinking—is itself a reflection of the contemporary crisis in values, assumptions, and beliefs and of the collapse of all integrated and simultaneously purposive historical interpretations.*

Centuries ago, in the great religions, man defined the norms that ought to guide the relations among men. Now, for the first time in recorded history, man is beginning—though just beginning—to liberate himself from the oppressive struggle to survive as a physical being. This has prompted a renewed concern with the more elusive, spiritual aspects of existence;† it has also

6. Scientific truth and knowledge are beneficial for society.	6. Scientific truth and knowledge may be harmful for society.
7. Myth and superstition are harmful.	7. Myth and superstition may be beneficial.
8. A society represents a harmony of interests, a *communum bonum*.	8. A society is composed always of conflicting interests.
9. Society is ruled by the consent of the people.	9. Society is ruled by the elite.
10. Democracy and the humanitarian social values serve to protect individual and community interests.	10. Democracy and the humanitarian social values are unfortunate mistakes that result in the rule of uneducated masses.

* Structuralism also involves a critique of Sartre's existentialism, which, in its stress on individual moral autonomy, was itself a reaction to the ideological emphasis on the individual's submissive identification with collective and purposive history-making.

† In the words of one of the participants in the Harvard University Program on Technology and Science: "With the advent of the affluent industrial societies science tends to replace economic productivity as a primary social goal. As science is able more and more to satisfy its material needs with less human effort, *it becomes more preoccupied with the spiritual and intellectual needs.* It must develop new goals and aspirations in order to remain viable as a social order. . . . Many times in the past scientists have believed that

created a state of agitation, in which systematic dialogue increasingly breaks down because of the lack of shared assumptions. Naturally, this is especially true of the intellectual community, though the reaction gradually communicates itself to the body politic. As a consequence, the majority of people abide by procedural political order only as long as that order works, but they have less and less internal commitment to it. (The passive behavior of the French people during the May 1968 collapse of political order is a case in point.) To be sure, there is much discussion today of the need to reassert human values, of the priority of man against the tyranny of political despots or dehumanizing technocrats, but in our time—as opposed to the situation in eras when religion or ideology was dominant—the means, the forms, and the inner significance of these goals remain extraordinarily undefined. (The International Philosophical Congress in Vienna in 1968 was, for example, dominated by the view that contemporary philosophy must be in the forefront of the "struggle," but *how* it was to contribute was never specified.)

It is doubtful, therefore, whether the growing concern with the abstract and the spiritual, and even the evidences of new interest in religiosity—in other words, all matters subsumed under the term "the quality of life"—will in the near future lead to the emergence of new formal ideologies or religions. Scientific complexity and skepticism—reinforced by the impressionistic effects of increased reliance on audio-visual communication (television) —work against the systematic and dogmatic qualities of an ideology. In this sense it is therefore right to speak of "the end of ideology." Religion and ideology were part of an age in which reality was still dogmatically compressible into intellectualized

all the significant questions had been answered, and the only task remaining was to fill in the details, to work out the full ramifications of the conceptual structure whose main framework was completely delineated. Yet each time the expectation has proved to be wrong. Each new major advance has revealed an unsuspected new world, a new conceptual structure embedded in the old, and subsuming it" (Harvey Brooks, "Can Science Be Planned?" Harvard University Program on Technology and Science, 1968, pp. 13–14 [italics added]).

compartments; both were reinforced by the urgent desire to translate the ideal into the real. What more probably lies ahead is a turn toward more personal, less structured, more subjectively defined attempts at a synthesis of the scientific and the spiritual—though perhaps nothing quite so mystical as Teilhard de Chardin's thinking. In any case, this appears to be the trend among contemporary Christian and revisionist Marxist thinkers.

Though it is individually enriching, there is the danger that this development might work against the durability of liberal democracy. Intellectual confusion and political disagreement, to say nothing of simple insecurity, might well stimulate a search for external sources of stability—which would take the form of either repression or the bestowal of confidence on a dominant personality. Moreover, "a society that carries eclecticism to the point where not only the total culture but the individual consciousness becomes a mere congeries of disassociated elements will find it impossible to make a collective decision as to what man shall make of man." [55] A leader can then be a substitute for the integrative tasks of society, which are otherwise performed by either a formal or an implicitly shared ideology.* In the absence of social consensus, society's emotional and rational needs may be fused—mass media make this easier to achieve—in the person of an individual who is seen as both preserving and making the necessary innovations in the social order. Given the choice between social and intellectual disorder—and by this is not meant anything that even approaches a revolutionary situation—and authoritarian personal leadership, it is very probable that even some present constitutional and liberal democratic societies would opt for the latter.

* Daniel Bell has described the social functions of ideology in the following terms: "Within every operative society there must be some creed—a set of beliefs and values, traditions and purposes—which links both the institutional networks and the emotional affinities of the members into some transcendental whole. And there have to be some mechanisms whereby those values can be not only 'internalized' by individuals (through norms) but also made explicit for the society—especially one which seems consciously to shape social change; and this explicating task is the function of ideology" ("Ideology and Soviet Politics," *Slavic Review*, December 1965, p. 595).

The temptation to choose security as an alternative to complexity may grow in the years ahead, because "the end of ideology," far from diminishing the importance of ideas and ideals in politics, is ushering in an age in which abstract issues concerning the meaning of personal and social life are again becoming central. It is precisely because institutionalized beliefs no longer both confine and define the framework of the dialogue that the dialogue is becoming more intense and far-ranging. The result is a renewed conflict of ideas, but not of institutionalized ideologies; renewed interest in religiosity, but not in organized religions.

In this new and passionate dialogue, established and widely used terminologies are increasingly useless. Terms such as capitalism, democracy, socialism, and communism—even nationalism—are no longer adequate to provide relevant insights. In ideologically dominated societies, such as the communist nations, this inadequacy expresses itself more and more in even overt attacks on the official ideology; in societies with looser, more implicit values, it prompts a search for some acceptable and relevant framework. In both cases the accent is on the need to combine the previously dominant emphasis on external man with renewed attention to his inner life. In both cases—as was true of Marxism in the industrial age—there is the felt need for a new intellectual synthesis.

It is symptomatic of our age that despite its intense turbulence it has not produced a relevant concept of revolution: a strategy of action designed to replace operative institutions and values with a new set; that is, both a method of change and the substance of that change. The industrial age did produce such a concept (Marxism), and it was later applied to countries in the process of industrialization. There is no such theory available to the post-industrial societies, nor has the New Left succeeded in providing one. Moreover, whereas in the past ideologies of change gravitated from the developed world to less developed areas—thereby stimulating imitation of the developed world—today the differences between the two worlds are so pronounced that it is difficult to conceive of a new ideological wave originating from the developed world and rapidly acquiring relevance for underdeveloped nations.

Total integrative revolutions were possible because integrative ideologies provided a framework for total change and reconstruction. The integrative ideology was in itself a reflection of an age in which authority rested on clearly established beliefs and institutions. The communist party, with its claim to infallibility, was thus the epitome of an age of integrated grand visions and authoritarian institutions. Rapid scientific change, the massive educational explosion, and the intense communications implosion are all factors that make for highly volatile beliefs and reactions and create a situation in which subjective feelings are more important than collective commitment to a blueprint for social action and organization.

Accordingly, for the present, both the fragmentation-unification tensions that are stimulated on the political, economic, and intellectual planes by the gap between the technological and electronic age and the persistence in a new era of institutions and social forms derived from another age point toward a time of turbulence rather than toward a time of fundamental revolution. The more developed world is facing a crisis of its liberal, democratic consensus; the communist world is finding it difficult to adapt its ideology; the Third World seeks a frame of reference in a modified form of socialism that substitutes emotion for orthodoxy. In the past the world lived in an environment of compartmentalized uniformity: agrarian societies, basically similar in socio-economic structure but differentiated in religions and cultures, were isolated from one another; today differentiated socio-economic realities, existing in an intellectual context of crumbling religions and ideologies, overlap perceptually. The psychic certitude of the past thus gives way to psychic tension; confidence of righteousness yields to feelings of guilt or resentful inferiority.*

* Thus, in the past when Christians and Moslems hated one another they did so in self-righteous confidence; today Third World citizens may hate Americans for their wealth but at the same time despise their own felt inferiority, whereas Americans feel guilty about their wealth but savor a feeling of technological superiority.

It is possible that in the present phase of intellectual turmoil there are for the first time the seeds of a globally relevant perspective. The assertively universalist ideologies of the nineteenth century were in fact highly parochial in their origins, and thus they quickly merged with nationalism. (This turned out to be particularly true of communism under Stalin.) The seemingly inner-oriented ideas and ideals that dominate—in a highly unstructured manner—the current dialogue are in fact much more concerned with the universal problems of man and with the reintegration of the spiritual and the material.

Man's vision of himself was at first highly primitive and fragmentary, reflecting thousands of small cultures. Out of these eventually emerged several religions with universal aspirations, though each was still culturally and territorially confined. The age of secularism gave rise to a more political vision, in which nationalism (elevated into a universal principle) was combined with largely European-derived ideologies that aspired to universal applicability. Whether our phase is a transition or the beginning of a more fundamental disintegration is likely to be very much influenced by what happens in the two major societies of our time—the United States and the Soviet Union—and by what happens to the two major contemporary visions of the modern world—liberalism and communism.

PART III
Communism: The Problem of Relevance

Marxism, born of the social upheaval produced by the combined effects of the industrial and nationalist revolutions, provided a unique intellectual tool for understanding and harnessing the fundamental forces of our time. As both a product and a response to a particularly traumatic phase of man's history, it supplied the best available insight into contemporary reality; it infused political action with strong ethical elements; it formed the basis for a sustained attack on antiquated pre-industrial social institutions; and it raised the banner of internationalism in an age increasingly dominated by national hatreds.

As the first state to have put Marxist theory into practice, the Soviet Union could have emerged as the standard-bearer of this century's most influential system of thought and as the social model for resolving the key dilemmas facing modern man. Yet today Soviet communism is a conservative bureaucratized doctrine. In China, the scene of the most extensive application of Marxist principles to extreme industrial backwardness, communism is a curious mixture of ethnocentric nationalism and ideological fundamentalism; in the more advanced West communism is vital only to the extent that it blurs its ideological identity by collaborating with its erstwhile ideological rivals; and in the East its ideological militancy feeds on a deliberate identification with the most fanatic nationalist passions. In sum, contemporary communism has sacrificed Marxism's Promethean commitment to universal humanism.

The tragedy of communism as a universal perspective is that it came both too early and too late. It was too early to be a source of true internationalism, because mankind was only just awakening to national self-awareness and because the limited technological means of communication available were not yet ready to reinforce a universal perspective. It came too late for the industrial West, because nationalism and liberal concepts of state-reformism pre-empted its humanist appeal through the nation-state. It came too early for the pre-industrial East, where it served as the ideological alarm clock for the dormant masses, stimulating in them increasingly radical nationalism.

Too late in the West, too early in the East, communism found its moment of opportunity in neither West nor East but in the halfway house of Russia. Its failures and successes, as well as its specific character, therefore, have to be seen in the context of that peculiar fifty-year tie between a would-be universalist doctrine and a highly specific Eurasian national setting. To the present-day world the practical reality of communism is mainly what Russia has made of it.

To modern man communism in China represents only a potential and does not offer a relevant example. Though some aspects of Chinese communism—its alleged puritanism, its seemingly permanent revolution, its ideological militancy—may appeal to the more disaffected and emotional Western intellectuals, as a social model China offers little guidance to those concerned with the problems of advanced industrial civilization. Still struggling with its own backwardness, suffering from political uncertainties, mired in conflicts with its immediate neighbors, increasingly Sinifying its Marxism-Leninism, China may be a revolutionary symbol for some, but it hardly offers a blueprint for coping with the social and psychological dilemmas posed by the post-industrial age.

To be sure, China may appear in a different light to some of the would-be revolutionary elites in the less developed nations. For some of them, China provides an attractive example of national discipline and ideological dedication, of a massive social effort to modernize in spite of technological backwardness. But even on this level the Chinese model is relevant only as an example of will and purpose, as a guide to the future, not as an example of how communism responds to the problems of modernity. The experience of the Soviet Union provides the only answer to that crucial test.

1. The Stalinist Paradox

One man dominated almost two-thirds of Soviet history, and his name is associated with both a system of rule and a particular approach to constructing communism. No examination of communism's contemporary role in the world, to say nothing of within the Soviet Union, can afford to overlook Stalin's role and Stalin's legacy. That legacy is represented by the Soviet state's current institutions and modes of operation, and even though almost two decades have passed since Stalin's death, any Soviet discussion of reform still inevitably revolves around the question of breaking with Stalinism.

This is quite understandable. The Soviet state and the Soviet society of today were created by an unprecedented social revolution deliberately carried out by the political elite. Violent and costly, that revolution should not be confused with the Bolshevik seizure of power in 1917, for it occurred more than a decade later. During the crucial years of 1930–1940, in the course of which Soviet society was reshaped to mirror the ideological aspirations of the political rulers, that revolution consumed at least six and a half million lives* as the new Soviet state took shape. It was that revolution which spawned Soviet Russia's present political elite. It was that revolution which is said to have constructed the first socialist society based on Marxism and to have laid the foundations for its eventual entrance into communism. It is also that revolution which begs the question whether that specific character was *necessary* to assure the industrial development associated so integrally with the creation of the new society.

The Necessity of Stalinism

The question of the "necessity" of Stalinism should not be confused with that of its "inevitability." In retrospect, inevitability can always be more easily detected in what did happen than in what did not. Stalinism became "inevitable" because Marxist power first took root in a specific Russian environment formed by an autocratic political tradition, intellectual frustration, and a strong propensity toward messianism. As a result, certain facets of Marxism were reinforced at the expense of others. It was Lenin's contribution, and the mark of his genius, to have

* The most detailed accounting is in Robert Conquest's *The Great Terror*, New York, 1968. He concludes that approximately one million persons were actually executed between 1936 and 1938 (p. 529), that at least two million more died in camps during these years (p. 532), to which one may also add the at least three and a half million who died during the collectivization (p. 533). My own calculations are that of the ruling party's 2.4 million members, no less than 850,000 were purged during 1937–1938 alone (*The Permanent Purge*, Cambridge, Mass., 1956, pp. 98–110). It should be noted that estimates made by others have been higher.

been able to adapt Marxism to his native Russia, and in so doing to have created both Marxist-Leninist ideology and the Bolshevik party.

Lenin's victory over his rivals within the Russian Marxist movement and, more important, his seizure of power upon the collapse of the old autocratic structure, laid the basis for the successful "de-Westernization" of Marxism, a victory of oriental despotic propensities over occidental democratic tendencies. His emphasis on dogmatic belief, on violence, on conspiratorial activity, and on the almost total subordination of the individual to the party (*partiinost*), as well as his intolerance of dissent and his paranoid suspiciousness (all to some extent characteristic of Marx's own behavior), both reflected and extended the brutal autocratic tradition in which he operated.

It can therefore be argued that Stalin's emergence as top leader—and particularly the oriental style and mood of his despotism[1]—was facilitated, if not dictated, by Lenin's concept of the party as an elitist group suspicious of the "trade-union mentality" of the workers and hostile to the inertia and conservatism of the peasants. Intolerance of opposition and insistence on obedience to the party facilitated the emergence of a bureaucratically skilled dictator capable of exploiting these traditions to paralyze would-be opponents and rivals. Writing from entirely different perspectives, Leonard Schapiro and Isaac Deutscher, who certainly did not see eye to eye either on Leninism or Stalinism, both conveyed the degree to which Leninism made Stalinism possible by inhibiting effective opposition within the party to Stalin's consolidation of power.[2] If Lenin did not make Stalin inevitable, he at least made effective opposition to him within the party impossible.

The question of the "necessity" of Stalinism is, however, a different one. It pertains to the problem of whether Stalinist methods—and the resulting Stalinist system—were needed to effect the socialist revolution and, particularly, industrialization. Even if it is assumed that Stalinism as a political system was "inevitable," it does not follow that the enormous human sacrifice that Stalin extracted from the Soviet people was necessary to modernize and industrialize Russia and the non-Russian nations of the USSR. That sacrifice may have been necessary to preserve the Stalinist system,* but to advance that proposition is to shift the ground of the argument and to make the case that to maintain Stalin's power Stalinist means had to be used. There is no gainsaying that argument.

It does not, however, provide an answer to the question whether Stalinist methods had to be used to modernize and industrialize Russia and the non-Russian nations of the Soviet Union. The question is important because the entire edifice of Soviet legitimacy—the authority and the power of the present Soviet elite—is derived from the claim that the past is essentially one of glorious and heroic achievement, only slightly marred by Stalin's occasional misconduct vis-à-vis some of his comrades. Despite the extraordinarily detailed and gory accounts of Stalin's crimes made available to the entire Soviet public during the Twenty-second Congress of the Communist Party of the Soviet Union in 1961, the tendency of the post-Khrushchev Soviet leaders has been to minimize Stalin's misdeeds and to stress the accomplishments of the thirties. The implication is that the party acted correctly throughout, and hence that its claim to power is derived from the essentially infallible leadership it has provided both in the past and in the present.

It is on this contention that the present Soviet political system bases its claim to morality and universality. To question the form of the transformation of the Soviet society is to question the legitimacy of the present rulers, albeit indirectly. Even more, it is to question the international relevance of the Soviet model, and particularly its Leninist-Stalinist concentration of power in the

* The Stalinist theory that class struggle intensifies as progress toward socialism accelerates—which conflicts with the notion that class struggle is a consequence of the existence of hostile classes but which justifies increased police terror—was functionally convenient to the interests of Stalin's policies and power.

hands of a small bureaucratic party elite. The events in Czechoslovakia in 1968, the Soviet attacks on the Chinese "Cultural Revolution" because it undermined the primacy of Chinese party officials, and the long-standing Soviet criticism of the Yugoslav dilution of party supremacy all show the extent to which the Soviet elite still considers its political model to be of broader significance. This link between domestic interests and foreign aspirations explains Soviet sensitivity to suggestions by both Marxist and non-Marxist scholars that the Stalinist mode of transforming Soviet society was wasteful, cruel, and—most important—neither outstandingly successful nor necessary.

Did Stalin have any alternative? At least some Russians—Marxists as well as non-Marxists—had envisaged means by which Russian industrialization could have been achieved in a manner less physically and morally costly than that pursued by Stalin, though on a comparatively ambitious scale. Even before the 1917 Revolution, Russian scholars were drawing up plans for the modernization of their country. Perhaps the most important plan was contained in the study concluded in 1918 by Professor V. Grinevetskii, rector of the Moscow Institute of Technology, which outlined a systematic program, to last several decades, for the development of the country. According to an extremely informative analysis of this study,[3] in addition to providing for deliberate state action, Grinevetskii placed greater emphasis than Soviet planners did on price signals and profit criteria as a means by which to arrive "in most cases at the same priorities, policies, and even specific investment choices as those selected by Soviet planners in disregard of these criteria." Indeed, the top priorities adopted by Soviet planners in the early five-year plans closely matched those envisaged by Grinevetskii: electrification, the relocation of industry and population eastward, hydroelectric development, canal construction, and so forth.[4] Though the standard Soviet claim has been that Soviet industrialization was derived from "the granite foundations of Marxism-Leninism," there is abundant evidence that Soviet planners, some of them Grinevetskii's former colleagues, relied heavily on his work, accepting his targets though rejecting his formula for a more flexible decision-making process and for greater (though not exclusive) reliance on price signals and profit criteria.

Within the communist party, there were also alternative plans for industrialization, most notably those coming from Bukharin and the so-called "Right Opposition." Somewhat like Grinevetskii, they advocated a policy in which positive inducements would be employed to encourage the peasants to increase their production and to make the urban population share some of the social burdens of industrialization, the timetable for which would be somewhat extended. They were particularly opposed to rapid coercive collectivization—the means used by Stalin to extract a surplus from the peasantry—and in that opposition they were later supported even by Trotsky, who initially had been a strong opponent of Bukharin. By 1930, Trotsky had concluded that the physical liquidation of millions of kulaks was an immoral "monstrosity," which was initiating a vicious circle of compulsion and violence that was bound to engulf the society as a whole and to discredit communism.[5] Perhaps even more damaging from the Soviet point of view have been the more recent observations of the otherwise orthodox and highly pro-Soviet Polish communist leader, Wladyslaw Gomulka. Speaking on November 23, 1961, he similarly labeled collectivization "as the beginning of the process of growing lawlessness, violation of socialist legality, the establishment of an atmosphere of fear, and the growth under these conditions of the personality cult, the cult of Stalin." *

* Whether collectivization facilitated rapid industrialization is a matter of debate among the economists. It is indisputable, however, that its extraordinarily brutal character precipitated a rapid decline in agricultural resources that might have contributed to investment. "The gross output of agriculture fell from 124 in 1928 (1913–100) to 101 in 1933, and was only 109 in 1936, while that of cattle farming declined from 137 in 1928 to 65 in 1933 and then rose slowly to 96 in 1936. Throughout the nineteen-thirties the grain crops did not exceed the pre-1913 level or were somewhat below it" (Deutscher, *The Prophet Outcast,* London, 1963, p. 99). A specialist in Soviet agriculture, in reviewing the recent Soviet reconsideration of that difficult period, reached the conclusion that "with larger grain and currency

It should also be noted that Stalinism put an end to a period of unprecedented creativity in Russian architecture, poetry, and the sciences. During the 1920s, in the immediate post-revolutionary phase, Russia exuded a sense of awakened, vibrant energy. The massive terror and the ideological orthodoxy of Stalinism prompted caution and conformity. Even in the ideological realm Marxist thought was reduced to an intellectually regressive catechism, for which Stalin's *Dialectical and Historical Materialism* (1938) served as the all-encompassing frame of reference.

A different range of issues is posed by the question whether Soviet development, though morally and physically costly, attained goals unmatched by any other society. This, of course, has special relevance not only to the internal historical legitimacy of the present system but particularly to its standing as a model for other societies. This claim has been disputed by some Eastern European economic historians as well as by those in the West. Among the Westerners, Walt Rostow has developed perhaps the most pointed (and controversial) challenge to Stalinist achievements in modernization. He argues that the communists "inherited an economy that had taken off" in industrial development in the two decades prior to World War I, and that "Stalin was the architect not of the modernization of a backward country, but of the completion of its modernization." [6] Moreover, he sees

---

reserves and the existence of a more effective socialized sector, the government's freedom to maneuver would have been considerably greater. The entire edifice of the industrialization program need not have collapsed and it would have been possible to avoid the catastrophic decline in livestock herds, the necessity of devoting huge amounts of scarce capital to the task of merely replacing the loss of draught power, and the tying up of much scarce administrative talent in the apparatus of control and compulsion.

"Whether the Soviet government would have been able to remain in power without the mass collectivization of 1929–30 is a problem in which an economist *qua* economist does not have much to say, but he is entitled to think that a non-Stalinist Soviet government might well have been able to do so" (J. F. Karcz, "Thoughts on the Grain Problem," *Soviet Studies*, April 1967, pp. 429–30). Thus, although the marketable share of agriculture might (or might not) be smaller in a non-collectivized setting, it is reasonably safe to assume that even a smaller share of a larger total output would mean a larger supply in absolute terms.

striking parallels in the pattern and pace of both American and Russian industrialization, the former commencing around the 1860s and the latter in the 1880s.[7] *

Similarly, Cyril Black, in his study of Russian modernization, has cited cumulative data showing that "in the perspective of fifty years, the comparative ranking of the USSR in composite economic and social indices per capita has probably not changed significantly. So far as the rather limited available evidence permits a judgment, the USSR has not overtaken or surpassed any country on a per capita basis since 1917 with the possible exception of Italy, and the nineteen or twenty countries that rank higher than Russia today in this regard also ranked higher in 1900 and 1919. The per capita gross national product of Italy, which is just below that of the USSR today, was probably somewhat higher fifty years ago." [8] Black's comparisons include countries that, like the Soviet Union, were badly devastated by wars and had to undergo extensive economic recovery. Other students of comparative socio-economic development have also tried to devise a scheme for ranking countries, and they agree that the Soviet Union today ranks somewhere in the middle twenties.[9] Black is led to the over-all conclusion that "other societies have achieved similar results at a substantially lower cost," and thus puts into question a major Soviet premise about its own past.†

---

* In such areas as steel, coal, petroleum, and electricity the over-all American rate has been somewhat higher, while in light industry and transportation the American performance has been spectacularly more impressive.

† Soviet achievements in space, in weaponry, or in the magnitude of its over-all industrial growth have been admirable. Moreover, the Soviet Union has made impressive strides in education, mass culture, and social services, and it has created a solid and extensive scientific base for the country's further development. Thus, it ranked first among the developed nations in the number of doctors per hundred thousand population, and it provided the highest per-capita annual social-security benefits (Statistical Office of the European Communities, *Basic Statistics,* Brussels, 1967, pp. 131, 153).

At the same time, it is useful to recall that in many respects the Soviet Union is a relatively average society as far as socio-economic development is concerned. The previously cited study by Black provides useful rankings of the Soviet Union in comparison with other states in such fields as education (in the 5–19 age bracket the Soviet Union ranked thirty-ninth among

Support for these generalizations has also come from a comparative study of growth in steel production as the key aspect of the industrialization process. It should be noted that Soviet economists, as well as political leaders, have frequently relied on steel as the major indicator of Soviet industrial growth. The author of this study, Stefan Kurowski, writing in communist Poland, offers extraordinarily detailed comparisons showing that under Stalin, Soviet steel production did not increase at a significantly faster pace than during the more rapid phase of the pre-World War I Russian industrialization, and that these rates approximated those attained by other countries, particularly Japan, during their corresponding phases of rapid industrialization.* More generally,

---

124 countries for which information was available in 1960), communications (in 1960 the Soviet Union ranked twenty-sixth in newspaper distribution per capita among 125 countries), in public health (in life expectancy the Soviet Union was thirteenth among 79 countries), and so on.

In regard to such indicators of modernity as the availability of air communications, radios, telephones, cars, highways, or computers, the Soviet Union was again in the lower ranks of the more developed countries. Thus, when compared with the more developed twenty-one countries (including the EEC and EFTA nations, Greece, Turkey, Finland, Spain, the United States, Canada, and Japan), the Soviet Union ranked twentieth in the number of telephones, seventh in the number of radio receivers, and twentieth in the number of passenger cars.

The Soviet lag in the more complex areas, such as computers, is equally striking. Thus, it has been estimated that by 1968 the United States had approximately 50,000–70,000 computers in use, of which (according to Paul Armor, "Computer Aspects of Technological Change, Automation, and Economic Progress," *The Outlook for Technological Change and Employment,* Appendix Vol. I to National Commission on Technology, Automation and Economic Progress, *Technology and the American Economy,* Washington, D.C., 1966, pp. 220–223) only 10 per cent were in use in the Defense Department, AEC, and NASA; the corresponding nonmilitary Soviet figure was somewhere between 2000 and 3500, or approximately as many as were then operating in Japan or West Germany, or the United Kingdom, respectively (see the comprehensive estimates in Richard V. Burks, *Technological Innovation and Political Change in Communist Eastern Europe,* RAND Memorandum, Santa Monica, Calif., August 1969, pp. 8–9). For a fuller discussion of the current problems of innovation in the Soviet Union, see pp. 155–159 of this book.

* Kurowski shows by projecting rates based on those from 1870 that Russian steel production would have grown between 1914 and 1920 to 11 million tons. In 1929 Soviet steel production had only reached the 1914 level, and by 1935—after Stalin's First Five-Year Plan and the six years equivalent to

relying on a more extensive comparative analysis that involves some dozen countries over the period 1780–1970, Kurowski argues that socio-political systems have relatively little to do with the acceleration in the production of steel and iron, and that in the acceleration of production there is a pattern of uniformity due to technical innovation.[10] This conclusion, quite naturally, provoked official ire,[11] for it touched upon the key issue in the Soviet past.

Imperial Pacification

Yet though Stalinism may have been a needless tragedy for both the Russian people and communism as an ideal, there is the intellectually tantalizing possibility that for the world at large it was, as we shall see, a blessing in disguise. As the state possessing the largest and richest land mass, inhabited by pliant yet very creative people, as the carrier of a strong imperial tradition, as a society skilled in warfare and statecraft, with or without Stalin the USSR was destined to emerge in the front ranks of world powers, with only another continental power, the United States, as its peer. It is thus highly unlikely, given Russia's traditions and the ambitions that the availability of power inescapably stimulate, that post–World War I Russia would have long remained stagnant, mired in a morass of inefficiency.

The question that therefore arises is what kind of Russia might otherwise have emerged. A democratic Russia, either liberal or socialist, does not seem to have been a real alternative. It would have required an unprecedented leap from autocracy to democracy—without an intervening period of democratic gestation—and in a setting of enormous social deprivation, dislocation, and confusion. It is difficult to see how post–World War I Russia, torn by national dissension, class conflicts, competing ideological ap-

---

those that separate 1914 from 1920—it reached 12.6 million (Stefan Kurowski, *Historyczny Proces Wzrostu Gospodarczego*, Warsaw, 1963, pp. 132–133.) Moreover, Kurowski compares Soviet and Japanese growth rates during both the 1928–1940 and the 1950–1962 periods in great detail. Again, he demonstrates striking regularities in rates of growth (pp. 134, 138, 175).

peals, and sheer physical misery, could have effectively institutionalized a democratic system, when such systems have failed in countries endowed with stronger democratic traditions and functioning under circumstances much more propitious to democratic growth.

Given the massive political awakening of the Russian people that had been stimulated by the industrialization of the preceding decades, by the beginnings of literacy, and by the experiences of the war, the only other alternative appears to have been an openly chauvinist and intensely imperialist dictatorial regime. When linked with economic expansion, similar phases in the political development of other great nations—Germany, Japan, the United States—resulted in aggressive, dynamic imperialism. Expansive nationalism provided the basis for popular mobilization and for a highly assertive, even aggressive, foreign policy. At the very least, Russia, in all probability aided by foreign investments (economic investment in states that subsequently became political enemies was characteristic of the capitalist era),* led by a modernizing, chauvinist dictatorship, might have experienced a burst of imperialist, nationalist energy that would also have made it a world power, perhaps both at lower domestic cost and in a fashion more threatening to the world.

This point deserves some elaboration. Stalin consummated the marriage of Marxism-Leninism and Soviet—particularly Russian—nationalism. The increasing stress on Great Russian state traditions, on frontiers, on national aspirations, on Russia's civilizing mission vis-à-vis the non-Russian Soviet nations, and the like, went hand in hand with the physical transformation of the Soviet communist party from one dominated by a rather mixed lot of cosmopolitan and internationally oriented intellectuals of Russian,

---

* For impressive evidence of Western participation in the early phase of Soviet economic growth, see Antony C. Sutton's *Western Technology and Soviet Economic Development, 1917–1930* (Stanford, Calif., 1968), which argues that "Soviet economic development for 1917–1930 was essentially dependent on Western technological aid" (p. 283), and that "at least 95 per cent of the industrial structure received this assistance" (p. 348).

Jewish, Polish, Baltic, and Caucasian origin into a party dominated primarily by Russian, and to some extent Ukrainian, peasants turned party *apparatchiki.* To these men, the Soviet political system simultaneously represented the source of their own social advancement and of their political power. Their loyalty to the system was not unlike that of many peasant priests (usually the youngest sons, for whom no land was left) to the Catholic Church in traditional societies: it was more institutional than intellectual. Ideology provided the integrative, intellectual perspective, but it was not the principal source of motivation and commitment as it had been to the international-minded intelligentsia who preceded them.

Accordingly, the new Soviet elite tended to be both conservative and nationalist, even when they sincerely believed themselves to be the advocates of an internationalist ideology. They could thus act in a manner essentially dictated by their own interests and nevertheless consider themselves true internationalists. To them Stalin's famous dictum that the test of a true internationalist is his loyalty to the Soviet Union was the ideal resolution of the tension that developed between Soviet nationalism and communist internationalism. No wonder that Brezhnev in effect revived the dictum in 1968 to explain the occupation of Czechoslovakia.

The cumulative result of this situation has been a pattern of mixed motivation and behavior, dominated since Stalin by state considerations that often cynically exploit the ethical universalism of Marxism. But the latter has also had to be kept alive, if only because it mobilized foreign sympathy for the Soviet Union and because it tapped the idealism of Soviet youth, making it easier for the regime to recruit adherents. Though the Soviet Union did exploit its Eastern European vassals, and though its financial and technical aid to China was not politically disinterested, the Soviet people genuinely believe (as they occasionally grumble to visitors) that the Soviet Union has aided both Eastern Europe and China as part of its obligation to communist solidarity.

Moreover, the internal violence employed by Stalin and the

educational effect of the communist ideology—even if initially not accepted by the masses—had a restraining effect on unbridled nationalism. At first both Stalinist terror and ideologically induced social changes perplexed and often alienated the people. The unprecedented 1936–1938 massacre of the top Soviet political, economic, military, and intellectual leadership inevitably reduced the vitality of Soviet society. Literally several hundred thousand of the most talented and best-trained people perished during those years. In addition, though the principle of internationalism was often violated in practice, it did restrain the inclination toward Great Russian nationalism, if only by forcing more covert behavior. Domestically, that principle helped to preserve non-Russian nationalities, despite Stalin's purges of their intelligentsia. Internationally, it helped to shape in Soviet leaders a state of mind that worked against the incorporation into the Soviet Union of Poland, Finland, and perhaps even other Eastern European states (at one point the Yugoslavs themselves volunteered for membership in the Soviet Union, and some Slovak communists, including Gustav Husak, proposed the same for Slovakia). This is a temptation that more traditionally nationalist and Pan-Slav Russian leaders might have found difficult to resist.

Paradoxically, therefore, though Soviet ideology has subsequently been reinforced and perhaps even increasingly dominated by the nationalism of the masses (particularly since World War II), the historical function of Stalinist communism may have been to restrain and redefine a phase in which the Russian people went through an intense nationalist, even imperialist, awakening. It forced that new mass nationalism to pay at least lip service to international cooperation, equality of all peoples, and the rejection of racism. Marxism not only provided Russia with a global revolutionary doctrine but infused it with a universal perspective derived from ethical concerns not unlike those stimulated in the West by the religious and liberal traditions.

Despite its monumental achievements, Stalinism sapped the human and emotional resources of the Russians, and a post-Stalin

Russia may therefore eventually enter into the world community as another spent, post-imperial power. Finally, by creating a particularly despotic model of communism and by insisting that all other Communist parties submit to it, Stalin not only set in motion the process of fragmenting communism but also vitiated much of communism's appeal at a time when the susceptibility of the more advanced West—the area originally seen by Marx as ripest for the historical transformation—might have made communism the truly dominant and vital force of our time.

2. The Bureaucratization of Boredom

The Communist Party of the Soviet Union has a unique achievement to its credit: it has succeeded in transforming the most important revolutionary doctrine of our age into dull social and political orthodoxy. That orthodoxy is revolutionary in rhetoric but conservative in practice. The political system, highly centralized but arrested in its development, is seen by some Soviet citizens as increasingly irrelevant to the needs of Soviet society, as frozen in an ideological posture that was a response to an altogether different age. Soviet society, in which elements of urban modernity are combined with extensive rural backwardness, is no longer undergoing rapid, revolutionary changes capable of mobilizing youthful *élan*; it seems, instead, bent on simply matching the higher consumer standards of the capitalist West.

Under those circumstances, it becomes ideologically more and more difficult to justify the historical legitimacy and the social utility of Soviet society's continued subordination to a political system embodying increasingly sterile nineteenth-century doctrines. Indeed, the ultimate irony is that the Soviet political system —having thrust Russia into the mid-industrial age—has now become the principal impediment to the country's further evolution. It keeps Russia in a mold that is industrial-bourgeois socially and dogmatic-authoritarian politically. For the USSR to become a truly modern society, the basic assumptions and structure of the political forms created to press industrialization must be changed. A more relevant vision of tomorrow than that provided by the official ideology is also needed to cope with the highly personal as well as the broader social concerns of the technetronic age.

The Innovative Relationship

At one point the Soviet political system was in a revolutionary relationship to society. Consolidated and subsequently subordinated to the will of one man, the political system imposed a process of radical transformation on society by combining modernization (largely through intense industrialization and mass education) with ideologically derived, novel social institutions and relationships. In effect, the function of the political system in Soviet society parallels what Marx described as the capitalist's principal role in history: "Fanatically bent on making value expand itself, he ruthlessly forces the human race to produce for production's sake; he thus forces the development of the productive forces of society, and he creates those material conditions which alone can form the real basis for a higher form of society, a society in which the full and free development of every individual forms the ruling principle."

Domestic revolutionary change fulfilled the ideological needs of the ruling elite without pushing that elite into foreign revolutionary ventures that might have jeopardized its power. The new ruling elite was apprehensive lest premature ideological zeal prove its undoing; yet it was also ideologically compulsive. Socialism in one country—Stalin's famous answer to Trotsky's permanent revolution—was a brilliant coup, for it fused the dedicated revolutionaries' genuinely ideological aspirations with their newly acquired taste for office. Socialism in one country allowed the new rulers to retain their ideological self-righteousness and their positions.

More basically, the new "one-country" concept defined a specific, innovative role for the political system in relationship to society. The political system became the principal source of dynamism for social change, setting goals and defining priorities. Once society had taken the desired shape, however, and began to mirror the official aspirations of the political rulers—who had in the meantime been transformed into bureaucratic officials—the momentum for social change started to wane.

In late 1952, Stalin hinted that in his view there was still need for further ideologically derived and politically directed social transformation. Subsequently, Khrushchev on several occasions strove to infuse the relationship between the political system and society with new programmatic content. At one time he suggested a dramatic reconstruction of the Soviet countryside into so-called "agricultural cities." Later he attempted to define new ideological goals linked to Soviet society's ultimate transition from socialism to communism. When that effort in social innovation—spelled out by the party's ideologues in the new party program adopted in 1961—turned out to be little more than a shopping list of additional material benefits to be enjoyed by the Soviet people sometime in the 1980s, Khrushchev turned his attention to the party itself and began to toy with the notion of redefining its role. In 1962 he pushed through a drastic reform that in effect split the party into two separate organisms, one devoted to agricultural matters and the other to industrial problems. As he explained it, "The production line is the main one. . . . The main thing in communist construction is economics, production, the struggle for the creation of material and spiritual goods for the life of man." [12]

Though Khrushchev's reform ran the risk of transforming the party into two separate, essentially managerially oriented hierarchies (and was for that reason immediately undone by Khrushchev's successors after his overthrow in late 1964), it did reflect a recognition that the relationship between the political system and the society had become dysfunctional, that if the political system was no longer defining new, grandiose, ideological objectives for society, then the system itself had to be reformed in keeping with the more routine, operational requirements of Soviet society, which had by now acquired the technical and industrial wherewithal for its own further, steady growth. Sensing that the party was in search of a new role, Khrushchev was prepared to make the necessary reforms.

Defensive Orthodoxy

Khrushchev's successors rejected his view and opted instead for relatively minor adjustments—primarily in economic planning and control—simultaneously re-emphasizing the imperative necessity of ideological orthodoxy and more vigorous ideological indoctrination. Under the post-Khrushchev regime there has been neither a definition of new ideological goals nor any major tampering with the political structure. As a consequence, official views on the state of Soviet society, on foreign affairs, on the problems of the future, and on the nature of contemporary communism contain strikingly little recognition of the novel problems that beset man, either in terms of his personal condition or as a member of the emerging global community. Difficult problems are simply swept under the ideological rug.

On the domestic front, the prevailing official view has been that the Soviet Union, having completed socialist construction, is now laying the foundations of a communist society, and that existing problems are essentially instrumental, needed to improve the efficiency of a system that in its basic assumptions and organization is officially considered to be the most advanced and just in the world. The lag in socio-economic development in some areas of Soviet life is ascribed either to the ravages of World

War II or to the failures of the pre-revolutionary regime. The writings of revisionist Marxist thinkers on the problems of personal alienation in an advanced urban society—to say nothing of anti-Semitism in a socialist society—are dismissed as inappropriate to Soviet conditions, or as malicious slander. The Soviet Union is said to have no generational problems, and only recently has urban crime been discussed as a phenomenon in its own right and not merely as a legacy from the pre-revolutionary era.

These views have been articulated in the context of intensified efforts to reassert and expand ideological training (thereby partially compensating for the decline of coercion as a key means of integrating Soviet society with the political system). Though the social scope of these efforts has been expanded, in recent years there is open acknowledgment of the fact that special attention has been focused on the new scientific community: "The party and the people want to see in scientists not only creators and organizers of scientific-technical progress but also political people, active fighters for the cause of communism." [13] In addition, there have been expressions of official concern over alleged ideological indifference among scientists and, what is even worse, over a tendency in these circles to consider technocrats the natural leaders of modern society.[14] Scientists have repeatedly been warned (and the very warnings reveal the attitudes of Soviet scientists) not to view themselves as "super-class humanists" but to identify closely with the class struggle and the people.[15]

The issue of "humanism" appears to have been a particularly sensitive one. Humanism, a central Marxist concern, can serve as a point of departure for a critique of both Stalinism and the present Soviet system. Moreover, the dehumanizing potential of modern science has given new urgency to the problem of defining humanism in the modern world. The official view, stated authoritatively in a series of major articles in the key ideological journals, has been unequivocal: "Socialism is profoundly humanistic because it eliminates the exploitation of man by man." Accordingly, "it is also humanistic when it erects the building of a new society at the price of extraordinary hardships in the persistent struggle against the old. It is also humanistic when conditions have already been created for the thorough development of the individual but society is still compelled to control the activities of a person and his labor discipline and, within the framework and in the interests of all of society and of the communist education of a particular individual, does not permit individuals to abuse the freedoms presented by socialism, does not permit people with an undeveloped sense of responsibility to violate the norms of the socialist community, suppresses the opposition of anti-socialist forces, etc." [16] This argument has been buttressed by the assertion that "the so-called 'eternal' values—freedom, democracy, humanism, individual dignity . . . are a weapon in the hands of the bourgeoisie to mislead and fool the masses," [17] and that the issue of Stalinism is essentially irrelevant.*

Views such as these have been expressed in the context of a broader emphasis on the argument that an ideological perspective on contemporary reality is absolutely essential in order to obtain accurate insight into that reality, and that scientific communism—as defined by the Soviet leaders—provides the only valid perspective. Although the latter is not a new proposition, there is novelty in the degree to which it has been linked in the more prestigious Soviet scholarly journals, as well as in mass media, with an attack on Western theories of ideological erosion, of the emergence of a general type of industrial society, and of the ubiquity of new bureaucratic political elites in all developed political systems. Soviet critics have made it clear that they view these theories as not only scientifically erroneous but politically harmful and probably designed deliberately to undermine communism.†

---

* "At the present time attempts are being made to discredit what was done in the process of building socialism by using the bugbear of 'Stalinism.' The 'Stalinism' bugbear is being used to intimidate unstable persons, to spread the thought that all firmness and revolutionary character in politics, uncompromisingness in ideology, and consistency in the defense of Marxism are, if you please, 'Stalinism' " (D. I. Chesnokov, "Aggravation of the Ideological and Political Struggle and Contemporary Philosophical Revisionism," *Voprosy Filosofii,* No. 12, 1968).

† For a systematic and well-documented Soviet criticism, see L. Moskvichev, "The 'Deideologization' Theory: Sources and Social Essence," *Mirovaia Ekonomika i Mezhdunarodnye Otnoshenia,* No. 12, 1968.

Soviet scholars have been particularly vigorous in rejecting the theory of "convergence" of the Soviet and Western, particularly American, systems. In the Soviet view, the crucial and distinctive element of the Soviet system—rule by the communist party as the expression of proletarian dictatorship—has been underestimated by Western thinkers, who have superficially focused on the external characteristics of a modern industrial society, without delving more penetratingly into the question of its socio-political essence. Though some of the Soviet criticisms are not without merit (and there is a curious touch of neo-Marxist determinism in some of the Western theories of convergence), it is striking how much intellectual effort has been invested in asserting and proving the distinctive character of the communist system. It once again reveals the importance attached to the notion that the Soviet past is linked to a future that is absolutely distinctive and not part of a broader stream of man's political evolution.* It also makes possi-

---

In the Soviet view, both the Marxist revisionists and Western theorists of ideological evolution, erosion, or deideologization of Soviet Marxism have essentially been engaged in a political stratagem designed to undermine the ideological foundations of Soviet power. The present author was particularly singled out for criticism in this connection. See, for example, Professor E. Modrzhinskaya's "Anti-Communism Disguised as Evolutionism" (*International Affairs* [Moscow], No. 1, 1969). She sees in Western sociological writing an effort to pave "the ideological way for subversion against Socialism. Among these theories are: the theory of stages in economic growth propounded by Walt Rostow (a well known U.S. reactionary politician and sociologist); the doctrine of the single industrial society, whose most famous propagandist is the reactionary French publicist and sociologist Raymond Aron; the convergence doctrine, and—the capstone of them all—the theory of evolution, which has been elaborated in greatest detail by Zbigniew Brzezinski, Director of the Research Institute on Communist Affairs at Columbia University. . . .

"The principal features of the evolutionary theory are set out in Brzezinski's writings of the last few years. . . . A distinctive and highly notable feature of the evolution theory is the desirable sequence of change: from ideology to politics leading to changes in the socio-economic system, and not the other way round, from economic changes to subsequent political transformation, as the votaries of convergence suggest" (p. 16).

* This emphasis sometimes leads to statements that verge on the comical, as when it was asserted in a major analysis of "Problems of the Last Third of the Century" that "Marxism-Leninism has no need to reconcile ideas with facts." The author—apparently in all seriousness—added that "according to

ble the argument that the Soviet system is free of the dilemmas that beset contemporary man elsewhere, and it frees Soviet communists from the responsibility of engaging in a cross-ideological dialogue about these dilemmas.

The official Soviet definition of foreign problems is characterized by similar intellectual inflexibility. This is not to say that the Soviet leadership and elite are misinformed or ignorant about basic facts or developments. There is no doubt that the level of Soviet overt and covert reporting of world affairs has improved considerably, and that factual misrepresentation—designed to meet anticipated ideological preferences—has declined. Specialized Soviet scholarly journals on Africa or Asia, Soviet analyses of the Common Market, or Soviet efforts to develop systematic studies of the United States go beyond purely ideological formulas and reflect the importance attached to the deeper understanding of regional developments. Some scholarly Soviet journals on world affairs (for example, *Mirovaia Ekonomika i Mezhdunarodnye Otnoshenia*) compare very favorably with their best Western counterparts in terms of systematic coverage, documentation, and scholarly rigor. Specialized research institutes, such as the Institute of World Economy and International Affairs, are apparently being more frequently consulted in the preparation of policy, and this doubtless contributes to greater sophistication in the decision-making process.

Yet, in spite of this, the Soviet conception of the broad framework of contemporary reality, as articulated by top leaders and even as presented in scholarly journals, remains fundamentally dogmatic. The basic premise continues to be the Manichaean notion of the antagonistic dichotomy between the socialist and the capitalist worlds (or between good and evil). Though war between these two worlds is no longer said to be "fatalistically inevitable," and the destructiveness of nuclear weapons dictates the

---

the recent decree of the Soviet Communist Party's Central Committee . . . the outstanding revolutionary events of the twentieth century have all been associated with Leninism" (V. A. Cheprakov, *Izvestia,* August 18, 1968).

necessity of peaceful coexistence—indeed, sometimes even closer cooperation is tactically desirable because of other considerations (for example, the Sino-Soviet conflict)—the underlying reality of our age is still said to be the competition between the two systems: "Two antagonistic socio-economic systems are pitted against each other today in a struggle of unprecedented scope and violence which affects the life of human society in all its aspects. The antagonists are capitalism and socialism." [18] Eventually one or the other will have to prevail,* and Soviet analysts are confident that they know which one it will be. This theme runs like a thread through all major speeches, foreign-policy analyses, or scholarly commentaries on world affairs.

It would be an error to dismiss the above as merely a ritualistic act of obeisance to doctrine, or to view it as a sign of fanatical and implacable militancy. Its importance lies in the influence of the ideological framework on more immediate, and otherwise quite well-informed, policy judgments. Though far from committing Soviet leaders to short-term militancy, the ideological framework does inhibit them from thinking of accommodation and stability as ends in themselves, since that would be tantamount to negating the communist view of history as a fluid, dialectical process. Accordingly, an official Soviet analysis of the issues covered in the first two chapters of this book would run along these lines: "The present era is dominated by the appearance of the world socialist system. Its emergence is a decisive force of change, not only accelerating the pace of socialist revolution but also successfully deterring the imperialists from countermeasures. War is therefore no longer inevitable, and peaceful rivalry between the two systems, and especially between the USSR and the United States, is possible. The eventual outcome of the competition is, however,

---

* Thus, a Soviet scholar, in an ambitious effort to analyze contemporary world affairs, asserts that "the outcome of the competition rules out accident. Victory or defeat are necessary, that is, unavoidable, and law-governed. Defeat comes but once in such competition. There will be no return match, no 'replay,' no chance of revenge" (Kh. Momjan, *The Dynamic Twentieth Century*, Moscow, 1968, pp. 107–108).

foreordained, given the inherent historical superiority of the communist system. In the meantime, in many areas more active cooperation is to be sought, in order to avert war or to promote economic or social development of the Third World. In some places the preconditions for the peaceful transition to socialism already exist; in some of the less developed countries a violent revolution will be necessary, but it would be a tactical error to precipitate it too soon (as urged by the Maoists or the Castroites)."

Authoritative Soviet analysts have, moreover, argued that they detect signs of intensified crisis in the more advanced capitalist states. "Political crises now occur far more often than, let us say, ten to twenty years ago, and no longer only on the 'periphery' but in the chief centers of imperialism. The socio-political crises in the capitalist states are now spreading under conditions of an exacerbated financial crisis and deterioration in the over-all economic situation of the imperialist camp." [19] An important new factor is said to be the growing radicalism of Western intellectuals, the majority of whom—unlike those of the pre–World War II era—are now "becoming a more active progressive force." In the Soviet view, this points to the further intensification of the internal crisis of the advanced capitalist world, a factor that is more important than the changes or even the revolutionary upheavals that are likely to occur in the Third World.

The decisive equation thus remains that of American-Soviet competition. Accordingly, the crucial operational question—leaving aside immediate tactical considerations—is not whether a given course of action will advance the cause of world communism but how it will affect the Soviet-American balance: in favor of the Soviet Union or against it? The Soviet policymaker senses no contradiction between Soviet interests and those of the international movement, and he thus experiences no ideological embarrassment in assisting anti-American elements otherwise ideologically foreign to communism or in seeking to reach accommodation with the United States on specific issues. This close subjective identification of purely Soviet state interests with the ideological cause, and the resulting goal-oriented flexibility in tactics, render impossible the simplistic judgment that the Soviets are either ideologically obsessed or ideologically cynical.

In regard to the ideological confrontation, Soviet leaders have ventured the opinion that "the contemporary stage in historical development is distinguished by intense sharpening of the ideological struggle between capitalism and socialism." This conclusion was formally expressed by the Soviet Central Committee in April 1968.[20] It was followed by a systematic development of the proposition that the world is witnessing "the rising role of ideology" and that ideological competition in international affairs is gaining in intensity. The Soviet invasion of Czechoslovakia in August 1968 gave rise to particularly extensive elaborations of this theme. It was explicitly argued that internal change in Czechoslovakia was abetted by Western policies of "peaceful engagement" that had as their ultimate objective the transformation of communism into social democracy. This policy was labeled by Soviet writers as the new Western strategy of "peaceful counterrevolution." [21]

The emphasis put on the continuing confrontation between the two conflicting ideological systems—and thus on the notion that contemporary reality can be understood in terms of such a dichotomy—is closely related to the Soviet Union's definition of its own role in international communism and of contemporary communism itself. In spite of the enormous changes in international communism precipitated by the Sino-Soviet dispute, by the decline of Soviet authority, and by the demoralization resulting from the military invasion of one communist state by another, the Soviet leaders have continued to uphold the orthodox concept of a single movement still led by Moscow. They have accordingly continued to press for "unity conferences" of as many communist parties as possible, even though the results have often worked against unity. They have also continued to assert a dogmatic interpretation of ideology and have consequently been under the necessity of excommunicating those who differ.*

---

* "Only one social theory, one teaching, is capable of expressing the content and direction of world processes in our epoch in depth—this is Marxism-

The result has been not only the oft-repeated condemnation of revisionists or of Chinese communists but the increasing intellectual inability to assimilate in doctrine either new revolutionary practice or the progressive evolution of communism in power. The Soviet attitude toward the rebellion of Western youth is a case in point. As soon as it became clear that these young people were not prepared to accept established communist leadership—and that their ideologues were critical of Soviet bureaucratism—the Soviet attitude became vehemently hostile. Marcuse was especially attacked for overemphasizing the role of the young and the intellectuals at the expense of the classical concept of a revolution by the working class.* In effect, Soviet theorists refused to take seriously into account the potentially revolutionary consequences of the educational upsurge in the developed world.

Similarly, when the Castroite revolution in Latin America moved into direct guerrilla action, the established pro-Soviet Communist parties objected, and they were supported by Moscow. Here, too, the preference was for the tried, city-based, party-directed, proletarian revolutionary model. When Czechoslovak political leaders began to suggest that Leninism, a product of specifically Russian conditions, was perhaps no longer the most suitable guide for the further evolution of Czechoslovak communism, the Soviet reaction was to charge deviation. Thus, in spite of many pronouncements concerning multiple roads to socialism, the Soviet party has remained wedded to the concept of dogmatic

---

Leninism. Only one philosophy is capable of interpreting all the contradictions of the present stage of historical development. . . . Communists have always regarded Leninism—and continue to regard it—not as a purely Russian but an international Marxist doctrine" (F. Konstantinov, "Marxism-Leninism: A Single International Teaching," *Pravda,* June 14, 1968).

The foregoing view permits Soviet ideologues to assert that "the philosophical 'thoughts of Mao Tse-tung' are philistine, often anarcho-idealistic eclecticism which has nothing in common with Marxist-Leninist philosophy" (A. Rumyantsev, writing in *Kommunist,* No. 2, 1969). It should be noted that Rumyantsev and Konstantinov are leading Soviet ideologues.

* These attacks sometimes took grotesque forms. Thus, a Radio Moscow commentator, Valentin Zakharov, devoted an entire program to the theme that Marcuse and Brzezinski were jointly involved—naturally in behalf of the CIA—in organizing "the Czechoslovak counterrevolution" in 1968 (Radio Moscow, August 19, 1969).

universalism, which is universal only in the sense that it sees the Soviet experience as fundamentally universal in relevance.

Perspective on Tomorrow

This rigidity both conditions and restricts Soviet thinking about the future. Studies of the future have become both fashionable and widespread in the West. They have involved systematic attempts to link technological projections with social forecasting, as well as with more critical, normative discussions. The philosophical ramifications of scientific discoveries, especially as they pertain to the human being, have become the object of a particularly intense dialogue. The political implications of technology have also attracted the attention of scholars and increasingly even of political leaders. Given the future-oriented thrust of Marxist thought, one would have expected the Soviet Union to be in the forefront of these investigations and analyses. This has only been partially true.

Systematic Soviet efforts to study the future were spurred by high-level decisions taken at the Twenty-third Party Congress. In its wake, special study groups were established for that purpose in a number of Soviet institutes—for example, the Soviet Academy's group for Social and Technological Forecasting. In addition, many informal groups were set up to bring Soviet scholars and intellectuals together. A special annual publication entirely devoted to the future of science was established in 1966, and its first numbers have included contributions by both Soviet and non-Soviet scholars.[22] Soviet scholars also established useful contacts with similar study groups and publications in the West, including the United States.

Solid work has been done by Soviet scholars, primarily in the area of technological-economic forecasting. For example, in 1964 the Soviet philosophical journal, *Voprosy Filosofii,* began publishing a series of articles on the theme of "The Scientific-Technical Revolution and Its Social Consequences." On the whole, these articles have been serious and frequently very informative treatments of such subjects as the methodology of forecasting, the organizational problems of science in the context of the scientific explosion, the role of cybernetics, comparative analyses of scientific development and projections for the United States and the Soviet Union, to say nothing of more specifically Soviet-oriented economic and technological prognoses.[23]

In contrast to these efforts, there has been a striking paucity of political, ideological, or philosophical studies focused on the interactions with projected technological-economic changes. There is no doubt that Soviet intellectuals are aware of the unavoidable link between the two,* but published Soviet discussions have been limited primarily to critical evaluations of Western literature on the subject. In their cruder forms—particularly when appearing in the theoretical organ of the party, *Kommunist*—these "evaluations" have been limited to denunciation.† More serious—though

---

* In a statement remarkably free of ideological cant, one Soviet scientist—and novelist—remarked, "The future has borne the brunt of all kinds of emotions: optimism, blind irrational hope, and black despair. It has been threatened by both hysterical seers and precise calculations. Attempts have been made to poison it or simply to annihilate it, to turn it backward, to return it to caves. It has survived. Today we have the opportunity to give it serious and thoughtful study. Today, perhaps as never before in human history, the future depends on the present and demands a new approach. It is fraught with crises we cannot assess today. Crises connected not only with a different conception of freedom, but also a different idea of individuality" (Daniil Granin, "And Yet . . . ," *Inostrannaia Literatura* [Moscow], No. 1, 1967).

In contrast, the five-volume work *Socialism and Communism,* prepared by the Institute of Philosophy of the Soviet Academy of Sciences in a comprehensive effort to sum up the likely shape of Soviet society under communism, refrains from any analysis of the social tensions brought on by the scientific revolution. It presents a uniformly blissful picture of the future.

† For examples of particularly primitive writings, see G. Gerasimov, "The Falsifiers of the Future," *Kommunist,* No. 2, 1968, for criticism of Aron, Fourastie, and others; or Yuri Zhukov's various articles attacking my earlier article, "America in the Technetronic Age." Soviet commentators were particularly incensed by my observation ("America in the Technetronic Age") that "the world is on the eve of a transformation more dramatic in its historic and human consequences than that wrought either by the French or the Bolshevik revolutions. Viewed from a long perspective, these famous revolutions merely scratched the surface of the human condition. The changes

still primarily negative—assessments have appeared in other journals, particularly in the organ of the Institute on World Economics. In both cases, however, the tendency has been to deny the possibility of either the evolution of Western polities into new post-industrial forms no longer determined by the capitalist phase of industrialization or the capacity of these new forms to overcome the individual crisis of alienation and frustration associated with the capitalist system.

This is why some Polish communists, though loyal to the common ideology, have noted critically that "we have to give a more specific answer to the question as to what really happens in modern monopolistic capitalism and what influence the technical revolution has on it." They have observed that communist theory has no concept of the transition from modern capitalism to socialism, that it has not faced the problem of the increasing technological obsolescence of communist economies as compared to those of the advanced West, that it has still to confront the fact that socialism—though it has proven its mettle in overcoming industrial backwardness—has yet to prove its capacity for scientific innovation, and that it has not given any thought to the significance of conflicts between generations.[24] In a far-ranging and thoughtful discussion, a Rumanian communist, appealing "For a Marxist Theory of the Technical-Scientific Revolution," put it even more bluntly: "In recent years the West has evidenced a more sustained concern with the theoretical elaboration of the essence of the scientific-technical revolution and its social and human connections. . . . We cannot as yet speak of the existence of a coherent, unified *Marxist* theory of the scientific-technological revolution."[25]

In short, Soviet political thought has failed to provide any systematic development of ideas concerning the future political and ideological evolution of the Soviet system itself or, for that matter,

---

they precipitated involved alterations in the distribution of power and property within society; they did not affect the essence of individual and social existence. Life—personal and organized—continued on much as before, even though some of its external forms (primarily political) were substantially altered. Shocking though it may sound to their acolytes, by the year 2000 it will be accepted that Robespierre and Lenin were mild reformers."

of the world revolutionary process under novel historic conditions. This is not only because intellectual dissent has been restricted to informal, "underground" forms of expression but primarily because there has been no open-ended creative political-ideological discussion among Soviet Marxists themselves. Soviet ideology is no longer shaped through the creative interaction of theoretical thought and practice—as was the case until Stalin's power became supreme—but is the product of a bureaucratic process of definition, a process entirely monopolized by career party officials. Ideology emanates from the offices of the Central Committee, where it is prepared on the basis of committee reports and staff papers before being submitted to the Politburo for group approval. An ideology whose content is determined by a political process is not likely to be preoccupied with speculative, and therefore potentially disruptive, issues. It has little to do with intellectual creativity and a great deal to do with bureaucratic imperatives.

Paradoxically, bureaucratic sterility in thought prompts intensified emphasis on revolutionary rhetoric and symbolism. Because the once revolutionary doctrine has become so intertwined with the vested interests of guardians who are themselves highly sensitive to Russian national interests, there is a tendency to take ideological refuge in increased emphasis on revolutionary symbolism. This is a manifestation common to all doctrines in their intellectual decline: as practice increasingly deviates from prescription, symbolism and rhetoric gain in importance. The consequence, however, is to congeal certain formulas and claims, making intellectual innovation more difficult, even when on the operational level ideological restraints are increasingly evaded.

The result is a condition of arrested ideological development, of ideological petrifaction rather than erosion, Marxist thought remaining vital only outside the Soviet Union.* The vision of to-

---

* This matches the Victorianism and grayness of much of contemporary Soviet life. Lincoln Steffens exclaimed, on visiting the Soviet Union in the early 1920s, "I have been into the future and it works!" Today more and more visitors to the Soviet Union come back saying, "I have been into the past and it is a bore."

morrow is reduced to meaningless and increasingly vague declarations, such as the conclusion to the official Soviet prognosis for the remainder of this century: "Armed with Marxist-Leninist thought and filled with historical optimism, the leading revolutionary forces of the world will march into the future." [26]

3. The Soviet Future

The crucial question today is: When will the Soviet Union break with the Stalinist legacy? Without such a break it will remain difficult for the Soviet leaders to diagnose the problems of their own society accurately and to make the Soviet Union truly relevant to the intellectual and international dilemmas of our time. Such a break need not require the abandonment of socialism or of Marxism, but it would require the transformation of a political system that today both reflects and is buttressed by an obsolescent and bureaucratized ideology of power into one more in keeping with the emerging humanist, universalist mood of our time. It is no exaggeration to say—though some anti-communists may be loath to admit this—that the peace of mankind depends in large measure on the Soviet Union's return to the occidental Marxist tradition from which the more oriental Leninism-Stalinism had diverted it, but not necessarily on the outright abandonment of Marxism.

Ideological change in the Soviet Union will inevitably be closely connected with socio-economic change, but it would be a mistake to view the latter as dictating the former. A Marxist framework of analysis is the one least suited to understanding communist politics, in which the political superstructure actually dominates the economic base. Political change in the Soviet Union will necessarily be influenced by the emergence of a new social elite, more technological in its orientation, but it will be even more affected by the changes in the internal character and outlook of the professional, ruling party bureaucracy, and by the degree to which this elite succeeds in coping with internal Soviet problems.

Internal Dilemmas

These problems are likely to develop on the levels of both economic-technological efficiency and political-ideological dissent. There can be little doubt that the Soviet economy will continue to grow in the years ahead, but it does appear likely that, barring some unforeseen development in either the United States or the Soviet Union, the absolute gap between the two countries will widen even further.* The growth will therefore probably be insufficient to satisfy the ideological ambitions of the political elite, and it is even less likely to satisfy rising social aspirations. These aspirations are certain to escalate as comparison with the West makes it more and more apparent that major sectors of Soviet society have remained extraordinarily antiquated.

Soviet backwardness is particularly evident in agriculture. Agricultural productivity has leapfrogged during the last several decades in most developed countries and lately even in a number of the underdeveloped ones. Not so in the Soviet Union, where pro-

---

* It can be estimated that if the GNP of the United States grows at 3.5 per cent per annum, by 1985 it will be over $1.5 trillion; if the rates of the 1960s continue, it will already be $1.7 trillion by 1980; if the Soviet GNP grows at the higher rate of 5 per cent, by 1985 it will be just under $800 billion; if it grows at the even higher rate of 7 per cent, by 1985 the GNP will be approximately $1.1 trillion. Thus the absolute gap will not narrow and could even widen considerably between 1965 and 1985.

In 1961 the Soviet leaders formally adopted a party program which, among other things, promised that by 1970 the Soviet Union will have surpassed the United States in industrial output. Clearly, this has not happened.

ductivity steadily declined and has only recently risen somewhat. The Soviet rural population is underemployed, undercompensated, and underproductive. The resolution of the Soviet agricultural problem is one of the more urgent—but also ideologically more sensitive—problems on the Soviet agenda. (The technological underdevelopment of Soviet agriculture is reflected in a labor-force distribution that places the Soviet Union considerably behind the more advanced sectors of the globe.)

TABLE 9. DISTRIBUTION OF LABOR FORCE

	PERCENTAGE DISTRIBUTION BY SECTOR		
AREA	Agriculture	Industry	Services
United States	8	39	53
Western Europe	14	45	41
Oceania	23	34	43
Japan	33	28	39
USSR	45	28	27
Latin America	48	20	32

Source: *International Labor Review,* January–February 1967.

In the industrial sector, more advanced than agriculture, the remarkable achievements of Soviet science in such areas as space and weapons technology have obscured a situation that is also far from satisfactory for a modern, industrialized society. It has been estimated that the Soviet Union (allowing for the differential in actual costs) has in real terms been spending approximately as much for research and development as the United States.[27] Moreover, Soviet scientific manpower has been growing at an impressive rate and now matches that of the United States. In addition, Soviet theoretical work in a number of fields, particularly physics, has been of the first order.

Yet the over-all socio-economic benefits of the Soviet scientific effort have been relatively meager. Though Soviet leaders were quick to capitalize ideologically on their initial space successes by claiming that they proved the superiority of communism (an assertion quietly allowed to fade after the American landing on the moon), the fact remains that the Soviet Union has not been able to produce technologically advanced products capable of penetrating economically rewarding world markets in the face of Western competition, nor has it satisfied more than the rudimentary needs of domestic consumption. Even in such a relatively elementary industrial field as automobile production, the Soviet Union has been compelled to rely on foreign help (currently Italian) to produce workable and economically feasible automobiles.[28] The rigid separation of secret military research from the rest of the economy, as well as the concentration of Soviet scientific researchers in institutes remote from industry, has meant that research breakthroughs have either never been developed, developed only for military purposes, or developed only after considerable delay.* The Soviet lag is unmistakable in computers, transistors, lasers, pulsars, and plastics, as well as in the equally important areas of management techniques, labor relations, psychology, sociology, economic theory, and systems analysis.†

---

* Soviet Academician V. Trapeznikov estimated that 98 per cent of Soviet researchers work in institutes, whereas 60 per cent of American researchers work directly in the relevant industries. He also estimates that approximately half the Soviet research discoveries are obsolescent by the time of their development (*Pravda,* January 19, 1967). See also the interview with Academician V. M. Glushkov, in *Komsomolskaia Pravda,* May 15, 1968, in which he calls for the rapid training of "systems managers," a skill in which he feels that Americans excel and which has no equivalent in the Soviet Union. He also urged the regular retraining of Soviet managers, again citing American precedents.

† "Certain sectors, including of course space and some military R & D, and an important part of the iron and steel industry, are technically very advanced; but many industries, particularly in the consumer goods sector, are far less technically developed than in major Western countries. . . .

"The impression which emerges from both Soviet and Western studies is that the Soviet Union is less technically advanced than the United States in all but a few priority industries, and that in a number of major industries the Soviet Union is technologically behind the industrialized countries of Western Europe" (*Science Policy in the USSR,* pp. 9, 476).

According to a study of the International Atomic Energy Agency, the Soviet Union, which in 1954 was the first nation to adapt nuclear energy for peaceful uses, had by 1969 been surpassed by the United States and the United Kingdom; by 1975 it will be behind the United States, the United Kingdom, Japan, Canada, Sweden, and Germany, with its megawattage approximately fourteen times less than that of the United States (*Power and Research Reactors in Member States*).

To correct this condition, the government initiated in 1968 a series of reforms designed to spur scientific research and development and to improve the quality of management. The Central Committee of the party passed a special resolution in October 1968 ("On Measures to Raise the Efficiency of the Work of Scientific Organizations and to Accelerate the Utilization of Scientific and Technical Achievements in the National Economy"), highly critical of Soviet research and development and initiating a series of reforms, which in essence upgraded the status of researchers working directly in industry to that held by scientists employed in purely scientific institutes, created research laboratories based in industrial enterprises, and offered bonuses and awards for innovation. As Academician Trapeznikov put it, "An important item in the resolution is the establishment of competition in scientific-technical ideas and proposals." [29]

It is far from certain that these reforms will suffice to generate a creative and socially significant burst of innovation and adaptation. Soviet scientists recognize that creativity requires "an atmosphere of free discussion, polemics, and airing of ideas, even if some of them are radically wrong." [30] This factor is in turn related to the ideological and institutional organization of society as a whole, and cannot be corrected merely by a few organizational adjustments. The OECD study, *Science Policy in the USSR* (1969), which reveals in a detailed, statistically documented manner the extraordinary disproportion between the scale of the Soviet effort and its relatively meager socio-economic consequences, reinforces the view that ideological-political centraliza-

---

As Burks puts it, "The curve of technological development in the West is exponential. Synthetic fibers, plastics, nuclear energy, transistors, digital computers, xerography, lasers, succeed one another in seemingly endless succession. As Western technology becomes more complex, furthermore, the time lag involved in its reproduction by East Europeans becomes greater. Borrowing time runs anywhere from two to fifteen years with the odds at least 50–50 that the product will be, in Western terms, obsolescent when it first appears on the Eastern market. In computers, the time lag for Soviet (not to speak of East European) borrowing varies between two and ten years" (Burks, p. 8). See also data cited on p. 133, *supra*, especially as it concerns computers.)

tion results at best in a capricious science policy and at worst in a catastrophic one.*

There can be no doubt that in the years to come the Soviet Union will accomplish many remarkable scientific feats, especially in the internationally prestigious realm of space investigations and in scientific areas related to defense research. Its military technology will also continue to match America's and in some areas will doubtless surpass it. This will be done by crash programs concentrating economic resources and scientific talent. The Soviet organizational structure is remarkably suited to such programs. But the crucial question is whether Soviet science and industrial management can provide Soviet society with the broad-gauged pattern of scientific innovation necessary both to assure internal progress and to advance the international position of the Soviet Union.

The forces opposing far-reaching scientific and economic reforms are formidable. They are primarily the bureaucratic party elite, especially the ideological sectors, and some of the upper echelons of the armed forces, who fear that decentralization would also mean the transfer of some key research institutes to nonmilitary uses. The upper echelons of party officialdom are still largely the products of the Stalinist era, and many among them got their start during the purges. Paradoxically, and contrary to Western speculation, the managerial elite has also been part of the opposition. The present Soviet managerial generation, trained to operate in a highly confined, hierarchical setting, is not predisposed to assume the greater personal hazards that a more decentralized, competitive system would necessarily involve.† Proposals for economic reforms have characteristically come mostly from the theoretical economists.

---

* An example of the latter result is the Lysenko affair and its disastrous effects on Soviet biology. An extraordinarily vivid and informative account of the affair is provided by the Soviet scientist Z. A. Medvedev, *The Rise and Fall of T. D. Lysenko,* New York, 1969. Medvedev's book was written in the Soviet Union, but its publication there was not permitted.

† Moreover, as Jeremy Azrael has convincingly argued in his *Managerial Power in Soviet Politics* (Cambridge, Mass., 1966), it must be recognized that

The problem of intellectual freedom prompts considerations that are more directly concerned with politics and ideology. It is impossible to judge the extent of fundamental, unorthodox dissent in the Soviet Union of the late 1960s and early 1970s.* In late 1968 two successive issues of the magazine *Problems of Communism* were devoted to the underground writings, petitions, protests, and appeals of dissenting Soviet intellectuals. They made for remarkable and profoundly moving reading, as did some separately published documents in which Ukrainian intellectuals protested the suppression of their country.[31] These publications indicated the existence of an active and articulate group of intellectuals, largely concentrated in Moscow and Leningrad, composed in some cases of the offspring of the Soviet political elite but more often of the children of prominent communists who had perished under Stalin. Though a number of these dissenters have been tried both privately and publicly in Moscow and Leningrad, they have not been deterred from

---

"occupational specialization can attain a high level without giving rise to social or political pluralism; that engineers and managers can be governed at least as much by transfunctional ideological and political commitments as by their 'objective' interests as incumbents of economic roles; that these interests can be largely, if not completely, satisfied within the framework of a political system that is neither democratic nor technocratic; and that men who are oriented toward the maximization of political power can successfully maintain a position of dominance over men who are oriented toward the optimization of economic utilities, although their doing so may require important sacrifices" (p. 175).

* It is important to differentiate here between instrumental, orthodox dissent and fundamental, unorthodox dissent. The two are sometimes confused by outside observers, with the result that instrumental dissenters are lionized for having run nonexistent risks and the government's tolerance of them is interpreted as the sign of a basic departure from the Leninist-Stalinist tradition. The classic contemporary example is Yevgeny Yevtushenko. His "dissent" has been primarily instrumental in content: it has aimed at making the relationship between the political system and society more compatible, without addressing itself to the question whether in fact the more basic, ideological underpinnings of the system needed rethinking and revision. In contrast, precisely because Alexander Solzhenitsyn's or Pasternak's works have had the effect of questioning the historical antecedents of the political system more searchingly, they have been objects of more assertive official displeasure.

protesting, and they did so again, at grave personal risk, following the Soviet occupation of Czechoslovakia.

For the time being and for some time to come, the intellectual and orthodox dissenters will in all probability remain a relatively small, isolated group. Like their predecessors in the nineteenth century, at the moment they do not appear able to attract broader popular support. The majority of the Soviet Union's urban population—only one generation removed from their rural setting—are characterized by a social orthodoxy based on a rather simplistic internalized ideology and by a sense of satisfaction in their recent social advancement. Moreover, in its social origins and ways of thinking, the party is closer to the masses than the masses are to the intellectuals.*

A very special and particularly perplexing kind of dissent is posed by increasing restlessness among the Soviet Union's non-Russian nations. The political significance of this phenomenon has largely been ignored by American scholars of Soviet affairs. Yet about one-half of the two hundred and forty million inhabitants of the Soviet Union are non-Russian, and many of them possess a distinctive sense of their own cultural heritage, their own language, territory, and history. Their intelligentsia, almost entirely Soviet-reared, tends to be increasingly assertive though not necessarily secessionist in attitude. It is beginning to demand a larger share in Soviet decision-making as well as a bigger part of the economic pie, and it is becoming increasingly leery of Russification. To some extent this Russification is deliberately

---

* "For all its modernization, the Soviet Union still contains a very massive 'dark' population aspiring to bourgeois amenities on the one hand, yet immersed in socialist rhetoric on the other. And within this population there is a strong element of 'grudge'—crude, primitive, often all too well-founded, a kind of legendary force in its own right—which views all privilege as corruption, and which is directed equally against the political and managerial elite of the party and against the intelligentsia. Here, however, the intelligentsia is at a disadvantage, for it still carries the traditional burden of guilt toward the people, and the lines of manipulation are in the hands of the party" (Sidney Monas, "Engineers or Martyrs: Dissent and the Intelligentsia," *Problems of Communism,* September–October 1968, p. 5).

fostered by Moscow, but it is also the natural result of industrialization and modernization. Official Soviet discussions of this problem, as well as attacks on the dangers of local nationalism, indicate that Soviet leadership is becoming apprehensive; indeed, a number of non-Russian intellectuals have been tried and sentenced in recent years. For the moment, the Soviet government has succeeded in confining nationalist tendencies to a relatively few intellectuals while evidence on the attitude of non-Russian party cadres tends to be ambiguous; however, the very scale of this problem, as well as the fact that nationalism tends to be infectious whether suppressed or tolerated, would suggest that in the years to come the Soviet Union might well be faced with a nationality problem graver in its political consequences than the racial problem in the United States.

The rumblings of ideological discontent within the scientific community have probably been more immediately disturbing to the party. The now well-known manifesto by the prominent Soviet nuclear physicist Andrei Sakharov, which was published in the West in mid-1968,[32] had apparently first been circulated among Soviet scientists and then revised by the author in the light of comments. The fact that subsequent Soviet responses to Sakharov took an indirect form, never mentioning him by name, and that he was not denounced by the usual device of a public statement of condemnation signed by his colleagues, seems to indicate that the government thought it preferable to avoid direct confrontation and public discussion.

This document is remarkable in that it not only challenges the right of ideological orthodoxy to continue but also attempts to offer an alternative vision of the future. In so doing, it exposes Soviet reality to a scathing critique. Sakharov's principal underlying assumption is well summarized by his assertion that "any preaching of the incompatibility of world ideologies and nations is a madness and a crime." He categorically rejects any restraint whatsoever on intellectual freedom and condemns "the ossified dogmatism of a bureaucratic oligarchy and its favorite weapon, ideological censorship." In rejecting intellectual subordination to the will of "the party's central apparatus and its officials," he also asks, "Who will guarantee that these officials always express the genuine interests of the working class as a whole and the genuine interests of progress rather than their own caste interests?" *

His thesis is that our age requires and compels increasing international cooperation—both to avoid a nuclear war and to overcome the dangers to mankind posed by hunger, overpopulation, and pollution—and that this cooperation will eventually come from the increasing convergence of the currently distinctive political and social systems. In this connection, he specifically asserts that, given the productive energies of the American economy, a revolution in the United States—in contrast to a similar upheaval in the Third World—would not be advantageous to the workers. His long-range vision for the remainder of the century involves a four-stage development: In the first stage the communist countries, and notably the Soviet Union, will become more democratic, overcoming the Stalinist legacy of single-party

---

* In criticizing the persisting backwardness of Soviet society, a condition which the officially idyllic view has ignored, Sakharov reveals the extraordinary fact that some 45 per cent of the population, or approximately 110 million Soviet citizens, live in underprivileged conditions. He compares this to the United States where "about 25 per cent of the population is on the verge of poverty. On the other hand, the 5 per cent of the Soviet population that belongs to the managerial group is as privileged as its counterpart in the United States," implying a condition of considerable social inequality in the Soviet Union.

Sakharov's observation is important because the attainment of social equality has long been a major Soviet claim. In fact, Soviet statistics and, more recently, sociological studies confirm the fact that in higher education the children of white-collar officials have considerably greater opportunities than do those of workers or of collective farmers. For example, in the late 1950s, 75 per cent of Moscow University students were children of officials; 20 per cent and 5 per cent were, respectively, the children of workers and of collective farmers. During this period the population distribution was approximately 20 per cent, 48 per cent, and 31 per cent, respectively (see the collective volume *Kulturnaia Revoliutsia*, Moscow, 1967, p. 151). Considerable disproportion also exists in levels of remuneration, with the Soviet minimum wage fixed as of 1968 at approximately $65 per month.

dictatorship; the second stage will see the transformation of the United States and other "capitalist" countries by reformers who will effect internal changes and adopt a policy of peaceful coexistence; the third stage will involve a massive Soviet-American effort to cope with the problems of the Third World and to promote disarmament; the fourth stage will see the remaining global problems attacked on the basis of broad international cooperation.

Sakharov's views, even if somewhat utopian, are noteworthy because they reveal how the world view of some in the new Soviet intellectual-scientific elite contrasts with the official perspective. Their importance, however, should not be exaggerated. His argument is simply inaccessible not only to the overwhelming majority of literate Soviet people but also to the majority of Soviet intellectuals. It may be assumed that where there are large concentrations of intellectuals (Moscow, Leningrad, Kiev, Akademgorodok, Obninsk), unorthodox viewpoints circulate somewhat more widely, but even there much depends on the degree to which at any particular moment the government is prepared to apply administrative pressure in order to enforce at least formal orthodoxy. Given the party's monopoly of communications, the extensive efforts to inculcate the official ideology, and the growing emphasis on nationalism, the government's view of the world and of Soviet society is still the basic source of information and interpretation for most Soviet citizens.

Alternative Paths

It is in the light of the foregoing considerations that possible alternative paths of Soviet political development should be evaluated. For analytical purposes, these have to be reduced to a manageable number and, accordingly, the discussion that follows will concentrate on five rather broadly conceived variants, with attention focused on the role of ideology and the party. The five developmental variants can be capsuled as (1) *oligarchic petrifaction,* (2) *pluralist evolution,* (3) *technological adaptation,* (4) *militant fundamentalism,* and (5) *political disintegration.*

Oligarchic petrifaction would involve the maintenance of the dominant role of the party and the retention of the essentially dogmatic character of the ideology. In effect, more of the same. Neither the party nor the ideology would be in a particularly revolutionary relationship to society; instead, the main thrust of the relationship would be for the party to retain political control over society without attempting to impose major innovations. Strong emphasis would be placed on ideological indoctrination and the confinement of ideological deviations. Political leadership could remain collective, for the absence of deliberately imposed change would not require major choices. The domestic result would be rule by an ossified bureaucracy that would pursue a conservative policy masked by revolutionary slogans.

Pluralist evolution would involve the transformation of the party into a less monolithic body, somewhat like the Yugoslav party, and the ideological erosion of the dogmatic Leninist-Stalinist tradition. The party would become more willing to tolerate within its own ranks an open ideological dialogue, even ferment, and it would cease to view its own doctrinal pronouncements as infallible. Its role would be more that of a moral-ideological stimulant than that of a ruler; the state as well as society itself would become the more important source of innovation and change. Because so much of the party's history has been contrary to the above pattern, in addition to sustained social pressure from key economic and intellectual groups, either a basic split in party leadership, or, paradoxically, a strong leader (like Tito) would be necessary to condition party officialdom into acceptance of such political and ideological pluralism.

Technological adaptation would involve the transformation of the bureaucratic-dogmatic party into a party of technocrats. Primary emphasis would be on scientific expertise, efficiency, and discipline. As has already happened in Ulbricht's East Germany, the party would be composed of scientific experts, trained in the latest techniques, capable of relying on cybernetics and computers for social control, and looking to scientific innovation for the preservation of Soviet security and industrial growth. Nationalism would replace ideological dogmas as the basic integrative principle linking society and the state. The younger, more technologically oriented leaders of the military establishment would, in all probability, favor this pattern. Political leadership, as in the first variant, could remain collective, though it would probably involve a wider coalition of party-state-military-economic leaders.

Militant fundamentalism would involve a revivalist effort to rekindle ideological fervor, which would in turn require a more revolutionary relationship between the political system and society. The notion of progression toward communism would have to be given new programmatic content, and hence politically induced social changes would be necessary. In all probability, this development would necessitate the application of force to overcome both actual resistance and sheer social inertia. Even if it fell short of Stalinist methods, the effort to shake up the Soviet system's rigidly bureaucratized structure would require highly centralized leadership, ideological militancy, perhaps a more hostile attitude toward the outside world, and something along the lines of Mao Tse-tung's "Cultural Revolution."

Political disintegration would involve internal paralysis in the ruling elite, the rising self-assertiveness of various key groups within it, splits in the armed forces, restiveness among the young people and the intellectuals, and open disaffection among the non-Russian nationalities. In the wake of the intensifying contradiction between the political system and society, the crisis that could arise would be made more acute by an inadequate economic growth incapable of satisfying popular demands. The petrified ideology—no longer taken seriously by the elite—would be incapable of providing the system with a coherent set of values for concerted action.

Looking approximately a decade ahead and using as a guide the present distribution of power in Soviet society, it would appear from the nature of the more immediate political-economic problems facing Soviet leadership and from the general pattern of contemporary Soviet social development that the Soviet leadership will seek to strike a balance between the first and the third variants. The combination comes closest to satisfying elite interests, the imperatives of social orthodoxy, and the needs of the Soviet Union as a global rival of the United States.

In the short run, development toward a pluralist, ideologically more tolerant system does not seem likely. The years 1964–1969 have even seen movement in the opposite direction. The political system is not in the near future likely to elevate to leadership a man with the will and the power to democratize Soviet society, and that society lacks the cohesion and the group pressures necessary to effect democratization from below. As the experience of Czechoslovakia has shown, democratization from below must be an organic process that links the intellectuals, the workers, and the students with some segments of the leadership in a deliberate effort to reform the political structure as well as the economic structure. Moreover, such a process must either draw on a democratic tradition (as was the case in Czechoslovakia) or create one by accepting the priority of legal norms over political expediency. For Soviet communism this would be tantamount to a new concept of politics.* Furthermore, the Soviet problem with non-Russian nationalities inhibits democratization: the Great Russian majority would inevitably fear that democratization might stimulate the desire of the non-Russian peoples first for more autonomy and then for independence. Given the thrust of Soviet social development and the interests of the present ruling elite, it is unlikely that an effective democratizing coalition could emerge during the 1970s.

---

* As one Czech scholar observed in commenting on the Czech experience with Stalinism, "One of the possible methods of preventing the recurrence of political trials in any form is a change in the concept of politics, with which is connected the birth of a new political system. I have in mind such a concept of politics as would not contain the elements of, or an assured basis for, displays of illegality of the kind that happened most frequently in the period of the political trials" (K. Kaplan, "Thoughts about the Political Trials," *Nova Mysl*, No. 8, 1968).

Militant fundamentalism under a one-man dictatorship, though perhaps somewhat more probable in the short run than a pluralist evolution, also would have to overcome enormous inertia and the collective stake of the party oligarchs in preventing the reappearance of one-man rule. Pressures toward such a rule could develop in the face of domestic upheaval or a major foreign threat, but a talented and effective political leader would have to be available. The present Soviet bureaucracy is constituted in such a way as to weed out and snuff out individual talent; it is no longer a revolutionary party in which individual courage and resourcefulness make for advancement.

Nonetheless, the fundamentalist alternative should not be dismissed out of hand, especially if it becomes the only alternative to political disintegration resulting from the petrifaction of the system as a whole. Protracted internal decay as a result of the leadership's inability to come to grips with current problems, continued failure to catch up with the United States in the scientific competition, and internal threats to national unity could in a context of increasing ideological indifference combine with an international security threat to spark a fundamentalist spasm from a section of the elite. Such spasms are characteristic of political faiths in their decline.

The alternatives of fundamentalism or of disintegration could be precipitated by a Sino-Soviet war. Such a war would inevitably impose major strains on the Soviet system. Even if won rapidly by the Soviet side, it would entail major economic costs and could even involve lengthy postwar counter-guerrilla activities. A protracted war would constitute itself a direct defeat for the Soviet regime, and it is almost certain that the regime would be toppled from power by dissatisfied elements in the ruling circles. Whatever its outcome, a war of this magnitude would be certain to trigger highly militant and volatile feelings within the Soviet Union, creating pressures on behalf of one-man rule or simply pulling the regime apart.

Given the conditions prevailing in the early 1970s, oligarchic petrifaction would be the probable consequence of continued rule by the present majority of the aging upper party bureaucracy (the average age of Central Committee members was over sixty in 1969, making them probably the oldest political leaders in the world, except for those of the Vatican and Mao and his associates), of the old-time army marshals (some of whom have more party seniority than the top political rulers), and of the party ideologues. This coalition represents not only the political but also the top social elite of the Soviet Union, in the sense that its power gives it prerogatives equivalent to those associated under capitalism with wealth: luxury, convenience, and prestige. Like any ruling class, it tends to become conservative and resistant to changes that threaten its position. Moreover—and this is a very important consideration—the Soviet middle class is highly bureaucratized and consists almost entirely of state officials who are rather conservative in their political and social mores and are only one generation removed from their proletarian or peasant origins. This class does not want major political change, though it does desire more material goods. It provides the underpinning for the conservatism of the leadership.

The upper stratum of the Soviet professional and scientific elite has, however, become too broad, too well educated, and too nationalistically ambitious to be satisfied with a pattern that merely preserves the *status quo*. Though concerned with political stability, it is also aware of the domestic and international imperatives for social and scientific innovation. In recent years this stratum has gained increasing access to the decision-makers and thus participates informally in a process of group bargaining, especially in policy areas requiring expertise. The organ of the Soviet Academy of Sciences has noted that "in recent times, the number of scientists called on to participate in the work of the governmental apparatus, even at the highest levels, has increased. They should be called on more often to organize production and to direct planning in the economic sphere." [33] Their innovative influence, added to the increasingly widespread political appreciation of the importance of scientific innovation, to national feelings of rivalry with the United States, and to the nationalist and security aspirations of the younger, more scientifically oriented military leaders, is already stimulating pressures for a fusion of the first (oligarchic petrifaction) and third (technological adaptation) variants, in an attempt to construct a novel kind of "technetronic communism." *

The example of Ulbricht's East Germany may become particularly relevant. Though in Rumania explorations of the scientific revolution's significance have led some communists to suggest that this revolution requires a new theoretical framework based on the principle of universality,[34] Ulbricht has attempted to combine scientific innovation with strict adherence to the Leninist-Stalinist ideological tradition. Political leadership has remained highly centralized, and ideological dissent has been firmly suppressed. At the same time, Ulbricht, perhaps more than any other communist leader, has emphasized that "the development of the socialist system, above all the implementation of the economic system as a whole, is to a growing extent a matter of scientific leadership. . . . We orient ourselves on the conscious scientific control of complex processes and systems by the people and for the people. We make use of cybernetics in this sense." [35]

During the second half of the 1960s, East German leadership made an intense effort to rationalize economic management in order to combine lower-level initiative with an effective system of controls and coordination. The Seventh Party Congress (April

---

* This process would provide the political expression for the impressive growth in both the over-all number of specialists engaged in scientific activity and services (including those with specialized secondary education) and in the number of those members of the political elite who have had extensive backgrounds in technical and scientific fields. Between the years 1950 and 1966 the former grew from 714,000 to 2,741,000 (*Science Policy in the USSR*, p. 679); George Fischer has gathered evidence showing that the latter are becoming the predominant group among the younger members of the Central Committee of the CPSU (*The Soviet System and Modern Society*, New York, 1968, especially pp. 125–34). Technical competence is as widespread in the Soviet political elite as legal background is in its American counterpart.

1967) set itself the task of developing a general conception of the relations between the various part-systems with the economic system as a whole; more than any other communist country, East Germany utilized cybernetics, operational research, and electronic data processing. Two years later, at the April 1969 Central Committee Plenum, Politburo member Kurt Hager proudly reported—and he repeatedly used this formula—that East Germany was not only ideologically sound but "correctly programmed."

In line with this "correct programming," the party has emphasized the importance of expertise among its members,[36] and the educational system has been reformed in order to link science closely with industry.* By the late 1960s, East Germany had transformed itself from one of the most war-ravaged societies into the most economically and ideologically advanced science-oriented communist state. After a fifty-year lapse, the combination of Prussian discipline, German scientific efficiency, and Leninist-Stalinist ideology has thus again made German communism a model for its eastern neighbors.

---

* Under these reforms universities and polytechnical schools have been transformed into new "science combines" directly linked with industrial enterprises. For example, the Technical University of Dresden works jointly with the nearby Radeberg computer factory, and other institutions of learning have been similarly linked with the basic industrial efforts of their cities or regions. In this reform a major effort was made to obtain student participation, and students are said to have made a number of constructive proposals along the above lines.

At the same time, Marxist-Leninist indoctrination has continued to be assigned high priority in the educational process, but stress has been placed on the necessity to combine it with scientific social forecasting: "It is necessary to impart to the leadership personnel of the socialist state a complex knowledge which enables them to carry out the party resolutions with a high degree of quality; this must be done on the basis of the social long-range forecast, in teamwork with the Socialist Economic Management Institute, the Social Sciences Institute, the 'Karl Marx' Party College, and other institutions" (a speech by Erich Honecker, member of the Politburo and Secretary of the Central Committee of the German Socialist Unity Party, April 29, 1969). Honecker's speech was remarkable for its emphasis on the technetronic features of a modern society and for its relative neglect of the ideological question.

In the Soviet Union, however, other considerations will in all likelihood impede the pace of a similar "technologization" of the Soviet political system. For one thing, the Soviet Union is a much bigger country, is more difficult to integrate, and has many more areas of socio-economic backwardness to overcome. In addition, over the last fifty years the ruling party has developed its own traditions and ideological style, and though it favors the acquisition of technical skills by its officials, it is likely to continue to resist the development of an essentially technical orientation among its members, since that would dilute the importance attached to ideology.[37] Moreover, perhaps intensified in the years to come by the Sino-Soviet dispute, the role of the security factor in policymaking and of the military in the political process might tend to increase. Indeed, if the security problem becomes more urgent and Soviet leadership remains collective, it will become increasingly difficult to deny the military direct participation in the political decision-making process. In that case, the fusion of the first and the third variants (striving to combine ideological rigidity with technological expertise) would also involve the transformation during the 1970s of the present communist party dictatorship into a communist praetorian oligarchy.*

The Problem of Vitality

The question then is: Will such a political development facilitate the resolution of the economic and political dilemmas confronting the Soviet Union? The answer to this question is bound to be even more speculative than the prognosis itself. On the whole, it would appear doubtful whether an attempt to combine ideological orthodoxy with technological innovation, per-

---

* This view is held also by some Yugoslav observers. Thus, V. Stanovcic, writing in the Yugoslav Central Committee weekly *Komunist* (September 26, 1968), has argued that the present Soviet system has proven itself unable to liberalize gradually and that as a consequence it will very likely "logically develop into a Bonapartist form of rule, with managerial-militarist groups assuming the role of 'line prescribers' and 'organizers' of society."

haps buttressed by increasing reliance on nationalism and the military, will create a setting propitious to intellectual and scientific creativity. Such an attempt is more likely to produce internal contradictions, with the ideologues and the technocrats often pulling in opposite directions. This will be especially true as concerns the complex issue of economic decentralization, increasingly recognized as necessary for economic reasons, but nevertheless feared for political reasons. The result will be either temporary compromises (such as have been characteristic of Brezhnev) or drastic policy shifts from one emphasis to the other. The consequent tension will widen the gap between the political system and society; the political system will appear unresponsive to internal dilemmas, and increasing social pressure will be generated for a more fundamental reassessment of the contemporary relevance of the ideological and institutional character of the Soviet state.

Accordingly, it may be expected that the 1970s will witness the spread to the Soviet Union of convulsions similar to those that Spain, Yugoslavia, Mexico, and Poland began to undergo in the late 1960s. The Soviet student population will have doubled during the 1960s (it increased by seventy-seven per cent between 1958 and 1965), and it is unlikely that the Soviet Union will altogether avoid student unrest. The late 1970s will probably see the sexual revolution spread to the more urban Soviet centers, and the party ideologues will not find it easy to accommodate within the prevailing official mores. These factors could create a broader social basis for the currently isolated ideological dissenters and, together with the likely growth in the self-assertiveness of the non-Russian intelligentsia, make for more visible social and political tensions. Given the authoritarian Soviet setting, a red flag spontaneously flown by Moscow students over their university will have much graver political symbolism than the same flag fluttering over Columbia or the Sorbonne.

But it will not be until the early 1980s that the first fully post-Stalin political leadership will enter the political arena. An aspiring forty-five-year-old leader in 1980 will have been only eighteen at the time of Stalin's death and twenty-one when de-Stalinization actually began in the Soviet Union. Though his generation will probably find its access to power blocked by political leaders ten or even twenty years older (the Polyanskis, Shelepins, Semichastnys, Tolstikovs of today), it will press for influence from the echelons immediately below that of the Central Committee. Given the more volatile domestic and global setting in which it will have matured, given its higher education, given the probably more flexible character of the adjoining Eastern European states, it is quite possible that the emerging political elite will be less committed to the notion that social development requires intense concentration of political power.

Nevertheless, even then evolution into a pluralist system is likely to be resisted by the entrenched political oligarchy. The introduction of political pluralism will at some point require a deliberate decision to open the Soviet Union to competitive ideas, to let each Soviet citizen read what he wants, to reduce the level of the party's ideological control, to decentralize decision-making and thus to share power with society: in effect, a major transformation of the system as a whole. Unintended consequences of economic-technological adjustments will not suffice to bring about significant political change. As in Yugoslavia or pre-1968 Czechoslovakia, at some point the political elite must decide to embark on deliberate political reforms.

Thus, barring an upheaval resulting from internal paralysis—and dramatically bringing about either social democracy or, more likely, a revivalist dictator capable of controlling internal dissent—the more probable pattern for the 1980s is a marginal shift toward the combination of the second (pluralist evolution) and third (technological adaptation) variants: limited economic-political pluralism and intense emphasis on technological competence, within the context of a still authoritarian government representing a coalition of the upper echelons of the principal interest groups. This could be the beginning of the return to the

Western Marxist tradition, but only a slow and cautious beginning at best.*

It would therefore be rash to expect in the near future a fundamental revision of the Soviet attitude toward the world. There will be change, but it will be slow. Moreover, the element of rivalry with the United States, reflecting the vestigial legacy of ideology and reinforced by middle-class-urban nationalism, is likely to continue to be dominant, even if tempered by growing Soviet recognition that increased United States–Soviet collaboration is dictated by the basic imperatives of human survival. The Sino-Soviet conflict may also have a double and contradictory effect: while intensifying the Soviet desire for a secure and peaceful western flank, it is likely to heighten Soviet security concerns, and thus strengthen the domestic position of the more conservative and nationalist elements.

This combination of eroding ideology and intensifying nationalism makes it unlikely that the Soviet Union will soon become involved either in militantly advancing the cause of world revolution or in actively promoting a policy of global cooperation. A more likely result is an ambiguous pattern determined by short-range expediency rather than by a broad, long-range perspective. In that context, precisely because the Soviet Union

---

* It might be relevant at this juncture to put to rest the popular analogy frequently made between the evolution of the French Revolution into a bourgeois democracy and the allegedly similar political consequences of the *embourgeoisement* of Soviet society. The analogy overlooks several salient differences between these revolutions. The French Revolution took place in a setting shaped by a rationalist, idealistic intellectual tradition and ineffective absolutism. The Russian Revolution was preceded by increasing intellectual fanaticism and utopianism, reacting to the absolutist and autocratic political setting. The French Revolution was effected by an idealistic and highly disorganized professional middle class; the Bolshevik Revolution by a highly professional, ideological, and disciplined party. The French revolutionaries did not have the time during their relatively short stay in power to reorganize French society fundamentally; the Bolsheviks, particularly under Stalin, ripped apart and rewove the entire social fabric, while effecting a far-reaching industrial and urban revolution. The French middle class was an innovative and intellectually restless class; the new Soviet middle class is Victorian, conservative, and orthodox. Last but not least, the legatee of the French Revolution, Napoleon, was defeated; Stalin was victorious.

does not appear likely to experience in the near future a domestic phase of open intellectual creativity and experimentation, its attractiveness as the socio-economic model for contemporary communism, one capable of intellectually and morally captivating the imagination of mankind, will probably continue to decline.

4. Sectarian Communism

In our age a universal ideological movement can only be a pluralist one. And if it is to be pluralist—that is, responsive to rapidly changing, differentiated global conditions and the resulting volatile intellectual mood—its ideological content must be highly generalized, more ethical than practical, and more humanistic than nationalistic. In effect, an ecumenical communism would have to be a deliberately pluralist communism. An international pluralist communism would in turn inevitably generate pressures for internally pluralist communist parties.

Pluralist communism does not exist and is unlikely to appear. Communist universalism has fallen victim to communist dogmatism. That dogmatism was compatible with universalism only as long as communism was an abstract attempt to define global conditions in the early stages of industrialization and found its political expression in disparate groups of intellectuals seeking power. Once these intellectuals had seized power in different states, dogmatism began to merge with the natural propensity of the new rulers to see the world through the prism of their own national power interests. Dogmatism, no longer operating on the level of universal abstraction but on that of national practice, facilitated the transformation of communism into sectarianism—with each sect insisting that its perspective was the truly universal one and establishing *internal* party discipline on that basis.

The Soviet Union led in transforming universal communism into sectarian communism, but the process developed naturally among all communist parties in power and even among the more established communist parties out of power. As a result of conflicting claims, mutual excommunications, occasional patched-up compromises, and active and latent conflicts, contemporary communism forms a mosaic almost as varied as the nations of mankind.[38] Far from helping to end the intellectual fragmentation of the globe, sectarian communism intensifies it.

Phases

Four broad phases can be discerned in the evolution of communism as an international movement since the creation of the first communist state in the Soviet Union. The first phase, corresponding roughly to the 1920s and the 1930s—but particularly to the 1930s, which witnessed the ideological restructuring of Soviet society—can be called that of *transplantation*. An essentially Western doctrine, responding to the specific conditions of Western capitalist industrialization, was transplanted to the Russian setting and redefined to meet the political needs of that setting. This involved domesticating and dogmatizing the imported and readapted ideology.

Domestication meant that formulations derived from specific Russian conditions, as defined first by Lenin and even more so by Stalin, increasingly permeated the doctrine; as a result, purely parochial considerations were dogmatically universalized. Dogmatization was largely the consequence of the primitive, autocratic setting into which Marxism was transplanted,[39] of the arbitrary personal traits of the top ideologues, and of the power needs of the new communist elite that found itself without what Marx saw as the foundation for socialist rule—the solid proletarian base that capitalist development had created in the West.

The second phase, the active *universalization* of the Soviet specific, corresponded approximately to the 1930s and particularly the 1940s. It saw the Stalinization of foreign communist parties, the forcible export of the Soviet version of communism to Eastern Europe, and the spontaneous expansion of the more oriental Leninist adaptation of Marxism to China, Korea, and Vietnam. Centralized by Moscow, international communism imitated the Soviet experience without taking into consideration conditions prevailing within the different nations. Indeed, Soviet insistence on a common mold became more intense precisely because a major gap existed between ideology and local conditions.

This state of affairs could not long endure, and national communist leadership groups came under growing domestic pressures for adjustments; in time the national leaders themselves began to see a divergence between their own needs and interests and Soviet prescriptions and demands. The result was the third phase, the *particularization* of international communism during the 1950s. It saw, first of all, the complete self-assertion of the Yugoslav leadership (in large measure because it had come to power through its own efforts), the partial self-assertion of the Polish leadership, the beginnings of such self-assertion by the Rumanians, and, most important of all, the increasing inclination of the Chinese leadership both to practice its own version of communism and to generalize the significance and relevance of its experience for other revolutionary communist parties.

The 1960s accordingly witnessed a new stage in the history of international communism. It was dominated by open tension between the process by which doctrine was relativized and the process by which specific points of view were made absolute. For the sake of unity, Soviet leadership seemed at first willing to tolerate increasing diversity; in the early 1960s it formally abandoned both its claim to leadership and its insistence on the need for a common general line.[40] A shift in the opposite direction, however, took place in the second half of the decade; it was perhaps generated by the fear that relativization was the first stage in the erosion of the ideology, and that the resulting ecumenical unity would be devoid of any political substance. Czechoslovak political developments in 1968 and the persistent Chinese challenge were in all probability the catalysts that precipitated the Soviet leaders' turn toward sectarianism: the reassertion of the absolute universality of certain common laws, largely as defined by the Soviet leaders themselves. The inescapable price that had to be paid was that those communist parties that could assert their own divergent position would do so—and would have to do so in the context of mutual ideological denunciations. Particularism, instead of being a stage toward ecumenism, was thus translated during the 1960s into the fourth and current phase, *sectarianism.*

Communist unity as of the early 1970s is thus devoid of any substantive meaning.* Western communist parties fortify their appeals for popular support by increasingly denying that the Soviet Union offers a relevant model. Indeed, the Italian and French communist leaders have come to realize that their parties will succeed only to the degree that they successfully convince the voters that a French or an Italian communist government would be different from the Soviet model. Despite persisting Soviet pressures, the ruling Eastern European communist parties continue to make quiet adjustments to domestic necessities, and in so doing they increasingly diverge from the Soviet model. The Chinese Communist Party not only practices its own brand of

---

* Failure to perceive this reality still prompts some Western conservative scholars to speak of "the foreign policy of communism," and to be critical of the view that communist ideology is no longer capable of mobilizing unified global support. See Hans Morgenthau, *A New Foreign Policy for the United States,* New York, 1969, p. 32. Presumably for the same reason, Professor Morgenthau argued in 1965 that the Vietnam war would bring the Soviets and the Chinese together.

communism but explicitly denies that the Soviet party is a communist party—indeed, it charges that the Soviet Union is in the process of restoring capitalism.

The Soviet decision in 1968 to snuff out Czechoslovak democratization was particularly fateful for international communism. Had the Soviet leaders permitted the liberalization of the essentially Stalinist model of the Czechoslovak communist state, a major and vitally important step in the democratization of European communism would have been taken. The democratization of Czechoslovakia would have significantly affected the other communist states, including the Soviet Union, eventually generating similar tendencies within them. This was the primary reason for the Soviet decision to intervene in Czechoslovakia. Roger Garaudy, a member of the Politburo of the French Communist Party at the time, was correct in stating that the Soviet leaders instinctively feared the democratization of Czechoslovakia precisely because they have been so committed to the Stalinist model of socialism that any attempt to adjust socialism to the conditions of more advanced societies has come to be viewed as a menace to socialism itself. Democratization went against the grain of their entire training and outlook; the occupation of Czechoslovakia was therefore not an error but a logical consequence of the Stalinist system.[41]

The spectacle of a democratic Czechoslovakia, ruled by a communist party tolerant of individual freedom (free travel, speech, press), would have had an enormous impact on Western communist parties. It would have encouraged these parties to effect their own internal democratization more rapidly, and it would have made them more appealing to their national electorates. This would have meant a major turning point in the history of communism itself. It would have created in the more advanced West a democratizing communism preoccupied with humanistically harnessing the technetronic challenge; it would have led to a militant, more revolutionary communism, violently reacting against the backwardness and social inadequacy of the conditions prevailing in the Third World. Unwillingness to tolerate Czechoslovakia has thus meant not only that the Soviet Union will for some time persist in a congealed, highly bureaucratized mold, but that there will be many sectarian communisms, each claiming that it expresses a universally valid message.*

Assimilated Communisms

The 1970s and the 1980s are hence likely to see increasingly diversified communisms merging with specific local conditions while fading as part of an international movement and a universal ideology. In Eastern Europe this might mean the appearance of some regimes that would more appropriately qualify for the label "social fascist" than communist; that is, ruling parties that reinforce their own dogmatism by forcing from their ranks those who in any way tend to deviate from the norm. Intensely nationalistic, the middle and upper echelons of their elite would be composed of socially and politically conservative first-generation middle-class officials who have vaguely internalized the official ideology—especially the belief in the paramountcy of the state—ruling in an alliance with an ideologically neutral, technologically expert class disdainful of the more "old-fashioned" intellectual humanists, and supported by the military. In addition to the Soviet

* Soviet spokesmen have occasionally argued that a democratic Czechoslovakia would have ceased to be a communist Czechoslovakia, that the communist party would have been put out of power. This is doubtful, though it cannot be either proven or disproven. Nonetheless, it is unlikely that other political parties could have actually appeared in Czechoslovakia, for neither the social basis nor the personnel for them appears to have existed. Indeed, as of 1968 the predominant attitude among the Czechs and Slovaks was in favor of working within and through a more democratic, pluralist communist party that would have been communist without being Leninist-Stalinist.

The Soviet argument, however, is deserving of note because it reveals something else. The charge is tantamount to an admission that democracy and the Soviet version of communism are still incompatible. It thus reflects not only a deeply ingrained bureaucratic suspicion of the popular will but the persistent incapacity of Soviet communist officials to relate meaningfully to the contemporary preoccupation with political and social equality, to the contemporary search for a new humanism relevant to the "scientific-technological revolution," which communists themselves admit that they have tended to neglect (see p. 152, *supra*).

Union, East Germany and perhaps Poland and Bulgaria are likely to approximate the above "social fascist" category.*

These regimes, however, are not likely to be stable. The ruling elites suffer from increasing cynicism and tend to be more and more fragmented; cliques, intrigues, and personal feuds dominate the internal political processes, which still lack defined constitutional procedures. Societies are becoming more restless under existing political restraints and are fearful lest their systems prove insufficiently innovative in technological areas. Moreover, a new and ever larger generation of students is beginning to leave the universities and to lay claim to power. The outbursts of 1968 are likely to be repeated in the 1970s. Should they occur in a setting in which Western Europe exerts a social attraction for frustrated Eastern Europeans, and in which there is political weakness and division in Moscow, the next wave of Eastern European unrest could be explosive on a regional, and not just national, scale.

In Yugoslavia the main source of uncertainty for the future is the possibility of dissension among the various nationalities, especially after Tito's death. That dissension could lead to a military coup designed to preserve the state, and Soviet leadership would then be likely to make a major effort to improve relations with such a praetorian Yugoslav regime. If that danger—which is quite real—is surmounted by a combination of political skill and continued economic growth, Yugoslavia will continue to evolve toward a more pluralist pattern and to cultivate closer contacts with the West—no doubt including something like associate status in the European Common Market. It may even begin to experiment with multi-party elections, and it is likely to be less and less doctrinaire about the classical issue of state versus private ownership.† Yu-

* It is interesting and relevant to note here that Central European fascism was primarily an urban development. For example, in 1937, 50 per cent of the members of the Hungarian Arrow Cross party were industrial workers, 12 per cent were professional and self-employed people, and only 8 per cent were peasants. At the same time slightly over half the population was peasant (Istvan Deak, "Hungary," in *The European Right*, Eugene Weber and Hans Rogger, eds., Berkeley, 1965, pp. 396–97).

† In the more developed parts of Yugoslavia there is already strong senti-

goslav theoreticians have already argued publicly that a multi-party system is a necessary mechanism for avoiding the political degeneration inherent in the communist party power monopoly. They have warned that "nothing is so irrational as a closed rational system which does not allow other ideas and contrary views to live, which does not permit any intellectual unrest." [42]

The example provided by such a Yugoslavia would be attractive to the more developed Eastern European states, such as Czechoslovakia and Hungary, and eventually to the currently most independent-minded member of the Eastern bloc, Rumania. The former are likely to continue quietly pursuing the road of democratization from within, eventually heading toward independence; Rumania is likely to consolidate its independence by increasing the scope of popular participation in the country's social and political life. All three countries increasingly appreciate the desirability of substituting a mixed economy for the highly centralized Soviet model. Moreover, Czechoslovak sociologists have recently been drawing attention to the transformation of their own society into one in which the intelligentsia, "the fastest growing group in society," is playing the decisive role. In their view, this necessarily compels a redefinition of the concept of "the dictatorship of the proletariat." [43] Hungarian sociologists, discussing the implications of the increasingly decentralized Hungarian economic model and of a similar increase in the Hungarian intelligentsia, have also called for a redefinition of socialism in the direction of "comprehensive social reforms, including broad sections of social life (political and cultural as well)." [44]

Moreover, the Eastern European states fear that scientific obsolescence may be the price that they will have to pay for remaining too closely associated with an Eastern bloc and for being cut off from extensive contacts with the West. (These fears are not

---

ment on behalf of widening the private sector in the economy. The group with the strongest anti-private-property feelings is that of the white-collar workers with the least education (see the public-opinion poll published in the Zagreb *Vjesnik,* December 24, 1968).

groundless. See Table 10.) This fear is shared even by East Germany, whose technological development is increasingly turning it toward Western markets, with the result that the regime's technological success is in tension with its political orientation.

In the West the bureaucratized and ideologically sterile communism of the Stalinist variety is likely to continue to fade in

TABLE 10. INVENTIONS REGISTERED PER 100,000 INHABITANTS (1964)

Country	No. of Inventions
Belgium	164
Austria	147
Denmark	131
Norway	121
Czechoslovakia	52
Hungary	20
Poland	10
Rumania	7

Source: Burks, *Technological Innovation and Political Change in Communist Eastern Europe*, p. 12.

socio-political relevance. The revolutionary standard has already passed into the hands of more ideologically volatile and activist groups; as a result, the established communist parties are likely to seek political relevance by minimizing their orthodoxy and emphasizing their acceptance of constitutional procedures.* Their fundamental problem is likely to continue to be that they have no attractive model of a modern highly sophisticated and pluralist communist power to offer as an example to their electorates; in addition, the significance of their programmatic message is further reduced by the fact that the West has preceded the communist states in experiencing the social and technological revolution.

Thus, both in order to exploit the tensions connected with the transition from the industrial to the technetronic society and to

* Or even participation in their national establishments. A moving account of the efforts of a devoted communist militant to arouse her party's officials to the plight of the Neapolitan masses and to stimulate a more revolutionary attitude in them is provided by M. A. Macciocchi, *Lettere dall'interno del PCI a Louis Althusser*, Milan, 1969. In her diary she describes her efforts to gain the confidence of the workers and—even more futile—to make the party bureaucrats more sensitive to the workers' abysmal conditions.

provide the basis for effective political action, the French and the Italian communist parties have been forced in dilute their orthodoxy. Some of their theoreticians have already emphasized the need to redefine the communist party as an altogether new party that would include the entire left, that would not be ideological in the strict sense of the word, and that would certainly not be Leninist in its bureaucratic structure. To the extent that these reformists have been thwarted by conservative party leaders, the communist parties in the West remain both sectarian and politically isolated; to the extent that the reformists have succeeded in gaining support, the communist parties in the West have moved toward diluting their nineteenth-century ideological tradition of dogmatic, integrated, and exclusivist grand visions.* These visions can no longer encompass either the new scientific revolution or the revolutions of the students and intellectuals, who have replaced the communists as the anti-establishmentarians of our time. Whatever the response, the basic fact remains that in the West the communist parties are no longer either innovative or revolutionary.

China and Global Revolution

Though it came too late in the West, communism has come too early for the East, or, more generally, for the Third World as a

---

* The first situation has been more true of the French Communist Party, and George Lichtheim was quite correct in stating that "if the role of Marxist doctrine in contemporary France can be reduced to a formula, it may be summed up by saying that from the vision of a revolutionary future it has turned into the critical contemplation of an eternal and seemingly unchangeable present" (George Lichtheim, *Marxism in Modern France,* a study by the Research Institute on Communist Affairs, New York, 1966, p. 169). The second situation is more applicable to the Italian party, in which the most explicit concept of the new broad party was developed by one of its theoreticians, G. Amendola, in a series of articles published in the fall of 1964 in the theoretical journal of the Italian Communist Party, *Rinascita.* In these articles he called for the creation of a single party of the left, which would be neither communist nor social democratic, neither shackled by ideology nor dominated by the party cadres.

whole. Instead of being the internationalizing and humanizing force that Marx conceived socialism to be, communism in the East is at best an inspiration for intensely nationalistic modernization or of revolutionary resistance to social exploitation; at worst, it is the basis for despotic fanaticism and massive oppression. As in the West, communism's virtues have more often been demonstrated when it has been out of power and has acted as a catalyst in the struggle against inequality, social injustice, or foreign domination. In power, it has tended to become extremely oppressive, fanatical, and intensely nationalistic.

Communism in the East, even more than in the West, has been a particularly important force in stimulating populist nationalism. This is quite understandable. Communism came to the Third World masses before their political awakening, and it has succeeded only where it has become both the external expression and the internal content of the new sense of national identity. Focusing on industrialization as the way in which to fulfill popular aspirations on both external and domestic levels, communism galvanized feelings of inferiority toward the more advanced West. Indeed, because of this, communism in the Third World has been especially vulnerable to the racism that—given the bitter legacy of the white man's imperialism—inevitably infected the new nationalism.[45] Racism, however, is one of the most primitive and irrational sources of motivation, and a communist ideology reinforced by it—whether in Asia or in Africa—cannot help but be deprived of both its universality and its rationality.

An altogether different challenge to communism's ideological and institutional global relevance has been posed by the victory of Chinese communism. Chinese communism has not only paralleled the claim of Soviet communism to be *the* pure communism of our time, but has been willing to back its claim with domestic revolutionary action. The "Cultural Revolution" of the late 1960s, which followed by a few years the "Great Leap Forward" of the late 1950s, was designed to overcome the ruling party's dangerous tendency toward bureaucratic stagnation and ideological petrifaction. The Chinese have explicitly stated that, in their view, the Soviet party had already become a victim of such petrifaction. The Cultural Revolution (the intellectual equivalent of the socio-economic shake-up effected by the Great Leap Forward) was designed to be the internal, domestic expression of the living and continuing revolution. Its over-all effect, however, was to do to the Chinese Communist Party what Khrushchev's aborted reforms of 1963 almost did to the Soviet party: to thoroughly disorganize it, and, with it, the Chinese economy as well.[46]

By denigrating the party and by simultaneously elevating Mao Tse-tung's personal rule and role, Chinese communism inevitably separated itself from the traditional communist mainstream—in spite of the Chinese theory that the geographic vortex of revolutionary leadership has over the years shifted from France to Germany to Russia and now to China. Moreover, unlike Stalin, whose role in the international communist movement was reinforced by a towering personal standing and by leadership of the only communist party in power, Mao was faced by a number of other ruling communist parties, all disputing his claim to orthodoxy and all eager to point out his doctrinal errors. The effect was to weaken China's international claim to ideological universality and to tarnish both the revolutionary prestige of the Chinese communists and their undeniably impressive achievements in the struggle to overcome China's backwardness.[47]

China's capacity to serve as a model of communism was further complicated by the unique character of China itself. The Chinese communists came to power not in a single country but in a vast society that represents a comprehensive and sophisticated civilization. Not only is that civilization highly distinctive but it has for a long time had its own concept of a world order in which China is the traditional center. Though the historical and universal categories of Marxist thought have been assimilated into that Chinese framework and become an extension of it, the cultural, linguistic, and racial distinctiveness of the Chinese has automatically made their communism much more difficult to export or emulate.

Moreover, unlike the Russians, who have often referred to Moscow as the "Third Rome," the Chinese have traditionally displayed no intense missionary zeal. Effective performance in the missionary role requires, in addition to personal inclination, some cultural, philosophic, and even ethnic kinship, to say nothing of a proselytizing tradition. It is no accident that, despite its missionary zeal, European-based Christianity was much less successful in its efforts to spread to Asia than was the East's Middle Islam. Perhaps a racial appeal—explicitly based on color and ideologically legitimized by the identification of the white man with imperialism—may create a bridge between Chinese proselytizers and foreign masses, but even that appeal is more likely to be effective in areas sufficiently distant from China not to be fearful of Chinese nationalism and China's cultural hegemony. Hence Africa, rather than Asia, may be a more promising long-range Chinese target.

These considerations provide some clues to the probable limits of China's revolutionary world role. Neither Chinese verbal extremism nor even China's crash program to establish a nuclear arsenal (the old question of intentions or capabilities) is as important as the fact that China has become a somewhat self-contained civilization-nation-state. China's power will probably grow in the years to come, and with it China's capacity to threaten its neighbors and eventually even the United States or the Soviet Union.[48] But it does not follow that China will therefore become an activist director of militant and globally relevant revolutionary processes. On the contrary, as memories of Chinese revolutionary achievements gradually recede into the past, China will find it more and more difficult to present itself as the historically relevant revolutionary model. China's aid will be accepted by needy revolutionaries, but it will probably become more rather than less difficult for the Chinese to convince the recipients of such aid that China has a universal mission.

Nor is it certain, as has been occasionally argued, that in the years to come communism will offer to the Third World an attractive model combining sustained economic development and social modernization with political stability. Even if China makes impressive strides and its GNP grows steadily at 5 per cent per annum, in the year 2000 it will still be among the poorer nations of the world. The fact is that its numbers, far from being a factor of strength, merely magnify the scale of its social and economic dilemmas. The relevance of Soviet economic experience to the Third World is also doubtful. Analysis of the Soviet experience strongly suggests that industrialization need not be derived from the impetus provided by extraordinarily coercive means or from the physical destruction of a social class. Moreover, it is important to note that Soviet industrialization occurred in a society that had some thirty years of prior industrial development behind it, that was endowed with matchless natural resources and a hard-working and disciplined population (but not *over*population), and that even before World War I had the advantages of solid statistics, relatively well-trained technical cadres, and preliminary plans for future development. (See our earlier discussion of "The Stalinist Paradox.") These conditions can rarely be matched by the Third World countries now undertaking to modernize and industrialize themselves. Whether China or Cuba (the latter, in any case, relatively well developed at the time of Castro's take-over) can provide examples of sustained growth and political stability is uncertain.

Of the countries where communism came to power without being imposed by foreign intervention (the Soviet Union, China, Cuba, Yugoslavia, Albania, Vietnam), only Yugoslavia has so far succeeded in achieving sustained economic growth, social modernization, and political stability without employing massive terror or experiencing violent power conflicts; even Yugoslavia, however, required extensive outside financial aid. Moreover, though the record of economic development of communist countries, particularly the more primitive ones, is good, it has not been better than that of some non-communist countries. In addition, most communist political systems (except for Yugoslavia, Vietnam, and Cuba) have been characterized by sporadic political instability, which in some cases had to be put down through Soviet intervention. Thus the over-all record is, at best, a mixed one and hardly sufficient to justify the argument that only the communists have found the key to effective modernization.*

Nor, for that matter, have they found the answer to effective revolution-making. Communism came to power indigenously in only one country not previously devastated by a major war—Cuba. In several other countries it came to power indigenously when communists picked up the pieces after these nations had experienced complete destruction of their state machinery and economy during a major war. Other than that, the communist revolutionary record since 1917 has been one of rather frequent failure,† while in Poland, Hungary, and Rumania it was the Soviet army that established communism.

Nevertheless, it is quite possible that in the years to come individual, highly nationalistic, perhaps even racist communist parties will come to power in some Asian, African, or Latin American countries by appealing both to the populist nationalism of the masses and the statism of impatient intellectuals. In his study *Communism and the Politics of Development,* John Kautsky has shown that "Communist party strength is lowest at the lowest stage of economic development, rises gradually with economic development, crests at a fairly high level of such development, and declines sharply with the highest level." [49] This generalization should not be mechanically applied to the Third World with the conclusion that communism will fade as soon as development has made substantial progress. A seizure of power could, for example, occur during the intermediary phase.

---

* In these respects, useful comparisons can be made between communist-ruled countries and countries ruled by modernizing non-communist elites; Poland-Spain-Italy; Rumania-Yugoslavia-Spain; Czechoslovakia-Sweden; Hungary-Austria; North Korea-South Korea; North Vietnam-South Vietnam; China-India; and so on. These comparisons are more revealing of certain uniformities than of significant disparities. The disparities are sharper when the comparison is made with non-modernizing, non-communist countries.

† A partial list of more significant revolutionary efforts by the communists includes: Hungary 1919; Poland 1920; Germany 1918, 1923; China 1927; France and Italy 1947; Greece 1948; Indonesia 1949, 1965; Bolivia 1966.

It is, however, unlikely that these seizures of power will be effected by the orthodox and formal communist parties, which in some countries (particularly in Latin America) are already becoming assimilated into the social establishment. The successful revolutionaries, though perhaps labeling themselves communists, will probably be loosely organized coalitions of impatient middle-class intellectuals, younger officers, and students. Instead of being adherents of a dogmatic and allegedly universal ideology, they are more likely to be men motivated by a vaguer and more volatile combination of radicalism, nationalism, and even some racism. Communist parties, though experienced in organizing exploited, disadvantaged workers and in transforming landless but nationalistically aroused peasants into revolutionary armies, have so far been unable to discipline, either ideologically or organizationally, the students and the intellectuals fermenting in the modern stainless-steel-and-glass universities. To these men, Fanon and Boumedienne, or Bolivar and Guevara, rather than Marx and Mao, or Marx and Lenin, are more relevant symbols. The revolutions to come will hence neither signify an automatic addition of strength to "international communism" nor represent a step forward toward the intellectual unity of mankind.

The ideologically more volatile, less disciplined character of these novel revolutionary forces would be in keeping with the broader trends already noted. Conditions during the early industrial age called for intellectual and organizational integration, but the dynamic congestion of the global city is inimical to a disciplined, centralized international organization whose purpose is to disseminate a particular system of thought and of values and to create a globally uniform social order on that basis. The fact is that proximity paradoxically dictates not uniformity but pluralism.

Moreover, the chances of truly revolutionary upheavals—radically and rapidly revolutionizing both social values and institutions—are in any case not high. In modern times only the French, the Mexican, and the Cuban revolutions can be considered as authentically indigenous and far-reaching internal revolutions that were achieved without the benefit of the cataclysmic dislocations wrought by the two world wars. Otherwise, even the most ineffective social and political systems have shown themselves to be highly resilient and difficult to overthrow. In most cases it has been found that social inertia can only be coped with piecemeal and that superimposed radical efforts to overcome it have prompted effective resistance.

At one time Soviet theorists toyed with the concept of the national democracy as a transitional stage toward a communist people's democracy. The overthrow of Ben Bella, Goulart, Kassem, Keita, Nkrumah, Papandreou, and Sukarno has compelled the Soviets to think in terms of much lengthier and more gradual revolutionary processes; at the same time, the Chinese and the Cubans have moved toward emphasis on various forms of guerrilla war, often in the face of open criticism from local communist parties.* Both cases have involved an implied admission of the increasing irrelevance of the classical revolutionary theory and a concession to social particularism, which—when linked to ideological dogmatism—means sectarianism.

Sectarianism is the negation of universalism. Communism may turn out to have been the last great integrative dogmatic faith. To the extent that some communist parties are today joining their national establishments, they are conforming to reality rather than forming it. To the extent that some communist parties are embracing racism and intense nationalism in the Third World, they are capitulating to reality rather than reshaping it. In either case there is a loss of identity which, once lost, is not likely to be regained. Thus, even if one is not a Marxist, it is not necessarily a

* The issues at stake were sharply posed by the secretary-general of the Venezuelan Communist Party, Jesus Faria, who stated in an interview printed in the Hungarian party organ, *Nepszabadsag* (February 17, 1968): "Experience has shown that the masses are withdrawing from the previous armed struggle. . . . Four million people are participating in the election campaign and we believe that we can orient the people better if we also participate in this campaign. . . . The ultraleftist groups in Venezuela, which disregard the combat readiness of the masses and persist in the slogan of armed struggle at any price, commit one mistake after another and find themselves more and more isolated."

cause for rejoicing to note that communism—which helped to enlarge the collective consciousness of mankind and to mobilize the masses for social progress—has failed in its original objective of linking humanism with internationalism.

PART IV
The American Transition

There is something awesome and baffling about a society that can simultaneously change man's relationship to the universe by placing a man on the moon, wage and finance a thirty-billion-dollar-per-annum foreign war despised by a significant portion of its people, maintain the most powerful and far-flung military forces in history, and confront in the streets and abet in the courts a revolution in its internal racial relations, doing all this in the context of the explosion of higher learning in its rapidly expanding and turbulent universities, of rotting urban centers, of fumbling political institutions, and of dynamically growing frontier industries that are transforming the way its citizens live and communicate with one another. Any one of the above aspects would suffice to transform the values and self-image of a society, and a few might be enough to overthrow its system. All together, they create a situation that defies analogy to other societies and highlights the singular character of the contemporary American experience.

Contemporary America is the world's social laboratory. The problems that the more advanced world is beginning to confront —and the Third World is witnessing—absorb America directly and often painfully. It is in the United States that the crucial dilemmas of our age manifest themselves most starkly; it is in the United States that man's capacity to master his environment and to define himself meaningfully in relationship to it is being most intensely tested. Can man master science for fundamentally humane ends? Can liberty and equality coexist, and do so in a multiracial environment? Can merit and achievement flourish without special privilege? Can technology be socially creative without inducing excessive social control? Can a society with diverse beliefs avoid complete disbelief? These issues dominate contemporary American life—the focus of global attention—and they prompt conflicting and often critical assessments of the meaning of the American experience.[1]

Unlike the situation in the Soviet Union, in America the challenge of change is highly visible. In the Soviet Union society is like a boiling subterranean volcano that strains against the rigid surface crust of the political system. In the more volatile United States, social, economic, and political forces openly clash, change, and interact on a broad front. The resulting turmoil is as creative as it is destructive, and it leads to metamorphic changes in that unique combination of order and chaos known as the United States.

In the next twenty years the population of the United States will approach three hundred million, of which approximately 80 per cent will be metropolitan and almost 50 per cent under twenty years of age. Intensely scientific in orientation, American society will have greater mastery of both terrestrial and spatial environment than any other society. At the same time it will have experienced intense social conflicts in which racial considerations will be paramount but in which antagonism between generations will also be a basic and painful burden. In all likelihood it will also be a society confronting an acute cultural malaise, uncertain of its aesthetic standards, and searching for common integrative values.

Contemporary America is in transition from the industrial to the technetronic age. As the world's first post-industrial society, the United States is no longer shaped by the same forces that have stimulated social change in the advanced countries ever since England first confronted the machine. This broad transformation is causing a crisis of established American values and institutions, particularly the tradition of liberal democracy, and as the nation's two-hundredth birthday approaches, it therefore calls for a redefinition of the American system.

Liberal democracy is a peculiar blend of the aristocratic tradition, constitutional legalism, and mass democracy. Unlike communism, it was not intellectually extracted from a telescoped and traumatic historical experience, and it is not embodied in a movement which draws its fervor and dedication from the deeply embedded Manichaean tradition. Rather, it is the product of slow growth—though occasionally accelerated by revolutionary upheavals in England, the United States, and France—which cumulatively created a broad tradition of social behavior, a set of only partially explicit values, and highly defined legal procedures and institutions. The aristocratic tradition put a premium on personal excellence and achievement, though in time standards of excellence changed and became less exclusive. Legalism, which in the past doubtless served to protect established interests, stressed regularity and objectivity in social relations and therefore gradually came to protect the individual. The democratic element, stimulated through universal suffrage, not only diluted the aristocratic component but infused liberal democracy with a strong concern for social welfare.

These components have combined in a loose and occasionally uneasy manner, and from time to time they have conflicted and clashed. In American history such clashes have been violent, though on the whole rather sporadic. The Civil War was the major exception, and its outcome effectively and rapidly destroyed the aristocratic element in American tradition, whereas the decline of European aristocracy was slow. The industrial revolution produced its own strains and violence, but the rapid pace of growth as well as the availability of European capital and of foreign markets eased the growing pains even as it enlarged and then consolidated the democratic component. The resulting social wealth and democratic freedom have made America the symbol of a new form of social organization, all the more attractive because its spectacular successes obscured its social blemishes.

This phase is coming to an end. The social blinders that have made America unaware of its shortcomings have been ripped off, and the painful awareness of American society's lingering inadequacy has been rendered more acute by the intensity and pace of change. In a word, America is undergoing a new revolution, whose distinguishing feature is that it simultaneously maximizes America's potential as it unmasks its obsolescence.

1. The Third American Revolution

It is easy to pinpoint the French and the Mexican revolutions, or the Bolshevik, the Chinese, and the Cuban revolutions. It is also not difficult to identify the first American revolution. From a colony that revolution created a nation; implicit though strongly felt beliefs gave birth to a Declaration of Independence and a Constitution, both of which articulated novel principles of political and social order.

Historical definition becomes more complex when dealing with the second American revolution. Precisely when did it happen and what did it do? Though that revolution cannot be pinpointed with the same accuracy as the first, it is a fact that an essentially rural, partially aristocratic, and even slave-owning society with a limited representative political system was transformed into an urban-industrial nation* whose relative legal-political-social equality extended—at least in form—to almost 90 per cent of its people and whose public ethos was dominated largely by widespread acceptance of social welfare, effected through governmental intervention. Thus, it too was a real revolution, though not as contained in time as the first. It took the Civil War, the industrialization of the country, the massive influx of immigrants, and, finally, the New Deal to transform American society. To call it a revolution is admittedly to stretch the definition of revolution, but there is no doubt that both the institutions and the values of the United States were thereby profoundly altered in a little over a century.

The third American revolution is even harder to define, for we are now in the middle of it and thus cannot be certain of its outcome. In one respect, however, it is easier to identify than the second, for its impact and its effect are more concentrated in time. The third revolution began gathering momentum after World War II, with the massive entrance into colleges of ex-GIs; with the concomitant explosion in higher learning and the growing acceptance of the social primacy of education; with the union of national power and modern science crowned by the harnessing of nuclear energy and the federal government emerging as a major sponsor of scientific investigation; with the sudden birth of rapid continental communications, ranging from the world's most modern and developed highway system, through rapid air passenger transport, to a uniquely effective instant transcontinental telephone

---

* In 1800 the rural population of the United States accounted for about 94 per cent of the total; in 1850, for approximately 85 per cent; in 1900, 60 per cent; in 1950, 35 per cent. It is estimated that by the year 2000 the rural population will be approximately 50 million out of a total of 300 million, or 17 per cent. In 1969, 73 per cent of all Americans lived on one per cent of the land (*Time*, January 24, 1969, pp. 18, 30–33).

system, and finally to a nation-wide television intimacy; with the transformation in managerial techniques wrought by the appearance of computers and other electronic devices that conquer complexity, distance, and even the diffusion of authority; and with the fading of industry as the most important source of employment for most Americans. Prompted by technology and particularly electronics, the third revolution is changing the basic institutions and values of American society and, as was also the case with the preceding revolutions, it is encountering resistance, stimulating violence, causing anxiety, and stirring hope.

In the process, it is creating three Americas in one. There is the emerging new America symbolized by the new complexes of learning, research, and development that link institutions of higher learning with society and create unprecedented opportunities for innovation and experimentation, in addition to sparking increased interest in the fine arts and culture, as is evidenced by new museums and art centers. Technetronic America is in the electronics laboratories and centers of learning along Route 128 surrounding Boston,[2] it is in the academic-scientific conglomerates around Los Angeles and San Francisco; and it is in the new frontier industries. The suburban middle class increasingly gravitates toward this America, though frequently resenting its scientism and nostalgically yearning for more community and stability.

Industrial America—the second America—is in the established factories and steel mills of Detroit and Pittsburgh, whose skilled blue-collar workers are gradually forgetting the traumas of the Great Depression and beginning to enjoy both security and leisure but are fearful lest their new social position be threatened from below. For this second America lives alongside the decaying slums of the industrial big cities, increasingly populated by a racial minority that is more difficult to absorb because the society was late in drawing it into the industrial age.

Finally, there is the original, the first America, the pre-industrial America of sharecroppers and migrant workers from the Mississippi delta and of obsolescent miners from Appalachia, whose income has fallen behind the American average. In this America access to education is considerably less than elsewhere in the nation, and racial discrimination is overt.[3] This America is seeking to enter both the industrial and the post-industrial ages, and to do so it must obtain the assistance of the new America, whose values and concepts it often mistrusts and rarely shares.

The new America is only now taking shape. "Today, not only does a child face a radical rupture with the past, but he must be trained for an unknown future. And this task confronts the entire society as well." [4] The current transformation also poses profound philosophical issues concerning the very essence of social existence, since it is largely derived from an unprecedented expansion of scientific power over both man's environment and man himself.* Studies of change[5] cumulatively reinforce the picture of a society undergoing a far-reaching, technologically induced revolution.

The Pace and Thrust of Progress

The facts reflecting change in America are familiar and therefore need not be related in detail. There is, first of all, the massive expansion in the sector of society concerned with science and knowledge. This means a significant growth—more rapid than that in the other sectors—in the number of scientists, college students, and, of course, the institutions that nurture them.† As a

---

* The discussion in the first section of Part I of this book is particularly relevant to understanding contemporary America, since it deals with the basic differences between an industrial and a technetronic society.

† The scale of that change can be illustrated by a few figures. College enrollments increased by 45 per cent in the years 1964–1969. In 1965 more than 50 per cent of all adults were high-school graduates; in 1900 the corresponding figure was only one per cent! (For background data, see A. J. Marrow, D. G. Bowers, S. E. Seashore, *Management by Participation*, New York, 1967.) The number of teachers increased from about 1.3 million in 1954 to about 2.1 million a decade later; the number of engineers grew from about half a million to almost a million. An OECD study of American science estimates that between 1963 and 1970 the scientific population of the United States will have grown from 2.7 million to 4 million, with doctorates

result, the university has emerged as the creative core of the massive learning-communications complex, the source of much domestic and international strategic innovation. In social prestige and influence, the university is displacing the equivalent institutions of the more traditional America: the church and big business.

The emphasis on science and learning goes hand in hand with the rationalization of techniques and the introduction of new teaching, managerial, computing, and communications devices, which are altering established practices and changing the methods used to store and retrieve accumulated knowledge. A national information grid that will integrate existing electronic data banks is already being developed [6] to pool the nation's accumulated knowledge. Increasingly swamped libraries may soon find relief by shifting to the ultramicrofiche technique, pioneered by NASA, by which a two-thousand-page book can be reduced to a transparency smaller than the average book page; this will make it feasible for every small college to possess a library inferior to none.[7] Though American educational theorists disagree about the degree to which the educational systems can adapt the new techniques, their debates reveal the extent to which technical assimilation rather than philosophical issues dominates their thinking.[8]

Contemporary business puts a similar premium on knowledge and the rapid adaptation of new techniques. This requires the pooling of resources, and collective organizational efforts, the frequent and systematic retraining of top personnel, and a close tie with the centers of knowledge. Linear programming, a systems approach to problems, coordinated teamwork, and a highly so-

---

in science increasing from 96,000 to 153,000 and those in engineering from 10,000 to 17,000. In 1869–1870, roughly at the beginning of America's industrial revolution, the number of all degrees awarded by institutions of higher learning was just under 10,000; in 1889–1890 it was 17,000; in 1939–1940, 216,000; a decade later it was 497,000; and in 1963–1964, 614,000. In the past twenty years investments in research and development have increased fifteenfold, expenditures in education sixfold, while the GNP has tripled (see Daniel Bell, "The Measurement of Knowledge and Technology," pp. 201, 206, 228; and *Reviews of National Science Policy: United States*, OECD, pp. 45, 54).

phisticated attitude toward human relations and labor psychology are becoming the dominant features of managerial processes. According to Lawrence Appley, chairman of the American Management Association, the number of managers involved in professional management societies and working with management consultants has risen from ten thousand in 1948 to over six hundred thousand in 1962.[9] Operationally, business less and less resembles a political hierarchy or a personal fiefdom; it is increasingly similar to a systematic scientific undertaking that not only produces what is known but systematically seeks to explore what is to come.*

In summarizing the social transformation wrought by technology, Daniel Bell listed five key areas of change: "(1) By producing more goods at less cost, technology has been the chief engine of raising the living standards of the world. . . . (2)

---

* "The new style of dealing with the future has no accepted, inclusive name, but the names of its more highly developed techniques have become familiar in the last ten years to most businessmen, government officials, military officers, scientists, and technicians. The techniques themselves, which are apt to be called 'systems analysis' or 'systems planning,' are now widely used both with and without the help of computers. 'Cost-benefit' or 'cost-effectiveness' analysis is a major ingredient of the new techniques; this involves ways of arraying ends and means so that decision makers have clearer ideas of the choices open to them and better ways of measuring results against both expectations and objectives.

"Among characteristics of the new pattern are these: (1) A more open and deliberate attention to the selection of ends toward which planned action is directed, and an effort to improve planning by sharpening the definition of ends. (2) A more systematic advance comparison of means by criteria derived from the ends selected. (3) A more candid and effective assessment of results, usually including a system of keeping track of progress toward interim goals. Along with this goes a 'market-like' sensitivity to changing values and evolving ends. (4) An effort, often intellectually strenuous, to mobilize science and other specialized knowledge into a flexible framework of information and decision so that specific responsibilities can be assigned to the points of greatest competence. (5) An emphasis on information, prediction, and persuasion, rather than on coercive or authoritarian power, as the main agents of coordinating the separate elements of an effort. (6) An increased capability of predicting the combined effect of several lines of simultaneous action on one another; this can modify policy so as to reduce unwanted consequences or it can generate other *lines* of action to correct or compensate for such predicted consequences" (Max Ways, "The Road to 1977," *Fortune*, January 1967, pp. 94–95).

Technology has created a new class, hitherto unknown in society, of the engineer and the technician. . . . (3) Technology has created a new definition of rationality, a new mode of thought, which emphasizes functional relations and the quantitative. . . . (4) The revolutions in transportation and communication, as a consequence of technology, have created new economic interdependencies and new social interactions. . . . (5) Esthetic perceptions, particularly of space and time, have been radically altered." [10]

To these should be added the new sense of self-awareness induced by society's increasing ability to see itself in the mirror provided by television, buttressed by increased reliance on statistical analysis,* and intensified by a systematic preoccupation with managing not only the present but the future. Moreover, for perhaps the first time in its history American society is beginning to acquire a national outlook on such matters as race and poverty; hence, inadequacies in one sector are no longer a matter of relative indifference to another region or class or minority. All this prompts a more deliberate, less haphazard effort to identify social inadequacies, and it thereby links moral outrage at social injustice with a more operational preoccupation with improving over-all social performance. Man's inhumanity to man was certainly easier to accept in a setting in which human relations were distant, class interests were compartmentalized, and social conscience was rarely aroused by visible injustice.

The consequence is not only undeniably rapid progress in many areas and increased social awareness of existing failings, but also the intensification of old problems and the posing of new challenges. The economic base that determines the average American's material lot has expanded in recent years at a pace that makes the American per-capita GNP increase at a rate greater than that enjoyed either by other advanced societies or by those

---

* It is useful to recall that a century ago a citizen would rarely, if ever, see the charts, graphs, and tables that a contemporary American reads almost daily in his press and that are a standard feature of any report or study.

that are becoming so.[11] This change has been accompanied in the years 1959–1967 by significant, and even accelerating, shifts in income distribution and in patterns of employment (see Tables 11 and 12). These shifts indicate the strengthening of the middle levels of American society, a development not only symptomatic of greater social egalitarianism but also significantly relevant to the political aspects of the current American transition (on which

TABLE 11. CHANGES IN INCOME DISTRIBUTION AND IN EMPLOYMENT

Percentage of Families with Income of:	1959	1963	1959–1963 Change	1967	1963–1967 Change
Over $15,000	3.1	5.4	+2.3	12.2	+6.8
$5000–$15,000	52.3	58.3	+6.0	62.7	+4.4
Under $5000	44.6	36.2	−8.4	25.1	−11.1

Based on "Consumer Income," *Current Population Reports,* Department of Commerce, August 5, 1968, pp. 2–7. The data in this table are based on income only, prior to deductions for taxes. However, the report states, "Even after allowance for changes in consumer prices, family income has risen by 3½ to 4 percent in each of the last 4 years" (p. 1).

TABLE 12. CHANGES IN EMPLOYMENT IN PERCENTAGES

	White-Collar	Blue-Collar	Service	Farm
1958	42.6	37.1	11.9	8.5
1967	46.0	36.7	12.5	4.8

Source: *Manpower Report of the President,* Department of Labor, Washington, D.C., April 1968, p. 232.

more later). In addition to these over-all percentages, note should be taken of the fact that as of the end of the 1960s Americans owned close to 70 million automobiles, that 95 per cent of American households had at least one television set and 25 per cent had at least two, and that over 60 per cent of American families owned their own homes.[12] Despite the indisputable persistence of poverty in the United States, American society is achieving an unprecedented affluence that touches all classes.

That poverty besets millions of Americans has been amply documented in recent years, and the majority's indifference to this problem has been at least somewhat shaken. The poverty line was initially defined, by arbitrary and very broad approximation, as income less than $3000 per annum for a family of four, or $1500 for an individual. There is no doubt that such a level involves acute hardship for most, and even malnutrition for many, but even more debilitating is the psychological sense of deprivation in relationship to the society's over-all wealth.* Nonetheless, here too the pace of economic growth, combined with more deliberate efforts, has brought progress: from 1961 to 1969 the group below the poverty line—as defined by the Social Security Administration and taking into account the rise in prices—dropped from 22 per cent to 13 per cent of the population.[13] Moreover, according to the Council of Economic Advisors' Report of early 1969, if 1961–1968 rates in reducing the number of poor persons are continued, "poverty" will be entirely eliminated in ten years; if the 1968 rates are continued, it will disappear in a little over five years at a cost of $9.7 billion annually (one per cent of the GNP and 5 per cent of the federal budget).

Poverty has plagued particularly, but not exclusively, the black Americans. In 1966 their nation-wide median income was only 58 per cent of the median income of whites; by 1968 this had grown to 60 per cent.[14] Blacks are the principal victims of poor housing, poor schooling, and unemployment. The urban slums, inhabited by a much greater percentage of blacks than whites (and blacks in the United States today are more highly urbanized than whites), impose living conditions reminiscent of the worst phases of industrialization—and all the more intolerable because they are no longer a part of economic growth but a vestigial reminder of an age which America is increasingly leaving behind.

Nevertheless, here too economic growth and the appearance of

---

* It is this psychological dimension that some foreign commentators neglect when they comment, with a touch of envy, on the United States' definition of poverty. For example, ". . . America draws its poverty line at levels that would be considered generous abroad. Amid all the sad statistics poured forth about the ghettos, it is worth remembering that in 1967 some 88 per cent of all black American families had a television set" ("The Neurotic Trillionaire," *The Economist*, special issue, May 10, 1969, p. 51).

new social values make accelerating progress visible. The obvious breakthroughs have been on the legal level of civil rights, especially in education and housing, but they have also taken place on the economic level. In 1961, 56 per cent of American blacks were classified as poor, but by 1969 the figure had dropped to 33 per cent; in 1956, only 9 per cent of Negro families had incomes of more than $7000, but by 1968 this had grown to 28 per cent, and the median income of a black family was $5360.[15] Between 1960 and 1966 the number of blacks in professional, technical, and managerial jobs doubled, and substandard housing occupied by blacks dropped from 40 per cent in 1960 to 24 per cent in 1968. According to a Gallup poll, between 1963 and 1969 the number of blacks expressing satisfaction with their jobs increased from 54 per cent to 76 per cent, and the number of those blacks satisfied with their housing rose from 43 per cent to 50 per cent.[16]

Extensive change is also taking place in America's over-all cultural life. Increased education, greater leisure, and perhaps an unconscious reaction to the danger that technology could breed cultural emptiness have led to a heightened interest in music, drama, and the visual arts. This has not only involved a spurt in the construction of art centers and renewed life for American museums but has also led to the extensive adoption of new techniques—such as video tape or stereophonic sound—to make easily available in the home cultural pleasures that previously required a great expenditure of time and money. In addition, closed-circuit television has opened up new opportunities for both local and even home-based university- or museum-sponsored adult education. Culture and education have therefore ceased to be aristocratic privileges; they have increasingly become an option available to more and more Americans—as well as a sometimes ostentatious symbol of new opulence.

Economic progress and elevated social expectations have precipitated an influx into colleges and universities of large numbers of young people from families with no previous background of higher education. Of the some 4.3 million family-supported college students in 1966, 63 per cent came from homes in which the head of the family had never completed a single year in college. More striking still is the fact that 30 per cent, or almost one-half of the above 63 per cent, came from homes in which the head of the family had not had even four years of high school.[17] During 1963–1969 the number of male blacks who had completed a high-school education increased from 36 to 60 per cent; the number of those who had obtained college degrees almost doubled in just two years, from 4 per cent in 1963 to 7.5 per cent in 1965.[18] As of the late 1960s, 83 per cent of sixteen- to seventeen-year-old black Americans were still in school, and the proportion going to college was higher than that for the same age bracket in Western Europe.[19]

To the extent that higher education has become the most important means of social advancement in America, the above figures are evidence of potentially significant upward movement.* Thus, as of 1969 some 37 per cent of all college students came from blue-collar, service, or farm families.[20] Educational background and intellectual-scientific achievement are increasingly becoming the measure of social worth. This development is of particular importance to race relations. Neither the huckster's short cut nor the Horatio Alger story offers much incentive or promise to millions of young blacks, but mass education, combined with the economy's expanded needs, does provide a wide channel for satisfying individual ambitions on a socially significant scale. Education could therefore serve as the point of departure for attaining a socially egalitarian and politically democratic multi-racial society. The attainment of such a society would be a historic victory

---

* One related and intriguing aspect of this development is the increasing entrance into the country's political elite of previously nonparticipating ethnic and racial groups. Jews, Negroes, Italians, and, to a lesser extent, Poles and Greeks, have been making an appearance in the national government on levels and on a scale previously rarely attained by non-"WASPS." While precise statistics are not available, these new "elites"—whose Americanism is sometimes as intense as it is new—may have had something to do with the reappearance of the activist, nationalist, dynamic orientation noted by David Riesman in his "Some Questions about the Study of American National Character in the Twentieth Century," *Annals of the American Academy of Political and Social Science*, March 1967, especially p. 47.

for mankind, for the brutal fact is that race relations are most vulnerable to the irrational forces of human motivation: the visual, instinctive, exclusivistic selection that operates almost automatically on the racial front.

The Uncertainty of Progress

But it must immediately be added that before America fully becomes such a society—indeed, in order for it to become such a society—the unassimilated legacy of industrial America as well as the unusual problems inherent in the American transition to a technetronic society must first be surmounted. The initially reluctant but increasingly widespread social recognition of the fact that the past has still to be settled with even while the new is being harnessed has created an inflammable situation that has already taken its toll and could grow worse.

An economic recession thwarting aroused hopes would have especially calamitous consequences for the stability of the American social order. Much clearly depends on the expanding economy's capacity to absorb and ameliorate existing tensions. Economic growth at a relatively stable and high rate of approximately three and a half per cent per annum, allowing for annual variations, seems to be the *sine qua non* for the continued evolution of American society toward a situation in which liberty and equality will buttress but not vitiate one another. This is particularly true of poverty and race relations, in which even social good will will be powerless to accomplish much in the event of a significant economic slowdown. The first victims of a recession will be the poor and the blacks, who always absorb a disproportionate amount of the suffering, owing to economic malfunction.*

Unfortunately, it is not even certain that the relatively strong pace of economic growth in the 1960s will suffice to liquidate the

* The 3.2 per cent unemployment figure at the end of 1968 meant that 21.5 per cent of all black teen-agers were unemployed (for whites the corresponding figure was 11.6 per cent); and that 3.4 per cent of black men were without jobs (for whites the figure was 1.6 per cent).

unfinished business of America's industrialization, both in absolute terms or relative to the growth of society at large.* Indeed, what amounts to the coexistence of two rather separate American economies—the lagging and even decaying industrial economy (increasingly exposed to more effective foreign competition, highly vulnerable to cyclical swings, and employing the poorer and less skilled workers) and the expanding technetronic economy (based on aerospace and other frontier industries and employing the better-trained, better-educated, and better-paid workers)—has made the assimilation and upgrading of the poorer segments of American society more difficult.

This gap is complicating the efforts to create a racial harmony based on both liberty and equality. The Negro should have been integrated into American society *during* the American industrial revolution. Unfortunately, that revolution came before America, if not the Negro, was ready for full integration. If the black American had represented only an economic legacy of the pre-industrial age, perhaps he could have been more effectively integrated into the industrial age. But racial prejudice kept him from acquiring the necessary skills. The problem is cumulative, and today the more advanced American urban-industrial regions are finding it difficult to integrate blacks—both a racial minority and America's only feudal legacy—precisely because these regions are moving into a new and more complex phase that requires more developed social skills. Paradoxically, it can be argued that the South today

---

* With a 4 per cent growth in GNP (in constant dollars, which is higher than the average growth since 1960), there are likely to be close to 17 million in poor households in 1974 compared to 26 million in 1967. Of these, more than 4 million will be families headed by non-aged working males compared to 10 million in 1967" (Department of Health, Education, and Welfare, *Toward a Social Report,* Washington, D.C., p. 47).

"In 1947 the poorest 20 per cent of the population received 5 per cent of the income, and it held this same 5 per cent share in 1964. . . . The second lowest fifth got 12 per cent in 1947 and 12 per cent in 1964. In short, 40 per cent of the American people were held to a 17 per cent share of the income throughout the entire postwar period. The 5 per cent at the top got about the same proportion as that 40 per cent" (Michael Harrington, *Toward a Democratic Left,* New York, 1968, p. 26).

stands a better long-range chance of fully integrating the blacks: American consciousness is changing, the black has awakened, and the American South is beginning to move into the industrial age. It might, if it moves rapidly enough, take the black along with it.[21]

The larger question still remains: Will the pace of development be rapid enough to meet the challenge posed by the simultaneous and mutually reinforcing processes set in action by the black American's awakening and by his disillusionment with the American system? Numerous public-opinion polls record the black's growing conviction that he has no choice but to opt out of the political system, to rely on exclusiveness, even on violence, as the basic means of progress.[22] This mood was absent from the experience of white immigrant groups, which on the whole aspired to enter the American community as rapidly as possible. In contrast, many blacks see in exclusiveness and in building a separate community the only way to the future—a future that to them no longer necessarily implies an eventual merger with the larger American society.

Nor is it certain that the entrance of large numbers of blacks into integrated universities will help to alleviate racial tensions. Though this development is necessary to promote full-scale participation of the black in the United States, several short-term factors point to an increase in racial tensions as a result of the increased educational opportunities for blacks. First of all, it is uncertain that black graduates will in fact obtain the positions they will feel entitled to;* secondly, this difficulty is likely to be magnified by the predisposition of some blacks to insist on separate "black studies" programs, not subject to prevailing academic standards, which will inevitably produce in growing numbers the American equivalent of the frustrated and badly educated pseudo-intelligentsia of the global ghettos; finally, as the American black

---

* New York City statistics indicate, for example, that white dropouts have better employment opportunities than black high-school graduates (*The Negro Almanac,* New York, 1967, chart on p. 292).

gains self-confidence and as his social position improves, he may temporarily be less responsive to the argument that his progress depends on cooperation with whites, and his sharpened awareness of social injustice is likely to be expressed in a more radical political posture that is indifferent to white sensitivities.

The problem of race relations gives added urgency to the broader question of the place of violence in American society. White society may continue to proclaim that "violence cannot build a better society," but the black will continue to see his inferior social condition as the basic reality. To the extent that violence precipitates bursts of reform designed by the white community to redress injustices, the argument that violence is necessary to black progress becomes stronger and stronger. On the other hand, this reliance on violence tends to blur the distinction, important to the functioning of any society, between political and criminal violence (was Eldridge Cleaver a political or a criminal fugitive?), and it prompts both legally formalized massive repressions by society at large and rationalizations of violence by the more liberal and educated segments; either result destroys society's capacity for discriminating between the necessity for order and the imperative of change.

A society's capacity for making such judgments is bound to be undermined by the degree to which it becomes psychologically inured to living with violence and to accepting violence as a means for solving its problems. That America's social history, as well as its political history, has been violent is not disputed. That America has been a more violent society than others is debatable.* But the

---

* The National Commission on the Causes and Prevention of Violence, in its report "Violence in America: Historical and Comparative Perspectives" (New York, 1969), states: "Despite its frequency, civil strife in the United States has taken much less destructive forms than in many non-Western and some Western countries. . . . The nation has experienced no internal wars since the Civil War and almost none of the chronic revolutionary conspiracy and terrorism that plagued dozens of other nations. . . .

"Although about two hundred and twenty Americans died in violent civil strife in the 5 years before mid-1968, the rate of 1.1 per million population was infinitesimal compared with the average of all nations of 238 deaths per

question of violence goes beyond statistics or even race relations; it involves the basic pattern of a nation's culture* and the way in which a society solves its problems.

Today the problems of poverty or of race relations demand adept psychological sensitivity to nuances and restraint in balancing many complex and competing individual and group rights. This is a point which many impatient reformers overlook. The assimilation of any ethnically or racially distinctive group into the majority culture is possible only in a context of stable institutions and values expressed in orderly procedures. It is possible to maintain majority domination by violence or to reverse the power relations between races by violent revolution, but to create harmonious race relations a society must be conditioned to accept change peacefully and to resolve social issues nonviolently.† But this

---

million, and less than the European average of 2.4 per million" (pp. 799–800).

On the other hand, a later report by the same commission points out that "a comparison of reported violent crime rates in this country with those in other modern, stable nations shows the United States rape rate clear leader. Our homicide rate is more than twice that of our closest competitor, Finland, and from 4 to 12 times higher than the rates in a dozen other advanced countries, including Japan, Canada, England and Norway" (as cited by *The New York Times,* November 24, 1969).

* Though it may not be more violent than other societies, contemporary America is psychologically permeated by violence. This is not only—and not even largely—because of the dramatic assassinations of the 1960s. It is above all attributable to American television, almost entirely controlled by three profit-oriented corporations and only loosely checked by the national government. In 1969 the University of Pennsylvania School of Communications reported in the research study prepared for the National Commission on the Causes and Prevention of Violence that in two weeks of viewing the three major networks from 4:00 to 10:00 P.M. it had counted 790 persons killed or injured in television dramas (not news reports), and that it had found 15 acts of violence for every hour of television viewing (as reported in *The New York Times,* July 6, 1969). To this dubious record should be added sensation-seeking "documentaries" such as NBC's "exclusive interview," prominently advertised in advance, with Sirhan Sirhan, Robert Kennedy's convicted assassin, filmed (according to NBC's advertisements) "the day after Sirhan was formally sentenced to die."

For a perceptive discussion of the television magnates' attitude toward their educational-social responsibilities, see Harrington, *Toward a Democratic Left,* pp. 19–20.

† This is not to deny that violence did play a constructive social role at

automatically tends to strengthen the forces that oppose change, whether these forces represent entrenched interests or, more generally, ingrained social or racial attitudes. A social setting in which a large part of the population comes to identify violence with change and to equate order with the absence of change is a setting in which an escalation of conflict becomes unavoidable.

The Futility of Politics

The responsiveness of political institutions to the need for change is of great import to America's future. Some citizens see the present American system as incapable not only of promoting the needed social changes but even of reacting to pressure on behalf of such changes. In such a setting, procedures and institutions that in times of stability are vaunted for their deliberateness become in times of more rapid change examples of delay, inefficiency, and even fundamental injustice.*

---

different stages of history. In overthrowing tyranny or in defying exploitation, violence has often acted as history's scalpel. The exaltation of historical violence should not, however, be carried too far. Barrington Moore, in his *Social Origins of Dictatorship and Democracy* (Boston, 1966), suggests that the physical cost of revolutionary regimes should not be held against them, for the absence of a revolution might have been even more costly. He does not, however, examine the possibility that the reforms undertaken by revolutionary regimes, often with monstrous brutality, might have been less physically costly if alternative schemes of reform successfully undertaken by other nations had been followed. Indeed, it can be argued that much of the violence undertaken by revolutionary regimes was in fact dysfunctional to the positive tasks they had set themselves. The real comparison, therefore, should be between the physical costs of alternative ways of changing society rather than between the cost of not changing it and the cost of changing it by very violent means.

Historical judgments aside, it is noteworthy that modern man is still educated in terms that promote aggressive feelings. In the West, films and television emphasize violence, and the teaching of history stresses wars, victories, defeats, and conflict between "good" and "bad" nations. These aggressive instincts are also expressed by children's games as well as by adult forms of entertainment. In communist countries ideology similarly stimulates aggressive feelings and hostility toward "evil" forces, thus continuing the more fundamental dichotomies introduced by the religious tradition.

* American justice is a particularly glaring example. It is as antiquated as it is often absurd. It appears to have benefited neither by the legal reforms

The government as an expression of the national will increasingly tends to be seen as unable to direct and coordinate national change effectively. It appears neither to articulate national goals nor to develop a sense of national direction. This feeling of uncertainty about national purpose is also magnified by the fading of the established political elite that has guided the nation since World War II. Primarily composed of men coming from the eastern seaboard and connected with legal, corporate, and high financial circles, the political elite provided a sense of continuity within the framework of a pragmatic liberal consensus on the nature and character of modern industrial society. The relative stability of the late 1940s and the 1950s reflected that consensus. Lately this elite has come under increasing challenge both from the newer, geographically more dispersed economic interests associated with the new scientific-defense and frontier industries, and from the more ideologically inclined intellectual forces, which are becoming more influential.

The breakup of the postwar elite highlights the dichotomy

---

carried out decades ago in Europe, nor even by the English pattern of relatively swift justice. Its extraordinarily cumbersome procedures, dominated by theatrical stratagems and showmanship and involving lengthy and complex appeals, lead to delays and even occasionally to results that defy the most elementary concepts of justice. The trial of Martin Luther King's killer —during which period Ray's lawyers competed in selling his memoirs—was a travesty; Sirhan Sirhan's protracted show in Los Angeles was hardly dictated by the needs of abstract justice; highly paid "exclusives" by the killers of Sharon Tate were a disgrace. Soviet secret trials are certainly deplorable, but are American judicial circuses really needed to protect the defendant and render fair judgment?

At the same time, the intermeshing of private and public interests, exemplified by the outside economic interests of congressmen and senators, reinforces many Americans' inclination to dismiss the political process as dominated by inherently conservative, socially unresponsive, profit-oriented interests. For example, 8 members of the House Commerce Committee have financial interests in railroads, airlines, radio stations, and moving companies, all of which come under their legislative purview; 90 members of the House, including 12 on the Banking Committee, have interests in banks, savings and loan associations, or bank holding companies; 77 members, including 19 on the Judiciary Committee, maintain private law practices; 44 members have interests in oil or gas companies, and so on. (*The New York Times*, May 11, 1969).

between the qualities necessary to gain political power in American democracy and those necessary to exercise effective leadership of that democracy. The courtship of the press and the mass media is a necessary concomitant of courting the masses, since the masses are influenced not only by direct appeal but also through the intermediary of an "image," which is in part built up by the media themselves. The desirability of this image puts a premium on advocating the immediately popular and the fashionable rather than on formulating broader objectives by focusing attention on basic philosophical questions concerning the meaning of a modern society. Since social consensus has been fragmented by the pace of change and society's value structure has itself become highly tactical, the larger strategic questions tend to be obscured.

To make matters worse, the American institutional framework has not kept up with the pace of societal change. Given the country's enormous transformation through industrial growth and communications mobility, its federal arrangements have become increasingly devoid of economic or geographic substance. These arrangements are kept alive by local traditional sentiment and vested interests, rather than by their actual functional utility. The price of this has primarily been paid by the new big cities, for whose growth the constitutional structure made little allowance and which have consequently been deprived of the means of coping with their dilemmas.

The national government, particularly because of the two-party system, has also found it difficult to develop the needed mechanisms for openly channeling the new major competitive forces on the political scene, and it still operates as if the political "game" revolved around the two relatively loose alliances of interest groups that largely reflected the industrial-rural dilemmas of the earlier age. In general, that arrangement had been effective in expressing, as well as moderating, the popular will and in striking a balance between continuity and change. Nonetheless, it is worth noting that in past times of stress and sharper choices the two-party system occasionally broke up, though only temporarily. It would appear that the breakup of the two-party system is again under way, precisely because the dilemmas of the country have become intensified by the extraordinary pace of change and by the widening spectrum of often incompatible choices it stimulates.

As a result, the industrial-rural or liberal-conservative framework no longer adequately encompasses existing competitive political forces: the agrarian–conservative–anti-communist and largely congressionally based bastion; the new industrial-military-scientific conglomerates that uneasily collaborate with the former on political-ideological grounds but are in conflict with it in terms of economic thrust; and the emerging, very loose, welfare–civil rights–intellectual coalition that shares some of the second's socio-economic dynamics but is in basic conflict with both the first and the second in the matter of priorities. The two latter forces have operated largely outside of direct participation in the legislative process of the country, and so reflect the degree to which the representative aspects of American democracy have failed to keep up with social change.*

Several political sub-Americas thus coexist uneasily, and though America is beginning to think of itself as an entity, each sub-America tends to project onto the whole its own perception of American reality. The relationship between these sub-Americas is therefore tense; each tends to seek its own political expression rather than to merge in the larger whole. In the 1968 presidential contest, Robert Kennedy personified the politics of anxiety, pas-

---

* The heavy representation of small-town lawyers is symptomatic of this condition. In contrast, the first National Assembly of France's Fifth Republic contained 67 professors and teachers, 48 medical men, 45 high professional civil servants, 34 lawyers, 32 workers, 27 businessmen, 25 scientists and engineers, 20 journalists, and so on. It is evident that from a representative standpoint the French Assembly more accurately reflected the character of a relatively modern society. The benefits of greater scientific competence in society's representative bodies are beginning to be recognized in Britain: "The House of Commons would benefit enormously by having, say, 50 engineers who could ensure that parliamentary discussions were more closely geared to the technical realities of the day," Anthony Wedgwood Benn, Minister of Technology, wrote in his weekly magazine *Engineering News* (quoted by the Associated Press, August 21, 1965).

sionately articulating the grievances of the underprivileged even though he shared the fears and uncertainties of established Americans who sensed and desired major change but did not quite know what that change ought to be;[23] Eugene McCarthy was the petulant spokesman of the politics of nostalgia, lackadaisically promising to take down the fences around the White House lawn, responding to the suburbanites' desire for a pastoral life and for social justice—provided the latter is implemented at a distance from them; Hubert Humphrey preached the politics of compromise between classes and races, and his passion evoked the class-conflict atmosphere of the New Deal; George Wallace expressed the politics of resentment, speaking for those Americans who felt that much of the social and racial progress was being promoted at their expense by Americans who were more comfortably established; Richard Nixon practiced the politics of caution, and he won because significant numbers of Americans from the several sub-Americas became fearful that "their" America was endangered and were uncertain as to what the new America might hold in store for them.

This inclination to stress personal interests reflected the impotence felt by some constituencies concerning the shaping of national policy. Many citizens sensed change but felt that they had little control over it. In a time of relative continuity, presidential and congressional elections served as an acceptable and personally satisfying method of expressing a highly generalized political preference. In a time of discontinuity and increasingly fragmented consensus,[24] national election campaigns became a less adequate form for expressing the popular will. The presidential election, especially given the importance television confers on personal looks and style, has for many become a national pageant rather than an exercise of basic choices meant to influence the nation's direction. These choices are instead made incrementally by administrative fiat or in congressional committees; since both these processes are largely removed from public view, they are more responsive to influences from the various special interests—with which administrators or congressmen are often in close relationship—than they are to the voters.

Related to this situation is the oft-noted remoteness, complexity, and impersonality of both public and private institutions. As the old traditional affiliations of the agrarian society crumbled, the industrial age produced its equivalents through unions and professional societies. But unions are no longer vital institutions,[25] and the "atomization" of modern life accentuates the citizens' feelings of impotence. Social institutions appear to provide neither an outlet for individual idealism nor a rapid response to collective demands. Moreover, the state or a big private organization inescapably schematizes social dilemmas in order to cope with their complexities; though this schematization permits a large-scale response, it frequently conflicts with the individually felt dimensions of the same problem and therefore limits the individual's freedom even as it fails to perceive the best solution to his problems. Thus, the more the state tries to help, the more it tends to reinforce the individual's feeling of impotence.

The result is paradoxical: the situation described stimulates a more intense public interest in politics while increasing the sense of the futility of politics; it fragments national consensus while prompting louder appeals for a sense of common national direction; finally, it simultaneously confronts the individual with the twin dangers of fragmentation and of excessive control. Indeed, national policy seems to fragment as national government expands.[26] As a result, many Americans feel that their freedom is contracting. This feeling seems to be connected with their loss of purpose, since freedom implies choice of action, and action requires an awareness of goals. If America's present transition to the technetronic age does not result in personally satisfying achievements, the next phase could be one of sullen withdrawal from social and political involvement, a flight from social and political responsibility through inner retreat and outward conservatism.

In the meantime, the scientific and technological revolution, itself so basically cerebral in character, still tends to affect American society in a largely unplanned fashion that is determined by decisions and impulses reflecting the values and interests of the earlier America. Intellectual power is mobilized to answer "how?" but not to ask "why?" America consequently risks becoming "a civilization committed to the quest for continually improved means to carelessly examined ends."[27] The political system has still to develop mechanisms and procedures to raise and answer the second question. Matters that fundamentally affect the national way of life, such as the construction of a supersonic aircraft, or that pose an ecological as well as a human threat, such as industrial pollution or radiation from atomic-energy plants, are handled by a decision-making process that inhibits the opportunities for an intelligent expression of the popular will. (According to the National Science Foundation's seventeenth annual report, less than 5 per cent of the more than 200,000 scientists and engineers employed by the federal government in 1967 were concerned with social or psychological disciplines. Moreover, according to the 1963 report of the Council of Economic Advisers, defense, space, and energy research were absorbing approximately two-thirds of the scientists working on the nation's scientific and technological frontiers. In addition, our society devotes relatively limited resources to a systematic concern with social problems, while it devotes enormous resources to economic, technical, and scientific matters. Table 13 tells part of the story.) Even higher education, by not focusing on the underlying questions but by emphasizing techniques, runs the risk of becoming miseducation: of creating large numbers of "educated" people who think they know the answers, but who in fact do not even know the truly important questions.[28]

The third American revolution highlights the sharp contrast between our technical success and our social failure, and it raises basic questions concerning the control and direction of the thrust of technological innovation. How are choices made? Why are they made? By whom are they made? What values are involved in these choices, and how can they be crystallized so that a coherent policy

TABLE 13. ANNUAL BUDGET IN MILLIONS OF DOLLARS

Industrial		Physical Health	
General Motors	20,210	Nat'l Cancer Inst.	186
Ford	12,240	Nat'l Heart Assn.	164
Standard Oil (N.J.)	12,190	Nat'l Inst. of Arthritis	141
General Electric	7,180	Nat'l Inst. of Neurology	119
Chrysler	5,650	Nat'l Inst. of Allergy	90
Mobile Oil	5,250	Nat'l Inst. of Child Health	66
Texaco	4,430	American Cancer Society	59
U.S. Steel	4,360	American Heart Assn.	37
I.B.M.	4,250	Nat'l Tuberculosis Assn.	27

Social and Psychological	
National Inst. of Mental Health*	31
Stanford Research Inst.*	18
Menninger Foundation	9.5
Planning Research Corp.*	8
Inst. for Social Research	5.5
American Inst. for Research in Behavioral Sciences	5
Brookings Institution	5
Human Resources Research Office	4.5
Mental Health Research Inst.	2

Source: Thomas Jefferson Research Center, June–July 1969, p. 5.
* Approximate portion of budget allocated to social problems.

can be shaped? These questions increasingly beset all modern societies, but given the extensive social scope of contemporary American science and technology, this challenge is especially important in the United States because it affects—and potentially threatens—the most intimate aspects of American life.

Since it appears true that "this society has chosen to emphasize technological change as its chief mode of creative expression and basis for economic growth," [29] it follows that this society's most imperative task is to define a conceptual framework in which technological change can be given meaningful and humane ends. Unless this is done, there is the real danger that by remaining directionless the third American revolution, so pregnant with possibilities for individual creativity and fulfillment, can become socially destructive.

2. The New Left Reaction

A revolution not only breeds its own children—it repels them. It is understandable that a society which puts a premium on change, which makes knowledge the basic vehicle of innovation, which vastly expands the institutions of advanced learning, which for the first time in history creates a large class of people free throughout their late adolescence and early maturity of the limitations inherent in the burden of self-support, which endows intellectual activity with a high degree of social prestige but no direct political power, should breed rebels who are the products of the very revolution that torments and repels them. The supreme irony of that loose and volatile socio-political phenomenon of contemporary middle-class America named the New Left is that it is itself the creation of the technetronic revolution as well as a reaction against it.

Infantile Ideology

The New Left, a complex and elusive entity made up of a rather fluid combination of individual sympathizers (especially from among the New York City literary establishment and some professorial circles) and a scattering of new organizations, of which Students for a Democratic Society (SDS) has become the best-known, is the political-ideological expression of a more extensive restlessness among American middle-class university youth. As of the late 1960s, membership in the more militant organizations was relatively limited, but in moments of stress (such as confrontations with the authorities) these organizations were quite successful in mobilizing broader support. Moreover, at different times and in response to different issues, the New Left was able to draw on the deep-rooted traditions of American populism, Quaker pacifism, and the pre–World War II largely immigrant-imported socialism and communism. The tension between generations as well as a widespread though passive alienation also prompted expressions of solidarity which occasionally created the impression of youth's massive identification with the goals of the more militant New Left.*

The outer boundaries of the New Left are, therefore, imprecise. At one time or another essentially reformist members of the political establishment, such as Robert Kennedy and Eugene McCarthy, were able to siphon off a great deal of the volatile youthful support that otherwise was attracted by the more extreme tendencies of the New Left. The New Left itself, however, tended to be more militant in its rhetoric, more sectarian in its organization, more intellectually and generationally exclusive than the broader coalition endeavoring to forge the "new politics" in America. The key difference, however, was the New Left's militancy—a militancy derived from the belief that reforms will no longer suffice.

It has often been said that the rather sporadic identification of broad segments of youth with the militant New Left reflected the more intense idealism and social consciousness of the current college generation, impatient with the crass materialism of its society and distressed by the political system's delay in moving against

---

* It should, however, be noted that the number of students participating in the more overt manifestations of militancy and strife was relatively limited. In the period October 1967–May 1969, one-fifth of the eruptions took place on six major campuses: Berkeley, San Francisco State, Columbia, Harvard, University of Wisconsin, and Cornell. Of the nation's 2374 colleges, there were outbreaks on only 211 campuses, and in a total of 474 such confrontations with authority 6158 arrests were made (according to data compiled for the United States Senate and reported in *The Washington Post,* July 2, 1969).

Dues-paying members of the SDS were estimated at about 6000; those vaguely sympathetic to some New Left appeals, at about 700,000; the total number of students, about 7 million (*Fortune,* special issue on youth, January 1969). The number of SDS activists was estimated in early 1969 as ranging between 70,000 and 100,000 (*Guardian,* January 11, 1969).

social injustice. This is doubtless so. The young have been active in the struggle for racial equality; they responded initially with enthusiasm to the call of global service in the ranks of the Peace Corps; they have flocked into the ranks of the many domestic efforts to mount a struggle against urban poverty and ignorance. It is equally true that the established system did not fully tap that idealism. The idealism of the young required a sense of deliberate national effort in order to give it fulfillment, and it was not to the young alone that this effort seemed to be lacking. Cumulatively, the resulting frustrations created an intense alienation, first from the political system and then from the socio-economic system as a whole. Both were denied moral legitimacy, and the combination of frustrated idealism and historical uncertainty created propitious circumstances for appeals based on passion and a desire for a simple dichotomic formula.

Major catalysts for youthful disillusionment with liberal democracy's determination and capacity to cope with either its old or its new problems were provided by the Vietnam war and the white majority's indifference to the black man's quest for equality. Both reinforced the argument that the existing system was preoccupied with self-preservation and not with change, and that federal funds were readily available for remote causes but not for curing America's immediate ills. Both also provided the young with convenient rationalizations for failing to come to grips with the intellectual complexity of our time and for turning their backs on the difficult and inescapably slow task of social renewal.

This same kind of self-serving intellectual rationalization for the more immediately convenient and emotionally gratifying posture of complete negation also plays a part in the broader student malaise, which the more militant New Left has been exploiting. Explanatory theories of student militancy have typically placed major emphasis on the psychological dimension of the crisis of values in contemporary America, on the stifling of the genuine idealism of the activists. For example, Robert Liebert has cogently argued that "it is necessary to understand the lives of the participants [in student militancy] in a 'psycho-historical' context. . . . The result is a sense of the tenuousness of life which is manifested more profoundly in its unconscious aspects. More specifically, it has provided them with a sense of urgency to effect change so that life can go on." [30] Similarly, Kenneth Keniston has stressed that in rejecting the existing society, the student is expressing "a revulsion against the notion of quantity, particularly economic quantity and materialism, and a turn towards concepts of quality. . . . Another goal of the new revolution involves a revolt against uniformity, equalization, standardization and homogenization. . . ." [31]

Student participants have also tended to stress the psychological dimension. Mark Gerzon's *The Whole World Is Watching,* a sympathetic account by a young Harvard undergraduate, put primary stress on the psychological aspect, noting that at both Harvard and Berkeley "the psychiatric units at the health services of the two universities, normally quite busy, found that the number of students coming in for psychiatric help declined dramatically during the period of concerted political action. The students, it must be concluded, found an external outlet for their intense concern and so were less caged in their own minds." [32] This did not mean that their personal problems were solved; they were, however, sublimated in something beyond the student. Gerzon also cited data showing that both militancy and drug-taking were more prevalent among students in the "soft" sciences, who were more preoccupied with the "habit of self-analysis" and less prepared for active participation in the more scientifically oriented society.[33]

There is doubtless much merit in this psychological interpretation of student militancy. The existing system and especially the emerging system put so extensive a premium on individual competition that anxiety is generated early in life. Part of the rebellion against authority in education can be attributed to the understandable desire of the young to get away from a competitive structure in which success or failure, at so early an age, has such potentially lasting consequences. At the same time, the weakening of the family structure creates pressures for compensatory sources of psychological reassurance, and peer groups become important in setting patterns of behavior and proclaimed beliefs.*

In addition, so highly rationalized a society as the American tends to be a dangerously boring society. Because of this, sheer boredom as the source of alienation—that oft-cited catch-all explanation—should not be underestimated as an important cause of restlessness. In our society "the excitement of the unexpected, the invigorating state of mind produced by shifts in pleasure, pain, tranquility and anxiety are largely missing. Underlying the rewards of being a cog in the wheel can be a sense of boredom and thinness of self." [34] To escape from it into a revolutionary "happening" can be freedom, and endless discussions exalting one's personal refusal to participate in the "automated society," the "gadget economy," and "corrupting affluence" become a form of group therapy.

This mood prompts a search for new sources of feeling and of authority, which the simultaneously impersonal and permissive existing institutions fail to provide. It creates a responsiveness to

---

* According to the President's Commission on Law Enforcement and the Administration of Justice (1967): "In America in the 1960's, to perhaps a greater extent than in any other place or time, adolescents live in a distinct society of their own. It is not an easy society to understand, to describe, or, for that matter, to live in. In some ways it is an intensely materialistic society; its members, perhaps in unconscious imitation of their elders, are preoccupied with physical objects like clothes and cars and indeed have been encouraged in this preoccupation by manufacturers and merchants who have discovered how profitable the adolescent market is. In some ways it is an intensely sensual society; its members are preoccupied with the sensations they can obtain from surfing or drag racing or music or drugs. In some ways, it is an intensely moralistic society; its members are preoccupied with independence and honesty and equality and courage. On the whole it is a rebellious, oppositional society, dedicated to the proposition that the grown-up world is a sham. At the same time, it is a conforming society; being inexperienced, unsure of themselves and, in fact, relatively powerless as individuals, adolescents to a far greater extent than their elders conform to common standards of dress and hair style and speech, and act jointly in groups—or gangs" (*The Challenge of Crime in a Free Society*, New York, 1968, p. 176).

highly generalized mobilization against the *status quo*. Paradoxically, the vaguer and more ambitious the demands, the closer and more rapidly narrowing the gap between the reality and hope.*

Finally, there appears to be an element of uneasy guilt and self-gratification in the motivation of some of the alienated young people, and this factor should not be ignored. It is certainly easier to condemn the social system as a whole than to participate in VISTA programs or the Peace Corps. Condemning the latter as an extension of imperialism becomes a self-serving explanation: the militants' "deep dissatisfaction with themselves and their inner confusion is projected against the institutions of the university first, and against all institutions of society secondarily, which are blamed for their own inner weakness." [35] This consideration is especially important in view of the economically secure, middle-class character of many of the youthful militants. Indeed, their self-indulgent life style somewhat belies their professed anti-materialism, especially as their material existence tends to depend on the relatively generous support provided either by their parents or by their colleges. There are accordingly some analogies between the restless American middle-class student and the Latin American student rebels, who are generally drawn from the upper classes and similarly quite certain that, given the social structure of their societies, they can count on a relatively successful and materially rewarding life, whatever the outcome of their studies.

The outlook of alienated but idealistic young people, in contrast to that of the activist political ideology of the numerically much smaller New Left, can perhaps be characterized as ideological infantilism: relying on psychology as their intellectual source, they use the current political slogans of the adult world (freedom, equality, and so on) but act as if the world were a

---

* Involved here was "the general American tendency, perhaps the human tendency, to assume that if things are presently bad, they were once better, rather than realizing that they are likely to be *considered* bad precisely because they are getting better" (Christopher Jencks and David Riesman, "The Role of Student Subcultures," *The Record*, Teachers College, Columbia University, October 1967, p. 1 [italics in original]).

given constant. For example, in Gerzon's book there is no discussion of how racial injustice can be eliminated, how the economy should create the needed wealth, or who should make the planes fly, the hospitals operate, the social system work. The book does, however, contain the usual emotional elements of an ideological system: the enemies are adults and technology, and the self-righteousness of the idealistic young is repeatedly stressed. The resulting doctrine is self-serving, since the tedious task of making society function is abandoned to others, and the future is left vague.*

Revolutionaries in Search of Revolution

The extreme New Left represents the phenomenon of middle-class rebellion against middle-class society. It is new in the sense that in exploiting the psychological unrest of some of the college generation it draws much of its support from a social group which is itself not yet engaged in producing social wealth and therefore cannot be represented as being exploited; on the whole, that group enjoys social and material security, but it is psychologically insecure, frustrated, bored, and guilt-ridden. This also appears to be the case with some older supporters of the New Left, particularly

* The psychological interpretation fits well some of the points made by Konrad Lorenz: "During and shortly after puberty human beings have an indubitable tendency to loosen their allegiance to all traditional rites and social norms of their culture, allowing conceptual thought to cast doubt on their value and to look around for new and perhaps more worthy ideals. There probably is, at that time of life, a definite sensitive period for a new object-fixation, much as in the case of the object-fixation found in animals and called imprinting. If at that crucial time of life old ideals prove fallacious under critical scrutiny and new ones fail to appear, the result is complete aimlessness, the utter boredom which characterizes the young delinquent. If, on the other hand, the clever demagogue, well versed in the dangerous art of producing supranormal stimulus situations, gets hold of young people at the susceptible age, he finds it easy to guide their object-fixation in a direction subservient to his political aims. At the postpubertal age some human beings seem to be driven by an overpowering urge to espouse a cause and failing to find a worthy one may become fixated on astonishingly inferior substitutes" (*On Aggression*, New York, 1966, p. 258).

those from the intellectual community, whose recently acquired social and material prestige is intensely threatened by a sense of political impotence and increasing fear of historical obsolescence.

The difficulty encountered by the militant New Left in reaching the "masses" is related to the current situation in the United States. During the 1930s, radical movements had a real basis for their hope to radicalize the American laboring masses, who were suffering from the deprivations of the Great Depression and only then beginning to develop their own organizational consciousness. There was, in effect, at least the potential for a historical symbiosis between radical ideology and the frustrated and impoverished masses.*

Today the situation is entirely different for very many Americans, though not for all: as has already been noted, the children of Americans without any higher education (the blue-collar workers of the still industrial, second America) are flocking into colleges, and contemporary society through its apparent openness reinforces the relative feeling of well-being created by its material advances. That second America increasingly sees its way clear to the long-range opportunities held out by the new scientific-technological society. It is simply not convinced by the New Left's argument that "more opportunity plus more democracy equals less freedom." [36] The New Left holds little promise for the second America, whose various anxieties tend rather to express themselves in a politically conservative and even anti-intellectual posture.

This leaves for New Left militants, still in search of mass support, only the first America, the pre-industrial and the industrially moribund America. But here the problem is complicated by the fact that much of that America is black and that American blacks are either inclined to take advantage of gradually enlarging eco-

---

* But only a potential. As Paul Buhle, the editor of *Radical America,* noted in the radical weekly *Guardian* (June 21, 1969): ". . . the most notable characteristic of American society, in contrast to that of Europe, has been the absence of a stable, class conscious proletarian movement."

nomic opportunities or to seek their identity through militant racial exclusiveness. In either case, the New Left tends to appear to many of them as a quarrelsome, not overly serious white middle-class diversion, perhaps of marginal nuisance value in shaking some white-establishment institutions and in stirring some white consciences, but generally lacking consistency, continuity, and defined political direction.*

The New Left might have become a more serious—and therefore more constructive—political force in the United States today if its prophets had been intellectually able to move beyond either their dated European radicalism or their newer escapist antirationalism.† For example, modern society poses especially

* The assessment of the SDS by David Hilliard, chief of staff of the Black Panther party, is revealing in this connection: "We don't see SDS as being so revolutionary. We see SDS as just being another pacification front that's given credit by the fascist establishment in order to cause disfusion [*sic*] in hopes that this would weaken the support for the Black Panther party. . . .

". . . we'll beat those little sissies, those little schoolboys' ass if they don't try to straighten up their politics. So we want to make that known to SDS and the first motherfucker that gets out of order had better stand in line for some kind of disciplinary actions from the Black Panther party" (interview in *Berkeley Barb,* August 4, 1969, as cited by *Guardian,* August 16, 1969).

† The intellectual roots of both Marcuse and Chomsky are grounded in nineteenth-century European radical dogmatism (on Chomsky and communism, see the particularly perceptive comments by Seymour Martin Lipset, "The Left, the Jews and Israel," *Encounter,* December 1969, p. 34).

In this regard, comments by Walter Laqueur are particularly pertinent to Marcuse's ponderous justifications for his preferred brand of dictatorship and to Chomsky's political banalities: "The American youth movement, with its immense idealistic potential, has gone badly, perhaps irrevocably, off the rails. For this, a great responsibility falls on the shoulders of the gurus who have provided the ideological justification for the movement in its present phase—those intellectuals, their own bright dreams having faded, who now strain to recapture their ideological virginity. . . . The doctors of the American youth movement are in fact part of its disease. They have helped to generate a great deal of passion, but aside from the most banal populism they have failed to produce a single new idea" ("Reflections on Youth Movements," *Commentary,* June 1969, p. 40).

This "banal populism" is expressed in the case of some writers (such as A. Mendel, in his trivial "Robots and Rebels," *The New Republic,* January 11, 1969) by an intensely Manichaean escapism and by attempts (for example, in the more intellectually serious effort by Theodore Roszak, *The Making of a Counter-Culture,* New York, 1969) to legitimize the antirational posture of some of the young as a new and enduring culture. The prevailing passion of the "gurus" is revealed by the sympathetic comments on Roszak's

complex problems relating to equality, an issue of major concern to the New Left; but those problems cannot be resolved by invoking nineteenth-century criticisms of capitalism.[37] In failing to assimilate intellectually the novelty of the current American transition, the New Left has made itself an essentially negative and obsolescent force. Indeed, the New Left's combination of Marxist rhetoric and exaltation of passion appears to have been designed to shock rather than to change society. This has created a situation deplored by even radical critics of the contemporary United States.* In addition, the New Left's exuberant rhetoric, coupled with the ideological immaturity of the young militants and the historical anachronism of its prophets, has resulted in a programmatic posture and ideological debates that occasionally verge on the hilarious.†

---

book by philosophy professor Robert Wolff. After noting that Roszak argues that "modern industrial society in general, and American society in particular, is ugly, repressive, destructive, and subversive of much that is truly human," Wolff goes on to say that the above proposition ". . . I take it, is now acknowledged to be true by virtually every sensible man and woman. Anyone who still imagines that the United States is the land of opportunity and the bastion of democracy is a candidate either for a mental hospital or for Richard Nixon's Cabinet" (*The New York Times Book Review,* September 7, 1969, p. 3).

* The *Guardian,* for example, condemned the SDS for its "intoxication with sectarianism, dogmatism, obscure rhetoric and empty sloganeering which tends to permeate the upper reaches of its leadership. Such practice can only further isolate the leadership from a membership which has never enjoyed a serious, national educational program designed to eliminate gaps in political consciousness that exist on the chapter level. . . . We question tendencies leading to the application by rote of important and intricate concepts such as the dictatorship of the proletariat and vanguard party, without regard for the present nature of U.S. monopoly capitalism or to adjustments which would have to be made in these formulations to be applicable to the world's most industrially advanced nation" (*Guardian,* July 5, 1969, p. 12).

† For example, at the SDS National Convention in 1969 the following dialogue took place: "The next speaker, Chaka Walls, minister of information of the Illinois Black Panther party . . . then began to explain the role of women in the revolution. 'We believe in the freedom of love, in pussy power,' he said. A shock wave stunned the arena, and PL responded with chants of 'Fight male chauvinism.' 'We've got some puritans in the crowd,' responded Walls. 'Superman was a punk because he never tried to fuck Lois Lane.'

"'Fight male chauvinism,' PLWSA and many others began to chant.

Cumulatively, the New Left has loosely linked the obsolescents, the abstainers, and the excluded of the technetronic age, but it has offered little prospect of a realistic response to this age's dilemmas. It is thus more interesting as a symptom of social change than for its programmatic message. It is an escapist phenomenon rather than a determined revolutionary movement; it proclaims its desire to change society but by and large offers only a refuge from society.* More concerned with self-gratification than with

---

Anger was so intense that Walls stepped down and left the podium to Jewel Cook, another Panther spokesman. Cook, not understanding what was wrong with 'pussy power,' quickly made matters worse. . . . Cook said: 'He [Walls] was only trying to say that you sisters have a strategic position for the revolution . . . prone'" (*Guardian,* June 28, 1969). PLWSA: Progressive Labor–Worker–Student Alliance.

Similarly, the Berkeley Liberation Committee's revolutionary program, designed to set a "revolutionary example throughout the world," contained the following thirteen points (*Oakland Tribune,* June 5, 1969):

"1—We will make Telegraph Avenue and the South Campus a strategic free territory for revolution.

2—We will create our revolutionary culture everywhere.

3—We will turn the schools into training grounds for liberation.

4—We will destroy the university unless it serves the people.

5—We will struggle for the full liberation of women as a necessary part of the revolutionary process.

6—We will take communal responsibility for basic human needs.

7—We will protect and expand our drug culture.

8—We will break the power of the landlords and provide beautiful housing for everyone.

9—We will tax the corporations, not the working people.

10—We will defend ourselves against law and order.

11—We will create a soulful socialism in Berkeley.

12—We will create a people's government.

13—We will unite with other movements throughout the world to destroy this racist capitalist imperialist system."

* Kenneth Keniston, though suggesting that youth really is shaping the future, has characteristically not indicated how it is shaping it, and thus appears to take their rhetoric for reality. (See his article "You have to Grow Up in Scarsdale to Know How Bad Things Really Are," *The New York Times Magazine,* April 27, 1969.) The same is largely true of Roszak.

Keniston, moreover, seems to be excessively influenced by prevailing moods. Thus in 1961 he wrote that "the drift of American youth, I have argued, is away from public involvements and social responsibilities and toward a world of private and personal satisfactions. . . . They will assure a highly stable political and social order, for few of them will be enough committed to politics to consider revolution, subversion, or even radical change . . ." ("Social Change and Youth in America," in *The Challenge of Youth,* Eric H. Erikson, ed., New York, 1961, p. 215).

the social consequences of its acts, the New Left can afford to engage in the wildest verbal abuse, without any regard for the fact that it alienates even those who are potential supporters. Its concern is to create a sense of personal involvement for its adherents and to release their passions; it provides a psychological safety valve for its youthful militants and a sense of vicarious fulfillment for its more passive, affluent, and older admirers.* Despite its increasingly Marxist-Leninist rhetoric, the New Left is more reminiscent of Fourier in content[38] and of Dadaism in style—and quite symptomatically so, since both Fourier and Dadaism were themselves reactions to a new age.

---

* For some the sexual revolution also became a partial substitute for political action. With political institutions too difficult to tackle, social conventions and the universities became convenient targets guaranteed to gain the desired mass-media coverage. As one actress explained the political significance of nudism in a statement to *The New York Times:*

"I considered (and still do) the naked human body the height of beauty, innocence and truth. I wished to oppose my nakedness to the intimate realism of Vietnam, in itself only symptomatic of the corruptions and hypocrisies of our time. The nude body on stage was the Truth; Vietnam, the Lie.

"Vietnam, Chicago, and Berkeley made me realize that my body could not be my own 'property' any longer, and that trust and vulnerability were our only salvation. I wished to say that, in reaching the natural end of their emancipation, women of my generation can no longer consider themselves as 'property.' "

A response by a black actress, asked to comment on the same subject, was much more to the point:

"This preoccupation with nudity under the guise of 'sexual liberation' is a white hang-up. Too many white 'artists' are constantly making a pretense of coming up with new forms, new ideas, and experiments. This is due to the fact that they are bankrupt when it comes to the tormenting business of artistic creation out of the human condition as it is. This task is much more difficult to confront.

"Any endeavor which employs the blatant and aggressive display of bodily nakedness in the glare of public voyeurism, all under the label of artistic merit, is not one step above those girlie magazine stores and movie houses on 42nd Street. It is what it has always been, pornography for thrill-seeking consumers. For the actor, this is nothing short of debilitating and exhausting to his artistic individuality.

"And as for liberation, sexual or otherwise, I as a black person am concerned with but only one liberation, and that is the total liberation of all black people. This is a *reality* which is quite *naked*" (Sally Kirkland and JudyAnn Elder, respectively, as quoted in *The New York Times*, June 22, 1969).

The Historic Function of the Militant Left

On balance, the militant New Left appears to be largely a transient phenomenon, a symptom of the tensions inherent in the interaction of the several Americas coexisting in a time of general American transition. In all probability, this transition will continue to spark additional violence, and the broader frustrations besetting some young people may prompt a more protracted alienation from the existing system. The decline in the attractiveness of business or government careers may deny the system a measure of social talent, but this alienation of some middle-class youth (especially from the better universities), the source from which America's elite is traditionally drawn, may well act as a social equalizer by opening up career opportunities for first-generation, post-blue-collar urban youth who have in recent years gained greater access to advanced education.

The long-run historic function of the militant New Left depends largely on the circumstances in which it will eventually either fade or be suppressed. Though itself ideologically barren and politically futile, it might serve as an additional spur to social change, accelerating some reforms. If it does, even though the New Left itself disappears, its function in the third American revolution will have been positive; if not, it will have been a catalyst for a more reactionary social response to the new dilemmas.

The anarchistic element in the New Left has often been noted. Less attention has been paid to its totalitarian predisposition. Yet both elements are influential in the New Left's behavior and mood. Despite the democratic rhetoric and proclaimed concern with equality, the demands of the New Left—in the perceptive words of a sympathetic observer—have been "fundamentally elitist and aristocratic, and should be frankly faced as such." [39] Its membership, in terms of both social composition and psychological make-up, is remarkably analogous to that of European groups which, in response to overwhelming complexity and times of stress, gravitated toward totalitarian movements. In Europe such groups were recruited from among marginal members of the middle class, the unaffiliated intellectuals, new and recently uprooted proletarians, and some of the more isolated trade unionists.[40] In America, given the new forces shaping its society, members have to a greater extent been drawn from among unaffiliated intellectuals, students—who in effect form a new class—and some members of the middle class, all of whom, unlike their European counterparts, are responding less to economic and more to psychological anxieties. These elements are united by their proclivity for total solutions and their boredom or impatience with incremental change.

The strong totalitarian tendencies of the New Left are evident from its conduct and prescriptions.* Yet it more accurately warrants the term "neo-totalitarian," because it has largely failed to forge sufficient unity to emerge as a relatively disciplined, organized totalitarian movement. Its totalitarian mood and aspirations have not yet been matched by totalitarian organization, even though the bitter internal factional conflicts and mutual expulsions are strongly reminiscent of earlier dogmatic movements.

Moreover, the sharp edge of the New Left's intellectual—and sometimes even physical—attacks has been aimed at those American institutions whose normal operation relies most on reason and nonviolence. The university, a peculiarly defenseless and vulnerable social institution—and in America the principal haven for liberal thought—has been a primary target because it offers the greatest chance for success with the least amount of risk. More generally, leading New Left spokesmen have been contemptuous of free speech, democratic procedures, and majority rule. They have left little room for doubt as to how they would handle their critics if the New Left were ever to gain power.

Though they seemingly conflict, the anarchistic and the totali-

---

* By no means the most glaring example of the latter is the explicit advocacy of repression of views divergent from those approved by the New Left. See Robert Wolff, Barrington Moore, Jr., Herbert Marcuse, *A Critique of Pure Tolerance,* Boston, 1965, especially pp. 81–110.

tarian strands of the New Left have been mutually reinforcing. The anarchistic component is in tune with the uncertainties connected with the rapid and baffling pace of change; the totalitarian component, derived from the Manichaean sense of absolute self-righteousness, provides a secure point of departure for confronting that change. It should be remembered, moreover, that totalitarianism rarely proclaims itself in advance; it emerges through practice. Since the French Revolution, the over-all political style of the Western world has called for reliance on slogans expressing devotion to freedom and equality. Even fascism claimed that its discipline made men free. The radical left has been shrill in proclaiming its commitment to true democracy, but the real test of democracy is not ultimate goals but the procedures used in attaining them.

New Left militants have thus threatened American liberalism in a manner reminiscent of the harm done to democratic American conservatism and liberal anticommunism by the McCarthy phenomenon of the 1950s. The New Left has jeopardized American social progress by providing a convenient rationalization for the more conservative social attitudes. Beyond this, it has brought to the surface and intensified—but not caused—the current crisis of American liberalism. That has perhaps been the most significant political result of the New Left's neo-totalitarian reaction to the third American revolution.

3. The Crisis of Liberalism

To a great extent, modern American liberalism has itself to blame for its present crisis. Long the almost exclusive philosophy of industrial America,* liberalism has not only dominated the

* "For along with its agrarianism the new nation was imbued with liberalism,

political discourse of the country but lately has been firmly ensconced in the seat of power, from which it has confronted the entrenched but largely defensive congressional rural-conservative forces. Swept out of office in 1932, the Republican Party needed thirty-six years, a world war, two Asian wars, and domestic racial-social unrest in order to regain the White House. (Eisenhower's victory in 1952 was a personal triumph, not a party one; he would also have won as a Democratic candidate.) Yet even then the Republican Party did so less by offering an alternative political philosophy than by capitalizing on the divisions within American liberalism and on the nation's uneasiness with liberal prescriptions and style.

The prescriptions and style were once a creative and humane response to the pressures and iniquities of industrial capitalism. About these dilemmas American conservatives had little to say, and American conservatism, preaching puritan homilies and extolling the virtues of free enterprise, did not succeed in making a full adjustment to the industrial age or to the massive social and political awakening it prompted. This left the field either to doctrinaire radicals, who largely drew on European experience, or to liberals, who sought to adapt the idealism and the optimism of the American tradition to the new industrial age. The success of the liberals preserved America's uniqueness—and this has been their crowning achievement.

Whig to the bone. Neither throne nor altar, nor, above all, reverence for the past existed as barriers to the new leveling forces unleashed by industrial technology.

"The political turning point was the defeat of the South in the Civil War, which ended forever any possibility of a nation based on agrarian values—and, indeed, destroyed forever the possibility of a conservatism that was anything other than intellectual preciousness or a shield for particular business interests. Bryan's constituents in the crucial election of 1896 were small farmer capitalists who were resentful of their disadvantaged position within the system rather than of industrial processes as such. When in the 1930's a group of southern writers responded to the American economic crisis and the attendant cultural crisis of industrial capitalism with their manifesto *I'll Take My Stand*, looking to agrarianism and rejecting both socialism and industrial capitalism in favor of small property, they found little resonance. Dixieland reacted to the Depression by standing in the vanguard of those supporting the state capitalism of the New Deal" (Victor C. Ferkiss, *Technological Man: The Myth and the Reality*, New York, 1969, pp. 65–66).

Without the liberal, America might well have either decayed economically or, perhaps even more likely, fallen victim to an antidemocratic social and political crisis. The genius of the New Deal liberal solution was to fuse the individualism intrinsic in American historical experience—an individualism that has inherently reinforced a conservative reluctance toward collective social action—with a sense of social responsibility as defined through the political process. In so doing, American liberals initially avoided the dogmatic rigidities of European socialists, though they have tended to share with them the inclination to rely on the government as the principal instrumentality for social reforms. This inclination, philosophical preference apart, was in any case dictated by the situation prevailing in America: the national government was the only instrument that was relatively responsive to the democratic process, that could be used to express and fulfill the welfare needs of the masses, that could blunt the sharp edge of economic and social inequality.

The Liberal Janus

In the process, however, the American liberal became increasingly a statist establishmentarian, confident of his prescriptions and convinced that he had discovered the way to manage social change. Indeed, the American liberal became a Janus-like creature, gradually acquiring two faces. The relatively pragmatic liberal who was rooted in the American democratic tradition and whose social values provided the broad framework for a nondogmatic approach to problem-solving came to be matched by a more ideological, eventually more dogmatic liberal, who was increasingly inclined toward abstract social engineering, prone to draw his intellectual inspiration from European left radicalism, ideologically hostile to the business community, and rather impatient with the nonideological "expedient" attitude of the pragmatic liberal power practitioner. The emergence of the second liberal was closely linked with the growth in prestige and influence of the American intellectual community after World War II. Increasingly, it was this more doctrinaire liberal who set the tone and who dominated American liberalism, though he was still unable during the 1960s to gain full control of the Democratic Party.

The accession of the doctrinaire liberal to prominence and political influence, if not to power—a development which coincided with the intensifying stresses in the American society—had much to do with a subtle but important change of tone in the liberal discourse. Both the procedural elements rooted in liberal democracy's attachment to legal order and the patriotic pride in America's constitutional achievements tended to be downgraded in favor of greater emphasis on rapid social change, on restructuring economic relations, and on a more general and highly critical reappraisal of the American tradition.

The doctrinaire liberal, moreover, was not innocent of the sin of intellectual arrogance.[41] Since neither the conservative nor the communist was able to match his social success, his self-confidence gradually developed into arrogance, often expressed by an intolerance of critics and an inclination to label as reactionaries all who deviated from the liberal norm as he himself defined it. This inclination became most marked in the academic world, an environment increasingly dominated by liberal intellectuals,[42] who were more inclined than the liberal power practitioners to conceptualize statist liberalism and to excommunicate deviants. As a result, a humane and creative creed gradually acquired overtones of dominant orthodoxy.

This made it more difficult either to perceive or to respond to new and unusual circumstances. The American liberal approached the dilemmas posed by the third American revolution with a New Deal strategy tried and tested during the recent industrial-capitalist crisis. There was little in the doctrinaire-liberal analysis of the problems facing the United States in the 1960s that departed from the principles and remedies developed in the preceding decades; there was little recognition of the growing responsiveness to social problems of societal institutions and organizations other than the federal government.

Moreover, the doctrinaire liberals were by and large late in recognizing the antidemocratic and antiliberal character of the New Left. Various factors played a role here, not the least of which was that in the past some of them had flirted with communism. Though Stalinism had eventually disenchanted most of them, the fear of being "outflanked on the left" remained a strong reflex, while the crudities of McCarthyism had made *anti*-anticommunism highly fashionable, socially acceptable, and politically less risky than fellow-traveling. Thus many doctrinaire liberals—unlike their pragmatic political counterparts, who were more in tune with the mood of the electorate—responded to the fact that the slogans voiced by the New Left *sounded* democratic; their undemocratic procedures were excused as examples of youthful exuberance and admirable idealism.

The downgrading of orderly legal procedure, on the ground that it had become a buttress of conservative institutions, contributed directly to the crisis of legitimacy of the American system. This crisis is clearly linked with the unwillingness of a major sector of the dominant liberal community to insist on legal procedures. The ambivalence of so many prominent liberals, and their inclination to rationalize abuses by militants—reflecting in part their highly permissive educational concepts—conveyed the weakening liberal commitment to what has traditionally been a vital ingredient of democracy: respect for majority rule as expressed by established democratic procedures.

The Price of Victorious Skepticism

This crisis of liberal values (and the New Left quite accurately diagnosed it as such and thereby gained confidence in its attack on liberal democracy) is in turn related to more basic causes. Liberalism was initially not only an expression of a relevant, modern, and humane response to the conditions created by industrialism but also an attack on the then prevailing orthodoxies. These orthodoxies, rooted in the traditional society, were a blend of religious views and conservative instincts reinforced by, and reinforcing, established church and rural-aristocratic institutions.

The liberal attack on these deeply ingrained orthodoxies and beliefs was part of the emerging mood of rationalism and skepticism. This mood was remarkably well suited to the needs of the new industrial age. Liberals reflected the spirit of the times in attacking institutionalized religion; they were fashionable in their anti-Catholicism; they were modern and modernizing in attacking the rural-aristocratic concepts of life. They were also remarkably successful, and by the mid-twentieth century the United States had become an essentially secular society, its mass media and its educational system dominated—except for parochial schools—by an essentially rationalist and skeptical philosophy.

Liberal success also marked the beginning of the liberal crisis. With success came evidence that the United States was becoming a society without any integrating values or integrating cultural institutions. The mass media could not replace religion as the source of integration, since their orientation was itself devoid of more fundamental concerns, and unalloyed nationalism alone was clearly a danger to liberal values. Skepticism was simply not enough when it emerged as the triumphant antithesis of traditional religion. The gravitation of some doctrinaire liberals toward the radical left was hence also partially a consequence of their success. Understandably unable to turn toward the values they had always combated, these doctrinaire liberals were attracted to the more intensely held beliefs of the radical left, since such beliefs were similarly derived from a rejection of the old. For most liberals, however, the turn to the extreme left was not an acceptable solution, for it involved a betrayal of their traditional democratic ideals. But what, they were forced to ask themselves, was to be the substance of a victorious skepticism?

Belief is an important social cement. A society that does not believe in anything is a society in a state of dissolution. The sharing of common aspirations and a unifying faith is essential to community life. This is a fact that the contemporary doctrinaire and skeptical liberal is beginning to confront, especially as a consequence of his ambivalence in defending procedural democracy.

Indeed, the chief beneficiaries of this liberal confusion have been the American conservatives who, though largely unresponsive to the social dilemmas of contemporary America, have reaped political rewards by advocating nationalism, private property, and constitutional order.

From the standpoint of the liberal who sees himself as a progressive force, belief is necessary to the effective social assimilation of change. The social costs of the absence of conviction and the paralyzing effects of skepticism as a ruling principle have been most graphically shown by the liberal's ambivalent response to the new black challenge. The liberal was in the forefront of the struggle for racial equality as long as it was opposed by the conservatives; once the conservative dams had crumbled and the black emerged with demands that were no longer defined for him by the white liberal, the liberal became baffled. This was the case in New York City's struggle over community control of schools, and it was also the case at Cornell University, where armed black students presented their demands in the form of an ultimatum. As a consequence, some liberals appeared to turn conservative: they rejected black demands for separate social institutions. Others turned into undifferentiated capitulators: they granted all black demands in an attempt to expiate their guilt as white men.*

Yet what society needed most in this time of transition was exactly what the liberal—uncertain of himself because his traditional enemy was prostrate—found most difficult to provide: a definition of his principles, an affirmation of his convictions, and a willingness to act on his devotion to liberal democracy. Ameri-

* It is truly remarkable that no prominent liberal educator was willing to say to his black students: "I will not engage in reverse discrimination by granting indiscriminately any demands that you choose to make simply because you are black. I will treat you as I treat all my students. The era of discrimination is over and I will not return to it under a new guise. I can understand the psychological roots of your demands, as well as some of your fears in having to compete with better prepared whites. I will, therefore, do everything I can to remedy the situation, even at considerable cost and organizational effort, but I will not grant those demands which will have the effect of perpetuating your exclusion from this society."

can blacks also needed such a response from the liberal, for the assimilation of any ethnic or racial group into society requires stable institutions and defined, though not dogmatic, values. The integration of blacks, difficult enough under most circumstances, becomes hopeless if existing institutions and values fail to provide a framework resilient enough to absorb the strains inherent in the unprecedented entrance of a large racial minority into equal societal participation. The emergence of radical, antidemocratic, and even racist young black leadership was doubtless primarily due to the white community's slow response to black aspirations; it was also, however, due to the growing contempt by the New Left and younger black leaders for democratic procedures and to their realization that such contempt could be expressed with impunity, given the liberal's own ambivalence about the legitimacy of democratic procedures and the meaning of democratic belief.

The ramifications of this situation were even broader and politically more painful to the liberal: they led to increased rejection of liberal values by the lower-middle-class blue-collar workers, who began to view the doctrinaire liberal as their natural enemy. To an industrial worker of the 1930s the symbol of the class enemy was a rich capitalist banker or industrialist. Even as late as 1948 Harry Truman was able to bring about an electoral victory by appealing to that sentiment. By the late 1960s that symbol was replaced: the class enemy was the black, backed by a dogmatic liberal intellectual, preferably a college professor.

There has been an undeniable element of justice in the white blue-collar American's resentment of the liberal's social idealism. The long delayed and imperatively needed racial revolution was launched in the United States by the comfortably established upper middle class at a relatively low cost to themselves; it was the less financially secure and less racially tolerant white working class who bore the brunt of the change in education, in housing, and in social mores. To many industrial workers it seemed that the rich were not sharing the economic costs of the revolution in hiring practices or in social programs, and that the militant liberals were unwilling to make the compromises necessary to obtain broader popular acceptance of painful social readjustments.* The resentment of the New Left by much of the American public thus tended to be coupled with white industrial labor's feeling of betrayal by the liberal forces, again to the advantage of the more conservative elements in American politics.

This sense of disaffection was intensified by the frustrations bred by the tendency to multiply governmental agencies in order to obtain positive social changes.† Here the practice of the pragmatic liberal merged with the ideological preferences of his doctrinaire counterpart. The combination of abstract theory with a remote, vast, and complex instrumentality had much to do with the alienation and irritation felt by white sectors of the American public.

---

* It is striking that it was only in the wake of the 1968 presidential elections that organizations such as the Americans for Democratic Action began to stress the need to remedy the liberal's neglect, and even abuse, of the industrial working class. On the eve of the presidential elections, a series of newspaper articles in *The New York Times* explored the ethnic and economic sources of northern-urban support for Wallace, repeatedly pointing its finger at the Slavic ethnic minority. Subsequently, it turned out that both in that election (in which, according to the NBC voting profile, Wallace obtained nationally 22 per cent of the Italian ethnic vote, 17.8 per cent of the Slavic, and 13 per cent of the Jewish [*Newsweek,* November 11, 1968, pp. 35–36]) and in the 1969 metropolitan elections the conservative swing was a much more generalized case of urban disaffection with the liberal approach.

† "We now have ten times as many government agencies concerned with city problems as we had in 1939. We have increased by a factor of a thousand or so the number of reports and papers that have to be filled out before anything can be done in the city. Social workers in New York City spend some 70 or 80 per cent of their time filling out papers for Washington, for the state government in Albany, and for New York City. No more than 20 or 30 per cent of their time, that is, almost an hour and a half a day, is available for their clients, the poor. As James Reston reported in *The New York Times* (November 23, 1966), there were then 170 different federal aid programs on the books, financed by over 400 separate appropriations and administered by 21 federal departments and agencies aided by 150 Washington bureaus and over 400 regional offices. One Congressional session alone passed 20 health programs, 17 new educational programs, 15 new economic development programs, 12 new programs for the cities, 17 new resources development programs, and 4 new manpower training programs, each with its own administrative machinery" (Peter F. Drucker, "The Sickness of Government," *The Public Interest,* Winter 1969, p. 8).

Nor was it always good remedial social policy for the underprivileged groups concerned. Just as the communists had erred in believing that social unrest (revolution) was the product of economic ill-being (exploitation), the doctrinaire liberal erred in assuming that economic progress would prompt social well-being. Both underestimated the psychological and spiritual dimensions. Some liberals sensed this, and experiments designed to combine social initiative, free enterprise, and governmental support (such as Robert Kennedy's Bedford-Stuyvesant effort) were meant to provide a new direction. Yet, though community action as a broad goal was a noble idea, in practice it too became a means of playing the game according to established political rules: organizing to gain power in order either to extract more public funds or to create a base for more radical politics.[43]

In the meantime, increased governmental intervention and deliberate social engineering—the latter derived from "theories" of social change and development—created a blend of operational incompetence, crosscutting group conflicts, social indifference, and political complexity that made for both a breakdown of public consensus and the alienation of the younger generation. Having finally obtained a unique opportunity to do much of what he had long aspired to do, the pragmatic liberal discovered that his intellectual arsenal, derived from a highly successful response to the crisis of an advanced industrial society, was exhausted; the doctrinaire liberal—confident that he had the right remedies and theory, impatient with the seeming conservatism of the more pragmatic power practitioner, and ambivalent toward the anarchism and totalitarianism of the New Left—undermined the liberal's base of support by destroying public confidence in the liberal's commitment to liberal democracy.

The contemporary liberal thus faces the threat of being deprived of his greatest assets: his optimism, his faith in America's future, his vision. In response to the crisis that he feels acutely—and has in many respects anticipated more correctly than the conservative—the liberal, especially the intellectual doctrinarian, tends more and more to withdraw into an ideological shell, savoring the pleasures of indiscriminate attacks on the nature of American society and thoroughly enjoying apocalyptic predictions of the imminent doom of this society.

A progressive society has been defined as one that involves an interplay of utopian goals and practical steps,[44] but the doctrinaire liberal seemed increasingly to offer society only a combination of pedestrian prescriptions and dogmatic solutions. His attitude toward space exploration, which linked the explosion of knowledge with deeply felt human aspirations, is symbolically suggestive. The doctrinarian's response to the adventure, challenge, and social opportunity provided by the space age was unimaginative, politically unwise, and psychologically anachronistic.* His call for concentrating all attention on America's unfinished terrestrial business simply ignored the psychological fact that a nation becomes more aware of its shortcomings as it expands—rather than contracts—its ambitions.

It was the frontier tradition that stirred the American imagina-

---

* President Kennedy's goal of reaching the moon was the object of particular scorn. For example, Lewis Mumford asserted that "the moon landing program . . . is a symbolic act of war, and the slogan the astronauts will carry, proclaiming that it is for the benefit of mankind, is on the same level as the Air Force's monstrous hypocrisy—'Our Profession Is Peace.' . . . It is no accident that the climactic moon landing coincides with cutbacks in education, the bankruptcy of hospital services, the closing of libraries and museums, and the mounting defilement of the urban and natural environment, to say nothing of many other evidences of gross social failure and human deterioration" (*The New York Times*, July 21, 1969).

In contrast, Michael Harrington noted that "there is a certain puritanism on the Left whenever the question of space comes up. It is the fashion to denigrate spending money on heaven when the earth is still so shoddy. But this view ignores two important points. First, if peace were to break out, a massive cutback in the billions for defense plus the normal growth of a full-employment economy would provide sufficient funds for rebuilding America *and* going to the stars. Second, space is not empty of social, scientific, and even aesthetic significance. It could conceivably provide room for human beings, vast new resources for the development of the world, and it will certainly incite a deeper knowledge of both man and the universe. Beyond these pragmatic considerations, there is a moral imperative which requires that humanity live up to the fullness of its powers, and men can rightly boast that they have always experimented and innovated" (*American Power in the Twentieth Century*, p. 31).

tion, created a society of movement and growth, and gave America its integrative myth. Scientific exploration, including exploration of space, has become the functional equivalent of America's frontier tradition, and such endeavor is immediately relevant to the educational and scientific attainments of the country. This is not to argue against greater social expenditures. It is, however, to argue that a broadly gauged improvement of American society will be a deliberate by-product of a society that thrusts forward with its acquired energy, that seeks altogether new objectives—including those beyond its immediate confines—thereby in the process achieving greater social consciousness and successfully confronting the unresolved problems of the past.

Even aside from the possibility that the technological impact of the space program may end up by contributing more to the resolution of city-ghetto problems than all the programmatic and sociological doctrines currently so fashionable, there is also an important international aspect to the space effort: a major world power such as the United States has to pioneer in those areas of life which are historically relevant and crucial. To the extent that ours is a scientific age, the failure of the United States to push beyond existing frontiers—and space offers a very dramatic challenge—would mean the loss of a major psychological motivation for innovation. Though it may not be popular to say so, the fact is that a continental society like the United States could not survive by becoming merely another Sweden; it would not survive internationally and it is not even certain that it would find a satisfactory balance between domestic material needs and spiritual aspirations. Space exploration is more compatible with the tradition of a pioneering country whose greatness has been linked with innovation in constitutional arrangements, in economic development, in continental exploration, and in scientific investigation.

To many Americans, contemporary liberalism offers neither principle nor progress. The crisis of American liberalism is hence both a crisis of confidence and of historical relevance.[45] It presents the bleak prospect that liberalism, historically the most vital source of innovation in contemporary American democracy, may become the critical expression of a doctrinarian minority—increasingly reactive in spite of its rhetoric—and a haven for philosophic protest against the dehumanizing effects of science, while the active shaping of the future passes into the hands of a socially somewhat conservative but technologically innovative elite.*

The End of Liberal Democracy?

A technologically innovative and politically conservative phase that would lead to some form of technological managerialism is only one possibility. Other alternatives could be more extreme. American socio-economic tensions could be aggravated by the loss of momentum in economic growth and therefore in the pace of scientific research and technological development—an important source of national pride. Racial strife, urban guerrilla activity, and alienation of the young, in addition to a profound national split over America's global role, could result in a further breakdown of national consensus and lead either the extreme left or the extreme right to capitalize on America's political disintegration by attempting to seize power.

On balance, the chances for the success of a serious revolutionary attempt do not appear to be very good. To become an effective revolutionary instrument the present New Left would have not only to relate more meaningfully to the new issues confronting our times but also to develop the techniques, the skills, and the organizational forms required to effect a revolution in the world's most modern, technologically advanced society. This would require the transformation of a somewhat petulant middle-class

* Though public opinion can shift dramatically, it is worth noting that in 1969 polls showed that a consistent majority of younger people and those with college education were in favor of increased space exploration; those opposed were most numerous among the more elderly and among those with grade-school education (cf. Gallup poll, as cited by *The New York Times*, August 7, 1969, and Harris poll, *The Washington Post*, August 25, 1969). At the same time, college graduates tended to favor more energetic law enforcement, including more wire tapping (Gallup poll, as cited by *The New York Times*, August 21, 1969).

youth movement, supported from a safe distance by some sectors of the more esoteric urban intellectual community, into an organization with a systematic theory of action that takes into account the specificity of contemporary America. SDS worship of Che Guevara, a tragic rural rebel, and its growing reliance on turgid Marxist-Leninist phraseology may be a compensation for its inability to make that adaptation, but it hardly augurs its emergence as an effective revolutionary force.

There is a significant difference between revolutionary activity and revolutionary success. Revolutionary activity—through terrorism, sabotage, selective assassinations, urban guerrilla strife—is possible and even likely in the early 1970s. It will come not from the New Left but from its emerging successor—the professionally Violent Left; not from the idealistic young people who infuse it with zeal and confusion but from those among them who have been hardened, disillusioned, and embittered by their experiences in prisons and penitentiaries. These men will be psychologically prepared for real violence, and they will dismiss as child's play the sitdowns and the raids on deans' offices. American society would then have to confront a major internal threat.

But even then the collective weight of political and social institutions, as well as the coercive might of organized authority, would in all probability prevail. As long as the New Left remains largely ineffective in its sporadic reliance on violence, it will be spared; should it become the Violent Left, suppression would be its almost certain fate. The fact is that revolutions are historical rarities, and in modern times their success has generally required a combination of internal social dissolution and external military defeat. The organization of power must itself break down, the elites must be split, the socio-economic system must malfunction, an alternative leadership must crystallize, and the more creative social forces must be, at least in significant part, convinced that a better alternative is available. Short of these conditions, reliance on revolutionary violence is likely to breed suppression, and even effectively brutal suppression.*

* On this point there is agreement among such dissimilar observers as the

The suppression of the Violent Left would almost certainly push the country to the right. Organized coercion would require the introduction of a variety of controls over the individual. If undertaken systematically by the legitimate institutions, the process would in all probability strengthen the conservative political forces; if undertaken ineffectively, it would probably prompt right-wing vigilantism, based on a variety of paramilitary formations. But even then a right-extremist coup seems most unlikely. Such a coup would require the development of a degree of organizational cohesion and conceptual relevance that seems beyond the capability of the extreme rightists—most of whom have been left behind by the pace of American change.[46]

The more likely probability, then, is that sporadic civil strife would lead to a polarization of public opinion, with the Democratic Party gradually becoming identified with some of the less extreme New Left positions and/or splitting, and the Republican Party striving to exploit this situation and to consolidate a national conservative majority. This could come about gradually; the more

---

National Commission on the Causes and Prevention of Violence and Barrington Moore, a severe critic of the present American system. The commission concluded that "collective violence seldom succeeds as an instrument for accomplishing group objectives. It can succeed when one group so overpowers its opponents that they have no choice but to die or desist. But modern governments are much more likely to succeed in such contests than their opponents.

"In the contemporary United States, attempts at revolution from the left are likely to invite massive repression from the right. The occurrence of violence in the context of protest activities is highly likely to alienate groups that are not fundamentally in sympathy with the protesters.

"The chronicles of American labor conflicts suggest that violence, when it occurred, was almost always ineffective for the workers involved. The more violent the conflict, the more disastrous the consequences for the workers" (conclusions of a report to the Commission on Violence in America, *The New York Times*, June 6, 1969).

Very much in the same vein, Moore warned that the prospects for an urban revolution in America are very dim and that successful radical revolutions have so far failed to provide "a lasting contribution to human freedom" ("Revolution in America?" *The New York Review of Books*, January 30, 1969, p. 10. See also the thoughtful study by Bruce Smith, "The Politics of Protest: How Effective Is Violence?" *Proceedings of the Academy of Political Science*, July 1968).

adventuresome aspects of the American dream would be preempted by the more conservative leaders (for example, Spiro Agnew's call for a mission to Mars), while lower-middle-class America's disillusionment with liberalism, resentment of the New Left, and fear of the blacks would prompt such an extreme concentration on order that concern with progress in race relations would become merely window dressing and eventually fade from the public agenda. The emergence of a more reactionary political response would neither be dramatic nor have the overt overtones of fascism.

This process could be accelerated by the doctrinaire liberals' determination either to remold the Democratic Party in their own image or to create their own political party. The insistence on a doctrinaire response to complexity and the impatience with more generalized compromises are characteristic social manifestations in times of historical discontinuity; as has been already noted, they are particularly representative of the young and of marginal members of society. The political consequence would be an even greater squeeze on the pragmatic, less ideological liberals, pressed from one side by the doctrinarians advocating large-scale social engineering and opting out of external challenges and from the other by the conservatives preaching the merits of social consolidation and of new scientific frontiers.

The latent anti-intellectualism of a great many Americans—intensified by college disorders, aggravated by the ambivalence of the intellectuals, and sharpened by class hostility toward the rebellious offspring of middle-class America—could also undermine public support for the country's educational institutions, thus matching the perilous challenge from the left with an equally perilous challenge from the right. The American university would become politicized: either constantly agitated over nonacademic issues, with its faculties and students passing resolutions on all sorts of extraneous matters and increasingly injecting political criteria into their intellectual pursuits; or subject to stricter outside control by conservative assemblies and trustees who would impose their political biases on the internal workings of academia.* The resulting destruction of the liberal university would itself be a grave symptom of the decline of American liberal democracy.†

In such a context, the already staggering task of creating an equitable multi-racial society could become hopeless. Present trends augur a worsening crisis unless a major social effort at amelioration is promptly undertaken.[47] Assuming public indifference or, even worse, public hostility toward such efforts, there are two equally horrendous prospects for white-black relations in America: suppression of the blacks and/or their separation. Either one could be undertaken only in the context of a more reactionary political atmosphere and would itself generate overwhelming pressures toward reaction. Suppression, including efforts at some form of separate resettlement, would involve major strife, for the American black is no longer pliant and, moreover, many whites would flock to his side. Though suppression could effectively be undertaken—especially in the wake of massive black uprisings prompted by desperation at the absence of progress—the price paid would be a tragic reversal of the process by which the scope of American democracy has deepened and enlarged over the course of the country's history.

Another threat, less overt but no less basic, confronts liberal democracy. More directly linked to the impact of technology, it involves the gradual appearance of a more controlled and directed

---

* Examples of this are provided by the Columbia University Senate's first major act in 1969, which was to express its judgment on the Vietnam war, and by the objections of UCLA's trustees to a young black philosophy professor because of her political associations.

† The long-range consequences of the attack on the universities appear to be of little concern to the New Left. For example, the demand for the separation of defense research from universities could create a separate complex of government-operated military research institutes whose secrecy would shield their operations from outside intellectual influence, as is true in the Soviet Union. This is precisely what has already happened in the case of bacteriological-warfare devices, which were developed in closed governmental research laboratories far removed from the overview of the scientific community. The removal of ROTC could similarly accelerate rather than slow down the emergence of a separate large professional career-officer corps—in other words, a warrior caste.

society. Such a society would be dominated by an elite whose claim to political power would rest on allegedly superior scientific know-how. Unhindered by the restraints of traditional liberal values, this elite would not hesitate to achieve its political ends by using the latest modern techniques for influencing public behavior and keeping society under close surveillance and control. Under such circumstances, the scientific and technological momentum of the country would not be reversed but would actually feed on the situation it exploits.

The emergence of a large dominant party, alongside the more narrowly focused and more intensely doctrinaire groupings on the right and the left, could accelerate the trend toward such technological managerialism. Such a large dominant party would combine American society's quest for stability with its historical affinity for innovation. Relying on scientific growth to produce the means for dealing with social ills, it would tap the nation's intellectual talent for broad target planning and exploit the existence of doctrinaire groups by using them as social barometers and as sources of novel ideas. Persisting social crisis, the emergence of a charismatic personality, and the exploitation of mass media to obtain public confidence would be the steppingstones in the piecemeal transformation of the United States into a highly controlled society.*

---

* This could also produce a historical paradox. The traditionally democratic American society could, because of its fascination with technical efficiency, become an extremely controlled society, and its humane and individualistic qualities would thereby be lost. (Such a society is the subject of Kurt Vonnegut's novel *Player Piano.*) On the other hand, the communist countries, because of their organizational inefficiency and the gradual loosening of political controls, might become more preoccupied with questions of humanism; their socialist inefficiency, combined with these more humane concerns, could eventually produce a more flexible social order in some of them.

It should, however, be noted that this extremely unlikely prospect is applicable only to the more advanced communist countries. The weight of the political tradition and great power aspirations of the Russian form of communism, as well as the relative socio-economic backwardness of most communist states, argue against it. For a critique of the concept of convergence, i.e., the evolution of a communist system into a traditional liberal democracy, see the concluding chapter of the book I wrote with Samuel Huntington, *Political Power: USA/USSR*, New York, 1964.

In different ways, both the doctrinarian and the conservative might find the temptations inherent in the new techniques of social control too difficult to resist. The inclination of the doctrinaire left to legitimize means by ends could lead them to justify more social control on the ground that it serves progress. The conservatives, preoccupied with public order and fascinated by modern gadgetry, would be tempted to use the new techniques as a response to unrest, since they would fail to recognize that social control is not the only way to deal with rapid social change.

Such an outcome—were it to come to pass—would represent a profoundly pessimistic answer to the question whether American liberal democracy can assimilate and give philosophical meaning to the revolution it is undergoing. This matter not only has relevance for the United States; it has larger implications: American success or failure may provide a significant indication whether a modern democracy with highly educated citizens can successfully undergo an extensive social change without losing its essentially democratic character. Fortunately, the American transition also contains the potential for an American redemption.

PART V
America and the World

America's relationship with the world must reflect American domestic values and preoccupations. A profound discrepancy between the external conduct of a democratic society and its internal norms is no longer possible; mass communications quickly expose the gulf and undercut the support needed for its foreign policy. Just as a nation preoccupied with the communist threat at home can conduct a vigorously anti-communist policy abroad, or a nation fearful of revolution can become intensely involved in counterrevolutionary activity, so a nation concerned with social justice and technological adaptation cannot help but become similarly committed on an international level.

In his *Second Treatise on Government*, John Locke wrote, ". . . in the beginning, all the world was America." Today all the world is America, in the sense that America is the first to experience the social, psychological, political, and ideological dilemmas produced by man's sudden acquisition of altogether unprecedented power over his environment and over himself. The third American revolution, occurring in an era of volatile beliefs and of rapidly spreading technological change, thus clearly dictates America's role: that of the social innovator, exploiting science in the service of man but without dogmatically prescribing the destiny of man. The success of America in building a healthy democratic society would hold promise for a world still dominated by ideological and racial conflicts, by economic and social injustice. America's failure not only would be a setback for trends under way since the great revolutions of the late eighteenth century but could signify a more fundamental human failure: man's inability to overcome his baser instincts and his capitulation before the complexity and power of science.

1. The American Future

If the problems that confront America were neither recognized nor anticipated, the inherent dangers would be even greater. Such is not the case. Contemporary America is perhaps more candidly critical and more demanding of itself than any other society: national reports pinpointing the society's failures, devastating critiques of national shortcomings, elaborate efforts at social stocktaking—all reflect a more introspective and deliberately sober national mood. Studies of the future, organized on a large scale (both by special academic commissions and by well-endowed private institutes), indicate mounting national recognition that the future can and must be planned, that unless there is a modicum of deliberate choice, change will result in chaos.* This

* The concern is not limited to intellectuals but includes businessmen as well. Thus, in March 1969 *Fortune* unveiled a plan to remedy the condition of "a second-rate nation with a civilization only half-built," offering a pro-

does not guarantee that a national response will actually be mounted, but it does indicate a more pervasive awareness among leading sectors of society of the need for a deliberate response.

The historical vitality of the United States system derives from the deeply rooted commitment of the American people to the idea of democratic change. The American tradition of free dialogue and of hierarchically unfettered expression of disagreement[1] has been an important factor in developing this responsiveness to change; it has made it possible to exploit protest movements (and thereby render them historically superfluous) by adapting and adopting their programs. This is to deny neither the element of violence in American history nor the oft-noted conservatism of the electorate. Nevertheless, the fundamental reality of American life has been the assimilation of the rapid change induced by the frontier, by immigration, and by industrial growth. A dynamic socio-economic reality has blended with a certain political conservatism and created a pluralist socio-political system that has in the past proven itself to be remarkably resilient in absorbing extraordinary change; it possesses a structural quality capable of generating and deciphering warning signals of mounting social stress.

Today's America has set higher standards for itself than has any other society: it aims at creating racial harmony on the basis of equality, at achieving social welfare while preserving personal liberty, at eliminating poverty without shackling individual freedom. Tensions in the United States might be less were it to seek less—but in its ambitious goals America retains its innovative character.

Though the New Left—and particularly the Violent Left—has

---

gram for extensive rehabilitation of the nation. It would require a massive public and private effort.

See also a more extensive study by Leonard A. Lecht, *Goals, Priorities and Dollars: The Next Decade* (New York, 1966), which outlines in extraordinary detail a plan for allocating the GNP for various tasks of national renewal, with special concentration on the scientific-technological and ecological structure of society.

temporarily served to fortify socially conservative or even reactionary trends, the impatience of the young is more and more likely to permeate the socio-political system, especially as they begin to occupy more influential positions and make it more responsive to the need for change and reform. Moreover, the increasingly international experience of the American intellectual and business elite has already prompted a greater inclination to consider contemporary problems within a larger framework, thereby drawing lessons for the United States from both the political evolution and the social innovation of other advanced countries.*

As a result, more Americans recognize that the two broad areas of needed and—it is to be hoped—developing change involve the institutional and the cultural aspects of American society. The former largely, though not exclusively, pertains to the political sphere, the latter to the educational domain, particularly as it concerns the content and the shaping of national values. More deliberate change in both realms would serve as a catalyst for reform in other areas of national life, providing both the framework and the motivation for the timely adoption of needed remedies.

Participatory Pluralism

The approaching two-hundredth anniversary of the Declaration of Independence could justify the call for a national constitutional convention to re-examine the nation's formal institutional framework. Either 1976 or 1989—the two-hundredth anniversary of the Constitution—could serve as a suitable target date for culminating a national dialogue on the relevance of existing arrangements, the workings of the representative process, and the desirability of imitating the various European regionalization reforms and of streamlining the administrative structure. More important still, either

---

* For example, it is now more candidly admitted that America has much to learn from Western Europe in metropolitan planning, in local urban planning, in regionalization, in the development of new towns, and in social and legal innovation.

date would provide a suitable occasion for redefining the meaning of modern democracy—a task admittedly challenging but not necessarily more so than when it was undertaken by the founding fathers—and for setting ambitious and concrete social goals.*

Realism, however, forces us to recognize that the necessary political innovation will not come from direct constitutional reform, desirable as that would be.† The needed change is more likely to develop incrementally and less overtly. Nonetheless, its eventual scope may be far-reaching, especially as the political process gradually assimilates scientific-technological change. Thus, in the political sphere the increased flow of information and the development of more efficient techniques of coordination may make possible greater devolution of authority and responsibility to the lower levels of government and society. In the past the division of power has traditionally caused problems of inefficiency, poor coordination, and dispersal of authority, but today the new communications and computation techniques make possible both increased authority at the lower levels and almost instant national coordination.‡ The rapid transferal of information, combined with highly advanced analytical methods, would also make possible broad national planning—in the looser French sense of target

---

* For example, 1976 could provide a target date for a massive effort to terminate poverty as currently defined, or to bring Negro education up to the national average; 1989, for ecological targets.

† For example, one simple—though admittedly unattainable—constitutional reform would go a long way toward making Congress more responsive to social evolution: the passage of a congressional equivalent of the Twenty-second Amendment limiting the presidential term of office.

‡ These techniques could also be used to improve electoral procedures and to provide for closer consultation between the public and its representatives. Existing electoral machinery in the United States—in regard to both registration and voting procedure—has simply not kept up with innovation in electronic communications and computation. Reforms (such as electronic home-voting consoles) to make it possible for representatives of the public to consult their constituents rapidly, and for these constituents to express their views easily, are both technically possible and likely to develop in view of growing dissatisfaction with present machinery. More intense consultation, not necessarily only on the national level or only in regard to political institutions, would further enhance the responsiveness of the American social and political system.

definition—not only concentrating on economic goals but more clearly defining ecological and cultural objectives.

Technological developments make it certain that modern society will require more and more planning. Deliberate management of the American future will become widespread, with the planner eventually displacing the lawyer as the key social legislator and manipulator. This will put a greater emphasis on defining goals and, by the same token, on a more self-conscious preoccupation with social ends. How to combine social planning with personal freedom is already emerging as the key dilemma of technetronic America, replacing the industrial age's preoccupation with balancing social needs against requirements of free enterprise.

The strengthening of local, especially metropolitan, government is already recognized as an urgent necessity for the democratic process in the United States. The devolution of financial responsibility to lower echelons of the political system may encourage both the flow of better talent and greater local participation in more important local decision-making. National coordination and local participation could thus be wedded by new systems of coordination. This has already been tried successfully by some large businesses.

The trend toward more coordination but less centralization would be in keeping with the American tradition of blurring sharp distinctions between public and private institutions. Institutions such as TVA or the Ford Foundation perform functions difficult for many Europeans to understand, since they are more accustomed either to differentiate sharply between the public sphere and the private (as has been typical of the industrial age or to subordinate the private to the public (as is favored by the socialists and some liberals) or to absorb the private by the public (as has been the case in communist states).

At one time the question of ownership was the decisive social and political issue of a society undergoing modernization. The forms of land ownership customary in the feudal-agricultural age were extended through force of habit as well as historical accommodation into the industrial age; owning a factory was seen as being largely the same as owning a piece of land. This eventually led to a severe conflict between old forms and modes of evaluating individual rights and the new requirements of industrial organization, of collective employee rights, and of changed sociopolitical institutions. Socialism was one extreme solution; in the more advanced West depersonalized corporate ownership and the limited sharing of authority with organized labor was the general pattern of accommodation. The question of ownership was thus redefined into one of control and regulation, while the issue of exploitation associated with ownership was replaced by new problems concerning the economic participation and psychological well-being of the employed.

In the process, even in America the federal government emerged as the key institution for restructuring social relations, and the question of the extent of the state's role in economic affairs became crucial. Unlike the agricultural age, during which few state institutions were involved in organizing and assisting man's daily existence, the industrial age produced both greater opportunities for national direction and a greater social demand for government-imposed social justice. More centralized direction by the state seemed the only alternative to chaos and the only response to social injustice.

Our age has been moving toward a new pattern, blurring distinctions between public and private bodies and encouraging more cross-participation in both by their employees and members. In Europe co-determination not only has involved profit-sharing but has increasingly led to participation in policymaking; pressures in the same direction are clearly building up in the United States as well. At the same time, the widening social perspectives of the American business community are likely to increase the involvement of business executives in social problems, thereby merging private and public activity on both the local and the national levels. This might in turn make for more effective social application of the new management techniques, which, unlike bureaucratized governmental procedures, have proved both efficient and responsive to external stimuli.*

Such participatory pluralism may prove reasonably effective in subordinating science and technology to social ends. In the past for some the introduction of the machine was the beginning of utopia; for others it meant the unleashing of evil. Similarly, today technology is seen by some modern conservatives as the beginning of a happy new age because it promises to free man from many social problems, while for the New Left technetronics is replacing property as the symbol of social evil.[2] Yet the crucial issue remains the ends to which science and technology are applied, and a society in which effective coordination is combined with decentralization is more likely to crystallize the necessary discussion and reflection. Scientific expertise can then be mobilized for social ends without granting scientists a dominating political role because of their scientific credentials.† Participatory pluralism will

* This is especially ironic since the government has sponsored the transfer of many technological innovations from defense to private industry (see R. Lester and G. Howick, *Assessing Technology Transfer*, NASA, Washington, D.C., 1966, especially pp. 42, 48, 76, and 79). At the same time, the *internal* bureaucratic procedures of many government agencies lag in technological innovation as compared with major banks or corporations. Bureaucratic rigidity appears to be a function of size and hierarchy. A study by sixteen leading research administrators reported in the spring of 1967 that small, independent companies have been much more innovative technologically than large companies (see Peter Drucker, *The Age of Discontinuity*, New York, 1969, p. 62.)

† On the complex question of the role of scientists in policymaking, comments by Don K. Price in *The Scientific Estate* (Cambridge, Mass., 1965) and by Sanford A. Lakoff and J. Stefan Dupre in *Science and the Nation: Policy and Politics* (Englewood Cliffs, N.J., 1962) are especially pertinent.

There is no reason to believe that scientific competence is sufficient for relevant judgments concerning all areas of social existence or public policy. Indeed, though somewhat exaggerated, the observations of a French social thinker on the dangers of excessive deference to the nonscientific opinions of scientists have some merit:

"We are forced to conclude that our scientists are incapable of any but the emptiest platitudes when they stray from their specialties. It makes one think back on the collection of mediocrities accumulated by Einstein when he spoke of God, the state, peace, and the meaning of life. It is clear that Einstein, extraordinary mathematical genius that he was, was no Pascal; he

automatically ensure neither political wisdom nor social responsibility, but it might make for a society that more nearly approaches both.

Anticipation of the social effects of technological innovation offers a good example of the necessary forms of cross-institutional cooperation. One of the nation's most urgent needs is the creation of a variety of mechanisms that link national and local governments, academia, and the business community (there the example of NASA may be especially rewarding) in the task of evaluating not only the operational effects of the new technologies but their cultural and psychological effects. A series of national and local councils—not restricted to scientists but made up of various social groups, including the clergy—would be in keeping with both the need and the emerging pattern of social response to change.*

The trend toward the progressive breakdown of sharp distinctions between the political and social spheres, between public and

---

knew nothing of political or human reality, or, in fact, anything at all outside his mathematical reach. The banality of Einstein's remarks in matters outside his specialty is as astonishing as his genius within it. It seems as though the specialized application of all one's faculties in a particular area inhibits the consideration of things in general. Even J. Robert Oppenheimer, who seems receptive to a general culture, is not outside this judgment. His political and social declarations, for example, scarcely go beyond the level of those of the man in the street. And the opinions of the scientists quoted by *L'Express* are not even on the level of Einstein or Oppenheimer. Their pomposities, in fact, do not rise to the level of the average. They are vague generalities inherited from the nineteenth century, and the fact that they represent the furthest limits of thought of our scientific worthies must be symptomatic of arrested development or of a mental block. Particularly disquieting is the gap between the enormous power they wield and their critical ability, which must be estimated as null" (Ellul, p. 435). For some suggestive analogies, see R. Todd, "George Wald: The Man, the Speech," *The New York Times Magazine*, August 17, 1967.

* This would go beyond the task set the National Commission on Technology, Automation and Economic Progress, authorized by Congress in 1964, and also address itself to the issues with which, for example, the British Society for Social Responsibility in Science has been grappling.

An editorial in *Science* (August 1, 1969) on "The Control of Technology" errs in implying that the above matter should be restricted to scientists. Social scientists, the clergy, and humanists should also be involved, and the Special Commission on the Social Sciences, established in 1968 by the National Science Board, could well be drawn in.

private institutions, will not lend itself to easy classification as liberal, conservative, or socialist—all terms derived from a different historical context—but it will be a major step toward the participatory democracy advocated by some of the New Left in the late 1960s. Ironically, this participatory democracy is likely to emerge through a progressive symbiosis of the institutions of society and of government rather than through the remedies the New Left had been advocating: economic expropriation and political revolution, both distinctly anachronistic remedies of the earlier industrial era.

The evolutionary emergence of participatory pluralism may not seem a sufficient response to those sectors of American society that have become entirely alienated—and it may appear as too much change to those who have a vested interest in the *status quo*. But for that large body of Americans who accept the concept of gradual change and who value procedural order, multiple patterns of social involvement could provide the desired creative outlet for a society that is increasingly becoming more complex and expert-oriented. In that setting it is even possible that the political parties as traditionally known in America will further decline in importance; in their stead, organized local, regional, urban, professional, and other interests will provide the focus for political action, and shifting national coalitions will form on an *ad hoc* basis around specific issues of national import.*

In the immediate future, the politics of street protest are likely to dominate the visible dimensions of American political life. Less visible—indeed, sometimes totally obscured by the prevailing rhetoric about the "repressive society"—is the gradual progress toward a new democracy increasingly based on participatory pluralism in many areas of life. Assuming that short-term crises do not deflect the United States from redefining the

* These coalitions are less likely to form along the traditional dividing line of Republicans and Democrats or—as more recently—of conservatives and liberals, but rather to divide according to basic philosophical attitudes toward the problems of modern life. In greatly simplified terms, the humanists and idealists on one side might be pitted against the pragmatists and modernizers on the other.

substance of its democratic tradition, the long-range effect of the present transition and its turmoils will be to deepen and widen the scope of the democratic process in America.

Change in Cultural Formation

The evolutionary development of American democracy will have to be matched by changes in the processes of forming and shaping the content of its national culture. As in the case of political change, cultural reform is more likely to come about through evolution—in part deliberately encouraged and in part stimulated by over-all social change—than through programmatic engineering. The element of deliberate and conscious choice may be even more important here than in the transformation of complex institutional arrangements, because in modern society the educational system and the mass media have become the principal social means for defining the substance of a national culture. This is particularly true in American society, which has downgraded such alternative sources of culture as churches and traditional customs.

The educational system has a special social responsibility in regard to black Americans. Here the simultaneous needs are to enhance the black citizen's dignity and to enlarge his long-range opportunities. These needs have occasionally clashed, but perhaps the short-term remedy will be to combine the black American's quest for his separate identity (through such institutional devices as separate courses and residences) with massive and scientifically oriented remedial training. The challenge today—and probably for several decades to come—is to help the black American skip the late-industrial stage of America's development, and this cannot be done unless sensitivity to his psychological needs is matched by a recognition of the necessity for a disciplined, focused intellectual effort. The two will be hard to combine, but it is in this area that eventual progress or disaster in America's race relations will be shaped.

Racial calamity will be avoided only if society at large defines more clearly the values it seeks, is willing to create a responsive framework to promote them, and is prepared to insist on respect for orderly procedure. Nothing could be more destructive than wide swings from permissive and guilt-ridden acquiescence to any demand made by black extremists—such acquiescence merely stimulates an escalation of extremism—to insensitive passivity or opposition to black demands for a fair share of participation in American society. A massive educational effort is the crucial factor, but to be successful it must be geared to the long-range thrust of American society's developmental needs.

The unprecedented spread of mass education in America raises the more general question whether mechanically extending the duration of education will suffice to meet both the psychological and technical needs of the emerging society. The social scope and duration of current mass education differs from the early-industrial emphasis on minimum mass literacy for males (and from the even more elitist medieval pattern of very limited learning for very few). Contemporary programs aim at the education of a high proportion of both sexes and call for periods of schooling lasting anywhere from ten to almost twenty years (in the case of more advanced degrees). In America higher education is carried on within a relatively self-contained organizational and even social framework, making for a protracted period of semi-isolation from problems of social reality. As a result, both organizationally and in terms of content, a divorce between education and social existence has tended to develop, leading to the already noted emotional and psychic manifestations of student frustration and immaturity.

By extending education on an *intermittent* basis throughout the lifetime of the citizen, society would go a long way toward meeting this problem. The duration of the self-contained and relatively isolated phase of initial education could then be shortened. Taking into account the earlier physical and sexual maturation of young people today, it could be more generally pursued within a work-study framework, and it should be supplemented by periodic additional training throughout most of one's active life.

A good case can be made for ending initial education (more of which could be obtained in the home through electronic devices) somewhere around the age of eighteen. This formal initial period could be followed by two years of service in a socially desirable cause;* then by direct involvement in some professional activity and by advanced, systematic training within that area; and finally by regular periods of one and eventually even two years of broadening, "integrative" study at the beginning of every decade of one's life, somewhere up to the age of sixty.† For example, medical or legal training could begin after only two years of college, thus both shortening the time needed to complete the training and probably also increasing the number attracted into these professions. Regular and formally required retraining—as well as broadening—could ensue at regular intervals throughout most of one's professional career.

Combining initial specialization with a subsequent broadening

---

* This cause could be either national or international, publicly or privately tackled. It would be in keeping with the humanitarian idealism of the young not to limit such service to national causes. One good way to handle the matter would be to maintain a list of acceptable humanitarian activities, service on behalf of which would be an acceptable equivalent for military duty.

† This change should focus the attention of the university on the broader integrative needs of the modern age. It would thus combine science with philosophy but no longer act as an intellectual cafeteria, offering studies ranging from physical education through classics, from "soul" courses to the latest specialized sciences. In effect, the roles of the "junior" college and of the university would become separate in time and place, probably to the advantage of both institutions. This would permit concentration on the larger social questions and keep higher education from being an aristocratic process; at the same time, it would allay some of the dangers inherent in the illusion that an educated citizenry is created by simply running a lot of people through the educational mill.

In addition, the traditional titles of learning, such as "doctor of philosophy," imply a terminal educational process and reflect the situation of an earlier stage in social history. Since learning will become a continuous, lifetime process that involves almost the entire community, degrees become a symbolic anachronism and should be drastically reclassified to indicate more accurately the various stages of specialized and generalized knowledge.

of philosophical and scientific horizons would somewhat counteract the present trend, which makes increased specialization and rising professional standing go hand in hand. This encourages a narrowness of general outlook. The trend could be gradually reversed by a situation in which specialization at the age of greatest absorptive capability would be followed by more intellectual integration at a stage of increased personal maturity. Such an approach would encourage the gradual emergence of an integrative, modernizing elite that would show greater concern with society's underlying humane values in an age in which intensive scientific specialization is fraught with dangers of intellectual fragmentation.*

The formal educational system has been relatively slow in exploiting the new opportunities for supplementary home-based education through television consoles and other electronic devices. It has also been suspicious of the growing inclination of nongovernmental organizations to develop their own learning and training programs. In different ways, however, both the black community and business are becoming more involved in education, for psychological as well as for professional reasons.† Greater multiplicity in educational training will make for a more pluralistic national community, and the increasing involvement of business companies in education may lead to a more rapid adaptation of the latest techniques and scientific knowledge

* "One of the paradoxes of the future is that while an increasing number of managerial decisions will be handled by automatic data processing, buttressed by clear and swift communications networks, the intelligent direction and coordination of large-scale systems will place an even greater premium than at present upon *the wise, artful, and broadly-experienced general manager* in organizations characterized by operational decentralization. In short, the proposition that effective decentralization can occur only where organizational centralization has become efficient will have become increasingly recognized, not as a paradox, but as a logical reality" (*The United States and the World in the 1985 Era,* p. 44).

† For example, Olin Corporation, noting in an advertisement that "there is no growth potential in ignorance," has instituted literacy and high school training programs in three of its plants. Other major corporations have similar training programs.

to the educational process. American business and, to a lesser extent, the government have already undertaken extensive programs of managerial "retooling" and retraining, thereby moving toward the intermittent educational pattern.

Change in educational procedures and philosophy should also be accompanied by parallel changes in the broader national processes by which values are generated and disseminated. Given America's role as a world disseminator of new values and techniques, this is both a national and a global obligation. Yet no other country has permitted its mass culture, taste, daily amusement, and, most important, the indirect education of its children to be almost exclusively the domain of private business and advertising, or permitted both standards of taste and the intellectual content of culture to be defined largely by a small group of entrepreneurs located in one metropolitan center. American television, in which a cultural monopoly is exercised by a relatively small group, reflects the insensitivity of the communications process to the tastes and philosophical values of much of America.*

Rising public dissatisfaction with this state of affairs indicates that perhaps some change has to come in this field as well. The geographical decentralization and dispersal of the television industry into more numerous units, the separation of broadcasting from program production, and the further extension of educational programming will probably be sharply opposed by existing interests; if past American experience can serve as a relevant guide, change will come by attrition and piecemeal reform,

* ". . . broadcasting has imposed upon American society what in the supreme civic sense may be a fatal contradiction. The extension of communication should be an extension of democracy. Yet while the participatory base of democracy has been broadening, the ownership and control of the means of communication have narrowed.

"It could be said indeed that far from being an expression of majority desire, as the networks say, television programs are the imposition of a social minority on the majority, the minority consisting of the fifty top advertisers, the three networks, and a dozen or so advertising agencies" (Alexander Kendrick, *Prime Time: The Life of Edward R. Murrow*, Boston, 1969, pp. 12–13).

rather than by wholesale readjustment. Here, again, scientific and technological developments may become the handmaidens of constructive change; they may make possible (through home video tapes, home-operated lenses, closed-channel programming) far greater diversity than is today available, as well as more extensive exploitation of the audio-visual media by more institutions and organizations. Instead of limiting intellectual horizons, television could become a diversified and intellectually enriching source of this society's over-all cultural growth.

Cultural change in our society may also be spurred by the growing female rebellion, accelerated by education and new sexual mores. The massive entrance of women into the professions, into executive positions, and into politics is probably only a generation away, and there is already abundant evidence of mounting restlessness because of current inequalities of opportunity. Such increased feminine assertiveness could spill over into American society's cultural front, enhancing somewhat the general social interest in cultural growth and standards.

Rational Humanism

The technological thrust and the economic wealth of the United States now make it possible to give the concept of liberty and equality a broader meaning, going beyond the procedural and external to the personal and inner spheres of man's social existence. By focusing more deliberately on these qualitative aspects of life, America may avoid the depersonalizing dangers inherent in the self-generating but philosophically meaningless mechanization of environment and build a social framework for a synthesis of man's external and inner dimensions.

Such a synthesis may eventually result from the current intense conflict between the irrational personalism of the "humanists" and the impersonal rationality of the "modernizers." The former group, source of much of the rhetoric of the literary community, the student activists, and the doctrinaire liberals, partakes of the tradition of skepticism and disbelief that played such a vital role in overthrowing the religious and philosophical hold of pre-industrial America on the values of industrial America; it seeks to fortify this tradition by a new emphasis on emotion and feeling. Given its Dadaist style and its Luddite-inspired historical posture, it is unlikely that this camp will long remain vital. The potential transformation of the New Left into the Violent Left will certainly not enhance its appeal to the American public. The latter group, more typical of the new business executives, the governmental-commercial establishment, and the scientific organization men, seeks to combine self-interest with a detached emphasis on rationalist innovation; since it fails to provide a satisfactory emotional or philosophical rationale for either, it alienates the more idealistic young people.*

The clash between these two orientations is destructive and threatening to American liberal democracy. It fragments the remnants of the consensus of the industrial age and polarizes articulate public opinion. Yet it also holds the promise of a new perspective that is better suited to the needs of the emerging American society, since it moves beyond the increasingly irrelevant framework that now confines modern man's outlook. This new perspective involves growing recognition that man's propensity for scientific innovation cannot be restrained—that as long as man's mind functions, scientific innovation will be one of its expressions. But it also involves a heightened awareness that as long as man conceives of himself as a distinctive being, idealism will be the central mode of expressing his spirit. The imperative need for both innovation and idealism is thus stimulating a ra-

* Modern psychology increasingly recognizes that the non-concrete, more abstract qualities of life, such as goodness, aesthetic beauty, and morality, are becoming more and more important in satisfying individual wants in modern society (see, for example, Abraham Maslow, *Motivation and Personality,* New York, 1954, and *Toward a Psychology of Being,* Princeton, 1962). However, the quest for these more abstract and emotional satisfactions often takes ludicrous forms. The late sixties have seen in America a proliferation of various institutes and seminars in which businessmen and others engage in special "sensitivity" séances, expose themselves to "brain-wave conditioning," undertake yoga exercises and sustained "meditation," and the like. These fads reflect the fracturing of the broader, more integrative frameworks of belief, as noted in our discussion in Part II.

tionalist humane outlook that is gradually supplanting both the liberal skepticism of some humanists and the conservative social indifference of some modernizers.

This rational humanism is expressed in several ways: first, in an emerging international consciousness that makes so many Americans and American institutions go beyond purely nationalistic concerns and become deeply involved in global problems of human growth and nourishment, and is prompting in American youth such a constructive preoccupation with problems of ecology; second, in a growing tendency—in spite of a still deeply ingrained anticommunism—to view international problems as human issues and not as political confrontations between good and evil; third, in a strong public idealism that is free of a utopian, impatient, and often intolerant desire to resolve all outstanding dilemmas immediately. In addition, it can also be seen in the fact that Americans, instead of trying to flee the problems of science, are attempting to balance their fascination with science and their reliance on it as a tool for dealing with human problems by a more intense concern with the personal qualities of life and by a quest for more philosophical and religiously ecumenical definitions of human nature. This suggests the likelihood of a revival of religiosity of a more personal, noninstitutional nature. Finally, the emerging rational humanism is historically contingent in the sense that it does not involve—as was the case with nineteenth-century ideology—universally prescriptive concepts of social organization but stresses cultural and economic global diversity. In so doing, rational humanism is likely to be historically more relevant than was the case with earlier responses to social dilemmas. Unlike the industrial age, when complexity and historical discontinuity induced ideological flights of the mind into atavism or futuristic utopias, in the technetronic age the greater availability of means permits the definition of more attainable ends, thus making for a less doctrinaire and a more effective relationship between "what is" and "what ought to be."

The great revolutions of the nineteenth and twentieth centuries sought both liberty and equality, but even in the absence of racial conflict it was found that the two were difficult to combine in an age in which the traditional institutions of a religious, aristocratic, and agricultural era were clashing with the effects of skeptical rationalism, legalistic democracy, nascent social consciousness, and the needs of a developing urban-industrial society. In America the linkage of liberty and equality was especially hindered by deeply embedded fundamentalist religious values that were reinforced by the ever widening gap between the progressing white community and the artificially arrested black community. Inequality became a self-fulfilling prophecy, as well as an economic necessity to the industrially developing North.

The positive potential of the third American revolution lies in its promise to link liberty with equality. This linkage is a process, and will not be attained all at once. Indeed, during the next several decades reversals and even increased tensions are to be expected. Nevertheless, though frequently obscured by passionate polemics, the emerging rational humanism is part of the "cultural revolution" that America has been experiencing, a cultural revolution more enduring and deeper than the one that initiated the term. Linked to political reform, the current cultural revolution could gradually enlarge the scope of personal freedom by increasing the sense of self-fulfillment of an unprecedented number of citizens and give greater meaning to equality by making knowledge the basis for social and racial egalitarianism. It could create the preconditions for a socially creative and individually gratifying society that would inevitably have a constructive world role to play.

2. International Prospects

Tension is unavoidable as man strives to assimilate the new into the framework of the old. For a time the established framework resiliently integrates the new by adapting it in a more familiar shape. But at some point the old framework becomes overloaded. The new input can no longer be redefined into traditional forms, and eventually it asserts itself with compelling force. Today, though the old framework of international politics —with their spheres of influence, military alliances between nation-states, the fiction of sovereignty, doctrinal conflicts arising from nineteenth-century crises—is clearly no longer compatible with reality.

Indeed, it is remarkable how rapidly the dominant moods have changed during the last two decades. The 1950s were the era of certainty. The two sides—Communist and Western—faced each other in a setting that pitted conviction against conviction. Stalinist Manichaeans confronted Dulles's missionaries. That mood quickly gave way to another, with Khrushchev and Kennedy serving as transitions to an era of confusion. Dissension in the communist world prompted an ideological crisis, while the West increasingly began to question its own values and righteousness. Communist cynics confronted liberal skeptics.

There are indications that the 1970s will be dominated by growing awareness that the time has come for a common effort to shape a new framework for international politics, a framework that can serve as an effective channel for joint endeavors. Yet it must be recognized that there will be no real global cooperation until there is far greater consensus on its priorities and purposes:

Is it to enhance man's material well-being and his intellectual development? Is economic growth the answer, or is a massive international educational effort to be the point of departure? Should health have priority? How is personal well-being related to the perhaps less important but more easily measured gross national product? Is there a necessary connection between scientific advance and personal happiness?

There is already widespread agreement about the desirability of cutting arms budgets and developing international peace-keeping forces. There is also a more self-conscious awareness of man's inherent aggressiveness and of the need to control it.[3] Totally destructive weapons make the effects of conflict incalculable and thus reduce the likelihood of a major war. Here, again, an emerging global consciousness is forcing the abandonment of preoccupations with national supremacy and accentuating global interdependence. In the United States this growing international awareness has sometimes taken the form of greater sensitivity to the influence of the "military-industrial complex,"[4] and it has effectively obstructed the unlimited development of biological-chemical weaponry and its use in combat. It has also stimulated pressures for a re-examination of defense requirements, while in other advanced countries, particularly in Japan and Western Europe, it has prompted strong pacifist movements.

Nonetheless, a realistic assessment compels the conclusion that there will be no global security arrangement in the foreseeable future. The most that can be expected and effectively sought is a widening of arms-control treaties, some unilateral restraints on defense spending, and some expansion in UN peace-keeping machinery. The conflicts between nations are still very real; readings of world change still differ sharply, and national aspirations remain divergent. Moreover, unlike the situation in Japan, Western Europe, and the United States, neither in the Soviet Union nor in China is there any public discussion of weapons development and defense spending. Secrecy and censorship impose restraints on views that diverge from the official position, and thus limit the influence of a growing global consciousness on policy choices open to the leaders of these states.

The picture is somewhat more ambiguous in the fields of economic and educational-scientific development. All major countries now accept the principle that they ought to aid the less developed countries. This is a new moral position, and it is an important component of the new global consciousness. Though nations still assert their sovereignty in fixing the scale of aid extended (most make less than one per cent of their GNP available), they have in effect created a binding precedent: the extension of aid has become an imperative. It seems likely that in the years to come, despite persisting conflicts among states, economic aid will grow in scale and be used less and less as a vehicle of political influence. At the same time, however, short of a very major crisis, it seems unlikely that aid will be forthcoming in amounts sufficient to offset the threatening prospects discussed in Part I.

In some respects technological-scientific developments augur more promise for the rapid global spread of educational programs and of new techniques. Television satellites are already making regional educational programs possible (as in Central America), and there has been progress in setting up regional technological institutes (this might eventually reduce the brain drain, which is caused in part by the temptations inherent in resident studies in the more advanced countries). The Development Assistance Committee of OECD offers the potential for a systematic approach to meeting the educational needs of the less developed countries, and unlike UNESCO it is not subject to political pressures from them.[5] Such an approach would be consistent with the emergence of a more cooperative community of the developed nations, one able to adopt a common development strategy. The spread of English as a global scientific language is accelerating the formation of a global scientific family, increasingly mobile and interchangeable.

Yet this progress could be vitiated in many countries by a social incapacity to digest and absorb the positive potential inherent in educational and scientific growth. Their inadequate economic resources—only marginally augmented by reasonably foreseeable foreign aid—may even cause some positive changes to backfire, prompting not social advance but costly conflict, not policy innovation but political paralysis. Indeed, our still limited knowledge of the factors inducing social development, and of the role played in that development by religion, culture, and psychology, hinders the formulation of an effective strategy for the dissemination of technical know-how and for the application of material aid.*

In this setting, which combines rudiments of order and elements of chaos, two general prospects, both more immediately relevant to United States foreign policy, seem probable: first, the Third World, though it will obviously continue to experience turbulent changes, is not very likely to be swept by a common revolutionary wave; second, the Soviet Union will in the foreseeable future remain too strong externally not to be a global rival to the United States but too weak internally to be its global partner.

The Revolutionary Process

The concept of an international revolution inspired by a common ideology had some meaning when the industrial revolution seemed to indicate that certain forms of social organization and of social crisis had a general application. That view combined a universal intellectual perspective with a geographically historical parochialism. It assumed, in part because information about world processes was relatively limited, that a common global framework could be postulated on the basis of the historical experience of a few Western countries. It is now increasingly evi-

* This is why there is special merit in the National Planning Association's proposal (1969) that a Technical Assistance and Development Research Institute be established in Washington to provide technical assistance to underdeveloped nations and to make a broad-gauged study of the problems connected with development.

dent that social conditions, as well as the way in which science and technology are socially applied, vary enormously, and that this variety includes very subtle but important nuances of cultural, religious, and historic tradition, in addition to economic and technical factors.*

Moreover, in Russia and in China the revolutionary intelligentsia of the late nineteenth and early twentieth centuries was itself in the forefront of the process of modernization. It represented the most advanced segments of society, and hence a political victory by it inherently involved a historical step forward for the society as a whole. This is no longer the case. The revolutionary intelligentsia in the less developed countries, to say nothing of its vicarious middle-class intellectual equivalents in the United States, often represents a social anachronism. As far as the modernization process is concerned, this intelligentsia has been left behind by developments in science and technology, in which it is largely "illiterate."

It is possible, therefore, that in some countries, perhaps even the more modern ones, these anachronistic intelligentsias may even succeed, by clinging to essentially aristocratic and anti-industrial values, in effectively blocking the modernization of their societies by insisting that it be postponed until after an ideological revolution has taken place. In this sense, the technetronic revolution could partially become a self-limiting phenomenon: disseminated by mass communications, it creates its own antithesis through the impact of mass communications on some sectors of the intelligentsia. In some of the developing countries this might eventually pit the traditional humanist-legalist trained intelligentsia, who are more receptive to doctrinal appeals, against the younger, more socially concerned and innovative officers, engineers, and students, who have combined to effect a modernization that is indigenous and socially radical, though programmatically eclectic.

---

* For earlier discussion of the prospects of revolutionary success, see pp. 48, 119, 188–191, and 248–249.

In Latin America the more extreme reforms may be more reminiscent of Peronism and fascism than of communism. By 1970 the student population will be approximately one million,[6] thus creating an ambitious and politically volatile base for reform. In addition, both the opposition of Latin American governments to United States economic and political influence[7] and their inclination to undertake radical domestic reforms may be expected to increase, but to do so within a framework that combines a more socially responsible Catholicism with nationalism, in a setting of considerable national diversity. This will produce a highly differentiated pattern of change, but even its radical manifestations are not likely to be modeled on communist countries, especially since the relative cultural sophistication of the Latin American elites reduces the appeal of the stodgy Eastern European or Soviet models. The officer corps, composed of socially radical and technologically innovative younger officers, is more likely to be the source of revolutionary change than the local communist parties, and Latin American discontent will be galvanized not by ideology but by continuing anti-Yankeeism—pure and simple.

In other parts of the globe similar social combinations probably will result in regimes that will compensate for the weakness of indigenous religious and intellectual traditions by being doctrinally oriented. Iraqi and Sudanese coups of the late 1960s, carried out by alliances of officers and intellectuals, will probably be repeated elsewhere in Africa and the Middle East. There is, however, some reason for skepticism concerning the genuineness and depth of the ideological commitment of these new regimes. Some of their ideology is shaped by extraneous factors (the question of Israel and of the Soviet attitude); some is merely currently fashionable rhetoric; much of it is highly volatile and subject to drastic changes.* Doubtless, these regimes will be assisted and

* Moreover, these regimes have difficulty in moving into what Huntington has called the second phase of a revolution: "A complete revolution, however, also involves a second phase: the creation and institutionalization of a new political order. The successful revolution combines rapid political mobilization and rapid political institutionalization. Not all revolutions pro-

exploited by the Soviets and the Chinese. (The latter, for example, have already made political inroads into East Africa.) Even so, it will still be more a matter of tactical cooperation than of actual control and a common strategic policy.

Similarly, in South and Southeast Asia revolutionary patterns are likely to have an essentially indigenous and differentiated character. It is quite possible that the two large political units—India and Pakistan—which combine a variety of disparate economic and ethnic entities, may split up. This will be especially likely as the present elites, whose internal unity was forged by the struggle against the British, fade from the scene. The waning of the Congress Party in India has been accompanied by intensifying ethnic stresses and by the polarization of political opinions. Should the Indian Union break down, southern Tamil separatism, probably left-wing radical in orientation, would be contested by northern Hindu right radicalism, perhaps more religiously oriented; each would tend to intensify the doctrinal and indigenous distinctiveness of the other. As happened earlier in China, any tendency toward communism that might result from such a confrontation would soon be culturally absorbed and perhaps overwhelmed by the weight of economic backwardness.

In China the Sino-Soviet conflict has already accelerated the inescapable Sinification of Chinese communism. That conflict shattered the revolution's universal perspective and—perhaps even more important—detached Chinese modernization from its commitment to the Soviet model. Hence, whatever happens in the short run, in years to come Chinese development will probably increasingly share the experience of other nations in the process of modernization. This may both dilute the regime's ideological tenacity and lead to more eclectic experimentation in shaping the Chinese road to modernity.

---

duce a new political order. The measure of how revolutionary a revolution is is the rapidity and the scope of the expansion of political participation. The measure of how successful a revolution is is the authority and stability of the institutions to which it gives birth" (Huntington, p. 266).

Many of the upheavals in the Third World will unavoidably have a strong anti-American bias. This is likely to be particularly true where American presence and power has traditionally been most visible. In areas near the Soviet Union and China, however, anti-Soviet and anti-Chinese attitudes are likely to predominate in the long run, irrespective of the character of the internal reforms and of the external complexion of the ruling regimes. This again highlights the point that the revolutionary process as such will not necessarily determine the foreign-policy stance of the new elites, which is more likely to be shaped by a combination of traditional antipathies, current fears, and domestic political needs.

Moreover, the basic orientation of the new elites will more and more respond to the intellectual impact of domestic changes in the more advanced world, changes directly and personally visible to these elites through travel, study, and global mass media. This intimacy with life abroad will further reduce the importance of integrative ideologies, which had previously provided a substitute for a clear vision of the future and the outside world. Ideological uniformity was the prescription for remaking a world that was both distant and largely unknown, but proximity and global congestion now dictate revolutionary diversity.

Accordingly, the real values—as distinguished from the rhetoric—of the aspiring elites of the developing nations will be shaped by tangible developments rather than by abstract generalizations. The success of the United States in shaping a workable, multiracial democracy while pioneering in science and technology, the ability of Europe and Japan to overcome the psychological and social stresses of mature modernity, and—last, but not least—the degree to which the Soviet Union breaks away from the doctrinal orthodoxy that inhibits its social development will be critically important in shaping the outlook of Third World leaders.

USA/USSR: Less Intensive, More Extensive Rivalry

The extent to which Americans view revolutionary changes abroad as automatically inimical to their interests reinforces the extent to which these seem beneficial to the Soviets and can be fitted into a global communist framework; conversely, the extent to which America views these changes in a neutral light diminishes the intrinsic attraction of the Soviet model for Third World revolutionaries and encourages indigenous factors to surface more rapidly. The Soviet attraction has already been weakened by the appearance of states more militant than the Soviet Union and of groups more activist than the pro-Soviet communist parties. The Soviet appeal has also declined because internal Soviet bureaucratization and dogmatic restraints on intellectual creativity and social innovation have made the Soviet Union the most conservative political and social order of the more advanced world.*

American-Soviet rivalry is hence likely to become less ideological in character, though it may become more extensive geographically and more dangerous in terms of the power involved. Increased direct contacts between the two nations, restraints imposed by mutual recognition of the destructiveness of present weapons systems, and lessened ideological expectations for the Third World could make American-Soviet relations more stable. Nevertheless, more and more areas on the globe could become the objects of moves and countermoves if the growth in long-range Soviet military forces, particularly conventional air- and sea-lift capabilities, extends American-Soviet rivalry to areas previously considered beyond the Soviet reach. Instability in the Third World could tempt either state to employ its power to offset or pre-empt the other, thereby creating situations analogous to the Fashoda

---

* Some Soviet scientists (particularly Kapitsa and Sakharov) have already warned of the resulting long-run cost to Soviet scientific and intellectual growth.

incident, which at the end of the nineteenth century almost caused a war between France and Britain at a time when these powers were moving (and continued to move) toward a European accommodation.[8]

On the whole, close cooperation between the United States and the Soviet Union seems a very unlikely prospect in the coming decade. This is only partially due to the different ideological and political character of the two countries. A communist America would in all probability remain a rival of the Soviet Union, just as Communist China soon became one. Given its size and power, a democratic and creative Soviet Union might be an even more powerful competitor for the United States than is the present bureaucratically stagnant and doctrinally orthodox Soviet system. Moreover, democratic nations are not necessarily pacifist nations, as American history amply demonstrates. Rivalry between nations is inherent in an international system that functions without global consensus—the result of centuries of the conditioning of man's outlook by competitive nations that insisted on their individual superiority, and particular values. Such rivalry is not likely to be terminated by anything short of a fundamental reconstruction in the nature of relations between nations—and hence in the character of national sovereignty itself.

At present, the formation of a new cooperative international pattern is getting little help from the Soviet Union, in spite of the fact that it considers itself in the forefront of historical progress and was until recently the standard-bearer of an ideology that had cut across traditional national lines. The irony of history is such that today the Soviet Union has a foreign policy that is intensely nationalistic and a domestic policy that calls for the domination of non-Russian minorities; it actively campaigns against regional patterns of international cooperation, grants a disproportionately small amount of help to the less developed nations (roughly ten per cent of United States foreign aid), and rejects a joint exploration of space (cloaking its own efforts in utmost secrecy).

Indeed, one of the unanticipated effects of the Sino-Soviet dispute may be a hardening of the Soviet outlook and a more paranoid view of the world. Though Soviet leaders want to avoid a two-front confrontation and are hence pushed toward accommodation with either the West or the East, the very scale of the Chinese challenge intensifies their fears, puts a premium on military preparedness, and stimulates an intense preoccupation with the sacredness of frontiers.*

Equally important but less generally recognized as a factor in inhibiting the Soviet Union from seeking more binding forms of international cooperation is the domestic weakness and insecurity of Soviet leaders. Even fifty years after its inception, the political system they head still lacks elementary legitimacy: its ruling elite relies heavily on coercion and censorship to retain its power, which is acquired not by regular, constitutional procedures but through protracted, bureaucratic infighting. (The struggles for succession are a case in point.) Because of the doctrinal incapacity of the Soviet political system to respond to the internal needs of social innovation, broad accommodation with the West, carrying with it the acknowledgment that the Leninist dichotomic vision of the world—which in turn justifies the Leninist concept of the ruling party—is no longer relevant, would inevitably cause far-reaching internal political instability in the Soviet Union and in Soviet-dominated Eastern Europe.

In large measure, this conservative Leninist attitude reflects Russia's delayed modernization and political development. In terms of the global city, the Soviet Union represents an archaic religious community that experiences modernity existentially but not quite yet normatively.[9]

---

* To appreciate Soviet fears, one would have to imagine a situation in which the United States was confronted by eight hundred million Mexicans who had nuclear arms and rockets and who were loudly insisting that the United States had seized vast expanses of Mexican territory, that the American system was inherently evil, and that the American government was their enemy. Such a situation would doubtless stimulate intense fears in the American public. Soviet apprehensiveness is further increased by the fact that Siberia —relatively undeveloped and uninhabited—serves as a magnet to the Chinese masses, and that Russo-Chinese territorial arrangements are of a historically dubious character.

Policy Implications

The foregoing general propositions point to several immediate implications for American foreign policy, in terms both of guiding assumptions and of the desirable foreign posture. Before elaborating, let us first posit these implications in their most succinct form: a posture based on ideological considerations has become dated; an American-Soviet axis is not likely to be the basis for a new international system; traditional spheres of influence are increasingly unviable; economic determinism in regard to the less developed countries or to the communist states does not provide a sound basis for policy; regional alliances against individual nations are becoming obsolescent; an extensive American military presence abroad is becoming counterproductive to American interests and to the growth of an international community; American diplomatic machinery—developed in the pre-global and pre-technetronic age—has become outmoded and requires extensive modernization.

Although American foreign policy has not been as undifferentiatedly anti-communist as its critics have found it convenient to assert,* there has been a strong rhetorical tendency in American official circles to reduce international problems to an ideological confrontation and to identify radical change as contrary to American interests. Henceforth, local transformations in various parts of the world are less likely to be seen as part of a universal threat; in addition, the gradual pluralization of the communist world will continue to accelerate differences among the communist systems. This will reduce reliance on active American intervention, making it imperative primarily in defense of concrete American interests or in response to an overt hostile act by a power with the potential to threaten the United States.†

---

* The charge that the United States has conducted its foreign policy on the assumption of a monolithic world communist conspiracy is dear to some scholarly critics. In point of fact, the United States pioneered in aid to Yugoslavia in the late 1940s; it was the first to initiate American-Soviet cultural exchanges, visits between heads of state, and so on.

† In more specific terms, it would be desirable and proper for the United

A less ideological perspective will reduce the American-Soviet relationship to its proper proportions. The principal threat the Soviet Union poses to the United States is military: a stronger Soviet Union therefore inescapably tends to threaten America; a weaker Soviet Union feels threatened by America. Since a war between the two superpowers would be mutually destructive, arms-control arrangements between the two countries are dictated by common sense. The continuing SALT (Strategic Arms Limitation Talks) between the United States and the Soviet Union can be seen as more than a negotiation between two rivals; inadvertently, precisely because they will be lengthy, the talks signify a *de facto* beginning of a joint commission on arms and strategy. Although limited in actual power, the "commission" gradually and perhaps increasingly will affect the way each side acts, stimulating greater mutual sensitivity to felt needs and fears.*

In the meantime, until a binding agreement is reached, American technological sophistication is sufficient to provide the neces-

---

States to aid Thailand with arms and equipment should that country be threatened by North Vietnam. The same response would apply to a North Korean threat against South Korea, or a threat by the Arab states against Israel. But in none of these cases should American forces be committed unless a major power, i.e., the USSR or China, becomes directly involved. Total American abstention would encourage aggression, but American aid should suffice to make the war either useless or very costly to the aggressor. To repeat—direct involvement should be reserved for situations in which a power with the capacity to threaten the United States is involved.

* Science and technology have already revolutionized the exercise of sovereignty by the two countries vis-à-vis each other. The utilization of the U-2s, and subsequently of reconnaissance satellites, vitiated the claim to unlimited sovereignty over national air space, somewhat undoing Soviet military secrecy. The acquiescence of the Soviet Union to the U-2 flights was necessitated by its inability to shoot these planes down; in spite of the May 1960 incident, the precedent of unilateral inspection was thereby asserted and has since become a practice followed by both states.

The inherent complexity of reaching an arms-control agreement is suggested by the following conclusion by a specialist in the field: "There is basis for hope [of a possible agreement] if both sides can accept the fact that for some time the most they can expect to achieve is a strategic balance at quite high, but less rapidly escalating, force levels; and if both recognize that breaking the action-reaction cycle should be given first priority in any negotiations" (George W. Rathjens, *The Future of the Strategic Arms Race*, New York, 1969, p. 40).

sary degree of ambiguity to the qualitative and quantitative power relationship between the two states. In the current phase of destructive parity, this strategic and psychological posture is needed in order to replace earlier reliance on manifest and credible deterrence born of American superiority in destructive power. Parity deterrence requires some ambiguity, just as superiority deterrence demanded precise credibility.

But outside this relationship the opportunities for a wide-ranging settlement are relatively restricted.[10] An American-Soviet axis would be resented by too many states and therefore tempt both Washington and Moscow to exploit these resentments. In effect, the more successful the efforts to create such an axis, the stronger the impediment to it. In addition, as has already been argued, the Soviet Union does not represent a vital social alternative that offers the world an attractive and relevant model for handling either its old dilemmas or—particularly—the new ones posed by science and technology. As a result, the most that America can reasonably seek is a gradual increase in Soviet involvement in international cooperation through such projects as joint space exploration, undersea studies, and so forth. Cumulatively, these may help shape a pattern of collaborative involvement that will eventually embrace other spheres.

Meanwhile, it is likely that American and Russian influence will decrease in areas that both nations have traditionally considered their own special domains. In a modern city "staked out" areas are possible only in relations among criminal gangs; in the global city sealed spheres of influence are increasingly difficult—or at least costly—to maintain. Eastern Europe is bound to remain attracted to the West, and only direct Soviet coercion can impede what would otherwise happen quite rapidly: the linkage of Eastern Europe to a larger European entity. Even Soviet force will not be able to halt this process entirely; the traditional cultural attraction of the West is too strong, and it is currently reinforced by growing Eastern European recognition that, because of the technological gap between the East and the West, Russia cannot effectively help Eastern Europe to enter the post-industrial age. This attraction is healthy, for the gradual expansion of Eastern European links with Western Europe is bound to affect the Soviet Union as well and lessen its doctrinal orientation.

The notion of a special relationship between the United States and Latin America is also bound to decay. Latin American nationalism, more and more radical as it widens its popular base, will be directed with increasing animosity against the United States, unless the United States rapidly shifts its own posture. Accordingly, it would be wise for the United States to make an explicit move to abandon the Monroe Doctrine and to concede that in the new global age geographic or hemispheric contiguity no longer need be politically decisive. Nothing could be healthier for Pan-American relations than for the United States to place them on the same level as its relations with the rest of the world, confining itself to emphasis on cultural-political affinities (as it does with Western Europe) and economic-social obligations (as it does with the less developed countries).

It would also be advisable to view the question of the political development of both the communist and the developing countries with a great deal of patience. Just as the infusion of American power may not always be the solution, so reliance on economic growth is no guarantee of either democratization, political stability, or pro-Americanism. As has been pointed out, political change in the communist states is not a simple by-product of economic development, and the susceptibility of the less developed countries to radical appeals rises as they begin to develop. Foreign aid and closer economic contacts are not a palliative for deep-rooted crises or a remedy for the ills of deeply entrenched ideological institutions.

This argues for an approach to international economic relations and foreign aid that is increasingly depoliticized in form, even if the ultimate underlying purpose remains political. If that purpose is to promote the emergence of a more cooperative community of nations, irrespective of their individual internal systems, then it would be a step in the right direction to give international bodies a larger role in economic development and to start eliminating restrictions on trade. Such action is all the more likely to be eventually successful because it is less overtly political and is not geared to expectations of rapid and basic political change achieved through direct economic leverage.*

A more detached attitude toward world revolutionary processes and a less anxious preoccupation with the Soviet Union would also help the United States to develop a different posture toward China. China and South Asia are heavily populated areas that have inherited from the past complex challenges to social organization, and are still struggling with these old problems at a time when the advanced world is beginning to confront problems of new dimensions. Until links are established with China—and these can initially be sought and directed through Japan and Western Europe—China will remain an excluded and a self-excluded portion of mankind, all the more threatening because its backwardness will increasingly be combined with massive nuclear power. Accordingly, the United States, instead of becoming an indirect Soviet ally against China—which is what Moscow obviously wants—should encourage efforts by other countries to seek ties with China. In addition, it should launch its own initiatives,[11] and avoid becoming entangled in overt anti-Chinese security arrangements.

Indeed, in our age international security arrangements ought to resemble those of large metropolitan centers: such arrangements are directed not against specific organizations or individuals but against those who depart from established norms. Thus, an association based on a concept of cooperative nations linked for a variety of purposes, including security, ought gradually to replace existing alliances, which are usually formulated in terms of

* This need not exclude the concentration of effort on specific states when prospects for economic development coincide with more strictly political American interests. In other words, international economic aid for humanitarian purposes can go hand in hand with more selective and more intensive efforts in regard to specific countries.

a potential aggressor, explicitly identified either in the treaty or in the accompanying rhetoric. Though initially this would be only a formalistic change—for the association of states would necessarily involve only those that share certain interests and fears—a deliberately open-ended structure, with the security elements only a partial and secondary aspect, would avoid perpetuating institutionally the inevitable but often transient conflicts of interests between states.*

Evolution in the forms of international security would facilitate the gradual restructuring of the American defense posture, particularly by concentrating American military presence abroad in a few key countries. Except in countries that feel themselves directly threatened, prolonged United States military presence tends to galvanize political hostility toward the United States even in traditionally friendly countries (like Turkey), and though that presence was once wanted by the countries concerned, it has tended to become an American vested interest. With the restraint imposed on the waging of an all-out war by the destructiveness of nuclear weapons and with the likelihood that sporadic Third World violence will replace the previous preoccupation with a central war, American forces stationed abroad on the assumption that they will be needed to assure the security of different nations from a common threat are less and less required for that purpose. With some exceptions (for example, South Korea, Berlin, or West Germany), by and large both global stability and American interests would probably not be jeopardized if the American defense posture became territorially more confined (this has been true of the Soviet Union, with little apparent damage to its security), and relied increasingly on long-range mobility.†

---

* This may be especially relevant to efforts to construct a system of cooperation in the Pacific. By itself, it is unlikely that Southeast Asia, even with improved economic performance, can create the foundations for regional security. But enlarged through Japanese, Australian, and American participation—and *not* specifically directed against China—some forms of cooperation could gradually develop, and the system might eventually involve more and more nations.

† Some stand-by facilities for international peace-keeping forces could be provided if, with the agreement of the host country, some vacated United

Finally, the opportunities and the dangers inherent in the scientific-technological age require subtle but important changes in American attitudes and organization. These changes will not come rapidly; they cannot be blueprinted in detail; they are unlikely to be achieved dramatically. Nonetheless, to play an effective world role America needs foreign-relations machinery that exploits the latest communications techniques and uses a style and organization responsive to the more congested pattern of our global existence.

This is hardly the case today. Our diplomatic machinery is still the product of the traditional arrangements that were contrived after 1815 and that were ritualistically preoccupied with protocol. It is predominantly geared to government-to-government relations, often neglecting the currently far more important role of social developments. It is no accident that newspapermen, less dependent on governmental contacts and more inclined to become absorbed in a given society's life, have often been more sensitive to the broad pattern of change in foreign countries than have the local American diplomats. Contemporary foreign relations increas-

---

States bases were taken over by the UN. It should in any case, be noted that American public opinion seems little disposed to back the use of American forces to protect foreign nations. In a mid-1969 public-opinion poll, which asked whether America ought to aid foreign states if these were invaded by outside communist military forces, those who were willing to rely on force were in the majority only with respect to Canada and Mexico (57 per cent and 52 per cent respectively); the figure for West Germany was 38 per cent, for Japan 27 per cent, for Israel 9 per cent (here the foreign aggression postulated was not necessarily communist), for Rumania 13 per cent; when combined with those willing to help short of force, the percentage for Canada was 79 per cent, for Mexico 76 per cent, for West Germany 59 per cent, for Israel 44 per cent, for Rumania 24 per cent, for Japan 42 per cent (Harris Poll, as cited by *Time*, May 2, 1969).

The national mood could easily change in the light of circumstances, but the above poll is significant in indicating a general attitude. It suggests a more selective approach toward military commitment and may have some bearing on the likely public response to the formation of a professional volunteer army. A large, conscript-based army was to some extent a reflection of the populist nationalism stimulated by the French Revolution, which saw every citizen as a soldier. This had greater meaning in an age of relatively unsophisticated weaponry and intense ideological motivation. With both factors changing drastically, the case for a more professional armed force, employed for more selective purposes, gains weight.

ingly require skills in intellectual-scientific communications, including the ability to communicate effectively with the creative segments of other societies, and it is precisely in these fields that the existing diplomatic training and procedure are most deficient.

Moreover, the entire tradition of secret dispatches and lengthy cables, which daily overwhelm State Department headquarters in Washington, has simply not taken into account the explosion in modern communications, the development of excellent foreign reporting in the leading American and foreign newspapers, and even the role of television.* In commenting on the 1969 Duncan report, which was similarly critical of the British foreign service, Canadian political scientist James Eayrs noted: "Too many people push too many pens across too many pieces of paper, filling them with worthless messages." [12] Thomas Jefferson once complained that he had not heard from one of his ambassadors for a year; the present Secretary of State could legitimately complain that he daily hears too much from too many unneeded ambassadors.

The United States is the country that most urgently needs to reform its foreign service and policymaking establishment, and it is best equipped to undertake such reform. It is the first society to become globally oriented, and it is the one with the most extensive and intensive communications involvement. Its business community, moreover, has also acquired extensive experience in foreign operations and has effectively mastered the arts of accurate reporting, foreign representation, and central control—without relying on enormous staffs and redundant operations. It has also pioneered in the adoption of the latest techniques, such as closed-circuit television conferences, shared-time computers, and other devices.

Though this is hardly the place to outline the needed reforms in detail, the point remains that, given the fundamental changes in

* This writer can state on the basis of personal experience while serving in the Department of State that in most cases a better or at least as good a picture of foreign developments can be obtained by reading the better newspapers—including, of course, the foreign ones—than by perusing the hundreds of daily telegrams, often reporting cocktail-party trivia.

the way nations interact, an extensive study and drastic reform of the existing, highly traditional structure and style of the American foreign service is long overdue. Wider diplomatic use of computers and direct sound-and-sight electronic communication should permit the reduction in the size and number of United States foreign missions, making them operationally similar to the more efficient international corporations. Washington's policymaking process needs to be similarly streamlined and freed from its tangle of bureaucratic red tape.[13]

3. A Community of the Developed Nations

These more immediately necessary changes must be reinforced by a broader effort to contain the global tendencies toward chaos. A community of the developed nations must eventually be formed if the world is to respond effectively to the increasingly serious crisis that in different ways now threatens both the advanced world and the Third World. Persistent divisions among the developed states, particularly those based on outmoded ideological concepts, will negate the efforts of individual states to aid the Third World; in the more advanced world they could even contribute to a resurgence of nationalism.

Western Europe and Japan

From an American standpoint, the more important and promising changes in the years to come will have to involve Western Europe and Japan. The ability of these areas to continue to grow economically and to maintain relatively democratic political forms will more crucially affect the gradual evolution of a new international system than will likely changes in American-Soviet relations. Western Europe and Japan offer greater possibilities for initiatives designed to weave a new fabric of international relations, and because, like America, they are in the forefront of scientific and technological innovation, they represent the most vital regions of the globe.

Though some scholars emphasize the vitality of European nationalism, the broad thrust of Western European development is toward increasing cooperation and—much more important—toward a European consciousness.* For the younger Europeans, Western Europe is already an entity in all but the political respect: though still anachronistically governed by a series of provincial chieftains (occasionally visited seriatim by the foreign potentate from Washington), their Europe is frontierless, open to unlimited tourism, to the almost unlimited movement of goods, and increasingly to the free flow of students and workers. To be sure, a positive regionalism is yet to mature, but the foregoing at least provides the needed psychological basis for a new Europe. The technetronic revolution has accelerated the appearance of this Europe, and the autarkic ideas of the industrial age have little or no hold on it today.

In Europe the impact of science and technology, though disruptive within some societies (particularly Italy, which is just completing the industrial phase of its development), has inspired increased cooperation; in Japan, however, which lacks the imme-

---

* This has been dramatically illustrated in France by polls which show that French public opinion, long held to be strongly nationalist, supports the emergence of a European government that would have decisive powers over a local French government in such areas as scientific research (66 per cent for a European government, 15 per cent for a decisive French government) and foreign policy (61 per cent and 17 per cent, respectively). These polls indicate that most Frenchmen favored retaining the French government's decisive role only in purely internal affairs, such as social policy, vacations, education, and so forth (Alain Lancelot and Pierre Weill, "The French and the Political Unification of Europe," *Revue française de science politique*, February 1969, pp. 145–70).

diate external outlet that European unification provides for the Western Europeans and which is subject to a highly visible American military-political presence, it has had an internally aggravating effect. It tends to sharpen the nation's internal political conflicts, polarizing public opinion and rendering the future orientation of the country uncertain.* The conflicts between generations evident in most of the advanced world have special gravity in Japan, given the cultural upheaval produced by its defeat in World War II and the only recently achieved balance between its traditions and modern democratic institutions. A revival of Japanese nationalism or a turn toward ideological radicalism would seriously threaten the highly tenuous structure of peace in the Pacific and directly affect the interests of the United States, the Soviet Union, and China.

Accordingly, an effort must be made to forge a community of the developed nations that would embrace the Atlantic states, the more advanced European communist states, and Japan. These nations need not—and for a very long time could not—form a homogeneous community resembling EEC or the once hoped for Atlantic community. Nonetheless, progress in that direction would help to terminate the civil war that has dominated international politics among the developed nations for the last hundred and fifty years. Though the nationalist and ideological disputes among these nations have less and less relevance to mankind's real problems, their persistence has precluded a constructive response to dilemmas that both democratic and communist states increasingly recognize as being the key issues of our times. The absence of a unifying process of involvement has kept old disputes alive and has obscured the purposes of statesmanship.

To postulate the need for such a community and to define its creation as the coming decade's major task is not utopianism.

---

* Thus, the center-right coalition that has governed Japan in the postwar period has gradually shrunk: in 1952 it obtained 66.1 per cent of the popular vote; in 1953, 65.7 per cent; in 1955, 63.2 per cent; in 1958, 57.8 per cent; in 1960, 57.6 per cent; in 1963, 54.7 per cent; in 1967, 48.8 per cent; and in 1969, 47.6 per cent.

Under the pressures of economics, science, and technology, mankind is moving steadily toward large-scale cooperation. Despite periodic reverses, all human history clearly indicates progress in that direction. The question is whether a spontaneous movement will suffice to counterbalance the dangers already noted. And since the answer is probably no, it follows that a realistic response calls for deliberate efforts to accelerate the process of international cooperation among the advanced nations.

Movement toward a larger community of the developed nations will necessarily have to be piecemeal, and it will not preclude more homogeneous relationships within the larger entity. Moreover, such a community cannot be achieved by fusing existing states into one larger entity. The desire to create one larger, formal state is itself an extension of reasoning derived from the age of nationalism. It makes much more sense to attempt to associate existing states through a variety of indirect ties and already developing limitations on national sovereignty.

In this process, the Soviet Union and Eastern Europe on the one hand and Western Europe on the other will continue for a long time to enjoy more intimate relationships within their own areas. That is unavoidable. The point, however, is to develop a broader structure that links the foregoing in various regional or functional forms of cooperation. Such a structure would not sweep aside United States–Soviet nuclear rivalry, which would remain the axis of world military might. But in the broader cooperative setting, the competition between the United States and the Soviet Union could eventually resemble in form late-nineteenth-century Anglo-French colonial competition: Fashoda did not vitiate the emerging European entente.

Movement toward such a community will in all probability require two broad and overlapping phases. The first of these would involve the forging of community links among the United States, Western Europe, and Japan, as well as with other more advanced countries (for example, Australia, Israel, Mexico). The second phase would include the extension of these links to more advanced communist countries. Some of them—for example, Yugoslavia or Rumania—may move toward closer international cooperation more rapidly than others, and hence the two phases need not necessarily be sharply demarcated.

Structure and Focus

The emerging community of developed nations would require some institutional expression, even though it would be unwise to seek to create too many binding integrated processes prematurely. A case can be made for initially setting up only a high-level consultative council for global cooperation, regularly bringing together the heads of governments of the developed world to discuss their common political-security, educational-scientific, and economic-technological problems, as well as to deal from that perspective with their moral obligations toward the developing nations. Some permanent supporting machinery could provide continuity to these consultations.

Accordingly, such a council for global cooperation would be something more than OECD in that it would operate on a higher level and would also be concerned with political strategy, but it would be more diffused than NATO in that it would not seek to forge integrated military-political structures. Nevertheless, a council of this sort—perhaps initially linking only the United States, Japan, and Western Europe, and thus bringing together the political leaders of states sharing certain common aspirations and problems of modernity—would be more effective in developing common programs than is the United Nations, whose efficacy is unavoidably limited by the Cold War and by north-south divisions.

The inclusion of Japan would be particularly important, both to the internal development of Japanese life and to the vitality of such a community. Japan is a world power, and in a world of electronic and supersonic communications it is a psychological and political error to think of it as primarily an Asian nation. Japan needs an outlet commensurate with its own advanced development, not one that places it in the position of a giant among pygmies and that excludes it *de facto* from the councils of the real world powers. The regular American-Japanese cabinet-level talks are a desirable bilateral arrangement, but Japan will become more fully and creatively involved in world affairs in a larger setting of equal partners.

Without such a larger setting, there is danger that the extraordinary pace of Japanese socio-economic development will become destructive. The automatic projections of Japanese growth into the future, made with increasing frequency in the late 1960s, are misleading; they do not make allowance for the destabilizing effect of the impact of change on Japanese traditions. There is a real possibility that in the 1970s Japan will undergo extremely upsetting internal conflicts unless in some way Japanese idealism is both stimulated and turned to goals larger than insular and personal hedonism. International cooperation, involving the sharing with Japan of responsibility as well as of power, could provide such an outlet.

Such a council would also provide a political-security framework in which the security concerns of each state could be viewed in a context that takes into account the inescapable connections between such matters as Soviet policy in Berlin and the Sino-Soviet crisis, Chinese nuclear development and its implications both for Japanese security and for East-West relations in Europe, and so on. Similarly, matters such as Japanese rearmament, possibly even Japan's acquisition of nuclear arms (thought by increasingly large numbers of Japanese to be likely during the second half of the 1970s),[14] could be viewed in terms of this broader significance rather than as a response to purely local considerations. Indeed, given the nature of modern scientific developments and communications, it is not too early to think of technological cooperation between Western Europe and Japan, as well as between both of them and the United States, in some fields of defense.

Political-security efforts would, however, in all probability be second in importance to efforts to broaden the scope of educational-scientific and economic-technological cooperation among the most advanced industrial nations that are becoming post-industrial and are in some regards moving into the post-national age. The projected world information grid, for which Japan, Western Europe, and the United States are most suited,* could create the basis for a common educational program, for the adoption of common academic standards, for the organized pooling of information, and for a more rational division of labor in research and development. Computers at M.I.T. have already been regularly "conversing" with Latin American universities, and there is no technical obstacle to permanent information linkage between, for example, the universities of New York, Moscow, Tokyo, Mexico City, and Milan.[15] Such scientific-informational linkage would be easier to set up than joint educational programs and would encourage an international educational system by providing an additional stimulus to an international division of academic labor, uniform academic standards, and a cross-national pooling of academic resources.

Steps in that direction could be accelerated by some symbolic joint actions. Space exploration is probably the most dramatic example of human adventure made possible by science, but cur-

---

* "Western Europe and Japan present the most immediate opportunities for the world-information-grid. The Europeans and the Japanese are both increasingly sensitive to the importance of information storage and transfer network, similar to the one now evolving in this country.

"The Europeans' success in this project will depend, in part, on their ability to modify a number of present restrictive attitudes. One is the lingering tradition of secretiveness in their research-and-development work. Another is the nationalistic inhibition in sharing regional information resources. It would be unfortunate if these attitudes held up formation of the network, since Europeans, over the long run, cannot think in terms of 'Italian research' or 'Norwegian research' any more than they are able to make a distinction between research done in California or New Jersey.

"There is every reason to encourage the Europeans to overcome these problems. The American information-transfer network should be linked directly into their regional system, permitting a broader exchange of information" (*Television Quarterly*, Spring 1968, pp. 10–11).

rently it is almost entirely monopolized on a competitive basis by the United States and the Soviet Union. The pooling of Western European, Japanese, and American resources for a specific joint undertaking could do much to accelerate international cooperation.[16] In addition, it may be desirable to develop an international convention on the social consequences of applied science and technology. This not only would permit the ecological and social effects of new techniques to be weighed in advance but would also make it possible to outlaw the use of chemicals to limit and manipulate man and to prevent other scientific abuses to which some governments may be tempted.

In the economic-technological field some international cooperation has already been achieved, but further progress will require greater American sacrifices. More intensive efforts to shape a new world monetary structure will have to be undertaken, with some consequent risk to the present relatively favorable American position. Further progress would in all probability require the abandonment of restrictions, imposed by Congress in 1949 and 1954, on the international activities of American corporations and on their foreign subsidiaries and plants. The appearance of a truly international structure of production and financing would have to go hand in hand with the emergence of a "theory of international production," needed to supplement our present theories of international trade.* Progress along these lines would also facili-

---

* Judd Polk argues that "what we need is not a theory of international trade that abstracts from production, but a theory of an international production which, being specialized, presupposes trade." He goes on to note that "the question is not one of intruding into the economy of others; it is a matter of releasing the production capabilities of all nations. The problems of production seen from the standpoint of an economy vastly larger than that of the nation are new to everyone. The United States cannot abandon its concern for the national balance of payments, but, as noted, it is beginning to perceive the urgent need for a system of international accounts as comprehensive as the present national accounts. It particularly needs to follow the whole picture of the international movement of factors of production. Just to feel this need is to have made extraordinary progress in a short 20 years, for there cannot occur a dislodgment of the dollar from its international function without a crippling dislodgment of the production and trade it supports. Nor can there be a practical improvement in this function except

tate the creation of a free-trade area, which could be targeted in progressive stages.

The Communist States

The Soviet Union may come to participate in such a larger framework of cooperation because of the inherent attraction of the West for the Eastern Europeans—whom the Soviet Union would have to follow lest it lose them altogether—and because of the Soviet Union's own felt need for increased collaboration in the technological and scientific revolution. That Eastern Europeans will move closer to Western Europe is certain. The events of 1968 in Czechoslovakia are merely an augury of what is to come, in spite of forcible Soviet efforts to the contrary. It is only a matter of time before individual communist states come knocking at the doors of EEC or OECD; hence, broader East-West arrangements may even become a way for Moscow to maintain effective links with the Eastern European capitals.

The evolution of Yugoslav thinking and behavior attests to the fact that the communist states are not immune to the process of change and to intelligent Western initiatives. Slightly more than twenty years ago, Yugoslav pronouncements were not unlike those of the Chinese today. Yet Yugoslavia now leads all communist states in economic reform, in the openness of its society, and in ideological moderation. In the late 1960s it joined GATT,* and Yugoslavia's association with EFTA†—and perhaps eventually with the Common Market—is a probability. While still committed to the notion of "socialism," Yugoslavia's views on international politics are moderate, and they have had a significant impact on communism in Eastern Europe.

Similar trends are slowly developing elsewhere in the com-

in the context of the cash and credit requirements of the new world economy" ("The New World Economy," *Columbia Journal of World Business*, January–February 1968, p. 15).

* GATT: General Agreement on Trade and Tariffs.

† EFTA: European Free Trade Association.

munist world. To be sure, they are opposed by entrenched bureaucrats, but in the long run the reactionaries are fighting a losing battle. Social forces are against them, and the conservative elites are on the defensive everywhere. It is doubtful whether they can reverse, though they certainly can delay, the trend toward a more open, humanistic, and less ideological society. The resistance of those regimes dominated by entrenched conservative bureaucracies will be further weakened if the West views the Cold War as primarily due to the fading self-serving doctrines of the Communist rulers, if it approaches the Cold War more as an aberration and less as a mission.

Over the long run—and our earlier analysis indicates that it would be a long run—Soviet responsiveness could be stimulated through the deliberate opening of European cooperative ventures to the East and through the creation of new East-West bodies designed initially only to promote a dialogue, the exchange of information, and the encouragement of a cooperative ethos. The deliberate definition of certain common objectives in economic development, technological assistance, and East-West security arrangements could help stimulate a sense of common purpose and the growth of a rudimentary institutional framework. (For example, through formal links in the economic sphere between OECD and the Council for Mutual Economic Assistance (CEMA); in the security sphere between NATO and the Warsaw Pact, and through United States–Soviet arms-control arrangements; or by the creation of an informal East-West political consultative body.)* [17]

A larger cooperative goal would also have other beneficial effects. For one thing, it is likely that the Soviet Union would initially demonstrate hesitancy or even hostility in the face of Western initiative. Therefore, an approach based on bilateral

---

* This is not only a matter of technological and multilateral determinism, as suggested by Pierre Hassner in his "Implications of Change in Eastern Europe for the Atlantic Alliance" (*Orbis,* Spring 1969, p. 246), but also a deliberate, though very long-range, strategy.

American-Soviet accommodation—as advocated by some Americans—might prove to be abortive and would consequently intensify tensions. But efforts to create a larger cooperative community need not be halted by initial Soviet reluctance, nor can they be easily exploited by Moscow to perpetuate the Cold War. On the contrary, Soviet resistance would only result in more costly Soviet isolation. By seeking to cut Eastern Europe off from the West, the Soviet Union would inevitably also deny itself the fruits of closer East-West technological cooperation. In 1985 the combined GNP of the United States, Western Europe, and Japan will be roughly somewhere around three trillion dollars, or four times that of the likely Soviet GNP (assuming a favorable growth rate for the Soviets); with some Eastern European states gradually shifting toward greater cooperation with EEC and OECD, the Soviet Union could abstain only at great cost to its own development and world position.

Risks and Advantages

The shaping of such a community may well provoke charges that its emergence would accentuate the divisions in a world already threatened by fragmentation. The answer to such objections is twofold: First, division already exists, and our present problem is how best to deal with it. As long as the advanced world is itself divided and in conflict, it will be unable to formulate coherent goals. The less developed countries may even be benefiting from the internal rivalries in the developed world, which incite it to compete in extending aid; but since such aid tends to be focused on short-term political advantages to the donor, it is subject to political fluctuations and may decline as the rivalry declines in intensity.

Second, the emergence of a more cooperative structure among the more developed nations is likely to increase the possibility of a long-range strategy for international development based on the emerging global consciousness rather than on old rivalries.

It could hence diminish the desire for immediate political payoffs and thus pave the way for more internationalized, mutilateral foreign aid. While the vexing problems of tariffs and trade with the Third World are not likely to disappear, they might become more manageable in a setting that reduces both the impediments to truly international production and, consequently, a given country's stake in this or that protective arrangement. The underlying motivation for such a community is, however, extremely important. If this community does not spring from fear and hatred but from a wider recognition that world affairs will have to be conducted on a different basis, it would not intensify world divisions—as have alliances in the past—but would be a step toward greater unity.

Its appearance would therefore assist and perhaps even accelerate the further development of present world bodies—such as the World Bank—which are in any case *de facto* institutions of the developed world geared to assisting the Third World. A greater sense of community within the developed world would help to strengthen these institutions by backing them with the support of public opinion; it might also eventually lead to the possibility of something along the lines of a global taxation system.*

More specifically, America would gain several advantages from its identification with a larger goal. Such a goal would tend to reduce the increasing danger of American isolation in the world; this isolation is unavoidably being intensified [18] by the problems associated with America's domestic leap into the future. Moreover, the United States cannot shape the world singlehanded, even though it may be the only force capable of stimulating common efforts to do so. By encouraging and becoming associated with other major powers in a joint response to the problems con-

* In my view, such a community would also provide a base for implementing more far-reaching and visionary proposals for global cooperation; for example, those contained in the stimulating "Bulletin of Peace Proposals" prepared by the International Peace Research Institute, Oslo, in the autumn of 1969.

fronting man's life on this planet, and by jointly attempting to make deliberate use of the potential offered by science and technology, the United States would more effectively achieve its often proclaimed goal.

The quest for that goal cannot, however, be geographically confined to the Atlantic world, nor should its motivation be even implicitly derived from security fears stimulated by a major outside power. One reason for the declining popular appeal of the Atlantic concept is the latter's association with the conditions of post–World War II Europe and with the fear of Soviet aggression. While such a concept was a bold idea at the time, it is now historically and geographically limited. A broader, more ambitious, and more relevant approach is called for by the recognition that the problems of the 1970s will be less overtly ideological, more diffuse—they will more widely reflect the malaise of a world that is still unstructured politically and highly inegalitarian economically.

Such an approach would also tend to end the debate over American globalism. The fact is that much of the initiative and impetus for an undertaking on so grand a scale will have to come from the United States. Given the old divisions in the advanced world—and the weaknesses and parochialism of the developing nations—the absence of constructive American initiative would at the very least perpetuate the present drift in world affairs. That drift cannot be halted if the United States follows the path which it is now fashionable to advocate—disengagement. Even if, despite the weight and momentum of its power, America could disengage itself, there is something quaintly old-fashioned in the eloquent denunciation of United States global involvement, especially when it comes from Europeans, who have shown a less than admirable ability to maintain world peace. Moreover, even the most brilliant indictment of United States policy cannot erase the fact that, despite its allegedly long record of errors and misconceptions, the United States has somehow become the only power that has begun to think in global terms and actively seek constructive world-wide arrangements. In this connection, it is revealing to note that initiatives such as the Test-Ban Treaty or the Non-Proliferation Treaty were opposed by governments habitually praised by some critics of United States global involvement. This country's commitment to international affairs on a global scale has been decided by history. It cannot be undone, and the only remaining relevant question is what its form and goals will be.

The debate on globalism did, however, perform one useful function. Though much of the criticism did not provide a meaningful policy program,* the debate prompted greater recognition of the need to redefine America's world role in the light of new historical circumstances. Thrust into the world by its own growth and by the cataclysms of two world wars, America first actively promoted and then guaranteed the West's economic recovery and

---

* Even a critic who identifies himself as sympathetic to the "isolationist or neo-isolationist" school concludes that the alternatives offered by the more traditional students of international politics, such as Lippmann or Morgenthau, have relatively little of a constructive nature to offer (Charles Gati, "Another Grand Debate? The Limitationist Critique of American Foreign Policy," *World Politics*, October 1968, especially pp. 150–51). Moreover, the propensity of even some perceptive writers to concentrate almost entirely on the shortcomings of American foreign-policy performance makes it difficult for them to account for its relatively respectable performance during the last twenty years as compared with, for example, that of the European powers. Thus, Stanley Hoffmann's massive (556 pages) and in places stimulating book, *Gulliver's Troubles* (New York, 1968), focuses almost entirely on the impatience, wrongheadedness, misunderstanding, self-righteousness, gullibility, condescension, inflexibility, and paranoid style of American foreign policy. This leads him, on a more popular level, to say in a magazine article ("Policy for the Seventies," *Life*, March 21, 1969) that "Americans . . . have been prepared by history and instinct for a world in black and white, in which there is either harmony or an all-out contest." He does not explain why, in that case, the United States and the Soviet Union were successful in maintaining peace, whereas in the past the European powers had failed to do so.

At the same time, traditionalists who emphasize the continued vitality of nationalism are inherently inclined to postulate policies that are no longer in tune with the times. Thus, on the very eve of De Gaulle's repudiation by the French people, Hoffmann could speak of a "fundamental rapprochement" with De Gaulle ("America and France," *The New Republic*, April 12, 1969, p. 22).

military security. This posture—of necessity heavily marked by military preoccupations—has increasingly shifted toward a greater involvement with the less political and more basic problems that mankind will face in the remaining third of the century.

John Kennedy caught the essence of America's novel position in the world when he saw himself as "the first American President for whom the whole world was, in a sense, domestic politics." [19] Indeed, Kennedy was the first "globalist" president of the United States. Roosevelt, for all his internationalism, essentially believed in an 1815-like global arrangement in which the "Big Four" would have specific spheres of influence. Truman primarily responded to a specific communist challenge, and his policies indicated a clear regional priority. Eisenhower continued on the same course, occasionally applying European precedents to other regions. These shifts were symptomatic of the changing United States role. With Kennedy came a sense that every continent and every people had the right to expect leadership and inspiration from America, and that America owed an almost equal involvement to every continent and every people. Kennedy's evocative style which in some ways appealed more to emotion than to intellect, stressed the universal humanism of the American mission, while his romantic fascination with the conquest of space reflected his conviction that America's scientific leadership was necessary to its effective world role.

Global involvement is, however, qualitatively different from what has to date been known as foreign policy. It is inimical to clear-cut formulas and traditional preferences. But this intellectual complexity does not negate the fact that for better or for worse the United States is saddled with major responsibility for shaping the framework for change. This point of view is subject to easy misrepresentation and is highly unpopular in some circles. World conditions do not call for a Pax Americana, nor is this the age of American omnipotence. Nevertheless, it is a fact that unless the United States, the first global society, uses its preponderant influence to give positive direction and expression to the accelerating pace of change, that change not only might become chaos—when linked to old conflicts and antipathies—but could eventually threaten the effort to improve the nature and the character of American domestic life.

To sum up: Though the objective of shaping a community of the developed nations is less ambitious than the goal of world government, it is more attainable. It is more ambitious than the concept of an Atlantic community but historically more relevant to the new spatial revolution. Though cognizant of present divisions between communist and non-communist nations, it attempts to create a new framework for international affairs not by exploiting these divisions but rather by striving to preserve and create openings for eventual reconciliation. Finally, it recognizes that the world's developed nations have a certain affinity, and that only by nurturing a greater sense of communality among them can an effective response to the increasing threat of global fragmentation—which itself intensifies the growing world-wide impatience with human inequality—be mounted.

There is thus a close conjunction between the historic meaning of America's internal transition and America's role in the world. Earlier in this book, domestic priorities were reduced to three large areas: the need for an institutional realignment of American democracy to enhance social responsiveness and blur traditional distinctions between governmental and nongovernmental social processes; the need for anticipatory institutions to cope with the unintended consequences of technological-scientific change; the need for educational reforms to mitigate the effects of generational and racial conflicts and promote rational humanist values in the emerging new society.

The international equivalents of our domestic needs are similar: the gradual shaping of a community of the developed nations would be a realistic expression of our emerging global consciousness; concentration on disseminating scientific and technological knowledge would reflect a more functional approach to man's problems, emphasizing ecology rather than ideology; both the foregoing would help to encourage the spread of a more personalized rational humanist world outlook that would gradually replace the institutionalized religious, ideological, and intensely national perspectives that have dominated modern history.

But whatever the future may actually hold for America and for the world, the technetronic age—by making so much more technologically feasible and electronically accessible—make deliberate choice about more issues more imperative. Reason, belief, and values will interact intensely, putting a greater premium than ever before on the explicit definition of social purposes. To what ends should our power be directed, how should our social dialogue be promoted, in what way should the needed action be taken—these are both philosophical and political issues. In the technetronic era, philosophy and politics will be crucial.

Reference Notes

I: The Global Impact of the Technetronic Revolution

1. Part of this section is adapted, in a revised form, from my "America in the Technetronic Age," *Encounter*, January 1968. In this connection, I wish to acknowledge the pioneering work done on this general subject at Columbia University by Daniel Bell and at Michigan University by Donald Michael.
2. Norbert Wiener, *The Human Use of Human Beings*, New York, 1967, pp. 189–90.
3. Testimony by Dr. D. Krech, *Government Research Subcommittee of the Senate Government Operations Committee*, as reported by *The New York Times*, April 3, 1968, p. 32; see also Gordon R. Taylor, *The Biological Time Bomb*, New York, 1967.
4. *The New York Times*, January 18, 1969.
5. Donald N. Michael, "Some Speculations on the Social Impact of Technology," mimeographed text of address to the Columbia Seminar on Technology and Social Change, 1966, p. 11.
6. Michael, pp. 6–7.
7. Sir Julian Huxley, "The Crisis in Man's Destiny," *Playboy*, January 1967, p. 4.
8. See Neal J. Dean, "The Computer Comes of Age," *Harvard Business Review*, January–February 1968, pp. 83–91. On the computer-initiated "profound revolution in our patterns of thought and communication," see Anthony G. Oettinger, "Educational Technology," in *Toward the Year 2018*, Foreign Policy Association, New York, 1968.
9. *The United States and the World in the 1985 Era*, Syracuse, N.Y., 1964, pp. 90–91.
10. See John P. Robinson and James W. Swinehart, "World Affairs and the TV Audience," *Television Quarterly*, Spring 1968.
11. Cyril E. Black, "Soviet Society: A Comparative View," in *Prospects for Soviet Society*, Allen Kassof, ed., New York, 1968, p. 36; A. B. Trowbridge, "The Atlantic Community Looks to the Future," *Department of State Bulletin*, July 17, 1967, p. 72.
12. "The Technological Gap in Russia," *The Economist*, February 9, 1969.

13. John Diebold, "Is the Gap Technological?" *Foreign Affairs,* January 1968, pp. 276–91.

14. For some examples of the predominance of American communications among the engineering-technical elite in Latin America, see Paul J. Deutschmann et al., *Communication and Social Change in Latin America,* New York, 1968, especially pp. 56, 70.

15. See Leonard H. Marks, "American Diplomacy and a Changing Technology," *Television Quarterly,* Spring 1968, pp. 7, 9.

16. Bruce M. Russett, "Is There a Long-Run Trend toward Concentration in the International System?" *Journal of Comparative Political Studies,* April 1968. For somewhat forced analogies to past empires, see George Liska, *Imperial America,* Baltimore, 1966; and for a highly critical appraisal, see Claude Julien, *L'Empire américain,* Paris, 1968, especially chaps. 1, 6–11; also Ronald Steel, *Pax Americana,* New York, 1967. For a criticism of the "imperial" approach, see Stanley Hoffmann, *Gulliver's Troubles,* New York, 1968, pp. 46–51.

17. *The New York Times,* November 17, 1968, cites government sources as indicating that 200,000 American civilians are serving abroad; for commitments, see *US Commitments to Foreign Powers,* Committee on Foreign Relations, Washington, D.C., 1967, especially pp. 49–71; for data on bases, see *The New York Times,* April 9, 1969.

18. Judd Polk, "The New World Economy," *Columbia Journal of World Business,* January–February 1968, p. 8, estimates that United States investment abroad accounts for total deliveries of some $165 billion.

19. Joseph Kraft, "The Spread of Power," *The New York Times Book Review,* September 22, 1968, p. 10 (a review of Amaury de Riencourt's *The American Empire,* New York, 1968).

20. In this connection, compare Harry Magdoff's *The Age of Imperialism,* New York, 1969, which sees America simply as a politically motivated imperial power, with the Rockefeller Foundation's *President's Five-Year Review and Annual Report, 1968,* which describes the Foundation's foreign activities. The Ford Foundation could also be cited.

21. Herman Kahn and Anthony J. Wiener, *The Year 2000,* New York, 1967, p. 149.

22. See Kahn and Wiener, tables pp. 161–65 and 123–30, for a fuller discussion of the assumptions on which these calculations are based. See also, however, Everett E. Hagan, "Some Facts about Income Levels and Economic Growth," *Review of Economics and Statistics,* February 1960. Hagan points out that comparisons between developed and underdeveloped countries are in some respects misleading and tend to exaggerate the disparities.

23. ILO conference, September 1968, as reported by *The New York Times,* September 3, 1968. For some equally staggering population projections for Latin America, see Louis Olivos, "2000: A No-Space Odyssey," *Americas* (OAS), August 1969.

24. *The United States and the World in the 1985 Era,* pp. 78–79.

25. Lester R. Brown, "The Agricultural Revolution in Asia," *Foreign Affairs,* July 1968, p. 698, and Brown's address before Kansas State University, "A New Era in World Agriculture," December 3, 1968. For 1967 data, showing food production outstripping population growth in the Third World, see *Ceres* (FAO Review), September–October 1968, pp. 17–18. For a more pessimistic assessment, see Myrdal, *The Asian Drama,* New York, 1968, pp. 417, 1029–49.

26. See *United Nations Yearbook of National Accounts Statistics,* 1966, Table 7B.

27. Myrdal, pp. 322, 540–41, 552 ff., 1585. See also *United Nations Statistical Yearbook,* 1967, for data on physicians per inhabitants in the early 1960s (p. 696); on number of occupied dwellings, average size, density of occupation, and general housing facilities (Table 202, p. 708 ff.); and on calories per day, proteins, and industrial consumption of cotton, wool, rubber, steel, tin and fertilizer in the years 1955–1965, covering general consumption (pp. 498–511).

28. For a discussion of some pertinent examples, see *Twenty-Third Report by the Committee on Government Operations,* House of Representatives, Washington, D.C., March 1968, hereinafter cited as *Report. . . .* Also *Hearing before a Subcommittee on Government Operations,* House of Representatives, Washington, D.C., January 23, 1968, hereinafter cited as *Hearing. . . .*

29. Joseph Lelyveld, "India's Students Demand—A Safe Job in the Establishment," *The New York Times Magazine,* May 12, 1968, pp. 53, 58; for an equally damning judgment, see also Myrdal, pp. 1784–90.

30. Myrdal, pp. 1645, 1649.

31. Raul Prebisch, "The System and the Social Structure of Latin America," in *Latin American Radicalism,* Irving Louis Horowitz, Josué de Castro, and John Gerassi, eds., New York, 1969, p. 31.

32. *Report . . . ,* pp. 7–8.

33. *Hearing . . . ,* p. 96.

34. *Report . . . ,* p. 17.

35. *Report . . . ,* p. 9, quoting the testimony of Dr. C. V. Kidd, head of the Physics Department of the American University in Beirut.

36. William Kornhauser, *The Politics of Mass Society,* Glencoe, Ill., 1959.

37. H. Jaguaribe, "Foreign Technical Assistance and National Development," paper submitted at Princeton, 1965, pp. 25–26, as cited in *Hearing . . . ,* p. 57; see also Irving Louis Horowitz, "Political Legitimacy and the Institutionalization of Crises in Latin America," *Comparative Political Studies,* April 1968, especially pp. 64–65.

38. See, for example, William H. Grier and Price M. Cobbs, *Black Rage,* New York, 1969.

39. Myrdal, p. 471; see also pp. 467–69 for urban-growth data compared with national growth; for fuller data on the growth of cities in

the Third World, see G. Breese, *Urbanization in Newly Developing Countries,* Englewood Cliffs, N.J., 1966.

40. Samuel P. Huntington, *Political Order in Changing Societies,* New Haven and London, 1968, p. 290, citing also Bert F. Hoselitz and Myron Weiner, "Economic Development and Political Stability in India," *Dissent,* Vol. 8, Spring 1961, p. 177, and Benjamin B. Ringer and David L. Sills, "Political Extremists in Iran," *Public Opinion Quarterly,* Vol. 16, 1952–1953, pp. 693–94.

41. Myrdal, p. 117.

42. For a useful and pertinent discussion of the relationship of violence and economic development, see Bruce M. Russett et al., *World Handbook of Political and Social Indicators,* New Haven, 1964, especially pp. 304–310; and John H. Kautsky, *Communism and the Politics of Development,* New York, 1968, especially chap. 10, "Communism and Economic Development," co-authored with Roger W. Benjamin. For a somewhat different breakdown of societies, see Cyril E. Black, *The Dynamics of Modernization,* New York, 1966, p. 150. For a much more optimistic prognostication, see Walt Rostow, *The Stages of Economic Growth,* Cambridge, Mass., 1960, p. 127.

43. Myrdal, p. 300.

44. A. Barber, "The 20th Century Renaissance," private paper, Institute of Politics and Planning, Washington, D.C., 1968, pp. 1, 8.

45. In Friedrich Engels, *Herr Eugen Duhring's Revolution and Science,* as cited by D. G. Brennan, "Weaponry," in *Toward the Year 2018,* New York, 1968, p. 2.

46. See Brennan, *ibid.*, p. 19. This possibility is developed further by M. W. Thring in his essay "Robots on the March," in *Unless Peace Comes,* Nigel Calder, ed., London, 1968, pp. 155–64.

47. Gordon J. F. MacDonald, "How to Wreck the Environment," in *Unless Peace Comes,* p. 181.

48. Victor C. Ferkiss, *Technological Man: The Myth and the Reality,* New York, 1969, p. 199; Michael Harrington, *American Power in the Twentieth Century,* New York, 1967, pp. 39, 43, 48; also the eloquent plea by Aurelio Peccei of Olivetti Corporation, "Considerations and the Need for Worldwide Planning," delivered in Akademgorodok, USSR, September 12, 1967 (mimeograph).

II: The Age of Volatile Belief

1. Pierre Teilhard de Chardin, *The Phenomenon of Man,* New York, 1961, p. 183.

2. See Claude Lévi-Strauss, *The Savage Mind,* Chicago, 1966.

3. In this connection, see Jacques Soustelle, *Les Quatre Soleils,* Paris, 1967. In lively terms, Soustelle attacks the progressive theory of history as expressed by Marx, Spengler, Toynbee, and Teilhard de Chardin.

For a more complex analysis, see Michel Foucault, *Folie et déraison*, Paris, 1961; American edition, *Madness and Civilization*, New York, 1965.

4. Teilhard de Chardin, pp. 178–79.

5. See, for example, Jules Monnerot, *Sociology and Psychology of Communism*, Boston, 1960.

6. In this connection, interesting data are provided by Jacques Toussaert, *Le Sentiment religieux en Flandre à la fin du Moyen-âge*, Paris, 1963.

7. "The writer knows of no instance in present day South Asia where religion has induced social change" (Myrdal, p. 103). See also Teilhard de Chardin, pp. 209–11, for a discussion of the passivity of oriental religions, and Kavalam M. Panikkar, *Hindu Society at Cross Roads*, Bombay, 1955.

8. Kh. Momjan, *The Dynamic Twentieth Century*, Moscow, 1968, p. 21.

9. Teilhard de Chardin, p. 257.

10. *Ibid.*, p. 211.

11. Rostow, *The Stages of Economic Growth*, pp. 162–63; see also p. 158, where Marxism is described as "a system full of flaws but full also of legitimate partial insights, a great formal contribution to social science, a monstrous guide to public policy."

12. Jacques Ellul, *The Technological Society*, New York, 1965, p. 290.

13. Karl Marx, writing in 1871, as cited by Lewis S. Feuer, "Karl Marx and the Promethean Complex," *Encounter*, December 1968, p. 31.

14. These terms were used by James H. Billington, "Force and Counterforce in Eastern Europe," *Foreign Affairs*, October 1968, p. 34.

15. Daniel and Gabriel Cohn-Bendit, *Le Gauchisme, remède à la maladie sénile du communisme*, Paris, 1968.

16. Leszek Kolakowski, "The Permanent and Transitory Meaning of Marxism," *Nowa Kultura*, No. 4, 1957.

17. *Praxis*, May–June 1967, p. 431.

18. Kolakowski, "Hope and the Fabric of History," *Nowa Kultura*, No. 38, 1957. For a recent and very perceptive analysis of Kolakowski's thought, see Leopold Labedz, "Kolakowski on Marxism and Beyond," *Encounter*, March 1969, pp. 77–88.

19. See Adam Schaff, *Marxsizm a Jednostka Ludzka*, Warsaw, 1965, p. 56, and p. 28 ff., where Schaff acknowledges his debt to Professor Erich Fromm for his improved understanding of Marxism. Schaff was expelled from the Central Committee of the Polish Communist Party in 1968.

20. This result makes it also reminiscent of fascism. See my "Democratic Socialism or Social Fascism?" *Dissent*, Summer 1965. See also the next chapter for further discussion.

21. On the problem of authority and legitimacy in contemporary Catholicism, see George N. Shuster, ed., *Freedom and Authority in the West,* Notre Dame, 1967, especially the contribution of the late John Courtney Murray, S.J.

22. Miguel de Unamuno, *The Tragic Sense of Life,* New York, 1954, p. 77.

23. Letter to Cardinal Konig, Archbishop of Vienna, January 14, 1969.

24. For an account generally sympathetic to the conservative point of view, see Ulisse Floridi, S.J., *Radicalismo Cattolico Brasiliano,* Rome, 1968. For a more general account, Ernst Halperin, *Nationalism and Communism in Chile,* Cambridge, Mass., 1965; and William V. D'Antonia and Frederick B. Pike, *Religion, Revolution and Reform,* New York, 1964.

25. These two words are the title of Garaudy's book *De l'anathème au dialogue,* Paris, 1965, discussing the Christian-Marxist dialogue.

26. As cited by the *Washington Post,* January 7, 1969.

27. For a similar point of view, see Emile Pin, S.J., "Les Motivations des conduites religieuses et le passage d'une civilisation prétechnique à une civilisation technique," *Social Change,* Vol. 13, 1966.

28. See Harvey Cox, *The Secular City,* New York, 1965.

29. *Ibid.,* p. 69.

30. Pierre Trotignon in *L'Arc,* Paris, No. 3, 1966–1968, as cited by Raymond Aron, "At the Barricades," *Encounter,* August 1968, p. 23.

31. Abbie Hoffman, *Revolution for the Hell of It,* New York, 1968. The best analysis of the ideology of the "student revolution" is the article by Leopold Labedz, "Students and Revolution," *Survey* (London), July 1968.

32. As cited by N. Molchanov, "Students Rebel in the West: The Meaning, the Causes and Goals," *Literaturnaya Gazeta,* November 6, 1968.

33. Paul Jacobs and Saul Landau, *The New Radicals,* New York, 1966, p. 7.

34. Speaking in 1967 at the Free University in West Berlin, as cited by Labedz, "Students and Revolution," p. 6.

35. *Ibid.,* p. 7.

36. Molchanov.

37. See Robert P. Wolff, Barrington Moore, Jr., and Herbert Marcuse, *A Critique of Pure Tolerance,* Boston, 1965.

38. Compare, for example, the demands of the Warsaw students, adopted in March 1968, with the demands of the Mexican students of September of the same year (*Survey,* July 1968, p. 114; *The New York Times,* March 28 and September 9, 1968).

39. This point is well made by Professor Z. Bauman, a well-known Warsaw sociologist expelled from Poland in 1968 after the student outbreak of March, in his introduction to a special documentary volume on

those events, published in Paris by Instytut Literacki, *Wydarzenia Marcowe 1968,* 1969.

40. See Melvin Lasky, "Revolution Diary," *Encounter,* August 1968, pp. 88–89.

41. *The New Left,* memorandum prepared for the Committee on the Judiciary, United States Senate, Washington, D.C., 1968, p. 23, citing also data from Jack Newfield, *A Prophetic Minority,* New York, 1966.

42. "The Hooligans of Peace Square," *Scinteia Tineretulúi,* July 5, 1968.

43. Black, *The Dynamics of Modernization,* p. 31.

44. On this, see also Kenneth Keniston, "Social Change and Youth in America," in *The Challenge of Youth,* Erik H. Erikson, ed., New York, 1961.

45. See Johan Huizinga, *Waning of the Middle Ages,* especially chap. 1 on "The Violent Tenor of Life," New York, 1954.

46. See Black, *The Dynamics of Modernization,* for descriptive and sequential analysis.

47. On this, for United States examples see Mark Gerzon, *The Whole World Is Watching,* New York, 1969, pp. 52–54, 73, 189–90; for a more systematic treatment pertaining to the Third World, see Donald K. Emmerson, *Students and Politics in Developing Nations,* New York, 1968, including a similar conclusion on p. 414.

48. Marshall McLuhan, *The Marshall McLuhan Dew-Line,* No. 1, 1968, p. 15.

49. See Paul Sigmund, ed., *The Ideologies of the Developing Nations,* New York, 1963, especially pp. 12–17. For a systematic evaluation of the appeal and meaning of the concept of equality within one new nation, see James C. Scott, *Political Ideology in Malaysia: Reality and the Beliefs of an Elite,* New Haven, 1968, pp. 194–96. For more general treatment, David Apter, ed., *Ideology and Discontent,* Glencoe, Ill., 1964; and Clifford Geertz, ed., *Old Societies and New States: The Quest for Modernity in Asia and Africa,* New York, 1963.

50. For example, see Léopold Senghor, *African Socialism,* New York, 1963.

51. Tom Mboya, *Freedom and After,* Boston, 1963, p. 262.

52. It is among them that Frantz Fanon's *The Wretched of the Earth* (New York, 1965) has the widest appeal. See also F. J. Marsal, "Latin American Intellectuals and the Problem of Change," *Social Research,* Winter 1966, pp. 562–92.

53. They have thus become "tutelary democracies." Cf. Edward Shils, *Political Development in the New States,* The Hague, 1965, pp. 60–67.

54. See the highly stimulating review of Michel Foucault's book, *Les Mots et les choses* (Paris, 1966), by Jean-Marie Domenague, *Témoignage Chrétien,* March 1968.

55. Victor C. Ferkiss, p. 241.

III: Communism: The Problem of Relevance

1. For insights into Stalin's character, see Milovan Djilas, *Conversations with Stalin*, New York, 1962; and Svetlana Alliluyeva, *Twenty Letters to a Friend*, New York, 1967.
2. See Leonard Schapiro, *The Origin of Communist Autocracy*, London, 1956; and Isaac Deutscher, *The Prophet Outcast*, London, 1963.
3. Leon Smolinski, "Grinevetskii and Soviet Industrialization," *Survey*, April 1968, p. 101. See also the critical comment by Alec Nove on Smolinski's analysis and Smolinski's reply in *Survey*, Winter–Spring, 1969.
4. Smolinski, p. 109.
5. Deutscher, pp. 100–115.
6. Rostow, p. 66.
7. Rostow, p. 95. See also pp. 96–97 for detailed tables by Warren Nutter, in which the persistent lag in certain areas of Russian industrial production is compared with American production.
8. Black, "Soviet Society: A Comparative View," in *Prospects for Soviet Society*, pp. 42–43.
9. Black, pp. 40–42, provides a useful summary of their findings and the basis for reaching the conclusions.
10. See the fascinating cumulative table, in Stefan Kurowski, *Historyczny Proces Wzrostu Gospodarczego*, Warsaw, 1963, p. 335.
11. See *Trybuna Ludu*, July 8, 1963, and *Nowe Drogi*, No. 8, 1963.
12. Speech of November 19, 1962.
13. N. Sviridov, "Party Concern for the Upbringing of the Scientific-Technical Intelligentsia," *Kommunist*, No. 18, p. 38.
14. P. Demichev, "The Construction of Communism and the Goals of Social Sciences," *Kommunist*, No. 10, p. 26.
15. E. G. R. Kosolapov and P. Simush, "The Intelligentsia in Socialist Society," *Pravda*, May 25, 1968.
16. D. I. Chesnokov, "Aggravation of the Ideological and and Political Struggle and Contemporary Philosophical Revisionism," *Voprosy Filosofii*, No. 12. This important article discusses the general state of contemporary Marxism as well as the significance of contemporary revisionism.
17. D. I. Chesnokov, "Current Problems of Historical Materialism," *Kommunist*, No. 6, 1968, p. 48. See also G. Smirnov, "Socialist Humanism," *Pravda*, December 16, 1968.
18. G. Khromushin, "Sharpening of World Ideological Struggle," *International Affairs* (Moscow), No. 12, 1968.
19. T. Timofeyev, "The Leading Revolutionary Force," *Pravda*, December 24, 1968. Timofeyev is the director of the USSR Academy of Sciences Institute of the International Working Class Movement and a corresponding member of the USSR Academy of Sciences.

20. *Pravda,* April 11, 1968.

21. S. Kovalev, "On 'Peaceful' and Non-Peaceful Counterrevolution," *Pravda,* September 11, 1968.

22. A useful source on Soviet "futurology" is the report by a Soviet scholar, I. Bestuzhev-Lada, "Les Études sur l'avenir en URSS," *Analyse et Prevision* (Futuribles), No. 5, 1968.

23. See, for example, A. D. Smirnov, "Socialism, the Scientific-Technological Revolution and Long-Range Forecasting," *Voprosy Filosofii,* No. 9, 1968; I. G. Kurakov, "Forecasting Scientific-Technological Progress"; and M. K. Petrov, "Some Problems of the Organization of Knowledge in the Epoch of the Scientific-Technological Revolution," *Voprosy Filosofii,* No. 10, 1968; and V. G. Afanasev, *Nauchnoe Upravlenie Obshchestvom,* Moscow, 1968.

24. "A Discussion: The Problems of the Unity of the Communist Movement," *Zolnierz Wolnosci,* January 21, 1969, particularly the contributions by S. Trampczynski; J. Urban, "Hands Close to Pulse," *Polityka,* June 9, 1969.

25. V. Roman in *Contemporanul,* January 3, January 10, 1969 (italics his). Roman, a member of the Central Committee and a former minister in the Rumanian government, is a professor and engineer by training. He is the author of several books on the scientific-technical revolution.

26. Cheprakov, *Izvestia,* August 18, 1968.

27. See C. Freeman and A. Young, *The Research and Development Effort in Western Europe, North America and the Soviet Union,* OECD, p. 33; also the exhaustive study *Science Policy in the USSR,* OECD, 1969.

28. For other examples, see *Science Policy in the USSR,* p. 95.

29. *Izvestia,* October 28, 1968.

30. Academician P. L. Kapitsa, *Komsomolskaia Pravda,* January 19, 1968.

31. *Problems of Communism,* July–August and September–October 1968. See also V. Chornovil, *The Chornovil Papers,* New York, 1968.

32. Text published in *The New York Times,* July 22, 1968. (Citations in the text are from this version.)

33. *Vestnik Akademii Nauk,* No. 3, 1966, p. 138.

34. V. Roman, "For a Marxist Theory of the Technical-Scientific Revolution," *Contemporanul.*

35. Walter Ulbricht, "The Significance and Vital Force of the Teachings of Karl Marx for Our Era," pamphlet, Berlin, May 2, 1968.

36. See Peter C. Ludz, *Parteielite im Wandel,* Cologne, 1968.

37. See, for example, the warning by P. Demichev, "The Construction of Communism and the Goals of Social Sciences," *Kommunist,* No. 10, 1968, p. 26. For a provocative discussion of the trend toward greater fusion of party bureaucratic experience with technical com-

petence, see George Fischer, *The Soviet System and Modern Society,* New York, 1968.

38. For an excellent general survey, see Richard Lowenthal, *World Communism: The Disintegration of a Secular Faith,* New York, 1966.

39. See in this connection the perceptive essay by Henry L. Roberts, "Russia and the West: A Comparison and Contrast," *The Slavic Review,* March 1964.

40. See the statement in *Kommunist,* No. 15, 1963, especially p. 26, which attacks the Chinese concept of an absolute line for the international movement, and the letter of the Soviet leadership of July 1963 to the Chinese leaders, explicitly rejecting the concept of a general line for the international movement. This period has been analyzed by me in my *The Soviet Bloc: Unity and Conflict,* rev. ed., Cambridge, Mass., 1967.

41. Roger Garaudy, *Pour un modèle français du socialisme,* Paris, 1968, pp. 148–49.

42. D. Susnjic, *Knjizevne Novine,* March 2, 1968. For useful summaries of Yugoslav views concerning a multi-party system, see also the RFE research papers of October 6, 1967, and May 21, 1968, both of which summarize the evolution of Yugoslav thinking on the subject.

43. For data on the growth of the Czechoslovak intelligentsia and for a discussion of its implications, see Z. Valenta, "The Working Class and the Intelligentsia," *Nova Mysl,* February 1968.

44. See the very thoughtful discussion by A. Hegedus, "On the Alternatives of Social Development," and "Reality and Necessity," *Kortars,* June, July 1967. For a conservative response to the above, see P. Varkonyi, "The Development and Problems of the Socialist Society," *Kortars,* November 1968. Even the more conservative response did concede the desirability of such discussion, which went much further than anything recently published in either the Soviet Union or the other more conservative Communist states.

45. See in this connection the revealing polemics between the Soviets and the Chinese on the subject of the revolutionary role of the American Negro: R. A. Remington, "Revolutionary Role of the Afro-American: An Analysis of Sino-Soviet Polemics on the Historical Importance of the American Negro," Center for International Studies, M.I.T., October 1968.

46. Tang Tsou, "The Cultural Revolution and the Chinese Political System," *The China Quarterly,* April–June, 1969.

47. Alexander Eckstein, *Communist China's Economic Growth and Foreign Trade,* New York, 1966.

48. O. E. Clubb, *Twentieth Century China,* New York, 1964, pp. 413–24. See also Ping-ti Ho and Tang Tsou, eds., *China in Crisis,* Chicago, 1967; and for a more general discussion, J. K. Fairbank, *The Chinese World Order,* Cambridge, Mass., 1968.

49. John H. Kautsky, p. 187.

IV: The American Transition

1. See, for example, Ronald Segal's *America's Receding Future,* New York, 1968; or Giose Rimanelli, *Tragica America,* Genoa, 1968.

2. A highly informative account is contained in the full-page article by Henry Lieberman, "Technology: Alchemist of Route 128," *The New York Times,* January 8, 1968.

3. An excellent and well-documented summary can be found in *The Advancing South: Manpower Prospects and Problems,* New York, 1968.

4. Daniel Bell, "The Measurement of Knowledge and Technology," in *Indicators of Social Change,* Eleanor Sheldon and Wilbert Moore, eds., New York, 1968, p. 149.

5. Notably Bell, above; also the more general, less documented reflections in the fourth annual report of Harvard University, *Program on Technology and Society;* and Victor Ferkiss, *Technological Man: The Myth and the Reality.* For an extremely useful summary of present trends in America, see *Toward a Social Report,* Department of Health, Education and Welfare, Washington, D.C., 1969. For a revealing and in places moving account of the impact of all this on some of the young, see Mark Gerzon, *The Whole World Is Watching.*

6. *Television Quarterly,* Spring 1968, p. 9.

7. For a fuller discussion, see *NASA: The Technology Utilization Program,* 1967, p. 10; and editorial in *Saturday Review,* April 19, 1969.

8. See Anthony G. Oettinger and Sema Marks, "Educational Technology: New Myths and Old Realities" (discussion and reply), *The Harvard Educational Review,* Fall 1968.

9. As cited by *Return to Responsibility,* a report by the Thomas Jefferson Research Center, Pasadena, 1969, p. 5.

10. Bell, p. 175.

11. *Toward a Social Report,* p. 43.

12. *Ibid.,* p. 42.

13. Bureau of the Census report, cited by *The New York Times,* August 20, 1969.

14. *Report of the National Advisory Commission on Civil Disorders,* Washington, D.C., 1968, p. 337. A breakdown of the distribution of the poor is contained in the report of the President's Commission on Income Maintenance Programs, released on November 12, 1969; see also *Joint Report* of the Commerce and Labor Departments cited by *The New York Times,* February 2, 1970.

15. Bureau of the Census report; Nathan Glazer, "The Negroes' Stake in America's Future," *The New York Times Magazine,* September 22, 1968, p. 31; *The Economist,* May 10, 1969, p. 51.

16. *The New York Times,* May 11, 1969. It should, however, be noted that in 1949, 59 per cent of the blacks expressed satisfaction with

their housing. This presumably indicates higher expectations in 1969. On housing, see *Joint Report* (note 14, above).

17. "Characteristics of Students and Their Colleges," a study by the Bureau of the Census, as cited in *The New York Times*, June 15, 1969.

18. Glazer, pp. 31, 90; see also *Joint Report*.

19. *The Economist*, p. 51.

20. *Toward a Social Report*, pp. 15–27; *Time*, October 31, 1969, p. 42.

21. But for a rather pessimistic projection and assessment, see "America's Frustrated South," *The Economist*, June 14, 1969.

22. See the special report "Black America," *Newsweek*, June 30, 1969, p. 23. For a broader analysis, see *The Politics of Protest* (The Skolnick Report to the National Commission on the Causes and Prevention of Violence), New York, 1968, especially chap. 4, "Black Militancy."

23. Gloria Steinem, "Link between the New Politics and the Old," *Saturday Review*, August 2, 1969, p. 19.

24. For a useful discussion of the fragmentation of political culture in democracy, see Arend Lijphart, "Typologies of Democratic Systems," *Comparative Political Studies*, April 1968.

25. Gus Tyler, *The Political Imperative*, New York, 1968.

26. For strikingly conflicting assessments of the impact of that expansion, see Emmanuel Mesthene, "How Technology Will Shape the Future" (*Science*, July 12, 1968), who argues strongly that the role of government is enhanced; and Ferkiss, pp. 146–47, who argues quite the contrary point of view. For a broad-gauged and stimulating discussion, see Peter Drucker, *The Age of Discontinuity*, New York, 1969.

27. From the introduction to Ellul, *The Technological Society*, by Robert K. Merton, p. vi.

28. See our earlier discussion, Part IV, p. 201.

29. Donald N. Michael, *The Next Generation*, New York, 1965, p. 16.

30. Robert S. Liebert, "Towards a Conceptual Model of Radical and Militant Youth: A Study of Columbia Undergraduates," presentation to the Association for Psycho-analytic Medicine, April 1, 1961, p. 28.

31. Kenneth Keniston, "You Have to Grow Up in Scarsdale to Know How Bad Things Really Are," *The New York Times Magazine*, April 27, 1969, p. 128. The foregoing reflects the argument of his larger book, *Young Radicals: Notes on Committed Youth*, New York, 1968.

32. Gerzon, p. 26.

33. *Ibid.*, pp. 52–53, 73, 185, 190.

34. Michael, *The Next Generation*, p. 41; see also Robert A. Nisbett, "Twilight of Authority," *The Public Interest*, Spring 1969.

35. Testimony of Dr. Bruno Bettelheim, professor of psychology and psychiatry, University of Chicago, to the House Special Subcommittee on Education, March 20, 1969.

36. See the argument developed by Edgar C. Friedenberg, "The Hidden Costs of Opportunity," *Atlantic Monthly*, February 1969, pp. 84–90.

37. See T. B. Bottomore, *Critics of Society: Radical Thought in North America*, New York, 1968.

38. See Daniel Bell, "Charles Fourier: Prophet of Eupsychia," *The American Scholar*, Winter 1968–69.

39. Friedenberg, p. 89.

40. William Kornhauser, *The Politics of Mass Society*.

41. For some perceptive comments, see Andrew Knight, "America's Frozen Liberals," *The Progressive*, February 1969.

42. For a discussion of the position of the liberal in the academic world, see Irving Louis Horowitz, "Young Radicals and the Professorial Critics," *Commonweal*, January 31, 1969, pp. 552–56.

43. For a good discussion, see particularly p. 54 of the special issue of *The Economist*, May 10, 1969.

44. From a lecture by Professor Joseph Blau, Aspen Institute of Humanistic Studies, January 1969.

45. Quite symptomatic is the title of the recent book by Arthur Schlesinger, Jr., *The Crisis of Confidence*, Boston, 1969.

46. A good account of right and left extremist groups is in George Thayer, *The Farther Shores of Politics*, New York, 1967.

47. For the outlines of the needed effort, see the *Report . . . on Civil Disorders*, especially pp. 225–26.

V: America and the World

1. For some comparative data, see *Toward a Social Report*, pp. 81–82.

2. Strong overtones of this view are to be found in John McDermott's "Intellectuals and Technology," *The New York Review of Books*, July 31, 1969; it is even more strongly argued in Theodore Roszak, *The Making of a Counter-Culture*, New York, 1969.

3. See particularly Konrad Lorenz, *On Aggression*, New York, 1966; also N. Tinbergen, "On War and Peace in Animals and Man," *Science*, June 28, 1968.

4. For a criticism of the radical attacks on the industrial-military complex, see Stanley Hoffmann, *Gulliver's Troubles*, p. 149.

5. See Frank S. Hopkins, "American Educational Systems for the Less Developed Countries," Washington, D.C., 1967 (mimeograph), and his proposal for an Educational Development Administration.

6. Irving Louis Horowitz et al., *Latin American Radicalism*. Student partisanship in Latin America is well covered in chapters 8–11 in Donald K. Emmerson, *Students and Politics in Developing Nations*.

7. See Claudio Véliz, "Centralism and Nationalism in Latin America," *Foreign Affairs,* October 1968.

8. See my article, "Peace and Power," *Encounter,* November 1968.

9. For a stimulating interpretation of Russian history and of its "lag" vis-à-vis the West, see Hugh Seton-Watson, *The Russian Empire, 1801–1917,* Oxford, 1967, especially pp. 728–42.

10. I share in this respect the conclusions reached by Theodore Draper in his "World Politics: A New Era?" *Encounter,* August 1968, p. 12.

11. See my article, "Meeting Moscow's 'Limited Coexistence,'" *The New Leader,* December 16, 1968.

12. Montreal *Star,* September 9, 1969.

13. For a fuller discussion, see my "Global Political Planning," *Public Interest,* Winter 1969.

14. See on this the public-opinion polls analyzed in *Peace Research in Japan,* Tokyo, 1968, pp. 25–71. They point to rising Japanese expectations of nuclear proliferation.

15. See in this connection the speech by Leonard Marks, director of USIA, "A Blueprint for a New Schoolhouse," November 8, 1967.

16. For detailed calculations of the likely financial share of contributors other than the United States, see *The Economist,* August 9, 1969, p. 13.

17. For a fuller elaboration of these proposals, see my "The Framework for East-West Reconciliation," *Foreign Affairs,* January 1968.

18. See the revealing analysis of foreign attitudes toward the United States in the polls cited by *The Future of U.S. Public Diplomacy,* report by the Subcommittee on Foreign Affairs of the House of Representatives, Washington, D.C., December 22, 1968, especially pp. 15–18.

19. Arthur Schlesinger, Jr., *A Thousand Days,* Boston, 1965, p. 559.

Index

DATE DUE

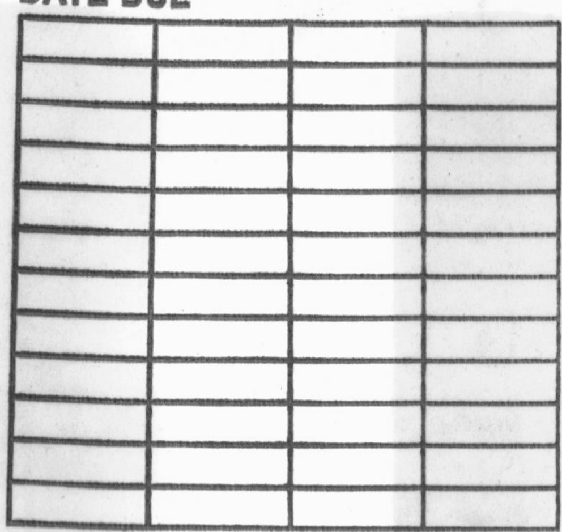